Praise for

the proper care

and

maintenance

of

friendship

"A lovely novel with moments of deeply moving insight into what it means to be a mother, a wife, and a friend. Read it and share it with your own friends—you'll be glad you did!"
—Nancy Thayer, *New York Times* bestselling author
of *The Hot Flash Club* and *Beachcombers*

"Offering words of wisdom from a dying friend, THE PROPER CARE AND MAINTENANCE OF FRIENDSHIP inspires us to focus on what's really important in our lives."
—Liza Palmer, international bestselling author
of *Conversations with the Fat Girl* and *A Field
Guide to Burying Your Parents*

"An amazing novel of love, friendship, and community. A truly joyous read that marks an impressive debut."
—Jane Porter, author of *Flirting with Forty*
and *She's Gone Country*

"Poignant, romantic, and funny…about the need for our closest friends to occasionally give us a shove in the right direction when we've lost our way. You'll recognize yourself in these women. I loved it."
—Claire LaZebnik, author of *Knitting Under the Influence*
and *If You Lived Here, You'd Be Home Now*

The proper care

and

maintenance

of

friendship

LISA VERGE
HIGGINS

NEW YORK   BOSTON

5 Spot
Hachette Book Group
237 Park Avenue
New York, NY 10017

www.5-spot.com

5 Spot is an imprint of Grand Central Publishing.
The 5 Spot name and logo are trademarks of Hachette Book Group, Inc.

Printed in the United States of America

First Edition: January 2011
10 9 8 7 6 5 4 3

Library of Congress Cataloging-in-Publication Data

Higgins, Lisa Verge.
  The proper care and maintenance of friendship / Lisa Verge Higgins.—1st ed.
    p. cm.
  ISBN 978-0-446-56351-2
  1. Best friends—Fiction.   2. Bereavement—Fiction.   3. Female friend-
    ship—Fiction.   I. Title.
  PS3558.I3576P76 2011
  813'.54—dc22
                                        2010011266

For the Sunday Night Ladies:
Nancy, Judy, and Cathy.
Amazing writers, wonderful friends.

~~ chapter one

When the rumbling Cessna heaved into the sky, Kate Jansen completely lost her nerve.

She seized the strap of her seat belt as the whole plane shuddered. Through the dirty window she glimpsed Jo and Sarah—her two best friends in the world—standing on the tarmac and shrinking swiftly into the distance.

"Now don't you mind all the rattling, Miz Jansen," Bubba shouted, patting the metal sides of the plane. "This old girl has brought me safely up and down again a hundred times or more."

Kate glared at her skydiving instructor. He sat facing her, dressed in his black-and-blue jumpsuit, looking like a giant mutant housefly. He'd just spent two hours shoving her off ever-higher platforms onto thick mats, to teach her the proper falling techniques in the airport's single hangar. He'd promised her that the jump would conquer her fear of heights, her fear of flying, her fear of *everything*. He promised her that the experience would completely change her life.

What the hell am I doing?

Breathe. *Breathe.* It had to be all right. Her friend Rachel

Braun had done this a thousand and thirty-six times. Solo. But Kate would be diving with Bubba strapped to her back, hooked to him at six points. Each hook could carry two hundred pounds, he'd told her, and so if four of them snapped off while they were tumbling toward earth, well, a little thing like her shouldn't worry.

The plane banked. Kate let go of the chokehold she had on her seat belt. She seized the ragged edge of the plywood she sat upon. A thousand little splinters pierced her palms.

She was going to kill Rachel Braun for this. And she would—if Rachel wasn't dead already.

The plane jerked in sudden ascent, and she cast about wildly, seeking escape—an exit, an out that didn't involve tumbling through the sky. Her gaze fixed upon a silver cross dangling from the rosary beads clutched in the other skydiver's hands. His name was Frank, Bubba had told her, a Franciscan monk who jumped a few times a year.

She wondered, in a panic, if a monk could take confession.

But what did she have to confess? She loved her life. She was a thirty-nine-year-old mother of three who had a comfortable home with a cranky heater and flaking plaster walls. Her life overflowed with PTA meetings and Christmas-craft fund-raisers. She baked bread on Sundays, slapping the dough with floured hands. Every other year or so, she'd do a twenty-mile walk for one of Sarah's charities.

She loved, most of all, her kids, whose faces she could summon up like spirits. Tess, trying to be cool while sucking on a hank of hair, her cropped hoodie clinging to her rib cage; Michael, moody and dark and brooding like Heathcliff; and Anna, little Anna, who gave small wet kisses like sparks.

Only a few hours ago, she'd signed fifteen pages of a contract that absolved the entire *universe* of any responsibility for loss of property, loss of limb, loss of *life*. It prevented anyone from even *asking* about her death—the death that would affect her three little beneficiaries, and her husband, too—who didn't know that she was currently approaching a cumulus cloud hovering a mile above the earth.

Suddenly the photographer stood up. He grasped the handle of the door just opposite the pilot's seat and yanked it open to a blast of sunlight and freezing air.

Ohmygod. Ohmygodohmygodohmygod—

"Don't go cold on me now, Miz Jansen," Bubba yelled over the roar. "Let's go over procedures one more time."

I can't do this.

"Remember, breathe through your nose."

I've got three kids to pick up from school this afternoon.

"We'll hook up, walk to the ledge, and somersault out." Bubba leaned in closer, so she could better hear the bellow of his voice. "Then get into the arch position right away."

The Franciscan stood up, palming the sides of the open door. He yelled something over his shoulder, and then made the sign of the cross. Papers on the pilot's clipboard rattled— two tore off and reeled into the wind.

Frank was gone.

Holy shit.

"C'mon, Miz Jansen." Bubba grinned as he reached over and unbuckled her seat belt. "Let's do this."

"No . . ." The wind sucked the word from her mouth. "No . . ."

But Bubba didn't hear her. He hauled her up with those ham-sized fists and then twisted her around like he was going to take her by the backside. She struggled to speak as she stood there with her knees buckling, bracing herself against the back of the plane, while he pressed his long, hard body against her and hooked her up to him—six little hooks.

She forced air past her throat. "I've changed...my mind."

"Ten minutes." He moved against her. "Ten minutes, and we'll be on the ground."

Kate's foot slipped off the plywood into a gully where the seats should have been. Something imploded inside her, shooting sparks to her extremities, making her cramp into a curled ball of terror, held up by six little hooks. She seized a beam of molded metal above a window, shouting, "You said... I could change my mind."

"You're not going to chicken out on me, are you, Miz Jansen?"

"I'm just...a housewife!"

"Right now you're a sassy thirty-nine-year-old woman," he bellowed, "with a big country boy strapped to your back."

"I've got *three kids*—"

"Congratulations. You must be a heck of an athlete, keeping those abs of yours."

"—I've got *responsibilities*." She couldn't breathe, and all the yelling hurt her throat. "I've got *obligations*. But Rachel died— she's *dead*."

Rachel, Rachel, why did you ask me to do this?

"Hey," the pilot barked. "We're over the drop zone! Get out!"

"Miz Jansen, you've got to make a decision *now*."

"Rachel...Rachel died," Kate stuttered, her whole body shaking. "That letter should have had instructions for her funeral. Dirty songs to sing over her grave. Not...not *this*."

Bubba yelled, "You opting out?"

"*Yes!*"

"You sure?"

"*Yes!!*"

Bubba sighed. She rose and fell upon the weight of it.

"Okay," he said. "We're done."

Kate stilled. She kept her grip on the molding, slippery now with sweat. She heard her breathing, felt the slight banking of the plane. "Really?"

"Oh, yeah. Really." Bubba worked the hooks. He spoke close to her ear so he could make himself heard without yelling. "You think you're the first to give up, honey? Hell, no. Happens all the time." He slipped the first hook free. " 'Specially with women like you. The ones staring down the barrel at their fortieth birthdays. Think they're going to hurl themselves out of airplanes to resurrect their wild youth. Never happens."

"I've got…three kids."

"So you said. It's too bad you didn't go. They'd never look at you in quite the same way."

"Better that I'm around to see them," she retorted. She straightened up, away from the cutting rumble of his voice. "Better I'm alive on the ground—"

"Oh, sure," he said. "Then you can go back to your soccer carpool. Flip out your foldable chair. Over a fancy coffee, tell those other moms all about how you *almost* jumped out of an airplane."

Hell, yes.

"And when you're done, you can go home and dust the moldings, maybe scrub a toilet. Figure out how you're going to cook chicken for dinner. Schedule a tune-up for your second car. Maybe slip in a load of laundry before bedtime. After all, you have to get that stain out of Junior's soccer pants. I hear Tide with bleach is the thing."

Stop.

She didn't need to hear it. She saw it, as clearly as she saw long wisps of clouds through the window. Oh, yes, the unfurling of the long years, marked by yet another beach-house vacation and another project involving toothpicks and toilet-paper rolls, another concert with the grammar-school band screeching "Hot Cross Buns." Smiling all through it. Yes, this was fun; yes, this is the life; yes, we're a hundred thousand times blessed. Year upon year passes in clockwork predictability, and the only things that change are the height of her kids, the baldness of her husband, and the width of her ass.

"Listen, asshole," she yelled over her shoulder, "stop the reverse-psych crap. Sure, I'm a housewife, but it's a hell of a better way to spend my time than chilling in a morgue."

"Like Rachel?"

Bubba yanked another hook free. He might as well have jerked it from her flesh. It left her speechless. Aghast. Grasping for words.

Failing to find them.

Then he pushed against her, sensing her vulnerability. He pressed his stubbled cheek against her hair. "What do you think your friend would give, Kate, for a chance to be up here again?"

Kate knew the answer. Rachel had lived for moments like this, made huge sacrifices for the adrenaline rush. Sacrifices Kate hadn't always agreed with.

But all that was over. All possibilities, for better or worse, were gone forever.

The pilot yelled, "Last chance, Bubba."

Last chance.

The plane dipped. The wind battered the jumpsuit against her legs. Kate Jansen glared out at those blue skies, at the ground so very far below. She glared up at the heavens. Didn't know whether to curse Bubba or Rachel or her wretched self for the foolishness she was about to attempt.

Bubba spoke, one last time.

"What'll it be ... wifey?"

chapter two

"Sweet Jesus, she's done it."

Bobbie Jo Marcum stood on the tarmac, leaning against a rental car, watching one of her best friends float out of the October sky. Even from a distance, Jo could see the grin splitting Kate's face, as the man strapped to her back manipulated the ropes in order to glide them both to the painted yellow target. They descended frighteningly fast, and hit the ground at a trot. Behind them, the parachute deflated in graceful red folds.

Jo gave Sarah a bump of her shoulder. "Kate Jansen, mother extraordinaire, has just jumped out of an airplane. What d'you think that means for us, sugar?"

"Never mind what it means for us," Sarah said, as she shaded her eyes against the sun. "Think of what it means for Paul."

"And those poor kids of theirs."

"She's overdue." Sarah ran her fingers through a kinky mane of hair that hadn't seen a stylist's scissors in ten years. "I don't think Kate has had a proper steam-blower since before Tess was born."

"Building up like a damn volcano."

"Last one I remember was years ago, that climb we all took in the Shawangunks, a few months before she got pregnant. Three bottles of red wine and a lot of yodeling."

"Yeah, and a striptease in the Hudson Valley sunrise." Jo grinned, remembering the frigid shower they'd all taken later, in a small mountain cataract. "Gawd, I love that girl when she's crazy."

"So did Rachel." Sarah's voice went soft, and she turned her clear gray gaze to Jo. "Guess there's no getting out of it now."

"I hear you, sugar. I surely do."

Jo let her gaze skid away. Go-for-it-all Kate had just thrown down the gauntlet by being the first to do what Rachel had asked her to do. If the stay-at-home martyr could jump out of an airplane, well, then, Jo had better do what Rachel had ordered in the ratty white envelope now folded in Jo's pocket.

It wasn't supposed to be like this.

Only a few days ago, she'd gone to Rachel's house. Rachel's family had been sitting shiva. Jo and Kate and Sarah had taken off their shoes and paid their respects, then wandered through a house with black-draped mirrors, tables full of hard-boiled eggs, and a swelling crowd of friends and relatives they didn't recognize. Jo kept expecting Rachel to jump out from behind a door.

Gotcha.

Once, a long time ago, Jo bet twenty bucks that snowboarding would be the sport that would kill Rachel—especially after the skiing accident in Colorado that left her in a body cast for two months. Kate put her money on skydiving—which would explain why Rachel had ordered Kate up eight thousand feet. Sarah, long dubbed their moral and social conscience, was bewildered by the betting until Kate explained that it was good juju to bet against survival. Sarah was most concerned about BASE jumping. She, the international public-health nurse, knew better than all of them the paucity of good health care in the countries that turned a blind eye to a sport that involved leaping off skyscrapers or very high bridges. So, for the nearly twenty years since they'd graduated from college, she and Kate and Sarah had held their breath on a death watch. But you can only teeter on the edge of worry for so long. After a while, it became a running joke, yelled over crackling satellite connections.

"Hey, Rachel, you still alive?"

Of course, Rachel hadn't died in any of those expected ways. Rachel's last terrible battle was the one adventure she'd kept secret, until the very end. Maybe that's why her death didn't seem real. Any more real than seeing Kate Jansen skid into the drop zone, buckled to a strapping hunk of man.

Sarah, breathless, skittered across the field to meet her. Her hand-dyed brown skirt flapped around her legs. Jo reached into the car's open window to push aside her cell phone, convulsing to the tinny chorus of "It's Raining Men," and hauled out a bottle of peppermint schnapps. Cracking it open, she savored a swig, then winced at the sweetness. It reminded her of ice-skating rinks and junior high and the boy who gave her her first kiss, Lonnie Clyde Barkley.

If only Rachel's instructions had been "Get laid." That would have been easy. Jo could have found someone in her BlackBerry, and if her contacts didn't pan out, there was always that hot divorcé in Accounting who'd been giving her the burning eye. He had a crest of silky dark hair and a butt that could crack walnuts. She'd been debating whether a fling with him was worth the inevitable complications. Unfortunately, Rachel hadn't let her off the hook that easily. Her instructions to Jo were simply . . . unbelievable.

Jo followed Sarah across the field, swinging the schnapps. Kate unbuckled herself from a rugged bull of a man, and Sarah flung her arms around her. Kate looked like someone had pulled her from the edge of the world. Flushed and wild-eyed and completely incoherent.

"I can't believe . . . Ohmygod . . . I just . . . I can't believe . . ."

When it was Jo's turn to hug, she felt the slamming of Kate's heart. Jo offered her the schnapps. Kate grabbed it and took the biggest swig Jo had ever seen her take. Except for one memorable evening in the spring of their senior year, when, stressed after finals, Kate had gotten so looped she'd worn her own bra on her head and sung "The Hills Are Alive" from the roof of their dorm.

Kate shook herself like a wet dog and thrust the bottle back at Jo. Then she let out a Kenilworth State University Rock Climber's Yodel that could probably be heard in Manhattan. The square-jawed rogue in the jumpsuit was grinning like he'd just given Kate a double orgasm.

Sarah swayed around, dancing, trying to get Kate to describe it.

"It was like . . . being suspended." Schnapps ran down Kate's chin; she didn't wipe. "The wind pushed me up."

"Come on." The hunk took Kate by the elbow and directed her toward the hangar. "Let's get you undressed."

"Oh, honey," Jo murmured, as she and Sarah followed, "don't talk like that. Kate's a married woman."

But I'm not.

He looked at Jo. The twinkle brightened in his eye. Jo savored the familiar tremor that shook her whenever she approached a man high on testosterone. It might be worth jumping out of a plane, she thought, to be pushed up against *that*.

"It was . . . Time stopped." Kate stumbled along. "It stretched. Nothing but air and noise. Ohmygod—"

"Looks like the schnapps is kicking in."

"Oh, no," the hunk said. "That's pure adrenaline. The best drug in the world."

"I JUST JUMPED OUT OF A PLANE!" Kate pulled away and twirled across the tarmac. "I JUST FREAKIN' JUMPED OUT OF A PLANE!"

"You know, you might want to think about taking our Accelerated Free-Fall course," the hunk began. "Then you can do it without me strapped onto you—"

"Now, darling," Jo interrupted, "what's the fun in that?"

"By myself?" Kate was hopping around like a kangaroo. "Really? How long does it take?"

"It's more extensive training, but if you're serious, we can talk about setting you up. . . ."

Jo narrowed her eyes as the hunk launched into his sales pitch. She skewered Kate with a good long look. No doubt it would put a damper on the moment to tell Kate that they didn't need another adrenaline junkie like their dead friend Rachel, or to suggest it might be a good idea for Kate to let her own husband know what she was doing while the kids were at school. But seeing Kate half crazed like this, totally cut loose, was becoming too rare a thing, like seeing the Tomato Queen catch the mud-slick sow at the pig scramble. It only happened on the blue of a moon if it fell on a Saturday. It reminded Jo of the good ol' Kate, the pre-wedding Kate, the pre-children Kate, the old friend whose vibrant personality was fading into legend.

"CAN YOU BELIEVE IT?! I JUST JUMPED OUT OF AN AIRPLANE!"

That airplane was landing now, roaring down the runway toward the same hangar they were heading toward. Kate danced ahead, and Sarah, laughing, danced with her, and every once in a while Kate would scream some variation of *"I just jumped out of an airplane!"*

Of course, this gave Jo some time with Mr. Hunk, who'd fallen back to keep pace with her. She gave him a sidelong look. Southerners were so thin on the ground here in New Jersey that Jo could recognize one from about fifty paces "So...is it Tennessee?"

"West Virginia." He gifted her with a lopsided grin. "How 'bout you?"

"Kentucky purebred."

"You're a long way from home. Feel like taking a ride yourself?"

"Oh, how you talk."

"I can give you a discount."

"Tell me you're not talking about airplanes." He had the grace to look sheepish. "You are talking about airplanes." She tried to hide her disappointment. She supposed it was a tough way to make a living, convincing normally rational people to hurl themselves into the void. "If it's all the same to you, I'll take my thrills on the ground."

Preferably on my back.

"Maybe we can meet up later," he said. "After work."

"That'd be nice." But Jo knew that kind of "maybe." That hopeful, sort of interested, can-we-do-this-without-me-making-any-effort kind of maybe. He was hot, but she couldn't muster the effort right now. She had plans this afternoon, and, unfortunately, they didn't involve a raucous roll with this hard-bodied adrenaline junkie.

Inside the office, a guy still in his jumpsuit was busy editing a DVD. Kate wrestled herself out of the yellow suit, made a frantic trip to the bathroom, commandeered the schnapps, then raced back to watch a video of herself falling out of the sky.

It was pretty incredible. No goggles could hide the fact that Kate had been terrified. Yet, as she leaned out of the airplane and the air pounded her cheeks, her expression shifted. She bloomed. The free-fall lasted less than sixty seconds; then the hunk hit her on the shoulder, and she deployed the chute, zooming high up, out of the range of the camera. Everyone applauded. The West Virginian handed her a certificate and a slim little DVD case, and Kate Jansen floated out of the hangar, her project completed.

A-plus, as usual.

Boy, Jo thought, it was really going to twist Kate's britches when she found out that the letters from Rachel were all mixed up. That's the only explanation Jo could come up with for what was written in hers.

"What now?" Sarah asked, her eyes lighting up. "Are we going for lunch?"

"Lunch—no." Kate quivered with vestigial adrenaline. "I couldn't eat. I can't eat."

"Sex is what you need." Jo tossed the empty bottle in the

garbage. In the back of her car, "It's Raining Men" kept up a constant chorus. "You should surprise Paul."

"Yes." Kate beamed. "That's exactly what I'm going to do. He's at work. I'll visit."

After a few hugs she was gone, zooming out of the parking lot faster than safety allowed.

Jo swung an arm around Sarah's shoulders. "I'll have lunch with you, sugar. It ain't going to be nearly as fun as Paul's lunch hour, but I'm what you're stuck with." And lunch was as good a way as any to procrastinate a little more. "Besides, we have to talk about Rachel's envelopes."

"I haven't gotten mine," Sarah said. "If Rachel sent it to Burundi, it's lost forever. Can't get a cow transported from Gatumba to Bujumbura without paying three times its worth in bribes."

"No, Rachel wouldn't take that chance. She would have sent it to your parents' house in Vermont. Where we used to send our letters, in the bad old days, before the blessings of e-mail. You haven't checked with your parents yet?"

"No. I suppose it'll find me, sooner or later. Just as yours will find you." Sarah's clear gaze met hers. Sarah had an arresting gaze; it was the most striking thing about her. Those unwavering gray eyes, the clarity of her freckled skin, and the way she probed your face, as if trying to read whether you were one of the good guys or one of the bad. Jo figured it must come in useful when you're a nurse among refugees.

Jo shrugged her shoulders as if the envelope she hadn't 'fessed up to wasn't sitting right in her pocket. *Yours will find you, too, Sarah,* she thought. *Kate and I will make sure of that.*

Lunch was a simple affair, a quick bite at a local diner.

Sarah scarfed down a cheeseburger and two root beers, as well as half of the French fries off of Jo's plate—explaining, as usual, that you can't get a good cheeseburger outside the U.S. of A. It was just as well, because Jo for the first time in a long time was too nervous to eat. She dropped Sarah off at the train station with promises to get together in the city next week, before Sarah caught a plane back to Burundi. Sarah boarded the train, and Jo wished she had half the calm that Sarah carried around her like a perfume.

Jo had turned off her cell phone during lunch. As soon as she turned it back on, it convulsed in her hand. She hooked up the Bluetooth and put the car in gear before she answered.

"Geez, Jo, where have you been? I've been leaving messages on your cell for hours."

Hector. Frantic again. She took a deep breath and put on her vice-president voice. "What happened at the meeting?"

"It was crazy, man, it was nuts. You wouldn't believe what crap they were coming up with for the Artemis account."

"Hector, I'm sure you came up with something good."

"Oh, sure, loads of ideas. Like giving all the guests trench coats and fedoras, having fingerprint powder and magnifying glasses as swag—"

"Oh, right. Gumshoe. That's what I want to smell like: Hell's Kitchen and stale cigarettes." Jo shot the rental into third gear, flexing her palm over the phallic shift. "It's a perfume called 'Mystery,' not a bad pulp novel. What else?"

"Randy thought we could do some artsy black-and-white shots of girls bent over in the shape of a question mark, with, well, their skirts hiked up just enough to reveal everything except...the mystery."

"Typical Randy. What did he suggest we do at the launch? Dress the girls up in cheerleader outfits with question marks on them? How 'Riddler.' No, thank you." Jo would close her eyes if she weren't doing seventy-five in a fifty-five-mile-an-hour speed zone. "Tell me there were more ideas."

"Jo, you weren't here. I did my best in your place."

"I know you did, Hector, and I appreciate how hard you're working in my absence. But come on, I know that crowd, there must have been something crazy enough to work."

"Sophie had one."

A cold chill ran down her spine. Sophie was an up-and-coming publicist with an eye on Jo's position. Jo's boss had already noticed the ambitious Nordic beauty, and with reason: Sophie was young and energetic and full of half-baked ideas. Some of which were not that bad.

"She wants to hire a model," Hector said, "the one who just got busted with cocaine? Karin, Kate, Kathy something. We can get her cheap, and by the time the launch gets off the ground—"

"Tell me you're joking."

"Sophie's idea," he sang, "not mine."

"Right."

"She says for the ads we can do a photo of the model's face, but mixed up like a puzzle. Mystery, get it? Who's the face of Mystery?"

Jo paused. The idea wasn't bad. It wasn't bad at all. She envisioned magazine advertising—*Vogue, Maxim, Glamour*—maybe even a bit more downscale. Repeated for a month or two to build up curiosity—although the idea of keeping the identity of the model under wraps was a logistical nightmare, full of nondisclosure forms and gags on the manicurist of the model's publicist, etc. But then, at the launch, Artemis could reveal the model. Preferably not Miss Drug Addict of the Month, of course, but someone...exciting, exotic. Mysterious.

"You like it."

"It has possibilities."

"Should I give her the go?"

"Absolutely not."

Hector was making noises on the other end of the phone, the kind of noises that went along with grimaces, eye rolling, covering of the phone receiver, general angst, and growing tension. She was sure he was sweating in his Brooklyn Industries T-shirt. "Jo, the meeting with the Artemis brass is looming."

"I know."

"You've been gone three days, and we don't even have an *idea,* never mind a proposal."

"Better no proposal at all than a bad one. And we've put together proposals overnight before."

"Yeah, and gave me angina in the process."

"Hector, you're twenty-eight years old, and you work out six days a week. It'll be sixty years before you know what angina is."

"Angina? It's you leaving me alone under deadline with these wolves."

"Howl away, Hector. See if you boys can come up with any-thing better—or at least a better runway model than what's-her-white-powdered-face."

Jo listened to her messages—sixteen!—half of which were

from Hector in increasing stages of hysteria as the creative meeting, in the background, burst into chaos. She erased the old messages from Sarah and Kate, arranging the gathering today at the small Fairfield airport. When she heard the raspy voice of a lawyer, however, she pulled over into the parking lot of a diner to write down the phone number. She punched it in immediately and waited an obnoxiously long time to get through.

"Miss Marcum? This is Barry Leibowitz. You wanted to speak to me about Miss Braun's last will and testament?"

"Yes, sir." Kentucky ways can't be bred out of a girl, and the man's voice telegraphed authority. "I was wondering if you were the individual who handled the envelopes that Miss Braun instructed to be mailed after her death."

"I was."

"Oh." Jo had figured that some secretary had dealt with that, not the five-hundred-dollar-an-hour lawyer himself. "Well, maybe you can help me. I believe there must have been some confusion after Miss Braun's death."

"Confusion?"

Jo mentally stepped back. "She died so quickly."

The lawyer paused. "I assure you, all her papers were in good order. Surprising, for such a young woman."

"I received one of those letters," Jo said, pulling it out of her pocket, "and I am quite sure she ..." Jo swallowed a sudden lump in her throat. "I mean, I think she *meant* to write it for one of the other two people."

"Two people?"

"Kate Jansen, perhaps. Or Sarah Pollard."

"Miss Braun didn't send just three envelopes," he said. "She sent dozens."

Dozens.

Jo stared at the huge clock over the doors of the diner, its hands fixed at nine. You'd think, if you had such a giant clock at a Jersey diner, you'd keep it working. Stuck forever at nine, it screamed, We can't afford to fix it.

You'd think, too, having known a woman for over twenty years, that you'd realize she'd made other friends. Dozens of them, even. Especially a woman like Rachel, who risked her life with every adventure and thus made deep, deep bonds with her fellow adrenaline junkies. Didn't she collect people as a child might collect marbles? *While training for this race, I met an amazing guy. He's a sixty-one-year-old triathlete and a practicing Buddhist....I met this waterman you wouldn't believe, Jo. He's like something carved out of limestone. He teaches surfing, and he lives in a bungalow in Maui....She's the first woman to attempt the big seven, but she's not stuck in the ghetto of motivational speaking; no, she's setting up an adventure travel company, and I'm thinking of joining....*

The fact that Rachel had sent dozens of letters suggested something even more alarming. Rachel had been thinking about this—planning for this—for a very long time. Which made Rachel's request all the more mind-boggling.

"We were careful with the sorting, Miss Marcum," the lawyer said into the silence. "You'll see that Miss Braun addressed all the envelopes herself."

Indeed, there was Rachel's handwriting, surprisingly girlish and left-leaning: "Bobbie Jo Marcum, Mogul Extraordinaire, 196 East 82nd Street #5D, New York, New York 10028." As intimate and personal as the letter itself. A fact Jo could no longer deny.

It just didn't make a lick of sense.

"Miss Marcum?"

"Yes, I'm here."

"Can we help you with anything else?"

Can you help me strangle a dead woman? "No, you've been quite kind. I thank you for your time, Mr. Leibowitz."

Jo disconnected the call and told herself it didn't matter. It wasn't going to happen anyway. There was no way Rachel's parents would allow her to interfere in the family like this. Kate Jansen had to jump out of a plane, sure, but all that required was two hours of training and about ten minutes of terror. Then it was over. What Rachel asked of Jo would last a lifetime.

She put the car in gear and headed toward Teaneck. This would all be resolved within the hour. She would show the letter to Rachel's parents. They'd be surprised and horrified, and then they'd all laugh about it. They'd laugh at how Rachel always tried to meddle in people's lives—change them for the better, of course—even from the grave. And then Jo would be absolved.

When Jo arrived, the windows of the neat colonial house were still shaded, as if the family was still sitting shiva. As she approached the door, Jo pulled down her clingy turquoise shirt and wondered if she should have worn something a little more respectful than a pair of low-slung jeans and slingback heels.

The door opened before she could knock. Rachel's cousin Jessie stood in the portal. "Oh, thank God, it's you." She moved aside so Jo could come in. "We've been waiting."

Jo stepped in. The house was in disarray; the black crepe

was still hanging on the mirrors, and plastic packages of food were piled on the dining-room table.

"I thought you'd be here earlier," Jessie said. "My aunt waited. I finally sent her out to run errands. She was nothing but tears, and I think we've had enough of that in this house."

"Jessie, sugar," Jo said, pulling out the envelope and waving it at her, "are you absolutely sure this is real?"

"Yes. *Yes*. I was there when Rachel made the decision."

Jo started. "You were?"

"Yes. I called the lawyer. I helped Rachel write it out. If you accept, it's a hundred percent legal." Jessie gave Jo an exasperated look as the young woman scraped a hand through bangs that badly needed cutting. "Rachel even told me that you'd try to weasel out of it."

Jo bristled. Jessie was about twenty-two years old and as full of herself as only a freshly minted college graduate could be. "I'm not 'weaseling' out of anything. It's just a big shock and a darn huge responsibility."

"I know. It's been mine these past few weeks. That's why Rachel specifically gave it to you."

"Frankly, I didn't think your aunt and uncle would allow it."

"Don't you know our situation at all?" Jessie's ponytail swung as she planted her hands on her hips. "My uncle broke his hip four months ago—"

"I know—"

"—and he's still upstairs in bed. He hasn't been downstairs in all that time. My aunt is looking at three or four more months of waiting on him, hand and foot. And she herself has diabetes. Why don't you think they'd allow this? They welcome it. And if my aunt walks through that door right now, you'd better act as if this is the greatest gift Rachel could ever give you. Because it is."

Jo straightened her spine. She hadn't come here to be lectured by some twenty-something. She got enough of that at work, from the bright young things wanting to take her place. "Why don't you do this, then? I hear you're not yet employed."

Jessie flushed. She dropped her gaze. "I would. I *offered*. But for some reason, Rachel chose you."

Just then, the back door squealed open, and the screen slapped shut. Through the kitchen rushed a scrawny little girl wearing a pair of flood pants, with her hair wild over her face.

"Grace, sweetie." Jessie caught the girl before she could fly out of the room. "Stay here for a minute."

The girl stuck a finger in her mouth. She had a dirty crust around her lips. She had Rachel's limpid brown eyes.

Jessie crouched beside her. "Do you remember we talked about Aunt Jo?"

Jo felt the impact of four anxious eyes.

"Well, sweetie, Aunt Jo is going to be your new mommy."

~~~ chapter three

Sarah hesitated before the computer. The monitor filled the battered desk. A layer of dust blanketed the top. An old friend of hers, now stationed in Bangkok, had given Sarah permission to crash in his New York apartment and make use of its few amenities. It had taken her a good half-hour to figure out that the outdated computer *did* have a modem, but it still used dial-up, at a very slow speed. Following the faded instructions taped to the monitor, she'd been dialing for another half-hour. Finally, she'd gotten a slow but steady connection.

Damn.

She backed away from the blue glow of the screen. The edge of the couch bumped her legs. She gathered the folds of her skirt and sank into the couch's perfect hollow, formed by a broken spring underneath.

In the camp outside Gatumba, such a steady stream of power would send her and Dr. Mwami scrambling. They'd charge the defibrillators, put the portable ultrasound scanner to good use, and find that woman who needed gallbladder surgery while the electrocardiogram was still working—all before a fuse blew, rain shorted out the cables, or a herd of migrating elephants crushed the generator.

But here, faced with such wretchedly reliable power, she wished for a thunderstorm. The screen blinked at her. Relentlessly. And despite the heaping piles of paper on the desk, Rachel's little white envelope shone bright like the moon in a Burundi night.

What are you afraid of, Sarah?

The truth, Rachel. The ugly, ugly truth.

Sarah seized her cup of orange-blossom tea. She corralled its warmth in her palms. For fourteen years, she'd avoided this situation. Fourteen years of living in blessed—and willing—ignorance. Not a darn bit of good could ever come of Rachel's last request: that Sarah track down Dr. Colin O'Rourke, Peace Corps volunteer, surgical wizard, passionate activist—and the only man that Sarah ever loved.

She closed her eyes...and remembered.

They lay under the mosquito netting, still breathing hard. Outside the hut, the insects of Paraguay screamed, slamming against the thatched roof, swarming in such density that they couldn't fly a clear path. Night birds howled in the forest beyond. Sarah was sure she heard the growl of a jaguar.

So different, it all was, from where she'd come from—from the muffled snowy Vermont nights she'd known growing up. Here the air was thick with life.

And that's how she felt—thick with life—lying with her head on Colin's shoulder, admiring the way his sculpted chest rose and fell in the gleam of the moonlight. She traced his muscles. Pectoralis major. External intercostals. Obliques. Not for the first time, she wondered why Dr. Colin O'Rourke chose to love her, an odd little farm girl on her first mission.

Sarah's teacup clattered as she set it down. The tea splashed over her hand. It smelled nauseatingly sweet. Her friend Tim—the owner of this apartment—had a perfectly functional coffeemaker but not a coffee bean in the whole place, so she was forced to drink this horrid herbal stuff. She jumped off the couch, pushed aside the beaded curtain that separated the living room from the kitchen, dumped the brew in the rust-stained sink, and mumbled an apology to the absent host for being such an ungrateful guest.

The computer waited, a blue ghost in the other room. Ready to reveal that Dr. Colin O'Rourke was now a balding proctologist in Kansas. Or a dermatologist in Tupelo, who ran marathons in his spare time. With a golf-club membership, four kids, and a pedigreed Shih Tzu named Porgy.

Perhaps, a lovely wife.

She braced her hands on the sink. Why couldn't Rachel leave her this one small eccentricity? Who did it hurt, really? Didn't everyone have something or someone that they held up between themselves and the jagged edges of the world, like a bright bit of rose-colored glass? Sarah ached to curl herself into a ball, clutch his memory against her breast like the last in a set of blown-glass Christmas ornaments, something shiny and exquisitely beautiful—and in terrible danger of shattering.

There was an option. She could pretend she hadn't received the letter yet. It wouldn't be difficult. This much Jo and Kate knew: The mail in Burundi was like the forty-year-old Volkswagen that had been donated for use in the camp; once in a while, to everyone's great astonishment, it worked. Most of the time, it didn't. She could hold off the task for months. Even years.

But despite too many years working in hellholes all across the globe, Sarah still couldn't shake off the minister's daughter in herself. She couldn't lie, and she didn't like to admit being a coward.

Well, she wouldn't do this alone. She batted her way through the beaded curtains and seized the receiver of Tim's phone. She dialed a familiar number, then turned her back to the computer screen.

"Jo Marcum."

Sarah checked herself. Jo had her business voice on—that clipped, citified, no-trace-of-Kentucky tone—but Sarah was sure she'd dialed Jo at home. "It's Sarah. You're working?"

"Catching up at home. Took too many days off. What's up?"

"I need a witness."

Jo made a breathy gasp. "You got your envelope."

"My mother just sent it to me."

"So, 'fess up. How thoroughly did Rachel screw you?"

"She wants me to track down Colin." In the silence that met her revelation, Sarah wandered to the desk. She ran her finger over Rachel's handwriting.

"Sarah...what did you just say?"

"I know it's unbelievable." Sarah tapped the envelope. "Rachel came to Africa last year. We spent a whole week together. We had some real heart-to-hearts. Now she's ripping mine out."

"Sarah, you've *got* to be kidding."

"I just don't understand why she'd ask me to do this, of all

things! I thought, after her visit, she understood why I didn't
ever want to—"

"Let me get this straight," Jo interrupted. "All Rachel asked
was that you *Google a guy?!*"

Sarah paused. There was acid in Jo's voice. More venom than
she'd expected. It was true that Jo and Kate had long given up
any tolerance for the subject of Colin O'Rourke. None of the
girls really understood why Colin stood between Sarah and
every lame, half-realized relationship she'd attempted since.

Apparently, not even Rachel.

"Okay." Jo was working herself up. "Kate has to jump out of
an airplane. And now you, my darling, are telling me that all
you have to do is *type?*"

Type? More like dig up a grave. Unearth what should be
left to memory. Stare at the rotted remains.

"Why are you calling *me,* anyway? Why for the love of Sam
Hill aren't you on a computer? You could get this over in about
ten seconds."

"Hey! Do you think you could be a little more unsympa-
thetic?"

"Sarah..." Jo paused; Sarah could hear Jo trying to restrain
herself. "Listen, sugar, you've been cow-eyed over this guy since
Paraguay." In the background, Sarah heard something thump.
Jo was apparently throwing things around. "We've *all* been telling you to hunt him down. Here, look—I'll do it for you—"

"No!" Sarah pulled the phone away from her ear. "I am going
to do this myself, Jo. I was hoping to do it—with a friend."

"Now?!" More thumping on Jo's end, like something heavy
going down stairs. "At this godforsaken time of night?"

Sarah paused. This, from a woman who rarely saw the inside

of her condo before midnight? She glanced at the cat-clock swinging its tail over the sink. "Jo, it's eight-thirty in the evening."

"Hold on."

Jo muffled the receiver, but Sarah heard her talking to someone, and then Sarah understood. *Of course.* Jo had company. Jo always had company. Jo gathered men as a wedding train might gather rice. She collected them idly, and then, occasionally, she'd shake them all off. Yet, whenever she wanted another, there he was.

Sarah had wanted only one.

"Jo, forget it." She tried to sound calm, easy. "I'll call Kate—"

"You do that." Jo walked briskly around her condo—Sarah could hear the clicking of her heels. "Oh, there she is. Grace? *Gracie!*"

Through the wire, Sarah heard a tremendous crash.

"Oh, shit!" Jo dropped the phone. "Shit! Shit—shit—shit!"

"Jo, is everything all right? Jo?!"

Sarah heard a high-pitched wail, and Jo swearing, and saying, "It's okay honey it's okay honey it's okay honey it's okay honey, I'll get a towel. It's okay honey it's okay. . . ."

Sarah listened, incredulous. Grace? The only Grace she knew was . . . Gracie Braun.

She caught her breath.

It couldn't be.

It didn't make sense.

It explained everything.

"Hang up," Jo said when she returned to the phone. Grace sobbed in the background. "I have to call 911."

"What happened?"

"There's blood everywhere. She fell. Now get off the phone—"

"I'm a nurse. How did she fall?"

"She tripped. In my living room. Coming down the last stair. Fell against the end table—"

"Did she lose consciousness?"

"I don't . . . No, I don't think so."

"Broken bones?"

"How the blazes do I know? She's bloody down to her knees. She's got a cut. On her forehead. It's welling like a Texas oil—"

"Near the eye?"

"No. Higher. By the hairline."

Sarah pulled the details from her. It seemed as if Grace had suffered a straight, two-inch slice that might need a few stitches. "Scalp wounds bleed like hell," she explained. "Don't let it get to you. Get a clean towel, apply pressure. Then drive her calmly to the emergency room. They'll have a plastic surgeon there to sew her up so well that you won't ever see it again."

"Shit. Shit." Jo paused, murmuring something to Grace. "All right. I have to go. Sarah?!"

"Yeah?"

"Don't you go telling Kate. About Grace being here."

Sarah paused, remembering an evening when Jo got all sarcastic about Kate missing a dinner because of her kid's soccer practice. "Jo, even you have to concede that in this she's an expert—"

"No! Do you hear me? No! Ain't I got enough going on? Just swear to me you *won't tell Kate.*"

Sarah reluctantly promised, then hung up. Puzzled. Not just about Jo's vehemence about Kate, but about Rachel's decision to leave her daughter with Jo. Long ago, Rachel had left the raising of her daughter to her own mother and father, at the house in Teaneck. Rachel traveled a lot. She'd decided that the best place for her daughter was in a stable home—with her grandparents in Jersey. Apparently, Rachel had changed her mind. But *Jo*? The best person to raise Grace should have been Kate.

Sarah retreated to the comfortable hollow of the couch, still clutching the receiver. She slipped off her sandals and curled her toes under her skirt. Outside, the cabs honked as they wove though the narrow street. Pedestrians murmured as they passed below her window, on their way to the more commercial area with its funky shops and restaurants. In the silence of this dusty apartment, the monitor still blazed its blue light; and the envelope still lay by the keyboard, shining.

One friend down. One to go.

She dialed a new number. It rang four times. Just as it was about to click over to an answering machine, Kate picked it up.

"Grand Central."

"It's Sarah."

"Hey." She dropped her voice. "Wasn't that wild this morning?"

"Incredible. I salute your courage."

"Anna, that number three is backward. Can you fix it, please? I don't know if it was courage or idiocy."

"Have you told Paul?"

"No." She paused. "Michael, finish that essay. Come on, two more sentences. No, I haven't told him yet."

"Kate!"

"I'll tell him, I will," Kate said, rapping twice on a door, "but only when he's receptive. Tess, you have to finish up in there. Anna's next for the bath. Bath night," she explained, drowning out Tess's complaints. "Crazy as usual."

"I got my letter."

"You have to find Colin."

Sarah started. "Am I that pathetic?"

"What else would she give you? It's about freaking time."

Sarah closed her eyes. "You know, in Burundi, my colleagues respect me. The patients gift me with goat's milk and bottles of banana wine—"

"He's holding you back, Sarah-belle. Michael, you can say the book was 'cool,' but now you have to give an example. How do you explain a book being 'cool'? Better to say the book was scary, or funny, or exciting, or boring. Easier to give examples. How long has it been? Fifteen years?"

"Fourteen." *Three months. Six days.*

"Anna, find one more thing that begins with 'f' and you'll be done, I promise. Paul, can you help her with this?" Kate puffed out some air, as if she was lifting something. "Unbelievable. She's in kindergarten, and she's coming up on an hour and a half of homework. So—did you Google him yet?"

"In my mind? About sixty times."

"Hold on. Paul, I've got more magazines in the rack in the living room. Use the kid ones—*Cricket* or *Spider*. No, Tess, I don't know where your hair dryer is. I took the kids out to dinner tonight. Crazy Jay's. They thought it was a birthday, it's been so long. Now I'm paying, though, because homework got started late."

Sarah hesitated. She didn't have a right to ask. Kate always had such a full load. Once, not long after Kate's second child was born and Kate decided to give up her job as a financial analyst,

Jo had snidely asked Kate what she did all day. By the time Kate finished listing the errands, Sarah was dreaming of the slow Paraguay afternoons spent grinding corn or rolling tortillas.

"I'm sorry, Sarah. I'm distracted. Can I help you with something?"

"Come over. I need a witness."

She hadn't meant to ask. She knew she shouldn't. She wasn't completely blind. She knew that whenever she returned to the States she wasn't quite in sync with the rest of this world, and that Jo, Kate, and Rachel always made special efforts on her behalf to stave off embarrassment or—in one particular case—arrest. To ask such a thing of Kate was to take advantage of her good heart.

But she needed a friend.

Sarah closed her eyes for a moment and wished she were home in Vermont, in that huge farmhouse with her parents and her ten sisters and brothers and her twelve nieces and nephews and her father the minister helping her pray on this, as he fired up the parish computer.

"Me?" Kate said. "You want *me* to come over?"

"I could use a buddy razzing me over my fixation on an ancient fantasy in order to get this done."

"Sarah, I...can't. It's bath night. And Michael has to work on his log cabin tonight or we'll never get it done by...I still haven't waded through the papers from their backpacks, and there's lunches to be made, and right now I'm putting in the first of three loads of laundry. Paul's helping with Anna, but he's—"

"I shouldn't have asked." Great. Now her buddies could add "pitiful whiner" to their opinion of her, along with "clueless" and "helpless." "I called Jo, but she had company."

Don't tell Kate.

"Into the city, too. At this hour. Parking's a nightmare."

"Really, Kate." She shifted her legs out from under her, set them firmly on the floor. "It's okay. It's not skydiving. I have to stop being a coward and just do this myself."

"So many damn papers...and tomorrow night's the PTA meeting, I haven't written up the agenda. Michael, I'll be right up, hold on. Yes. Hold on. Tess, I told you, look in the linen closet!"

"Kate, I'll let you go."

"*No.*"

It must be a full moon. Everyone was acting weird.

"Don't hang up. Just...just give me a minute."

Sarah heard her walking. Heard her thinking. While chaos and noise reigned in the background.

"Yes." Kate took a deep breath, as if she were rising out of a vortex. "Yes, Sarah. I'll come. I'll be there within the hour."

Indeed, within the hour Kate barged into the apartment wielding a bottle of wine. She was still sporting the T-shirt and yoga pants she'd worn under her skydiving jumpsuit that morning. Sarah rifled through the kitchen drawers and pulled out one of the six wine openers. As Kate pulled out the cork and poured two glasses, she eyeballed the garage-sale furniture, the Zulu mask on the wall, and the pressed-tin ceiling. "Some place you got here."

"It's a free bed. Tim's not home often. And he's always offering this place up to friends."

"Look. I'm making footprints. So this is what a dirty house looks like." Kate glanced at the computer, which was still on, though the connection was broken. "Geez, what's that, a reject from the 1960s?"

"Unfortunately, it works. I had a good connection when I called you, but it's dial-up, and I don't want to stick Tim with a big bill. I figured I'd try again, once you were here to do chest compressions if I pass out."

Sarah typed in the number and waited for it to dial. This time, she got through right away. "Sit down. It takes at least one glass of wine to load the home page."

Kate found the comfortable spot on the couch immediately. Sarah sat at the other end. She took a sip of the wine; it was probably a fine vintage, though she wasn't much of a drinker. Minister's daughter and all.

"All right, Miss Sarah. This is going to hurt. Are you ready?"

"I've heard doctors say that, right before they take out the bone saw."

"What do you want to find out? I mean, what would be the best thing you could discover?"

Sarah swirled her drink. One day, Colin had been playing soccer with the kids of the village. A line of sweat darkened his shirt right down the center of his back. He hadn't shaved in about a week. For a moment, he'd glanced at her, over his shoulder. Grinning.

White teeth, wild hair.

"I'm hoping," she said, "that he still has six-pack abs."

"Don't get snarky."

"All right, all right." The truth, then. "I'd want him to be happy."

"The Internet isn't going to tell you that."

"Maybe it would. I do know the man." Every square inch of him. From the V-shaped scar on his neck, just below his ear, to the long feet with their funny toes. To the fierceness of his intellect, and the fullness of his heart. "If I were to find out that he's still involved in some kind of relief work," she said, "I'd know he was happy."

"What if he's married?"

The word had the force of a grenade. Sarah jerked forward and clattered her wineglass on the coffee table. That was it, wasn't it? That was the root of it all. He was thirty-nine years old. She couldn't imagine how a man like the one she'd known in Paraguay could remain single, childless, through fourteen years. Their time together was a sacred thing in her memory, and it overshadowed every relationship she attempted. But maybe—just maybe—Colin had never felt as fiercely, and loved as thoroughly, as she had.

After all, he never came back.

"If he's married," Sarah said, the word rolling thick in her mouth, "then his wife is the luckiest witch in the world."

"And your task is over. Right here, right now, in this room."

A lot more than that will be over. She rubbed her brow so Kate couldn't read her face. Kate didn't live her life; Kate wouldn't understand. And Sarah wouldn't burden Kate with the latest story of what had happened at the camp in Burundi, only a few weeks ago. Sarah had witnessed man's inhumanity before—humanitarian aid siphoned off to warlords at ports, medical supplies lifted by eight-year-olds to fuel their addictions, budget constraints in the midst of a measles epidemic—but never anything like that poor little girl found in one of the camp's muddy alleys.

She was such a tiny little thing. She had two crooked braids, secured by wooden beads. And a rape fistula Dr. Mwami wasn't sure he could repair.

Sarah squeezed her brow and poured darkness over the memory. She forced herself to exhale the breath she'd been holding. Then she took that ugly memory and shoved it deep down into that place that held all the others, where it could fester.

This was why she *needed* the memory of Colin, she told herself. She needed to know that goodness and honesty and dedication still lived in the world. She was afraid of what would happen to her sense of balance if she discovered that Colin had left the business of international relief, that he'd settled into an easy life as a gout-footed general practitioner with a cabin on the shore of Lake Michigan.

"Okay, Sarah, now let's get to the hard part."

"Childbirth?" she asked, shaking the gloom away. "Twisting a Guinea worm out of an infected leg?"

"What if he's single?"

The idea flowed through her, dissolving the last shreds of darkness like a river of light. She hadn't allowed herself to consider Colin's availability. Because to consider it meant there was a possibility for more, and no reasonable girl would ask for more than heaven could give.

Kate swirled her wineglass toward the desk. "Look. The computer is booted. Get up and type his name."

"But—"

"He was the greatest lover you ever had. Oh, please, don't blush. You admitted that to us that night we conned you into doing a second shot of vodka. You even told us about that toe thing he did—"

"Is there nothing sacred?"

"Hey, didn't you catch me and Paul on the washing machine that night in—"

"Enough!"

"So," Kate said, her grin growing sly, "have you thought about what it would be like to be with him again?"

Sarah filled her mouth with wine. Potent and dry. She thought about his body, wiry, long, strong.

"Even just once," Kate said. "Just one more time. Even if nothing else happened." Kate leaned forward. "Because isn't that what Rachel wanted for you, Sarah? To either move ahead . . . or, at least, leave him behind."

Sarah put down her empty wineglass. The monitor blinked at her. The home page had downloaded. Her gaze fell upon Rachel's envelope. With a burst of courage, she slipped into the computer chair and typed "Google."

Kate loomed behind her. "You know, when I got my letter, I couldn't believe what Rachel had me doing."

"When you meet her in the afterlife," Sarah muttered, "push her off a cloud."

"I mean, I've got three kids at home. Huge responsibilities. I don't have the right, anymore, to risk my life. My life isn't mine."

For heaven's sake, this computer was slow. It was still loading the very simple, very plain page.

"I'm a slave to dust bunnies. And overenthusiastic twenty-something kindergarten teachers who think they have a right to screw my weekends with 'family projects.'"

The box for the search engine finally appeared. Sarah went cold. Cold that had nothing to do with the October breeze coming through the open window.

"But Rachel was right." Kate slid her glass on the desk, scraping an inch of fuzz. "It wasn't much of a risk at all. It was a well-managed risk. And in those few minutes and the hours since I plunged from eight thousand feet, I've felt more alive, more intense, and more clear-eyed than ever before. I'm not living the life I should, Sarah. Things *will* change."

Type it in. Dr. Colin O'Rourke. No. Colin Quinn O'Rourke.

"Things will change for you, too." Kate put a hand on Sarah's shoulder. Warm. Firm. Confident. She spoke into her ear. "Go ahead, Sarah. *Jump.*"

His name blinked at her from the little box. Dr. Colin Quinn O'Rourke.

Love of my life.

She tapped the enter button.

Kate wrapped her arms around her. She clutched Kate's forearm and leaned back against her. Her heart raced. Such a silly thing. She was acting like a child; she couldn't look at the screen. She knew it would take a while to load. She was tempted to ask Kate to preview it, to tell her the worst.

Kate leaned close. "Gawd, this thing is slow."

"*Tranquilo.*" Sarah spoke more to her racing heart than to Kate. "The news will come."

Then there it was. Colin's name. Running up and down the screen. Twelve hits altogether.

And seeing his name there, so steady, so real, changed everything: It turned her fear into hunger. She jerked forward in the seat. She seized the mouse. She scrolled down the entries, soaking in the snippets of information, processing them, seeing how they all fit together.

Then she came to the last. Kate gasped. Sarah covered her mouth with her hand.

"Oh my God."

chapter four

"Oh my God."

Jo grabbed the frame of the hospital bed just as Dr. Mulcahey stabbed what looked like a fishhook into Grace's forehead.

Grace—who'd been listening to the plastic surgeon chatting about the virtues of SpongeBob—turned her gaze to Jo. Jo froze. *Don't look terrified.* Jo intentionally unclenched her grip on the bed rail. *Smile. Everything's fine, just dandy.* The doctor must have numbed Grace up good; the kid couldn't possibly feel a thing. And is that . . . is that Grace's skull under all that ragged skin?

Don't faint.

The doctor's gaze never flickered from the gash. "Keep still, now, Grace, just another minute." Stab. Tug. Flash. "Nurse, why don't you take Miss Marcum back to the front desk? I understand she's got some paperwork to finish."

Jo gave in to the tug of the nurse's hand, realizing only after she was beyond the curtains and out of Grace's sight that her jaw ached because she'd been grinning like an idiot.

She followed the nurse down the blazing white hall, contemplating the idea of fainting into one of the molded plastic chairs. She was a Southern girl, after all, and fainting was a Southern girl's prerogative. It instantly absolved a woman of so very many responsibilities.

But Bobbie Jo Marcum didn't faint. Couldn't faint. At least not yet. Because the desk troll was glaring at her from the end of the hallway.

This squat and implacable medical administrator had halted her when Jo first rushed Grace into the ER. Grace had been bleeding all over both of them. The gatekeeper, ignoring the screaming child, had demanded the answers to so many pesky questions. Like when Grace was born. *In February, right, kiddo? Was it really June?* Where Grace was born. *Uhh . . . Teaneck?* Whether her immunizations were up-to-date. The kind of things a mother would know, but not a new guardian—or a pedophilic kidnapper.

Now the troll waved in the air the plastic card that Jo had tossed her as a distraction, just before Jo had barreled past the desk and shoved Grace in the arms of a surprised nurse.

"We don't take frequent-flier miles, Ms. Marcum."

Clearly, a broad smile and a sweet apology weren't going to work. Nor would flattery, Jo thought, sweeping her gaze over the troll's bleached green scrubs and iron-gray hair. So Jo simply poured herself into a chair and allowed herself a fleeting fantasy about St. Lucia in February.

The troll returned her attention to the computer screen. "Your full name."

"Bobbie Jo Marcum." She fished out her driver's license. "'Bobbie' with an 'i-e.'"

"Relationship to the patient?"

"I guess I'm her legal guardian."

"You guess."

"It's complicated."

"Try me."

"My friend died. Rachel Braun, Grace's mother." Jo remembered the letter. *I know you're going to think this is a mistake....* "In her will, she made me Grace's guardian."

"Got a copy of that document?"

Jo indicated her slim leather clutch. "You think that'd fit in this purse?"

"Adoption papers."

"Oh, please." Jo felt a sudden urge for nicotine. "Rachel died only recently."

"What about the father?"

"He was an anonymous tablespoon of semen in a test tube."

Iron Woman didn't flicker an eyelash. "Any other family? A blood relative who can verify your claim?"

Claim?

"She's got grandparents in Jersey, with a whole barrel-full of medical problems of their own." And likely to have heart attacks should they get a call with the news that another Braun was in the hospital. "I can manage the bills, if that's what you're worried about."

Just then, Jo noticed three officious-looking people turn into the hall beyond Grace's room. Not doctors. Clearly not doctors. Two of them talked together, in low and urgent tones, consulting their clipboards as they strode up the hall. The third was dressed in blue, sporting a badge. Jo watched them as they approached Grace's room, then turned into it as a group.

Oh, sweet Jesus.

She'd seen that type before. Whenever her mother was forced to file for benefits, they'd arrive, park their cars in front of her double-wide, stride across the drive, and eye her home with an anthropologist's horrified curiosity. Then they would take a good long look at her, in her borrowed clothes, and ask her mother—indiscreetly sniffing her breath—if she was sure she could care for a child . . . under the circumstances.

"Listen, I'll call the lawyer." She pulled out her cell phone. "Barry Leibowitz of Leibowitz & Rabin in Hoboken. They'll verify the will—"

"You can't use that cell phone in here."

"Then I'll use your phone—"

"This is an emergency-room phone, Ms. Marcum. Step outside to make your call. Have the lawyer call back at this number."

Jo marched through the automatic doors. As she flipped open the phone, she felt the sizzle of authoritative eyes on her back. Glancing over her shoulder, she noticed that one of the guards had followed her out of the building—as if he were suddenly in need of a breath of fresh air.

She punched in the number for the lawyer and got an answering machine. Clearly, Barry Leibowitz had no criminal practice. It was nearly ten-thirty at night, and his perky message left no emergency number for late-night bailouts. She flipped the phone shut and took a deep breath before making the one call she hadn't wanted to make.

"She's *where*?!"

Jo kept her voice neutral. "It was an accident, Jessie. I heard a noise, I looked up, and there she was wandering in my hallway. She didn't hear me call her name. She just kept walking . . .

right to the edge of the stairs." Jo flinched, remembering the crack of Grace's head against the glass table. "I insisted on a plastic surgeon—she's getting stitches right now."

"And *where* are *you,* calling *me,* while Grace is being *sewn back together*?"

"I'm doing my doggone best not to interfere with the function of every X-ray machine in the hospital."

"You should be at her bedside. She's seven years old. She must be scared to death! I'm coming in." Jessie panted, clearly running up some stairs. "What the hell were you doing, Jo? You had her for less than a day—"

"Jessie, if you don't answer my questions right now, Gracie will be spending the night in a New York City foster home, and I'll be banging a tin cup against the bars of a jail cell."

"What?!"

"Picture it. I come in here with a bleeding kid. She's got a different last name. She looks as much like me as a possum does a mountain goat. I don't even know Grace's birthday—"

"June fifteenth."

"—I don't know what grade she's in—"

"Second!"

"—or if she has allergies or previous hospital visits or medical insurance. They think I'm some sicko kidnapper, and they've got social workers lining up outside her hospital room."

Jessie went silent. Behind Jo, the security guard shuffled his feet against the sidewalk.

"So maybe," Jo continued, "you should have filled me in on a few vital details when you shoved her suitcase in the back of my car this morning." Jo turned over the scrap of paper the troll had given her, and wrote down Grace's birthdate and grade. "Now tell me her medical insurance number, so I can give the troll something to work with, until you call her directly with the rest of the information."

"Uh...hold on."

"Jessie!"

Too late. Jessie abandoned the phone; Jo heard her receding footsteps. Jessie must be off to tell Grace's grandmother Leah, who for the past three months had done nothing but visit the sick.

Jo sagged against the brick wall. Great freakin' mom she was turning out to be. And wasn't that predictable? Jo had grown up fatherless in the shadow of a chicken-processing plant, wearing Salvation Army clothes. Baby fever, she'd once told Rachel, was one fever she would *never* catch.

"Hey, I'm back." Jessie fumbled with the phone. "You still there?"

No, I abandoned Grace and bought a ticket to the Caymans.

"Okay. I found a folder in my uncle's office. Marked 'Grace.'"

"You didn't tell Leah and Abe."

"Are you crazy? Like my aunt and uncle don't have enough to deal with. Okay. We got a birth certificate. We got a couple of report cards—"

"What's the name of the school?"

Jessie told her, then continued to rifle through the papers. "We got...I guess this is a chart of immunizations. It's in the stuff Rachel sent to register Grace for school. And here's a business card....I know this guy. Dr. Migliore. He must be Grace's pediatrician. Want his phone number?"

"You think?"

"Oh, yeah. Here's Grace's health insurance card."

"A little nugget of gold."

Jessie paused. "I suppose I should have sent this off with you."

"Hey, they *did* teach you something at that fancy city school."

"I didn't expect you'd need it quite so *soon*."

"Sugar, right now I've got a security officer breathing down my neck, and though he's hot in a jackbooted kind of way, I'm a little too distracted to think about hooking up." Jo spun on a heel to eyeball the officer. "Right now, I'm going back into the hospital to check on Grace. You are going to call this number and give all that information to the tro—to the lady at the desk. Then, just maybe, I won't have to spend a night under a bare bulb undergoing interrogation—and Child Protective Services will let Grace out of its dirty clutches, okay?"

Jo gave Jessie the number and then snapped the phone closed, straightened her shoulders, and swept by the security guard. The automatic doors whooshed open, and the first thing Jo heard was the sound of the emergency-room phone ringing. The troll picked it up and then gave her a significant glance. Jessie was obviously a quick dialer.

Jo approached the desk, envisioning a velvet rope and a bouncer beyond. She knew how to deal with invisible barriers. Spent most of her life crashing them. So she just kept walking with unquestioned authority. She strode by the troll, turned the corner, and clacked her way down the hall. Her shoulders tensed. But no one followed her; no one stopped her. And as she neared Grace's room, the police officer and two social workers emerged in conversation.

The woman in the group caught her eye and met her in the hall. "You must be Mrs. Marcum?"

"Ms."

"I'm Bonnie Spencer. From Social Services." Earnest look, dangling earrings and all. "My colleague and I just finished talking to Grace."

"Is it your policy," Jo said, summoning her inner warrior, "to interview a minor without a parent or legal guardian present?"

The woman's smile tightened. "Since she seems to have neither, we took the risk."

Touché.

"Guys," the social worker said, nodding to her colleagues, "would you give us a moment?"

The men left, and Bonnie Spencer from Social Services gave Jo a discreet but thorough look-over that suggested that a certain breed of social workers went to the same school, where they were taught to gauge people's worth by reading their clothes and their body language and the tics of their faces under pressure—and destroy entire families with these conclusions.

"Grace is a quiet little girl," the social worker said, "but when I let her talk through her Lovey, she confirmed your story."

"Well, hallelujah, I've been sprung by a stuffed rabbit. May we go home now?"

"When the doctor is finished. Tell me, have you ever caught Grace sleepwalking?"

"This was her first night at my house."

"I see."

Jo tried to keep her gaze steady. It wasn't easy. She knew, just as well as this social worker, that in her Manolo Blahniks and silk sweater she didn't exactly cut the figure of a Good Mommy.

"You should keep an eye on her behavior." The woman rifled through the pockets of her suit jacket. "This little trip-and-fall may have been an accident. Or it may have been a way of getting attention. Or she may be sleepwalking. I don't think she has fully processed the loss of her mother yet. Children grieve very differently than you or me."

Jo took the card she offered. "Tell me this is the phone number for Mary Poppins."

"No. It's for Dr. Rodriguez. She's a very good child psychiatrist, one of the best in the city. I suggest you make an appointment with her as soon as possible. It'll help to get a professional opinion."

Then she left, her soft-soled shoes making no noise as she padded down the hall, leaving Jo standing there realizing she wasn't just going to be the sole caretaker of a seven-year-old girl; she was going to be the only guardian of a *grieving*, sensitive seven-year-old girl, which meant she might as well kiss the counselor's ass—she was sure to screw it up.

Why, Rachel?

Jo had grown up owning three changes of clothes. Now she had her dry cleaning and laundry picked up every Monday and returned every Thursday. She'd grown up sharing an outhouse. Now a nice Portuguese lady cleaned her toilets every week, whether they needed the wash or not. She'd ditched her childhood Sunday-newspaper route for afternoons listening to bluegrass and reading the *New York Times*, particularly to see if any of her own parties had made it into the Style section. She'd long ago reached a place she used to only dream of.

Her life was perfect, just as it was.

And Rachel had known it.

"Miss Marcum, are you all right?"

The plastic surgeon stood before her, holding Grace's chart.

No. "Yes. Just distracted. Did you finish the stitches?"

"All five of them." Dr. Mulcahey pulled a pen out of her lab coat pocket and wrote something on Grace's chart. "She's a tough kid. Very serious. Didn't cry, didn't squeal, a perfect patient. Give her acetaminophen when she gets home. She's, what, fifty, fifty-five pounds?"

Hell if I know.

The doctor did a quick calculation and wrote down the dosage—in milliliters. Jo wondered when acetaminophen had started coming in a liquid.

"And make an appointment at my office," she continued, tearing off the discharge papers, "to have the stitches taken out next week."

Jo hoped all these doctors had Saturday hours. But she couldn't think about that right now. She pulled herself together and walked into Grace's room. Grace's wound was closed. The ends of the thread splayed in odd directions. The nurse standing by the bed glanced up as soon as Jo came in and gave her a look that said, *Where the hell have you been, leaving this kid alone?*

"Ah, here she is, Grace," the nurse said. "Bet you want to get home to your own bed, huh?"

A spark lit in Grace's eyes. "Am I going home now?"

"Yeah, kiddo." Jo grabbed Grace's coat. "We're going to hail one of those funny yellow cars again. The kind we took here? The one that went so fast? The man in it will take us back home."

"To Nana's house?"

Jo shook out the coat and slipped Grace's arm into a sleeve, taking advantage of the motion to hide her face. "Back to boring old Nana's house? Oh, no. You'll be staying with Aunt Jo for a while. It'll be an adventure." It certainly had been so far. "Hey, but what's this?" Jo squinted at the stitches, then pretended to pick at them. "Girl, you've got a caterpillar on your head!"

Grace lifted one hand and ran a finger over the stitches, greasy with antibiotic ointment, as if she had just become aware of their presence. Her eyes went wide, and she drew up her knees, crossing her brown-bear slippers.

Shit.

"Just kidding, kiddo, it's covered by your hair. Why, by this time tomorrow it'll be like there's nothing there at all." Jo tugged the girl's nightgown over her knees. "Come on, now, help me get your other sleeve on."

Jo hustled her out, ahead of the tears, chatting mindlessly all the way to the elevator. After a stop at the hospital pharmacy, where Jo puzzled over a myriad of choices of children's pain reliever and finally purchased some orange-flavored Tylenol ("Cherry," Grace said, "makes me throw up"), she hailed a cab and headed home.

Manuel, the doorman, crouched to Gracie's level. "How you doing, Gracie? Everything put back together?"

Jo answered for the silent kid. "She's all stitched up."

"She's what? Stitched up?" He squinted at Grace, cocked his head, then mugged a bit as he pretended to pluck at her stitches with his fingertips "Uh, Gracie, I hate to be the one to tell you this, but you've brought something home from the hospital."

Oh, no. Oh, no—

"You've got a caterpillar on your head!"

Jo braced herself.

Grace laughed.

She laughed?

As they headed into the elevator, Manuel called after Grace: "Don't press the button, Gracie, you're too little to press the button—no, don't press that button!" Grinning, Grace poked it. Jo waved as the doors shut. Then, brightly, Jo told Grace not to press the "8"—"No, don't press the '8'!"

Grace shrank in the corner of the elevator.

Wearily, Jo pressed the "8" herself. Tomorrow, she told herself. Tomorrow will be better.

Inside the condo, Grace wandered to the scene of the crime. The end table lay on the floor. The glass top stood cocked against the banister. Magazines covered the rug. Grace stared at the spots of blood on the carpet.

"I'm going to clean that all up, honey, don't you worry. Upstairs now."

"Don't want to go upstairs."

"Aren't you tired? You've had such a big day."

She chewed on the tip of her rabbit's ear. "Don't like the dolls."

"The dolls?"

"The ones in the big glass cabinet."

Jo frowned. She'd forgotten about the corner curio in the

spare room, filled with china dolls dressed in Victorian costume. A hobby she'd taken up not long after she'd gotten her first job.

"You can play with them tomorrow," Jo said, "if you'd like."

"They stare at me."

"They have great eyes, don't they? They blink, too."

Grace tightened her grip on her bunny.

"I mean, if you move them, they blink. They don't blink on their own."

Geez. Now the demon dolls.

Grace ran her fingers across the armrest of the couch. "Nana lets me stay on the couch when I'm sick."

"What?"

"I get to watch cartoons."

A dozen thoughts flashed through Jo's mind, most of them to do with manipulation and setting bad examples and starting off on the wrong foot, but under the influence of a pair of averted brown eyes, she figured she couldn't be any worse of a guardian, so she fetched a comforter and said, "You can sleep here, *on my white couch,* if you really want to."

Jo settled Grace in front of an all-night cartoon station and scrubbed her carpet clean. When Grace finally fell asleep, splayed like she'd been shot out of a cannon, Jo dimmed the lights and poured herself a scotch. She slung it back in one grateful gulp.

She told herself she needed the alcohol for its sedative effect. It wasn't going to be comfortable sleeping in that modern living-room chair, a piece she'd bought more for style than for comfort. But what choice did she have? She certainly couldn't leave Grace down here alone. What if the kid woke up during the night and needed to go to the bathroom? She'd knock over a vase, or trip over the carpet, or walk into a wall. What if the kid wanted a cup of water? She'd pull over a chair, reach for a glass, drop it, shatter it on the tile floor, then step down in her bare feet, and then there'd be a second trip to the emergency room—

How am I going to do this?

Her own mother had done it alone. She'd worked day shifts—and, later, night shifts—shuttling Jo among friends in town, or settling her in unofficial and unregulated day cares that they couldn't really afford, until she was just old enough to be a latchkey kid. What was she, nine years old? She remembered Mom coming in after 10 p.m. smelling like henhouse and blood, still shaking off feathers. She'd worked for minimum wage, back at a time when a soul could live in Kentucky on minimum wage, cutting chicken breasts off the bone. Sweet Jesus. Jo had sworn as a teenager that the last thing she'd do was be poor in a Kentucky town.

But Jo wasn't living on minimum wage.

In fact, Jo made a really, *really* good salary.

Then Jo thought about Kate. Hyperefficient Kate, ferrying her clean kids from one sport to another, keeping a dust-free house, baking cookies to serve with low-fat milk after school, serving up a square family meal every damn night. Kate, who lived in her big rambling house with her bring-home-the-bacon husband, and behaved as if her own life had stopped with the birth of her first child.

Jo set her glass on the counter, then braced her palms on

the beveled granite countertop. She took a good look at her reflection in the stainless-steel microwave in its custom-made cabinet.

She reminded herself: She was Bobbie Jo Marcum, Mistress of Her Universe. Twenty-two people owed their livelihoods to her. Fortune 500 corporations paid her obscene amounts of money to launch their newest products at impossibly chic blowout parties. She had to stop thinking of motherhood as Kate did—as something overwhelming, something impossible, something so all-consuming that her own ambitions stopped for it. She had to treat the sudden appearance of Gracie in her life just like any other eleventh-hour project. It wasn't going to be simple, it would require great organizational skills and a search for professionals, but that's what she got paid for. That's what she was good at.

Maybe, just maybe, that's why Rachel chose her instead of Kate.

Besides, Jo knew there wasn't a damn problem in the whole world that couldn't be solved with money.

> Curled up on my bed
> In my cramped old room,
> Teaneck, New Jersey

Dear Kate,

If you're reading this, darling, then my last desperate treatment has failed, and I'm gone.

I'm so sorry you had to find out this way. I wish I'd told all of you about the cancer earlier. I was so convinced I could beat it. I pictured it like another mountain I had to climb. I didn't want you fussing over me, and worrying, when surely I'd be back to my old self, and soon.

It's strange, the things you think about after you get the bad news. When the doctors first told me, the one thing I wanted to do—more than anything—was to go skydiving. Skydiving has a way of clearing my mind, focusing energies, and revealing what's really important in life. Boy, did I need that.

So I called you, Kate. You were the first friend I thought of. For years I've been trying to get you to come with me. There's a reason for that. Kate, for a long time I've had the sense that you're overwhelmed by your own life. You need to rise above it for a little while, so you can see it more clearly. But you begged off. Maybe you remember? You needed to attend a soccer tournament with Tess. But someday, you promised. Someday.

Someday is here, darling. There are no cell phones where I'm going, so this letter is my very last request. Go skydiving, Kate. I'll be with you in spirit when you tumble out of the plane. I'll be with you when you pull the chute. You won't see me, Kate, but I'll be there anyway, watching you come alive again.

Will you do that for me?

Love,
Rachel

chapter five

Kate flew again—this time, nearly solo.

The wind sucked the breath right out of her. The loose jumpsuit battered her body. Bubba flew on her left, gripping one arm and one thigh. A lean young buck by the name of Keifer tumbled to her right, holding her just as tight.

I'm alive.

A single thought, electrifying her mind. Oh, she understood that she was tumbling at terminal velocity toward the ground, with all its bristly trees and electric wires and concrete surfaces. And she remained keen enough to watch Keifer's hand signals and heed the lessons of four hours of training. But all that was as automatic as her beating heart, as subconscious as breathing—what she felt above all was the fierce tingling certainty of being *alive*.

She lifted her head to grin at the camera on Keifer's helmet. The wind caught under her lips and snatched away her laughter. Somewhat below and to her south, two trainers released another student. After a few moments, the student pulled his cord. A red parachute exploded into the sky.

She breathed through her nose and experienced this, her

body careening through the atmosphere, high above the world. She felt capable of anything, *everything*—yet in control of nothing—the way she'd felt a long, long time ago. Before she was married, mothered, mortgaged. Here in the sky, the weight of those years peeled away from her—one after another—stripping off and reeling into oblivion.

Keifer signaled. She signaled back. All at once, the men's grip eased. They swept away from her, suctioned by the wind.

She tumbled alone.

I'm doing it. Kate flexed her arms. She wobbled, then steadied. The air itself cradled her up. She had only three seconds.

One.

Why had she never done this before? Rachel had tried to talk her into it so many times. Every time Rachel started training for a bike race or a rock-climbing expedition or went for her scuba-diving certification or to learn CPR with the American Red Cross, she had always asked Kate to join her.

Two.

But first it was the demands of her job that had stopped Kate, and after that her husband, and too soon after that she had a baby and then another baby, and then another baby, and then there was a mortgage and college funds and first communions and PTA—

Three.

Grief welled up. She let it happen; she wanted to *feel.* That's why Rachel had done this to her. Amazing how a jump could clear the fog from her head. And now Kate wanted to feel this intensely forever.

Pull!

With a whistle, the cords unfurled. The blue cloud of the

parachute caught the wind and billowed. Abruptly the chute yanked on her harness, snatching her vertical. In a second, the roaring of the wind stopped, the suction in her lungs gave way, and she settled back into her body.

She floated through the sky, marveling at the white haze of the horizon, the gold and red foliage sprouting amid the green carpet of the world. She welcomed the grief; she even welcomed the guilt. Over how much she and Rachel had drifted apart. Over how many times she'd said no. Over her own fierce, frowning opinions of Rachel's choice to bear a child without a father—an idea Rachel had presented over dinner as if it were just another trip to the Brazilian jungle.

Today...right now...with the limits of her world as far as the horizon, Kate could almost understand.

The drop-zone target glowed bright yellow on the tarmac. It expanded beneath her. Following the hand signals of her floating mentors, she gripped the risers and pulled them the way she'd been trained, to aim closer to the target.

But her gaze wasn't on that little yellow target. It was on an iridescent Volkswagen Beetle parked off the edge of the runway, behind a high, razor-wire-topped fence. Just beyond that fence grew a thick oak, and through the webbing of branches, she glimpsed the car that held her unsuspecting husband.

He'd come.

Just like she'd asked him to—luring him with the promise of a lunchtime backseat tryst in a deserted airport parking lot—neglecting to tell him one tiny little detail: She'd be arriving by parachute.

She yanked the right handle. She pulled it down and across her chest. The other two students, already aground, leapt and waved at her from the pool of their parachutes. She kept her gaze on the flash of metal between the branches. As she skimmed lower, the tree drifted out of her sightline. Then she glimpsed Paul, a lanky figure draped against the hood.

Her heart swelled. She'd been waiting for this moment since she'd first jumped out of a plane. Of course, she was nervous about his reaction to the sight of her falling from the sky, but she kept reminding herself that they'd both been adventuresome, once. After college, they'd backpacked through Europe, sleeping in flophouses and working the wine-grape harvest just to extend their stay. Once, they'd gotten lost hiking in the Adirondack Mountains for three full days. For their honeymoon, they'd surfed the killer waves off Oahu's Makapu'u Beach. As soon as he got past the surprise, he'd be thrilled to see her floating down from the sky.

She couldn't think about him now; she had to concentrate on landing. The scenery whipped by swiftly, and she was coming down fast. One of the instructors waved, signaling her to pull the left riser, to *pull*. The target loomed. She should be a good girl, land where she was told. It was her first freefall, too early to start hot-dogging it. She'd be judged on how well she landed.

But the devil on her shoulder won.

She veered left on the final turn and straightened her arm. One of the instructors shouted. She ignored him. And kept ignoring him, even when the painted yellow target swept past beneath her feet.

Under her, the smooth asphalt ended in old paving, cracked and split by weeds, and still she flew above it, buoyed by a low-lying gust of wind. The asphalt deteriorated to chunks and then to rubble. She touched down, dragging two ruts through the debris, until she caught her foot in a fissure and stumbled. She righted herself and then stumbled again as the parachute overshot her, unfurling on the weedy lot no more than twenty yards from her own husband.

From behind a high chain-link fence, Paul flashed a lazy grin and applauded. Kate searched his face, waiting for him to realize who stood before him. His features stilled for a moment, but it wasn't the stillness of recognition. This was the kind of expression he wore when an idea came upon him suddenly, at dinnertime, with a spoonful of peas halfway to his mouth. She suspected that later he would hole up in the home office and work on how to simulate the billow of a parachute—as realistically as possible—in his next computer game.

From the target drop zone, Bubba and Keifer came running.

"I'm fine, I'm fine!" She brushed off her jumpsuit, then unhooked the harness. Free of the parachute, she curled her hand around her helmet and pulled it off. Her hair tumbled in the wind. Very much like Lola Lipstick, the buxom wasp-waisted sword-wielding heroine of one of Paul's more "mature" computer games.

Paul froze mid-clap.

She strode straight for him—striding swiftly, with purpose, as if she could pass right through the chain-link fence and slam up against him. Then she opened her arms as she hit the fence, seizing two fistfuls of links.

She couldn't stop grinning. "Hey, darling."

He made a strangled noise and stumbled back, smacking against the hood of the VW. He braced himself upright. His blue eyes blazed with incomprehension...and shock. "What the *hell*?"

She pressed her body against the fence, feeling the pressure of the grid dig into her breasts. "Hungry for lunch, darling? I am. I'm just *starved*."

Paul blinked at the yellow jumpsuit, and then glanced beyond, to the parachute deflated upon the ground, and then still farther beyond, to the instructors grinning at a respectful distance. He looked like he'd been beta-testing a new game that had just, inexplicably, jumped six levels.

"Kate...What did you just do?"

She leaned away from the fence long enough to unzip the jumpsuit all the way to her crotch. Her shirt rode up to show the wink of a navel. "I jumped from an airplane—with a little help—from eight thousand feet."

He shook his head reflexively. She noticed the barber-short cut of his hair. He'd recently had it trimmed. When they were young, he never used to cut it until the shag brushed his collar.

His hand slipped on the hood of the car. He lost his footing and fell back, his hip thumping on the hood. "Why," he said, his voice hoarse between breaths, "why the hell did you do that?"

"Because of Rachel."

"Rachel," he parroted. A line of concentration deepened between his brows. "Rachel's dead."

"It was her last request. She asked me to go skydiving." She lifted her face to the sun. "So I went skydiving."

"I can't get you to back up your freakin' hard drive, but one word from Rachel..." His voice sounded strange, strangled.

He pushed away from the car, clasped his hands on his head, and swiveled on one foot. He paced a dozen steps, then crouched over like a baseball catcher, searching for answers in the dirt. She could almost hear him thinking, thinking, working his way back down the levels, searching for the algorithmic root of the problem.

Suddenly he shouted, *"Have you lost your DAMN MIND?"*

Her euphoria dipped, like a sudden plunge through an air pocket. Of course, he was shocked. Of course, he was confused. She'd made very sure these past days not to give him a clue about what she was doing. But in her fantasies, she'd dreamed of a different reaction. She'd imagined something like the conclusion of Paul's last multilevel adventure game—where the warrior woman throws herself into the arms of the most worthy of her heroic sidekicks amid an exploding shower of stars.

This wasn't working. She needed to get closer to him before his anger ruined a golden opportunity. She pushed away from the fence, searching down its length for the gate. "Paul, don't be angry."

"Don't be angry?" He lifted his head long enough to glance at the sky, where another Cessna circled the drop zone. "It's not like you used my computer screwdriver to open the molasses! I just saw my wife and the mother of my three children *jump out of an airplane.*"

"I took four hours of training today." She squinted down the long length of fence. Was that a gate all the way down there? "I had a professional diver on either side of me, both guiding me down. I had two chutes. The main one and a reserve. If one hadn't worked, the other would have—"

"Is this supposed to *reassure me*?"

"I know how to hover. I know how to check my altitude. I know when to pull the cord. I know how to eject the first chute and pull the reserve if something goes wrong. I spent an hour learning how to jump out of the plane. You know, it doesn't matter; I could have been killed on the drive to this airport. I could collapse from a brain aneurysm tomorrow. We can die anytime, just like Rachel—"

"You did this before," Paul interrupted, shooting up to his full, lanky height. "You did this on Tuesday. Before you came to my office."

She scraped her fingers across the fence, the memory of their sex-on-the-desk putting a smile on her face.

Paul swore. Fiercely.

I need to get close to him. She swiveled on her heel and strode for the gate. Out of the shadow of the oak, the heat of the sun hit her shoulders. She peered up at the blue sky. She'd been up there. Only moments ago. Free-falling, the wind beating on her face. She felt it still, but the feeling was melting into memory. How she'd balanced so well on the updraft of air. What would it have been like if she'd changed positions, or straightened up? Maybe she could control the fall if she wanted to. She could have flown across the sky. With a few more hours of training, she could do it herself, count down to the deployment, and maneuver the handles to drop right into the center of the zone.

What would it be like to live like that always? To be present in the moment. To be fully and unsparingly alive.

Paul fell into pace with her, striding fiercely on the other side of the fence. "You didn't tell the kids?"

"Of course not."

"It's good to know you haven't *totally lost your mind.*"

Paul had worn body spray; the scent wafted between them, warmed by his body. She began to tingle in all the right places: She wanted to make love with him right now, in the backseat of that tiny car, even if he was angry. She wanted to shake him out of his senses, shake some sense back *into* him. Today he looked so good in his starched white shirt and officious blue tie—dressed up like Mr. Corporation—and, oh, how she wanted to strip him out of it. Beneath the uniform beat the heart of a laid-back surfer boy with an aptitude for math, a careless sense of time, and a wicked sense of fun. He'd been following the straight and narrow path, charmingly so, since the day Tess was born. But in college they'd had a habit of meeting in the laundry room at three in the morning: she without underwear, and he armed with olive oil and a handful of quarters.

Oh, how she wanted that man back.

Paul, striding furiously to keep pace with her, yanked at his tie. "Listen, if this is some kind of midlife-crisis thing, I'm all for dumping the Bug and buying a sporty red convertible—"

"It's not a midlife crisis! I just decided to do something fun, something *different,* like we used to."

"Go roller-skating, then. Go to the opera. Take up kickboxing. But for this, you should have asked me."

"So you could set up a flowchart and talk me out of it?"

"Marriage. Team. United front."

"I already knew what you'd say." She rattled the reasons on her fingers. "I can't do this. I have three kids. You'll kill me. I can't fit it into my damn schedule. It's too dangerous—"

"Kate, it's one thing buying an ugly pink paisley couch without consulting me—"

"A couch you came to *love,* I might add—"

"—because a couch isn't going to splatter your intestines all over the tarmac."

"When was I supposed to bring this up, anyway? While you're racing to catch the train and I'm wrestling the kids into their coats for school? It wasn't exactly on the list of 'information to be exchanged' while you're helping Mike with his log project and I'm fighting with Tess over algebra homework."

"Lame, Kate. Lame."

He was right, of course. She had intentionally hidden this from him, fearing he'd react this way. But she'd been struggling to find a way to explain how she was feeling so that it would make *sense* to someone who hadn't hurled himself out of an airplane.

She strode with more force, digging tracks in the rubble, and tried arguing from a different direction. "Do you remember when you went away with your buddies last month? For your annual golf weekend?"

"Yeah?"

"You had to buy airline tickets, make reservations at the hotel, set up tee times, and pack your bags—"

"Is there a point to this?"

She bit down on an angry retort as she side-kicked a chunk of rubble out of her path. "When I spent a single night in the city, after Rachel's funeral, I had to do the same. I made arrangements to stay with Jo, called for dinner reservations, packed my bags. But I had a few more things to do as well." The blur of it all, in the midst of shock. "I had to arrange two sleepovers. I called six moms so I could find three of them willing to shuttle each of our kids to soccer, piano, Tae Kwon Do, and then back home again, so that no one would be inconvenienced that first afternoon. Then I arranged for that high-school girl to come in to serve the kids' dinner. A dinner I pre-cooked, with elaborate reheating instructions, so you all wouldn't starve. I stocked the fridge with food and did three loads of laundry so nobody would be wearing dirty underwear—"

"I'm waiting," he interrupted, "for the part about *skydiving*."

"The point," she said, wishing the gate closer, "is that, with skydiving, I didn't *have* to make a hundred thousand arrangements. I just went out and did it. Think about it, Paul. When you want to do something, you just do it. When I want to do something—even something simple—it's an effort that inconveniences a dozen people and involves a spiderweb of fragile scheduling arrangements. Sometimes I just feel so *trapped*."

Kate stopped in her tracks and gave him a long, steady look. Paul tended to lose himself in deep thought, and rise up abruptly, and with great puzzlement, into the world. As she scanned his oh-so-familiar face, with its craggy cheekbones and sharp jaw, she knew he wasn't entirely with her, here, in the present—she knew he wasn't getting it.

But he always did have the most amazing blue eyes. As a smitten young woman, she'd spent hours reeling in their open skies.

"Tell me," Paul said, with absolute incredulity, "that you're just kidding."

She stumbled, as if she'd been punched in the solar plexus. The ground tilted beneath her feet. She seized a handful of links, seeking balance, as the horizon shifted. The last of her euphoria dissipated like smoke.

Paul flexed his strong fingers, ticking off his points, one by one. "We've got the perfect life. We've got a four-bedroom house. We've got three great kids. We have a healthy bank account. None of us are dying of cancer—"

"I know, I *know*," she interrupted, pushing off the fence and striding once more toward the gate, "I know we're comfortable. I know we've got insurance policies, a retirement plan, and sex like clockwork on Tuesdays and Saturdays—"

"You get to stay home with our kids," he continued, swiveling on one foot, walking backward so he could glare at her. "We have two vacations a year—"

"Yes, yes." She sighed. "And *do* I love them, I really do, though we spend them in the same town, the same hotel, in the same room, where I make lunch every single day, and we go to the same take-out restaurants every night."

"The kids love it!"

"Chicken-of-the-Sea on Monday. The Clam Shell on Tuesday. The Hammerhead on Wednesday—though Tess will occasionally change from her usual dish of fried cod to butterfly shrimp—"

"You need to talk to Sarah," he said angrily, reeling away, "and get some perspective on life."

She squeezed her eyes shut, thinking of Sarah and her stories of parasites and female circumcision. "Paul, I'm not complaining—I *know* we have a good life. A pretty-near-perfect life." She raked a hand through her tangled hair, frustration rising, because she knew it didn't make sense to feel as she did, amid such plenty. But wasn't it true that material things didn't always bring happiness? Wasn't it true that she and Paul had felt much closer, much more in love with each other, when they were living on ramen noodles and sleeping in youth hostels?

"Listen," she said, "I went skydiving today, and not just for Rachel. Tuesday was for Rachel. Today was for *us*."

For the way they used to be, before marriage, motherhood, and mortgages fixed them in their roles. Before responsibilities filled up their days and drove out all spontaneity. For the way she used to feel when Paul glanced at her from across a crowded room; or, at a dinner party, when, under a table, he took her hand in his.

"For the love of God." He jerked the first button of his shirt free. "Can't you just leave the massage oil on the bedside table?"

"Paul, it's not that simple."

"Isn't it?"

"No!"

"Listen, Kate. Listen." He dropped back to walk at her pace, his chest rising on a deep breath. He ran his fingers along the links, brushing her fingertips where they met in the gaps. "I know Rachel's death rocked you."

"Of *course* it did—"

"Last week I found the peanut butter in the refrigerator. And yesterday you put Michael's underwear in my drawer."

Did you notice me chewing my nails to nubs? Or tossing in bed until two a.m.?

"But, from this moment on, let's behave like rational adults," he continued. "No more jumping out of airplanes. Promise me that."

"But I *love* it." She braced herself. He wasn't going to like this. "And the free-fall course is two phases. I just started phase I."

"Phase I?"

"If I want to get my USPA A License, I've got to go through two phases, of twenty levels each."

"Your *license*?"

He sounded so incredulous, so dismissive, that prickles of anger worked up her spine. "You know, fifteen years ago, you would have applauded me for jumping out of an airplane."

"Fifteen years ago, we didn't have three kids and a mortgage."

"Fifteen years ago," she repeated, as she finally reached the gate, a six-foot cutout in the high fence, "you would have jumped with me."

"Fifteen years ago, we thought we had nothing to lose. We were *children*. We thought we were *immortal*—"

She shook the gate, glaring at the chain twisted around the posts, and the heavy lock binding it closed.

"—but we're not kids anymore, Kate, and here you are planning to risk your life on a regular basis—and risk the happiness of your three kids as well. And for what?" Paul slapped his fingers over hers, through the links, squeezing them to stop her from shaking the fence. "For what, Kate? For a really good lay?"

She ripped her fingers out from under his. "How about for a really good marriage?"

Paul went utterly still.

Damn.

She shoved herself away from the fence, away from him, away from the echo of her words. This wasn't going as planned. She'd wanted to make post-skydiving love with him—a wild, swift joining—and then hit him with the next tiny bit of important information while he was still bleary and post-coital. Then, at least, he'd have been moderately receptive. *No, no, no!* She didn't want to wade into the thickness of these issues, not now, maybe not ever. Even in the best of circumstances, it would have been a struggle to explain to him what had happened to her since her first jump, on Tuesday.

Rachel had said in her letter that skydiving would clear Kate's mind, focus her energies, and bring her in touch with what was really important in life. Well, in truth, Kate barely understood what she was feeling. She just knew she was in the grip of emotions so fierce that they flooded common sense and they *had to be obeyed.* She had to follow her instincts, wherever they took her—to go back was impossible. How could she explain to Paul something so gnarled with complications, so viscerally emotional, so intensely important? The only thing she knew for sure was that, in the crazy, overscheduled madness of her life, she was losing someone.

And it wasn't Rachel.

It was Paul.

She paced in a tight, uneven circle. "Paul, when was the last time you took me on a date?"

His voice, resonant and angry: "You're changing the subject."

"It *is* the subject. It's about our marriage. Think about it."

"I don't have to. Just two weeks ago, we went to that Portuguese place in the city—"

"—with your clients."

He glared at her, a furrow deepening between his eyebrows. "We went for sushi. On our wedding anniversary."

"Seven months ago. And I made those plans. Called for

reservations two months ahead of time. Hired the babysitter. Took a bus into the city—"

"Is there a point to this?"

"Yes." She rubbed her forehead, where a dull ache threatened. "I know our life is comfortable. Wonderfully so." That's why it had taken a leap out of an airplane to get her to notice that something wasn't quite right. "Our routine is so comfortable, Paul, that I can see its bullet-straight path right to the end. It's the two of us in our old age, eating dinner on Saturday nights at the local Applebee's in absolute silence—"

Paul interrupted. "Who the hell is that?"

Kate swiveled on her heel. Bubba jogged their way. He'd slipped out of his jumpsuit. He looked lean in a tight T-shirt and a pair of jeans. "Hey, Kate," he yelled, "the video's done, and we're all waiting for you back at the hangar."

"I'm coming."

"Bring your friend, too. We've got some kicking footage."

"Just give me a minute."

Bubba eyed them both, backed up, then turned to jog back to the hangar.

"Is it Sven, then?"

"What?"

"Mr. Universe there—he's the one rattling your cage."

"Don't be an idiot, Paul."

"Then it's about Lola Lipstick, isn't it? You give me the hairy eyeball every time you see one of the prototypes—"

"Forget it."

She turned away and headed after Bubba. This had been a bad, bad, bad idea. Paul wasn't going to get it now, and he wasn't going to get it later, when she told him her plans.

Fifteen years. Wears away a marriage like water over rock.

"Kate. Kate!"

"I have to go." She stopped anyway, pulled by the intensity of his voice. "Bubba is expecting me."

"Kate, listen." Paul clutched the links, shaking them. "All right. All right, you win." He shifted uneasily. "Can't do it this weekend, but next Saturday, we'll go out. A date. Just you and me. I'll get reservations. The Highwood Manor—"

"I'll be busy next Saturday." She gave up all hope of easing him into the truth. "It's all arranged. I got my shots today."

"Shots? *Shots?*"

"I've already called your mother. She's flying in to watch the kids. I've arranged everything around your schedule. I'll have the pantry full and the clothes washed and the long-term projects finished and the Halloween costumes done, too, just in case I stay over a little—"

"Stay over?"

"Paul, when I went to Rachel's funeral I realized something. It was the first time in years that I went away, alone, with my friends. How pitiful is that? I only see my friends when one of them is dead."

"You're leaving us."

"Don't complicate this, Paul. I'm not your father. I'm not leaving you, I'm just going on *vacation*. Sarah needs me, so I'm going to make up for lost time. You don't even have to worry about money. It's in the budget—I've arranged to work Christmas hours at the mall, wrapping presents, to help pay for it—"

"This is about Rachel again, isn't it? If she's got you mountain-climbing or BASE jumping—"

"This has nothing to do with Rachel. I'm doing this for *us*." Grinding a foot in the dirt, she turned around and strode right up to the fence. She stopped inches from the links, inches from his angry face, inches from all that powerful muscle, close enough to feel his heat. "Listen to me. Sarah's not going to need me the whole time we're there—she's either going to be very busy or on a quick plane back to Burundi. But *I'm* staying the whole time. And I want you to join me." She met his angry blue gaze and held it steady. "But this time, Paul, I'm not making the plans. This time, *you* have to make it happen."

He curled his fingers into the links, staring at her as if he'd never seen her before in his life.

"On Tuesday," she said, "Sarah and I are flying to India."

chapter six

After telling a bald-faced lie to a Customs officer, Sarah confirmed what she'd begun to suspect during the twenty-hour trip to Bangalore: Bringing Kate to India was a mistake.

"Kate, walk straight." Sarah stumbled, unbalanced by Kate's weight and the drag of Kate's overstuffed suitcase. She shoved her taller friend upright. "Fake it for a few more minutes. We're almost out of Customs."

"It's so hot."

"Yeah, well, say a couple of grateful prayers for that." Sarah resisted the urge to glance over her shoulder, to the officers whose gazes she felt boring into their sweaty backs. "If the air conditioning in this airport was working, you'd be the only one drenched in sweat, and we'd still be back there, arguing with the viceroys."

"Yeah, but couldn't you think up a better lie than telling them I'm drunk?"

"Better they think you a drunken tourist rather than a diseased one." Sarah gave Kate's gigantic suitcase a yank. "I just saved your ass from Indian quarantine. Keep walking."

"I'm not sick."

Sarah closed her gritty eyes and willed one more drop of patience. Her back ached from so many uncomfortable hours on a cramped, stinking airplane. "Kate, how many shots did you take last week? Diphtheria and tetanus? Polio? Hep A? Meningitis?"

"Gotta take the typhoid capsules—"

"Oh, no. The only pills you're taking are aspirin. Stop grabbing my backpack. You're pulling me down."

"Which door?"

Sarah looked at the single door leading from Customs to the main area of the airport. Then she looked at Kate, shiny with sweat, her face flushed right up to the hairline, her gaze unfocused, drunkenly trying to put one foot in front of the other. Her nurse's eye told her: a hundred and one, maybe a hundred and two. Starting to get delirious. The doctor who'd given her all those shots in such a short time should be flogged. Kate could be out of it for days.

Days. Days when Sarah would have to nurse Kate to health, cocooned in the cushy Western hotel Kate's husband had insisted they book, the same hotel where Colin's conference was taking place. How easy it would be to hide herself in an air-conditioned room and let the opportunity of seeing Colin...just slip right by.

Rachel's voice, clear as a gunshot.

Coward.

An image of Rachel bloomed in Sarah's mind: Rachel, in full climbing regalia, grinning from the top of a craggy rock face, watching Sarah—sweaty and exhausted—struggle at a tricky pass.

Hurts like hell, doesn't it, Pollard? Push through it, kid, because heaven's all the way up here.

Sarah shifted Kate's weight and plowed forward, following the signs to ground transportation. Well, Sarah knew that finding Colin was going to hurt like hell. She'd done nothing but think about him, staring out the airplane window as the world flew by. He was here, now, somewhere in Bangalore. Walking within the same ten square miles. Flesh and blood. No longer just a shimmering memory.

As she plunged herself, and Kate, and Kate's ridiculous suitcase into the chaotic terminal, she wondered if he was passing through this very crowd. Strolling amid the bright-sari-clad women. Dodging the same laughing children who swarmed around them. Perhaps picking up a colleague from the airport, another speaker in the panel on "Team Management of Cleft and Craniofacial Anomalies." Or maybe he was perusing the wares of the kiosks—like the one she dragged Kate past, fragrant with incense. Or the next, piled high with sandalwood sculptures. Maybe he was at the spice seller's just across the way, purchasing cumin, coriander, or saffron.

I must be out of my mind.

Kate groaned, "Are we there yet?"

Sarah had stopped cold, right in the middle of the terminal. Men with suitcases shouldered past, bumping them without apology. A woman in a blue sari muttered something as she shepherded her flock of children past them.

She couldn't think about Colin right now: She had to triage. The first priority was getting through the phalanx of porters and touts and rickshaw drivers clustered by the doors to the pre-paid taxi booth, where she was sure they wouldn't be cheated—and then to the hotel, to get Kate hydrated, medicated, and in bed.

A tug on Kate's suitcase informed her that they were already under attack.

"Let me take this for you, madame, I have a very, very good taxi—"

"Thank you, but no," Sarah said, giving the suitcase a firm yank. "We've got a metered taxi waiting—"

"A metered taxi will cheat you," he said, and the purity of his English accent put her on alert. "Me, I'll take you into Bangalore for free."

She blinked up into a pair of laughing brown eyes in a face as dark as mahogany. Her heart made a strange little leap as she recognized his growing smile. He wore his usual battered cotton shirt and a pair of well-worn khakis. In Africa, even at a distance of five kilometers or more as he bounced along in his jeep, she'd recognize him by the silhouette of his finely shaped head. But Sarah didn't believe what she was seeing, because there was no reason for Samuel Roger Tremayne, the British/Nigerian supplies coordinator for the Burundi refugee camp, to be standing in front of her in a Bangalore airport.

"It's good to see you, too," Sam said, gently tugging the handle of the suitcase. "But we'd best stop the chatter and get to the car. I'm parked double, and the bobbies around here don't like that much."

He disappeared into the crowd.

Kate asked, "Did that hunk of man just steal my luggage?"

"What? No." Sarah readjusted Kate's weight, her mind racing but not quite catching up. "No, he's a friend—a colleague."

"You're unbelievable. You've got agents of the Sarah Survival Network even in India."

Sarah ducked around a cluster of travelers huddled over a guidebook, straining her neck to keep Sam and the battleship of a suitcase in sight. "Sarah Survival...who?"

"SSN." Kate aimlessly waved her hand, narrowly missing Sarah's cheek. "It's the way you get from one end of the earth to another with empty pockets and maxed-out credit cards."

"He shouldn't be here." Sarah shouldered through the doors of the terminal into a dense wall of humidity. She muscled Kate through a line of cab drivers. Sam unlocked the trunk of a white car, a far cleaner model than he usually drove. "He's supposed to be in Burundi," she said pointedly, as they got within earshot, "watching over the camp while I'm gone."

"Dr. Mwami is well stocked for the time being," Sam said, hurling the suitcase effortlessly into the trunk of the car. "And I needed a holiday."

"Sarah, are you going to introduce m—"

"A holiday, Sam? In Bangalore?"

"Let me tell you about the beaches in Goa, Sarah-belle." He swung the back door open and gestured for Kate to slip in. "They're within driving distance from here. They're dotted with shacks that serve icy beer and food spicy enough, even for me. I found a clean place to sleep for three dollars a day. And the beaches are full of white sand, as soft as a woman's skin."

Sarah felt her fair skin flush. She dipped her head to avoid Sam's eye, protecting Kate as she helped her into the backseat. "Last time I spoke to you," Sarah argued, swinging her own backpack into the car, "all you could talk about was quitting the business, telling me how you were dying for bangers and mash and cricket on television."

"The Indian Cricket Squad will be training on the outskirts of the city today, there'll be matches later in the week—"

"Dr. Mwami told you I'd be here, didn't he?"

She looked up too fast. He'd slung one arm over the door and braced his other hand on the roof of the car, trapping her in the circle of his heat. She could see the faint ridge of the scar on his cheek, the one he'd gotten as a boy, the one that made Rachel confess, after she'd met him last year, that Sam had the sleek, exotic look of the singer Seal and twice the sensuality.

But she and Rachel judged people differently.

"The good doctor," he said, as a muscle moved the scar in his cheek, "may have mentioned your plans."

"And on the strength of that, you came to Bangalore."

"India is not Burundi, Sarah-belle. Who is going to save you from the cons of the big, gritty city? Who else will bail you out," he said, as his gaze flickered past her, "after you're thrown in jail for parking double in a restricted zone?"

Sarah picked up the hint. An officer approached, gesturing with his baton to move the car. She closed Kate in and swiftly slipped into the passenger's seat as Sam raised his hands, feigning ignorance. He folded himself into the driver's seat and stepped on the gas.

Sam swung the car into the flood of traffic. Sarah gripped the dashboard and felt a familiar tingle of anger. Sam had the unique ability to do this to her—make her feel prickly, unnerved. Off-balance.

"You shouldn't have come, Sam," she said. "I don't need to be rescued."

"Who said anything about rescuing you?" Sam swerved to avoid a rickshaw jerking too quickly into the flow. "I need a vacation, you need a driver, and here I am."

"I could have hired one."

"You'd be cheated."

"A native driver would know more about these roads than you do." A light loomed at an intersection. "It's green."

"I know enough about the roads," he said, cutting off a battered taxi to get through the light, "and I won't have my hand out for baksheesh, nor will I be driving you to some uncle's incense shop when it's a temple you want to see—"

"Did Dr. Mwami tell you *why* I was coming?"

Sam took his eyes off the road for only a minute, but the steady look he gave her informed her he knew *everything*.

Her insides went liquid. It wasn't possible. Sam *couldn't* know. She'd told Dr. Mwami *where* she was going, but not *why*—she wasn't about to admit to her boss that she was chasing down an old flame. Yet Sarah felt the heat of Sam's knowledge, and it melted her into utter mortification. Sam was a man who carried, in his head, a map of ever-shifting, critical information about three government and six rebel movements that made him indispensable in supplying their isolated and often beleaguered refugee camp with food, fuel, and medical necessities. What Sam didn't know, Sam would—and apparently did—discover.

Sarah turned away from those all-seeing eyes. She pressed her head against the glass, gazing at the Bollywood posters plastered on the auto-rickshaw speeding beside them. Her throat ached from thirst; her body ached from lack of sleep; grit scoured her eyes with every blink. Kate started singing in the backseat, a strange jumping melody that only she understood. And now there was Sam to contend with—Sam, an unnerving complication in her life, and a man who also happened to have been in Paraguay when she and Colin were lovers.

Kate's fingers curled over the front seat, and she hauled herself up so she could rest her chin on the edge. "Sarah, are you going to introduce me, or do I have to puke all over the back of this car to get your attention?"

"Sam, this is Kate, an old friend of mine." Sarah eyed the oncoming light. "Yellow, but you can make it."

"Pleasure's mine, Kate," he said, flashing his I'll-charm-a-goat-from-a-Hutu grin in the rearview mirror as he powered past a lumbering truck. "You are the one with all the children?"

"Just three. How many do you have?"

"Oooh, none. That I know of." He leaned on his horn as a rickshaw driver made a dangerous swerve into what most Westerners would consider Sam's lane. "Did the flight do you in, or did Air France fill you with wine?"

"Kate's suffering from idiocy," Sarah interjected, as the bleary Kate melted to his charm—literally, her head slipping so she rested her cheek on the edge of the front seat. "She took too many vaccinations in too short a time."

"Ah, well," Sam said, "Nurse Sarah will have you up and touring the maharaja's palace in a day or two. I've seen her work. There's none better."

"Red, Sam. *Red*."

Sam slammed on the brakes and skidded, coming to a stop with the nose of the car poking into the intersection. "You've got to be quicker than that, Sarah. We'll end up in some Indian hospital—"

"—which will have some of the best doctors in the world. And it'll be my punishment for getting in the car with a color-blind driver."

The slumped Kate emitted a high-pitched squeal.

"Mostly blue-green," Sam explained quickly. "But yellow-red gets me on cloudy days. But it's only eight kilometers to the hotel, and most of it highway from here, so don't you worry."

Kate's voice went up an octave. "Sarah?"

"Sam is our logistics man in Burundi," Sarah explained. "He sees that our camp is properly supplied. Occasionally, he runs guns through checkpoints by stashing them inside medical machinery."

"Now, Sarah," Sam said, his voice full of warning, "don't be giving Kate the wrong impression."

"Am I?"

Kate popped up. "You're a gunrunner?"

"Sarah is like a princess in a tower. She wraps herself up in a nice, safe fantasy about how things *should* be done, without taking a good hard look at the situation on the ground. By the way, Sarah, how is that dialysis machine working?"

"Fine."

"And the mobile sonogram?"

"Just peachy." Sarah winced as the light changed and Sam surged left, cutting off another truck, slamming her into the door. "How's the last batch of Kalashnikov assault rifles working, Sam? I thought I heard a whole bunch of them, just before I left, over the Rwandan border."

"I'm in a car," a swooning Kate murmured, "with an African gunrunner."

"I don't run guns. And I'm English, Kate, English. My mother is Nigerian, my father English. Raised in Sussex—"

"—and trained at Oxford," Sarah added, "and thus should know better."

"I'm speeding through the streets of Bangalore with a Nigerian renegade." Kate melted into the backseat. "Now I can die happy."

~~~~

Sam let out a slow, long whistle as he pulled up to the front entrance of The Chancery, the finest hotel in Bangalore. "I'm going to have to talk with the regional department head," Sam said. "Clearly, he's paying you a lot more than he's paying me."

"Paul's idea." Sarah nearly tumbled out of her seat as a white-gloved attendant opened her door. "Paul is Kate's husband. He wouldn't let me make any arrangements other than giving him the name of this hotel. He's even paying for it."

"He said," Kate muttered, hauling herself up, "that Sarah would put us in a cheap hostel with iron beds and squat toilets—"

And I probably would have, Sarah thought, retrieving her backpack from an attendant's hands.

"—and I'd wake up in the middle of the night to the sound of a rat chewing on my toothpaste."

Sam met Sarah's gaze across the hood of the car, and his

mouth twitched. "You won't be having trouble like that here, Kate, you can be sure."

"I suppose," Sarah asked pointedly, "that you're booked here, too, Sam?"

He jerked his head toward the teeming street. "I'm down the road a bit. In a place with more local color."

"Thanks for the ride, then." With a tingle of relief, Sarah pulled Kate's arm across her shoulders and shifted her until she held the bulk of her weight. "We'll be seeing you—"

"Now, what kind of gentleman would I be," Sam said, tossing the keys to the attendant, "if I didn't stay and see you both settled?"

Sarah set her jaw. She turned away and dragged herself and Kate through the front doors of the hotel. She didn't want Sam here. Not *now*. But it would take a lot more energy than she currently had to convince Sam to leave her alone. It was useless to argue with him when he got like this. He'd been just as cheerfully stubborn when she'd insisted on making that trip into the mountains six months ago to deliver the meningitis vaccine. Sam argued that the trip was too dangerous to do alone; there'd been skirmishes between armed groups from both the Hutu and the Tutsi. Worn down by his cheery insistence, they'd gone together. The trip had been uneventful.

Except for that kiss by the lake.

To hide her sudden flush, Sarah poured a limp and sweaty Kate into one of the lobby chairs. "Watch Kate for me," she mumbled, turning on her heel. "I'll check in."

She crossed the cool, brightly lit lobby, her sneakers squeaking on the polished floor. Western Muzak played through hidden speakers. Surrounded by smoked glass and gleaming, rosy wood, Sarah thought that, but for the few exquisite hand-loom rugs hanging on the walls behind the registration desk, she could be in a Sheraton in Topeka, or a Hilton in Berlin. All local color remained firmly outside the doors.

Then she came to an abrupt stop. Near the registration desk stood a placard welcoming all attendees to the International Conference on Craniofacial Surgery. The placard listed, among the speakers, a surgeon by the name of Dr. Colin O'Rourke.

Seeing his name in bold black letters brought back, in full force, the surging pride she'd experienced when she'd first searched for his name on the Internet. Oh, what he'd accomplished since he'd left Paraguay. Five hard years of general-surgery training, followed by a two-year residency in plastic surgery, and then yet another year specializing in craniofacial surgery. Double board certification. Then years of world travel, associated with an organization that specialized in correcting severe cleft-palate abnormalities and misshapen heads of children who would otherwise never live an ordinary life.

And what all this meant to her was that Colin hadn't changed. He was the same dedicated, determined man he'd been when he'd swept into that hut in Paraguay and, despite the risks, saved Werai's battered leg. She had imagined—expected—hoped—dreamed of—great things from him. Fourteen years of wild expectations. She was sure no man—no human—could meet her ridiculously inflated imaginings. Yet, on paper, he'd exceeded every one of them.

And tomorrow, she thought, pulling documents out of her backpack to hand to the man behind the registration desk—tomorrow, after she'd scrubbed off twenty hours of airplane grit, slept her mind clean, and braced herself with a high-protein breakfast—tomorrow, when she wouldn't feel light-headed just at the sight of his name on a placard, she'd hunt him down.

When she finished registering, she turned around with a key card in hand and glanced to where she'd left Kate and Sam and saw, instead, three men, bent in obvious concern over Kate's limp form, and Sam standing stiffly apart.

Oh, God. Sarah crossed the lobby as her mind raced. Had Kate lost consciousness? She hadn't seemed hot enough for febrile convulsions. The side effects of so many shots could be serious—had Kate taken the live polio vaccine rather than the genetically engineered one? Sarah mentally flipped through the vaccinations, their known side effects, and their more rare complications. *I never should have brought her here; she's not herself. She hasn't been acting right since she jumped out of an airplane—*

"Sam," she gasped, "what happened?"

He looked tight-faced. His eyes were strangely blank.

"Sam?!"

"She's fine, Sarah," he said curtly. "These men are doctors."

Sarah crouched next to the chair and noticed with relief that Kate was conscious. In fact, Kate was grinning up at the doctor gripping her wrist in his hand, searching for a pulse.

"Look, Sarah-belle," Kate said, with a strange giggle, "I'm being examined by Indiana Jones."

The doctor rumbled a low, earthy laugh. "Clearly she's delirious."

Maybe it was the laugh. Maybe it was the broad American accent. Or maybe it was the sight of those tanned, tapered fingers, probing Kate's wrist. Deft, limber fingers. Knowing hands. A surgeon's hands.

Colin.

~~~

Things like this happened only in dreams. She had no weight; she had no substance. His gaze was her only anchor. It fixed her in place. Around him, the world receded.

Time had slipped a few strands of white into his hair, and he'd clipped it to his collar rather than let it grow shaggy. She noted the shadow of his clavicle visible through the opening of his crisp white shirt, the faint throb of a vein in the column of his throat, and the V-shaped scar just below his ear. In a heartbeat he'd been yanked from the midst of her fantasies and poured into the flesh-and-blood creature looming only inches from her face.

Colin. The skin at the corners of his eyes crinkled. That webbing hadn't been there when she'd known him in Paraguay. Certainly, he'd spent the last fourteen years laughing to earn those merry creases. She could almost hear that laughter: through the long stretch of his surgical residency, while he gently teased sweet-tempered children in the hours before he stitched their faces back to normal.

As recognition flickered in his gray gaze, she noticed the amber nimbus around his pupils, those whiskey-colored rings that set his eyes apart from all others. He swayed back in disbelief, and then his face warmed with a bright, growing realization. She watched him. She watched fourteen years, like water flowing between them, pass like a flash flood. And then they were staring at one another as if no time had passed at all.

"Sarah?" He shook his head, a quick and almost impercep-
tible shake. "Sarah Pollard?"

"Colin."

His name came out as a whisper. So insubstantial, yet she
heard it, saturated with promise.

From a distant place came another voice. And yet another.
Awkward laughter, muffled to her ears. She tried to force the
distractions away, but Colin eased himself up and broke the
spell.

The world rushed in upon her. She heard the chatter of a
crowd. Small groups of men and women flowed in through
the hotel doors. The elevators rang as they slid open. Kate
hummed in the chair. Colin's companions watched her with
avid curiosity. Just beyond them, Sam also watched—with an
expression both fierce and stiff.

"I'm surprised speechless," Colin said to his colleagues, not
taking his eyes off her. "Gentlemen, this is Sarah Pollard, an old
friend of mine. We were in the Peace Corps together, in South
America. Along with Sam here. About, what, fifteen years ago?"

She straightened up. She had weight again; she had substance. The throbbing in her back intensified. She became
achingly aware of her finger-combed hair and wrinkled muslin shirt as Colin introduced her to his colleagues, whose
names she didn't register and thus immediately forgot.

Kate stopped humming long enough to moan.

Colin the doctor leaned in, all concern.

"It's the vaccinations," Sarah explained, trying to clear the fog
from her senses. "She took five of them, practically all at once."

"Which ones?"

Like a good nurse in an emergency, Sarah rattled them off.

"All within the past week," she added. "She started feeling sick on the airplane. We arrived only a few hours ago."

I came for you.

Sam stepped in. "If you have your room, Sarah, let's get her to bed."

"I'll help." Colin took Kate's hand and coaxed her to her feet. "I can examine her more thoroughly in private."

Colin's colleagues made polite noises and then melted away. Slipping an arm around her back, Colin guided Kate's uncertain steps toward the bank of elevators. Sarah trailed behind, trying not to stare. He wasn't as taut and lean as he'd been in Paraguay—but the bulk he'd put on in the interim was clearly muscle. He had an athletic trimness, an un-self-conscious physique that spoke of occasional mountain biking, weekend pickup basketball, even rock-climbing.

This is not how she had envisioned their first meeting. On the way up to her room, he chatted easily with a semi-responsive Kate. He coaxed her upright. He expressed his surprise at seeing both Sam and Sarah here, his gaze traveling between them. He asked what relief group they were working for, how long they'd be staying, and whether they'd come for the conference. Sarah answered in vague generalities—she worked for Doctors Without Borders now. She hadn't come for the conference. When she fell silent, Sam filled the void. Sam told Colin that he'd been assigned to Burundi about a year ago, supplying Sarah's refugee camp as well as several others. That's how he and Sarah had connected again.

Not for the first time, Sarah suffered under the blight of her fair skin, which mortified her with every flush.

In the room, after getting Kate settled in the bed, Sarah

stole some privacy by slipping into the bathroom with her own backpack to scour her face, put a comb through her hair, and try to stop her heart from pounding.

I came for you.

"She should be fine," Colin said when Sarah re-emerged. Kate had fallen asleep. "I'll check her again tomorrow morning, before the conference sessions begin." Then he tilted his head in a way so familiar that Sarah flattened a palm against the wall in a sudden attack of vertigo. "I had to dig through her luggage for the aspirin," he said, sheepishly, gesturing to Kate's open suitcase. "It was tightly packed, so—"

"I'm sure she won't mind."

"She doesn't travel light, or often, I suspect."

Sarah shook her head. Her earrings, clusters of amber beads, clattered. "It's a very long story."

"Then have a drink with me." His gaze lingered on her for just a fraction of a second, before he added, glancing at Sam, "Both of you. We've got a lot of catching up to do."

Kind Colin. Always inclusive, always generous, always doing the polite thing, though she knew by the way his gaze clung that he wanted to talk to her, and her alone. That knowledge was enough to start a slow, lazy swirl of heat low in her abdomen. But timing was everything. She needed to breathe, collect herself, even for just a few minutes.

"Perhaps tomorrow," she said. "We just arrived, and I really should stay with Kate—"

"Go with Dr. O'Rourke, Sarah," Sam said suddenly. "You two have much to talk about."

Sam? His face was unreadable; his hands were fists in his pockets.

"Don't worry about Kate." Sam shrugged a tight shoulder. He picked up the television remote, then sprawled on the second bed. "I'll keep an eye on her. I'm sure she'll be thrilled to wake up in a strange hotel room with a Nigerian gunrunner."

Colin laughed.

And Sarah was lost.

Moments later, on the first floor, in one of the hotel's two restaurants, Colin slipped onto a barstool and ordered a sherry. She ordered the same, because it was easier to say, "I'll have what he's having," than to actually think up something for herself. She felt as if someone had severed the connection between her mind and her tongue.

"Here's to old friends." He lifted his glass. "And good times."

She took a sip. Powerful, sweet, burning. She felt his eyes upon her, like hot roaming hands.

"You haven't changed a bit." He reached up and brushed a thumb over her nose. "Maybe a few more freckles."

Her drink clattered against the bar. She gripped it more firmly. He must remember. He'd tried to count those freckles once. The ones on her legs. He'd played connect-the-dots with his tongue until—

He cleared his throat and slid the drink onto the bar. "Funny seeing you and Sam here."

"Yes."

"One or the other, maybe. The world is small, and there are only so many relief organizations. But both of you. Together."

"Mmm."

She thought, So was this what it was going to be? The two of them, sitting so close, talking about nothing. Chattering away, filling the silence with small talk, after all that had passed between them?

"Sarah?" He settled his gaze on her and waited a moment. "Well?"

"Hmm?"

"You and Sam—are you a couple?"

"A couple?!"

"The way he looked at you in the hotel room, I thought maybe you were. But then he let you come here with me."

"No, no, we're not...Sam and I are just"—*a flash of memory, of the lake in the rain*—"we're just colleagues."

"Vacationing together," he mused. "In Bangalore."

"Uh-huh."

She left it at that. She didn't need to complicate an already complicated situation by detailing the unnerving relationship she'd developed with Sam this past year, a turmoil of unbidden emotions and, yes, she supposed, some plain old-fashioned physical attraction. It had absolutely nothing to do with what was going on right here, right now, in this bar, across a stool from Colin.

Sarah peered into the amber liquid of her drink and wished for one moment she could be like Jo. Free and easy with men, knowing the secret language of barstool chatter and body language. Knowing how to telegraph her own deepest desires with the flick of her eyelashes, the twitch of a smile, the gape of her shirt, or the swing of a bare leg. But though Sarah could speak English and Spanish and Guaraní and a few words of passable Bantu, in this, she was as ignorant as a Tutsi virgin given over to her husband in exchange for some cattle, goats, and hoes.

Get him talking about himself, sugar. Nothing a man likes better.

"Tell me," she said, with Jo's voice still ringing in her ears, "what this conference is about."

Colin began talking about his work. He was presenting and demonstrating some advanced surgical techniques, in the hopes that the junior doctors could use them for the more severely deformed craniofacial abnormalities they faced in the poorer sections of India. The more he talked, the more Sarah realized that he'd been nervous, too. His shoulders relaxed. He used his hands, and he sipped more freely on his drink. He talked about the week he'd already spent traveling the countryside; he talked about the work they'd be doing in the days to come. He told a story about a boy he'd operated on last year at a similar meeting, a boy he'd visited, a boy now thriving because for the first time he could eat solid food without the risk of choking.

When he paused, she said, "You've come a long way from stitching together Werai's leg in the backwaters of Paraguay."

He laughed, even flushed a little, and her heart turned over, for he was always modest about having saved not only the boy's life but also his leg. Without touching upon why he'd left, he talked about what he did after—the surgical residency, the specialties, the board certifications, all that résumé fodder she'd managed to dig up on the Internet. He leaned toward her, using his hands, his shoulders, his head, the whole of his body, and she watched him with her heart swelling in her chest, because this was the Colin she remembered best. The man whose work was his passion, the man who lived his ideals.

She wanted him.

It wasn't the sherry, though she was on her second, and she'd always been an easy touch with the booze. It was *him*, in all his clean, strong glory, resurrected from her dreams.

"…and I've spent all this time talking about me, and I still don't know a thing about you."

She met his gaze. A fierce yearning shot through her. The shock bolted between them, swift and hot, leaving in its wake an aching need for well-remembered pleasures.

Then, abruptly, Colin leaned back in his chair. Leaned away from her, from the sizzle that remained. Uncertainty rippled over his features. He traced his chin with one hand. "Sarah," he began, on a half-sigh, "there is one more thing—"

"No."

Sarah slid her hand over his, where he gripped his knee. She slid her fingers between his. She felt his frisson of uncertainty, but she willed it away. *Forced* it away. She would summon the great lusty will of Jo in this. She hadn't come halfway across the world to whimper and cave. She hadn't come halfway across the world on Rachel's urging to pay lip service to Rachel's last wishes. She hadn't come halfway across the world just to say good-bye.

"Don't you want to know," she said softly, feeling her lips swell under his gaze, "why I'm here?"

He looked dazed, almost dazzled. "I had wondered."

"I came for you."

She lifted herself out of her seat. She aimed for his mouth, that strong, curved bottom lip. She lifted herself and caught him by surprise. Caught his mouth and pressed hers on his, not caring that the bartender hovered nearby, not caring that many of his own colleagues were also having drinks in the room, not caring about anything but the heat of his breath and the moistness of his mouth as he responded.

Now it was his turn to have a voice full of husky promise. "Sarah."

She pressed her forehead against his and slid her fingers behind his neck, feeling the crisp curl of his hair against her fingers. "Do you have a room?"

Breathlessly, "Yes."

"Take me there."

He sat still, just for a moment longer. Just a moment's hesitation. She felt how solidly he fixed himself on that chair, even as he breathed hoarsely against her cheek, even as his fingers flexed on her waist. He wanted her. He resisted her. She ignored it—just as she ignored that feeling at the back of her neck, that tingling of guilt, that knowledge that she was not playing by the rules.

He had been her lover first.

She pressed closer, and let her breasts oh-so-lightly brush his chest. He'd always loved her breasts, small as they were—closer to the bone, he'd said, dense with nerve endings, he'd said. Exquisitely sensitive.

He slid off the chair. His body scraped against hers. She felt his spine soften, right under the grip of her fingers.

Then she knew. She would have him tonight. And maybe, in the course of time, it would be she herself—Sarah Elizabeth Pollard—who'd be Colin's beloved fiancée. Instead of that distant California woman—the one he was due to marry in three short months.

chapter seven

"Okay, okay, okay, get this," Hector said. "It's a puzzle, but the pieces are all mixed up so you can't see who it is, but you can see enough to know it's someone young and hip, because they're wearing designer, but we haven't decided on who yet—"

"I got it, Hector." Jo adjusted the earpiece to her phone just as her laptop beeped the arrival of a new e-mail. "But—"

"Hold on, hold on, I haven't got to the good part yet. Here's the thing: The whole puzzle? It's in the shape of a puzzle piece. It's a puzzle in a puzzle piece. Isn't that brilliant?"

"Nice."

"In the magazine ads we'll add at the bottom, 'Who's the face of Mystery?' Or 'Can you guess the face of Mystery?' We haven't come up with anything really banging yet. Casey's talking about having a sweepstakes to guess the winner. You know, one of those things where everyone sends in a postcard with a guess and then we randomly pick one winner from the group that guesses right. We can give them swag, some kind of product case—"

"Nix that." Jo shifted forward on her couch and scanned

the rough draft of the project proposal, scrolling down the page. "Too *Family Circle*. We're aiming at soccer moms hiding navel rings, and teenagers with tongue studs."

"Fine. That geek in Graphics is working on the video presentation. He says he's got some fresh ideas about how to mix the pieces. When are you going to give us some face time?"

"Tomorrow."

From her makeshift office in the living room, Jo glanced upstairs, where Grace rustled about the spare bedroom like a squirrel. Twice Jo had meant to sneak up and peek through that door to see what on earth the kid was doing, but both times she'd been interrupted by phone calls. Now Jo could tell, by the sumptuous smell of warm cheese wafting from the kitchen, that Benito, the cook she'd hired for the day, was putting the finishing touches on lunch. She'd check on Grace when the food was ready.

Jo tapped her pen on the day's ink-blotched schedule, the one she'd started at six in the morning and had been filling ever since, operating in her fiercest Mistress of the Universe mode in order to pull her life back together. "I'll have everything worked out by the end of today, Hector. But listen, this proposal is useless if we don't find a face. Who did you catch?"

"No one. I called those people you mentioned, but not a single bite. And get this, that soul singer with the big rear asset? She's working on her own perfume."

"Shit."

"Maybe that's what they'll call it. And that girl band you suggested, well, I talked to the lead singer. She still thinks it's all about the music."

"What about that starlet from that Sundance movie, the one who played the lesbian vampire?"

"No callback. Listen, Jo," Hector said, "you'll probably hand me my balls on a platter, but Sophie might be right about that supermodel."

Jo bristled. Sophie's impression on this project—*Jo's* project—was like a spreading cloud of poison. "Are you talking about the model with the fried nasal passages? The only mystery about her is where she's hiding her stash."

"But she's cheap now. And desperate. By the time the perfume is launched, she'll have done rehab, sobbed on Barbara Walters' shoulder, and finished her community service. She'll be walking the runway for Versace again—"

"—and backstage she'll be cutting lines on her boyfriend's butt. No way. The model we choose is *everything*. We've got to find someone else—"

"In ten days?!"

"Who's got a movie coming out? A CD? A midseason TV series to launch?" Jo's doorbell rang, and she checked her watch. "Find someone looking for a tie-in, Hector. You work the phone on your end, and I'll work on it on mine. We'll talk in an hour."

The fireplug of a man standing in her doorway wore a red polo shirt and a pair of navy pants. He couldn't be more than an inch or two above five feet, and all of it was muscle. His shoulders bulged so fiercely that they threatened to consume his shiny bald head.

He consulted his clipboard. "You Bobbie Jo Marcum?"

"Yes."

"George from SafeKiddies.com." He flexed his arms. The muscles that stretched from his neck to his shoulders twitched in a way that was not quite human. "I'm here to give you an estimate on how to protect your kid from everyday household dangers."

"Come on in." Jo strode toward the couch and pushed her laptop aside. She cleared papers off a stretch of coffee table, only to realize that the fireplug hadn't even crossed the threshold.

"Is this the place?" He eyeballed her bilevel condo. Dropping the clipboard to his side, he ran his hand over his head. "Oh, geez. Oh, geez. How long you had it like this, lady?"

Jo glanced around. Piles of papers teetered on the couch. Dishes, spoons, and bowls littered the kitchen table. Her jacket had slipped off its peg and lay in a puddle on the floor. A couple of sweaters festooned the banister. "It's been cleaner," she admitted. "Maria comes tomorrow."

"Any kid could catapult himself from there," he said, gesturing to the second level. "They'd crack their head on that glass table of yours and splatter like ground meat."

Benito, singing Sinatra in the kitchen, stuttered mid-riff.

George said, "Kid's not here, right?"

"She is here," Jo said. "She's playing in her room."

"Alone?"

"Well, yeah." She blinked. "Grace is seven years—"

"Are there blinds in that room? With cords?"

"Of course."

"Naked outlets, like these? Bookshelves to climb on, like these?" He seized a shelf, rattling the books and photos. "You know how quick a kid could pull that down on herself? How do you know she's not fried to ashes right now, or laying there in a pile of her own fractured bones?"

Jo managed a tight Southern smile. Why couldn't SafeKiddies .com send some hot young gym rat? She really didn't have time for characters. "Because," she said, pausing long enough to hear the rustling she'd been listening to all morning, "I can still hear the little darling."

"Could be convulsing in her death throes."

"I'll just have to check on her, then." Jo's phone vibrated, and sang a rousing chorus of "I Will Survive." "George, is it? You'll have to excuse me—I've got to take this call. Why don't you get started on that estimate?"

"Geez, lady, look at that table—it's gonna take a boatload of wrap to cover that." He consulted his clipboard and tugged a pen from behind his ear. "It's a wonder the kid hasn't slit her wrists on those edges. And those stairs. That's an eight-foot drop. The opening's wide; that'll be a custom gate for sure."

Jo turned away and met Benito's arched gaze above a bowl of tossed salad. She rolled her eyes and then glanced at her caller ID before answering the phone.

"Jessie, did you find those papers?"

"Look, I tried to get you what you needed," Jessie began, "but it's going to take some time."

"Time is something I don't have a whole lot of, Jessie." Jo wandered into the kitchen. She peered through the oven window to where something was bubbling and just starting to brown. She was starved. She hadn't eaten since 7 a.m. "I can't keep Grace out of school any longer. There are laws against that in Kentucky—I suspect New York is no different."

"The doctor will send the immunization forms. But the

office needs a few days. I called Grace's old school for transcripts, but they have to send them directly to the new school. So you need to tell me what school she's going to. I need the full address—"

"Fax them. It's faster."

The fireplug bustled about, whistling through his teeth as he fingered edges and pushed aside curtains and shook his head at the exposed radiator under the window. He let out a shout of dismay when he measured the space between the balusters on the second level.

"Well, okay." Jessie sighed. "But there's another problem. I can't find her birth certificate."

"Jessie, sugar, that's one piece of crucial information."

"You know how bad Rachel was about papers. It's nowhere. I've looked and looked. I'll have to write to the city clerk's office to get a certified copy."

"It's October." Jo hungrily eyed the pile of carrots on the table. "This kid's got to go to school."

"It could be a week. Or two."

Jo scooted out of the way as Benito opened the oven door and squinted at the dish. "That's unacceptable," she said.

"I know. She's got to be about twenty pages behind in her math and spelling workbooks. That's where I'd be if I could ever find a damned teaching job. You'd better start her on those subjects at home."

"Honey, I'm no teacher." Jo shook her head. "Not for what you want her to learn, anyhow."

"Then talk to the principal, or hire a tutor. Now, look, I have to go. I'll get that stuff to you as soon as I can."

Jo pulled the earpiece off and tossed it on a granite

countertop, then leaned against it. A tutor now. Another body to hire. Another expert on the project. A project that was going way over budget.

This sure wasn't the way her mother had done it, raising Jo alone in that small-town backwater. A Manhattan nanny ran thirty-two to sixty-four thousand a year. The laundry service added another weekly cost, as did the delivering of groceries for a refrigerator that usually stood empty. Childproofing this condo wasn't going to be cheap, either, if she could judge by the way the fireplug was flashing his measuring tape. It was darn lucky that she'd spent so many years fully funding her retirement account, and keeping a "just in case I'm fired" account with nearly a year's salary tucked away. She was a vice-president of a major media company—she got paid well, she could absorb all this...but she sure as heck hadn't planned for it. It certainly made Rachel's motivation for giving her Gracie a lot more understandable.

"No window guards?" the fireplug cried out. "You got no window guards? She could sail right out and become anchovy pizza right on Eighty-second Street—what are you here, tenth floor?"

Jo sank onto one of the three barstools that edged her kitchen table. "Benito, how 'bout mixing me a big ol' margarita?"

"No, no, no margarita." He pushed out his lower lip. "Doesn't mix with the lunch."

"Tell me lunch has bourbon in it."

"You hired me to cook for a child. I cook macaroni and cheese." With padded hands, he opened the oven and pulled out the white casserole dish. "You say she no eat, I give you something she won't stop eating. Look," he said, tipping it toward her before he settled it on a trivet. "The finest home-made elbow macaroni—my father's recipe—drowning in the freshest of cheeses: smoked Gouda, Parmesan, a bit of sharp cheddar, and a drop of Worcestershire sauce just to give it a bite, then crusted with bread crumbs and browned to perfection. She will eat, yes, she will eat!"

"Benito, you're a genius."

"That's why you hired me."

At a hundred and fifty dollars, it'd be the most expensive macaroni and cheese ever made. Benito touched his fingers to his forehead and rolled them toward her, then went back to peeling curls of carrots that he shaped into roses.

Pouring a fresh cup of coffee, Jo got back to work. She searched the Internet for grade-school tutors. There were a huge number of companies that arranged private tutors for all age groups. (Kindergarten? *Kindergarten?* Why would a kid need a tutor for kindergarten?) Jo did what she'd been doing all morning: She chose the organization with the biggest ad.

The doorbell rang while she was in the middle of a phone conversation with a perky young woman extolling the virtues of her company's college-age tutors. Jo told her to send someone over this very afternoon, and then she disconnected the call and opened the door.

To Biker Brünhilde.

At least, that's the name that came to mind to describe the brick house of a woman standing in her doorway. She wore a fitted black leather jacket and circulation-cutting black jeans tucked into black boots. Her white-blond hair was spiked up with gel, and she carried a purse the size of a credit card.

"Mrs. Marcum?"

"Ms.," Jo corrected.

"No, I'm no miss. You can call me Gretalda."

"Gretalda?"

"The agency sent me." She thrust out a piece of paper. "Where is the little one? Come take me to the *kindlein*."

"She's in her room." Jo sidestepped as Gretalda marched into the house. "We'll talk first."

"But where's the child? I want to meet her. I'll have a look at the little one I'll be watching."

Jo managed yet another tight smile as she perused her papers and sat, decisively, on the couch. "I see you were at your last position for eight years."

"*Ja.* Two little *kindlein*, nice Jewish family, Upper East Side. No discipline in the house." Gretalda eyed the chair for crumbs and then perched on the edge. She tucked her purse over her camel toe. "Kids run wild, so wild."

"Is that why you left?"

"Oh, no! I left when Jason went to college. Columbia University, he went, my little *schüler.* You have two children?"

"Just one."

"Oh. One children are problems. No one to play with, think I be their playmate. Who's that?"

Benito set a glass of milk on the table beside a plate of the macaroni and cheese. "Lunch," he said, tossing a dishcloth over his shoulder, "is served."

"You have cook?" Gretalda's forehead crumpled into accordion folds. "You have one child and a cook?"

"Thank you, Benito. I'll get Grace in a minute—"

"Don't wait long," Benito said. "It's just the right temperature *now.*"

Benito was a sous-chef at Poulet, a trendy SoHo restaurant, which brought a lot of prestige but not much money. Which explained the willingness to make macaroni and cheese for a private client, and the snotty attitude as well. Jo's face was beginning to ache from all the false smiling.

"And who is this other man, wandering around?" Gretalda glared at the fireplug and his measuring tape. "You doing carpentry? I won't stay in a house with all that banging and dust." She patted her ample chest. "Not good for my asthma."

"Gotta get rid o' these right away." The fireplug ran his fingers through the river stones in a bowl on the sofa table. "The kid puts one o' these in her mouth, inhales, and that's it—she's as blue and dead as if you'd stuffed her in a garbage bag."

Jo jerked up. "Why don't I fetch Grace for lunch?"

She grabbed the railing—the one with balusters apparently too far apart—and took a leaping step up. *I'm Mistress of My Universe. I handle twenty-two employees. Among my staff I have a guy with a vial of blood hanging from his neck. Another is a practicing Wiccan. At least two of my employees are Young Republicans. The rest are pure save-the-manatee Manhattan liberals. We all get along. The CEOs of large corporations depend on me to run their Christmas office parties, their product launches, their PR campaigns, their international retreats. I can do this. I can run my life and Grace's, both at the same time.*

Jo pushed open the door. "Hey, kiddo, lunch is ready."

Dim gray light filtered through the slats of the drawn blinds. As her eyes adjusted to the lack of light, Jo noticed the fort in the corner of the room—a tangle of cloth and chairs and ropes. Only when Grace poked her head out from under a sleeve did Jo realize that the fort had been constructed with her freshly delivered dry cleaning.

Jo's breath froze in her lungs. She noticed the knotted wrinkle of a blue silk Versace skirt and the crinkled sleeve of a Ralph Lauren jacket. "Grace," she stuttered, "what...what are you doing?"

"I made a fort." She hid one eye behind a watered-silk sleeve. "I wanted to use those bags, but he took them away."

The fireplug had been here. A pile of hangers and plastic sheaths jutted out of the garbage pail. The rope pulls of the blinds were knotted high up like big bows.

He couldn't have rescued her Vera Wang?

"He said if I used the plastic," Grace muttered, "I'd suffocate like a dead puppy."

Jo took a deep breath and told herself it was okay. The clothes could be freshly pressed. They could be cleaned and ironed and put back in new plastic, and hidden in her own closet. This was not Grace's fault; it was Jo's own fault. Buying the kid toys was on her list, but not until later in the day.

"Don't mind him," Jo said, willing herself calm. "He's trying to make this place safer."

"Is it true that an eye can really pop out? 'Cuz that man said the point of a hanger—"

"Now, don't you go listening to him. My grandma would say he's full of fish stories. Time to come out of the fort now, kiddo. I've got lunch downstairs—"

"Not hungry."

More like *never* hungry. Gracie hadn't eaten more than a candy bar since she'd arrived. Though there was something around her mouth right now, something gray and mushy, like oatmeal. Where'd she get oatmeal? "It's your favorite"—according to Jessie—"macaroni and cheese."

Grace withdrew into the designer fort. Deep inside. So deep behind Jo's favorite black pants that Jo had to crouch to see her. Grace knelt on a rainbow pile of silk shells, and she was making two scruffy-looking stuffed animals talk to one another. Grace bounced them up and down. The rabbit had a ratty old ribbon around its head. The bear had a tear along its neck that was leaking small white balls.

"C'mon, Grace," Jo said. "I'm going to need a boatload of help with this macaroni and cheese. The cook made enough to feed Lee's army."

"Teddy says that I shouldn't go down there, because it's like last time."

"What's like last time?"

"Like when there were lots of people around. The day Aunt Jessie told me Rachel went away."

Jo registered several things. One, Grace was talking about her mother's funeral; two, Grace called her own mother "Rachel"; and, three, the kid was talking through a stuffed bear.

Well, Jo had spent enough time with a pint of ice cream in front of cop shows to know that this was some sort of coping mechanism. Maybe, from those actors who played district attorneys, she could pick up a few tips on how to handle grieving children.

Jo sat down gingerly, avoiding the other half of the Ralph Lauren suit, and intentionally didn't look at Grace directly. "That was some day, wasn't it? So many people around. So much noise. Everyone petting you like you're a darn pony."

Grace pulled on the ears of the floppy rabbit.

"Growing up, I had an aunt Lauralee. She was always trying to kiss me, and she had a big fat cold sore on her lip. Whenever she'd come over, I'd skitter right down to the basement to hide."

Grace pulled, pulled, pulled. Poor rabbit was going to lose those ears, and Jo depended on tailors to do anything that required a needle and thread.

"And the basement was full of spiders," Jo added. "Big hairy ones, the size of possums. I was scared to death of them, too, but that's how much I needed to get away from her."

And away from her complaining of how no good Jo's daddy was, leaving at the first sign of trouble, forcing her and her mother to live in a one-room dump. And didn't she curse the day Mom met him, look at her living in this filthy apartment with no backyard for Jo—

"And my uncle Gabe," Jo continued, "had a nose all swollen and red like it wasn't part of him at all. It was like a great big red cauliflower coming at you."

Jo thought she saw a smile. Fleeting, indistinct. It was something. Or a flutter of something. She leaned in a little, and pointed at the injured bear. "Is that Teddy?"

"Teddy Michael Joseph Braun."

"He's looking mighty hungry."

"Teddy is hungry." Grace plucked at the string unraveling around his neck. "But he wants to eat right here."

Under the shade of Dolce & Gabbana. *No way.* "Tell Teddy there are only three people here, and as soon as he sits down at the table, two of them will leave." Benito was done. And surely the fireplug was finished terrorizing everyone by now.

Grace's gaze slid by hers, and then retreated behind a sheaf of tangled hair. Didn't she comb it? Don't seven-year-olds comb their own hair? "Tell Teddy," Jo continued, "that by the time he finishes his lunch, the third will be gone."

The boomer biker babe wasn't going to work anyway. Fortunately, Jo had scheduled two more nanny interviews in the afternoon. Meanwhile, the smell of the mac and cheese wafted up from the kitchen. Jo was growing hungry, so Grace must be starving. By Grace's feet was a shoebox, partially torn into pieces, which served as the stuffed animals' bed. The kid toed it around. Then, without a word, Grace shuffled out of the fort.

Jo sighed with relief. She reached out to take Grace's hand, but Grace's hands were full of stuffed animals. So Jo settled for leading the way out of the bedroom into the brightness of the condo, where Gretalda and the fireplug were deep in conversation.

"...skidding across this waxed floor, see, and he's got his wet hands out to break his fall, and one finger goes right into the outlet. Zap. Shish kebab."

"That's what happens when no discipline."

"Kid's nothing but a pile of smokin' ashes."

"These kinds, they let them run wild."

"All they needed was a small plastic cover. A buck fifty for three. Save the kid from going crisp."

"It's getting cold, Jo," Benito said, as he spotted her coming down the stairs. "Nothing worse than cold melted cheese!"

Gretalda and the fireplug stopped their conversation and stared. Benito clanked the last pot on the dish drainer, and then, drying his hands, eyeballed them. Jo put her hand on Grace's head. "Folks, this is Grace. She's one hungry girl, so we're going to let her eat while we finish up."

Gretalda looked the kid over, from the bristly black stitches of Grace's scar to the tops of her ankle socks, visible above the flood hem of her jeans. Jo suddenly noticed Grace's dirty knees and her faded T-shirt. A well-loved shirt, apparently, for upon it lay the crinkly ghost of a number.

Mentally, Jo added clothing to the list of things to buy. Then she led Grace toward the table.

"Here you go." Jo lifted Grace up onto the barstool as Grace set her stuffed animals on the table. Behind her, the fireplug hissed.

"First thing to go ought to be those stools, lady. She's likely to tip backward and bash her head like a melon—"

"I'll surely take that under consideration." Jo handed Grace a spoon. "Look, Grace, Benito made roses out of the carrots!"

"If everything's done here," Benito said, threading the dish-cloth through the oven handle, "I'll be on my way. I've got to soak pinto beans and marinate the squab or Pierre will chop off my—"

"That'll be fine, Benito, thanks." Her phone sang. She answered it while pawing through her purse for cash. The perky tutor girl had found three candidates; they were coming in this afternoon.

Gretalda lumbered her leather to Grace's side. "What a cute girl you are. How did you get that cut on your head? Aren't you eating your lunch?"

Grace stiffened. She held the spoon in her fist. A clean spoon.

"Lady," the fireplug said, "I'm done here. I got enough to work out an estimate, but it'd be criminal if I left here without—"

"I'll be with you in a minute." Jo closed her phone and

started counting out money for Benito. Out of the corner of her eye, she noticed Grace's untouched plate. "I thought you were hungry, sweetie?"

Grace tightened her grip on the spoon and said, in a small, odd voice, "You said you made me macaroni and cheese."

"Yes, isn't it good? Benito made it just for you—"

"This is *not* macaroni and cheese."

Jo meet Benito's gaze, then folded the bills and held them out. "Sure it is, sweetie."

"There's yucky brown stuff."

Benito stiffened.

Jo flashed him an apologetic look. "Oh, that's just the crust. It's browned cheese and bread crumbs, from toasting in the oven. This is *special* macaroni and cheese."

"Why don't you eat your lunch, huh?" Gretalda fisted a serving spoon, took a heaping pile of the mac and cheese, and shoveled it into her mouth. "Good food," she mumbled, bobbing her head wildly. "Good, so good."

"Look, Grace," Jo said, coming around her, "we can take the brown part off."

Grace had gone white, which only emphasized the gray mush around her mouth. It had a few colors in it. Blue and red. Colors suspiciously like the torn-up shoebox upstairs.

Cardboard? Grace was chewing cardboard?

"Look, sugar," Jo said, as she peeled the brown crust off the top of the casserole. "Underneath it all, it's pure macaroni and cheese—"

"No, it's *not!*"

Grace slammed the spoon. It shot out of her hand and spun off the table.

"Now, Gracie—"

"No!" Grace stood up on the rails of the stool and banged her fist against the table. "It's *not*!"

Jo took a step back. Benito skidded to a stop halfway to the door.

"You, *kindlein*, you don't talk to Mother like that—"

"You *lied*!" Grace curled her fists around the edge of the table as if she would overturn it, tugging, tugging. "*It's not macaroni and cheese!*"

"Grace—"

"*It's not macaroni and cheese! You told me macaroni and cheese!*" She slammed her fists on the table, knocking her plate. It flipped, and spewed food across Grace's shirt. "*I want macaroni and cheese. I want macaroni and cheese!*"

Jo stood shocked into silence. Gretalda collected her purse and turned on her booted heel. The fireplug and Benito skittered after her.

"*I want macaroni and cheese!*" Grace squeezed her eyes shut; her tangled hair flew around her reddened face. Hands in fists, standing up on the stool, she banged the table, screaming, "*I WANT MACARONI AND CHEESE! I WANT MACARONI AND CHEESE! I WANT MACARONI AND CHEEEEEEEEEEEEEEESE!*"

Jo's blood went cold.

Behind her, the front door closed with a click.

∼∼ chapter eight

I *am riding an elephant in India.*

Kate let the thought roll through her mind, keeping in rhythm with the sway of the elephant. Lush vegetation formed a canopy over her head. Raindrops from the morning's squall pattered onto her loose cotton pants. The taste of strong coffee—served tooth-achingly sweet before they left Bandipur—lingered on her tongue.

I am riding an elephant in India.

The elephant's mahout—a rail-thin young man by the name of Naseem—called a brisk command as a wild peacock stepped into the pachyderm's path. The elephant lumbered on, unconcerned, but the bird swiftly skittered to the undergrowth, trailing his sapphire feathers like the silken train of a Bollywood star.

She closed her eyes and tilted her head back. She breathed in the jungle air, perfumed with rosewood, sandalwood, and teak. One of the guides had told them they were visiting the wildlife refuge during the best part of the year, after the monsoons, when the purple flowers of the jacaranda burst into bloom, the Indian bison and the wild boar went into rut, and the whole forest swelled with life.

If it weren't for the insects, the chattering of the German tourists on the next elephant, and the occasional waft of the elephant's intestinal eliminations, she'd wonder if this was just another fever dream.

But it wasn't. She really was *here*. Across an ocean and a continent. In a foreign country. Buzzing across her mind was the niggling little worry about the fate of Mikey's log cabin, Anna's seed project, and Tess's complicated soccer carpool arrangements. Was her mother-in-law remembering to dole out the vitamins, test the kids on spelling, and remind Paul of the PTA meeting he had to attend in her absence? With an ease that would have shocked her a week ago, those buzzing concerns faded in the noise of the jungle.

Tonight she would sleep among tigers. There would be time enough later for guilt.

She cast a glance over her shoulder at Sam, swaying behind her. "Tell me you're glad I talked you into coming."

"In Burundi, it's cooler," he muttered, swatting away a fly. "And the jungles are more beautiful."

"I wouldn't know. I haven't stepped out of New Jersey since George Michael left Wham!" She sifted her fingers through her hair and felt the sun's heat trapped in the strands. "I'm glad you came anyway, Sam."

"It's the least I can do, since Sarah"—he ground out her name with more than a bit of emphasis—"has abandoned you."

Kate let that pass. Sarah had other things on her mind. She hadn't returned from her evening conversation with Colin. You didn't have to be a CPA to add up what was going on. Or, Kate thought, sliding a glance at Sam's proud head, why Sam had been moody all morning.

"It's best Sarah isn't here," she said. "Now you can be my witness."

Sam cocked his head. "A witness to what?"

"To my abduction."

"Bloody hell. I knew you needed another day to recuperate."

"And waste my first vacation in fifteen years lying about a hotel room? No way." Perched so high, on a grass mattress covered with a silken blanket, Kate felt like a maharani—a maharaja's woman—being guided through the jungle to some distant palace. There she'd be fed grapes, fanned by nubile young men, and then thoroughly ravished. "You've heard the stories, Sam. About Veerappan and his gang of thirty. He trades in illegal ivory, poaches sandalwood, and kidnaps screen idols. He and his men haunt this jungle. They say he has fifty wives because he searches, endlessly, for the one woman who'll be the ruby of them all."

"Kate, you're a romantic."

Kate ducked to avoid a frond of greenery, and the collection of bugs feasting upon it. She never thought of herself that way when she was shoveling baked ziti into paper bowls at the school cafeteria. She supposed she *used* to be a romantic. Back in the days when she took eight weeks of a belly-dancing class just to surprise Paul with a veil dance on their fifth anniversary.

Yet another talent sacrificed on the altar of motherhood.

"Did it cross your mind," Sam asked, "that this bandit of yours will murder the rest of us?"

"Don't ruin my fantasy."

"And what would you want, Kate, with being one wife among many?"

"I hear harem life can be lovely. All those veils, and jewels, and communal baths—"

"You're mixing cultures."

"You never hear about those women washing dishes, or cooking meals, or doing laundry, or running errands—"

"They wait around for the attentions of one shared man."

"Frankly, I can see the use of a second wife."

"Are you still feverish?"

"As long as she's the one who does all the chores. Really. She could bring one kid to soccer while I bring the other to gymnastics. She could stay home and watch the baby while I go to the gym. And if I've got a headache—"

"Now, that's just bollocks—"

"Besides, if Veerappan has the same intense brown eyes as Naseem here—"

"Listen to you." Sam barked a laugh. "And Sarah insisted that Rachel was the crazy friend."

"Rachel *was* the crazy one."

She had a sudden, slicing memory of a ski trip in the Rockies, and Rachel's broken body in the snow.

"Can you hear me? Rachel? Can you move? Shit! You've broken your leg."

"Sugar-coat it for me, would you, Kate?" Her breath was short and her skin pale, but she was laughing. *"Some stunt, eh?"*

"Some freakin' stunt is right. What the hell were you thinking?"

"You're swearing. You've been spending too much time with Jo."

"If only you'd spent the afternoon in the stands with her, wrapped in a blanket, with some hot chocolate in a thermos." Kate waved over the rescue snowmobile. *"Ever think of doing that for fun?"*

"This is going to kill my snorkeling plans for next week."

"Snorkeling? Is that all you can think of? For God's sake, did you ever wonder what would happen to all of us if you were killed?"

"Actually, yes." She grinned, bloody from where she cut her lip. "Yes, I have."

Grief squeezed Kate's heart. It hurt, but, in a strange way, it felt good to experience the emotion so intensely. "You'd have liked her, Sam. She lived life boldly."

"I met her when she visited Sarah last year. But here's what I don't understand: If Rachel was the crazy one, then what is Kate Jansen doing here, swatting away flies in the jungle with a complete stranger?"

"Living, for the first time in a long, long time." Kate drew her legs up higher. "I bet, before today, you've never heard a single story about me."

Sam paused only a fraction of a second. "Sarah mentioned you—"

"You're a terrible liar. Sarah never mentioned me, because there's nothing to say." When did that happen? When did the old rock-climbing, multiple-master's-degree Kate lose her edge? "I'm no more exciting than an advertising demographic. Middle-aged suburban white woman."

He gave her a quizzical look. "Don't know too many demographics camping in the Indian jungle."

"Rachel is dead; someone had to take up the colors."

"Well, I tell you now: Don't ask me to bungee-jump. It's enough that we're crossing this jungle—which, for all I know, may be a major smuggling route for opium—with what appear to be armed Tamils—"

"Tranquilo, Sam," she murmured with a laugh. "We'll be fine."

His mouth twitched into a small grin, a grin that softened with melancholy. "That's just what Sarah would say."

~~~

Three hours later, limp from exertion, Kate and the rest of the crew—who'd left the elephants behind once they reached denser terrain—trekked within sight of the camp. It was a makeshift place, with a view down to a muddy watering hole. One rough shelter stood in the middle, waterlogged and mossy, just big enough to protect the inhabitants from rain. A wide ditch surrounded the camp itself. Their guide informed them it was to keep the wild elephants from wandering in—or the tigers from jumping over.

Kate grinned. It was perfect.

Two men in white sarongs tended a series of fires. Something mouth-watering simmered in the pots hanging over them. As Kate dumped her backpack in a growing pile, a third man, similarly dressed, approached with a tray of drinks. *Jal jeera*, Sam told her, taking a precautionary sip. He'd sampled it in the marketplace the day before. Thirsty, Kate gulped it down, savoring the refreshing mix of mint, salt, and cumin.

Settling by the fire, Kate and Sam chatted with the Germans, who were avid birdwatchers and, it turned out, believed Sam and Kate were married. Kate, feeling mischievous, didn't bother to deny it.

Dinner came on a broad, stiff plantain leaf. Sam instructed her to lap up a sweet, milky concoction on the lower right side of the leaf first. Then, with the help of the guide, they puzzled their way through the sweet-and-sour chutneys, the curries, the round, spiced chips, the seasoned grilled fish, and a mouth-searing dish called *sambhar,* all washed down with coconut milk drunk from the husky nut. The meal was an explosion of peppercorn, cinnamon, cardamom, and green and red chilies, and—like any meal actually prepared *for* her and not *by* her—mind-numbingly delicious.

The jungle grew dark, pitch-dark. The light of the fires became the light of the world. Insects screamed in the canopy. Kate fingered a betel leaf—a digestive, the guide insisted, and no more narcotic than a Marlboro—then put it down. The staining of her teeth aside, she wanted no artificial stimulants to dull her experience of the night.

Then, in open defiance of the park's rules—no loud noises, no playing music—one of the men pulled out a sitar; another, a tall lean drum. The sitar player chanted a rhythmic, seductive song. It was old music, exotic and compelling. It slithered through her, making her hips liquid.

Sam whispered in her ear. "Let's break another rule."

She raised a brow. He carried his bag and bedroll tucked under his arm. The light played across the dark planes of his face. He smiled in conspiracy, making her wonder if he was taking this husband/wife thing a little too far. Though she knew Sam's romantic interests lay elsewhere, Kate quivered with a frisson of excitement at the thought that someone as hot as Sam might look at her as more than a dull housewife abroad. Hey, it was just a fantasy—and a safe one, at that.

"C'mon." Sam headed away from the light. "You can see the stars better away from the campfire."

Kate grabbed her own bedroll and followed. In the dimness on the other side of the shelter, Sam unrolled his blanket and revealed the bottle inside.

"It's called *fenny*," he told her. He pulled a Swiss-army knife from his back pocket and made short work of opening it. "I got it in Goa. It's a liqueur made from the juice of a coconut."

She unfurled her bedroll next to his. "And you hiked with it twelve miles into the jungle."

"Camping is dull, Kate. Nothing to do but drink and... well." His teeth flashed in the darkness. "You're married. Those German girls think we're married. Clearly, no bonking for me."

He held the bottle out to her. She fisted the neck and took a deep swig. Choking on the burn, she sat on the spread and handed the bottle back. "And I thought you were gay."

Sam spewed a mouthful of *fenny*.

"Oh, I knew I was wrong the moment I met you, Sam, even if I was half dead from fever." Kate lay down on the blanket, to better take in the smear of stars. "But before that, all I'd known was what Sarah told us, and so I assumed—"

"Sarah knows *quite* well where my preferences lie."

"Listen, we heard your name mentioned this past year, but in Sarah's way. Now, anytime Sarah mentions a guy, we probe a little, because, hey, we've been wanting to drag that girl back into life for a long time—but she always brushed off our questions, and when we figured out that you didn't have a wife or a girlfriend, well, what else could we think?" She stretched out, languid, on the blanket. "We had to assume that you were her gay buddy."

"So much for the virtue of patience." Sam curled his hand around the neck of the bottle and upended it. His throat worked as he took a hefty gulp. "In my business," he said, the liquor making his throat husky, "to talk about the opposite sex like that—like a friend—means something entirely different."

Three streaks of light shot across the sky. The heat of the alcohol spread, seeping from her stomach through her veins. Sam was a looming, warm presence, a tall, vibrant man, and she found herself longing for Paul. Young Paul, never preoccupied. Before-children Paul, who'd take his time with her, in the darkness, under the open sky.

"I'm serious, Kate. It's different out here. People come and go in this business that Sarah and I are in." Sam planted the bottle on the blanket between them and rifled through his bag to pull out a pack of cigarettes. "People come out of their brick houses into a new country that has no indoor plumbing. There's hunger and disease and sometimes there's shooting. It's always dangerous. And for two weeks or two months or six months, they live very differently than they've ever lived before. They take huge risks. Sometimes they fall arse over tit in love."

Kate closed her eyes. "I knew I should have joined the Corps with Sarah."

"Sounds cracking, yes." He lit a cigarette, and the tip glowed in the night. "But listen to this: I spent some time in the Congo. I loved a girl there."

"You just spoke the opening line to a romance novel."

"Well, here's how it ends. When this girl's two months were over, she went back to Kansas. For a couple of months, she rang me up every night. But as she sank back into her old life, the calls tapered off. She started talking about our time together as if it was a dream." Sam planted the cigarette just off the corner of his blanket, at an angle in the hard-packed dirt, so the smoke curled up as it burned. "That's what happened to all her memories of the black Brit she'd loved in the Congo. She shoved the whole relationship up on a shelf marked 'Wild Oats Sown in Youth.' She was married to a corn farmer in less than a year."

Kate turned her head to see his profile against the sky as he lit a second cigarette. She'd forgotten how booze and darkness lowered the usual social barriers to intimate revelations. "Sam, I'm so sorry."

"Don't be. That kind of thing happens all the time. We call it 'crusader sex.'"

"Crusader what?!"

"It's a hunger for connection in a dodgy place," he explained, planting the second cigarette by her feet. "It's bound to happen when you're forced outside of your own comfortable life. You feel a tug towards a stranger, a burn for deeper connections."

Kate understood, better than he knew. It explained why, tonight, surrounded by jungle, stretched out on a blanket underneath the stars, her body was prickly with misplaced sexual awareness, and she couldn't get the memory of Paul's lanky body out of her mind.

She spread her hand over her belly.

Paul, why didn't you just come here with me?

"You know," Kate said, as Sam reached for a third cigarette, "those things will kill you."

"Yes, but it'll take a while." The tip glowed red in the darkness. "In the meantime," he said, as he planted the third cigarette in the dirt by her head, "the smoke will surround us and keep mosquitoes away."

"Ah."

"Occupational hazard," Sam explained, as he stretched out

a friendly distance away. "After your first bout of malaria, you learn to be disciplined about bed nets and repellent. After your first bout with crusader sex, you practice a different sort of discipline. Patience and self-denial. Especially around the one you most care about." He laced his fingers behind his head. "Which is why I make a point of steering clear of hungry-eyed ladies on their first overseas outing."

"Um...is this when I promise to be careful?"

Sam rumbled with laughter. "Oh, no, I wasn't talking about you, Kate. Any fool could see that you're at the reeling end of a long, strong rope—soon enough, it'll be tugging you back. I was talking about Sarah. And me. Working together for a year, and not once..."

He let out a long, ragged sigh.

"Oh, Sam." Kate felt herself melt a little. "Don't blame yourself. Sarah hasn't been able to get very far in *any* relationship," though she, Rachel, and Jo had encouraged every fledgling little hope. "We figure she just can't get past Colin."

"Oh, yes, our good Dr. O'Rourke. Now, there's a perfect example of overblown crusader sex."

"No, no, no way." Kate propped herself up on one elbow. "He's no flash in the pan. She's worshipped him forever."

A muscle, burnished by moonlight, moved in Sam's cheek. "Sarah is a woman of great loyalty and strong convictions. But Dr. O'Rourke is her one blind spot."

"You know, this Indian booze is pretty strong, but I'm following the conversation well enough to know we're both talking about the same man. The surgeon who stitched a kid together using spit and bits of twig. The guy who convinced a whole village to give the kids the measles vaccine—"

"Sarah did that," he said sharply. "O'Rourke arrived with the vaccines after Sarah had already spent months working on the mothers. She'd earned their respect and their trust." He made a low, angry sound in his throat. "She never takes credit for her own successes."

Kate knew that was true. The most infuriating thing about Sarah was her modesty.

"The worst part of this," Sam added, "was that I was the one who drove the bloody bastard right up to her door."

Kate bolted upright. "You were there? In Paraguay?"

"Oh, yes." The pale starlight glazed the sharpness of his cheekbones. "That's when I first met both of them."

Sam went silent, but it was a tense silence, and his gaze drifted through the wavering haze of cigarette smoke, to some indistinct point beyond a southern constellation. Kate stayed still, hoping he'd tell her his side of the story. She'd heard Sarah's side, of course, to the point of being able to mimic it, dreamy sighs and all. Over the years, the tale had taken on the sheen of a myth. And Kate couldn't help being just a little selfishly excited, at the prospect of being—*finally!*—able to understand the hold that Colin had on Sarah.

"Sarah had been alone in the camp for a while." That muscle flexed in Sam's cheek, more fiercely than before. "I'd see her once or twice a month, whenever I dropped off supplies. The Guaraní don't usually take well to outsiders. They only tolerated me because I came infrequently and usually brought things they needed. But they treated Sarah like a young aunt, almost instantly. She's Sarah." He shrugged. "She has a quality."

"Like her feet don't quite touch the ground."

"Mmm." Sam took a breath, and his chest rose, then fell, as he blew it out on a sigh. "So one day I arrived with a boot-full of vaccine and another Peace Corps volunteer, a doctor sent to talk the locals into getting their children vaccinated. He was a nice enough chap. We chatted about the usual things—how long you in for, how pretty are the birds, were there any pubs. He didn't strike me as anything special.

"So we get to the village, and there's something going on. The women are wailing; I can hear them half a mile out. Kids flowed out of the village and tumbled all over our car. They're speaking Guaraní, and I only knew enough to understand two words—crocodile, *caiman,* and boy, *mitõ.* Clearly, some kid was hurt."

Kate curled her fingers around the neck of the bottle. She held it out to Sam, but he waved it away.

"So Dr. O'Rourke is out of the jeep like a shot. The kids knew he was a doctor—any white guy around there had to be an engineer looking to find oil, or someone from an NGO. So they dragged him into one of the huts, where Sarah was struggling to stop this kid from bleeding out.

"O'Rourke peels away the cloth and pokes at the leg. Sarah is covered in blood, and her face is gleaming with tears or sweat, but she's not looking at me, she's staring at the doctor."

"She told me," Kate said, slapping her thigh as one of the growing swarm of gnats pierced the halo of cigarette smoke, "that she thought he'd dropped straight down from heaven."

"Yeah, riding shotgun in *my* jeep." Sam sat up and rifled around in his pack. "Anyway, Colin starts talking about taking this kid to a hospital. Now, some of the doctors, they come to these camps, and they think there's a chemist around the next bend. They're asking for bandages and antibiotic ointment and can't you get me a pair of tweezers and where's the penicillin? Some doctors, they arrive, and they think they can punch out for lunch.

"So I tell him a hospital is a hundred hard miles away, and he's staring at me as if I'm crazy. But—I'll give the man his due—it only takes a minute for him to figure it out." Sam thrust a small tube at her—mosquito repellent—and settled back on his elbow. "Then he starts barking orders. Sarah and I are the only ones who understand English, so we're digging out morphine and the sutures, and for the next six bloody hours this guy sews this kid's leg back together. And there's Sarah standing right beside him, looking up at him like he's the sun."

As Kate slathered the fierce-smelling stuff on her skin, Sam pulled the *fenny* to his chest, but he didn't drink it. He twirled it, making whorls in the blanket. "I saw her fall in love that day."

Kate heard his regret, shimmering in the air.

He laughed, a brief, mirthless laugh that died with a shake of his head. "You know what's the real irony in this, Kate, my girl?" He fixed the bottle to his lips and took a long, deep sip, then wiped his mouth with the back of his arm. "I come to find out that Colin didn't even do the right thing. Colin broke every medical rule there was, trying to stitch that boy back together. The safer, the better decision would have been to amputate quickly and close the boy up. Instead, he risked six hours of surgery in a filthy hut. The infections that followed should have killed that kid, slowly and more painfully. The chances that boy would survive were one in a million."

"But he did."

"Yes. Colin performed his miracle."

"Right before the eyes," Kate murmured, handing him back the tube, "of a minister's daughter."

"A minister's daughter who can't comprehend deceit." Sam tossed the repellent toward his pack with more force than necessary. "Sarah didn't see it coming. When it was time for the doctor to leave, he made the usual promises. He'd keep in touch, he said, they'd meet up again. Pretty lies."

"Maybe he meant them."

"Good intentions wouldn't buy you a pissing pot in Gatumba." He finished the dregs and dropped the bottle on its side on the blanket. "The doctor returned to the States and put her heart up on the shelf, marked 'Wild Oats Sown in Paraguay.' And that was that."

"But not," Kate murmured, "for Sarah."

Sam flopped down upon the blanket again, lacing his fingers under his head, searching the open sky to avoid her gaze. He flexed his shoulders, as if a rock jutted into his back through the blanket. Kate wondered when Sam had realized he loved Sarah. Was it in the past year, since they'd become reacquainted? Or had he been shadowing her since Paraguay, hoping for her heart to change?

And Kate's own heart moved, as she thought of Paul, Paul and herself, as they'd been the evening they'd met—locked, riveted, joined. That very first evening, they'd known with certainty, *This is the one*; this was forever. How terrible it must be, to feel that way and not have the feeling reciprocated. How terrible it would be to lose that connection forever.

A worry pricked her, a small thing, like the twinge of a

splinter. Paul was so very far away. And they'd parted on such bad terms.

She shook off the memory. She wouldn't let it ruin her first vacation in years. Paul just needed a few days to come to his senses before he finally bought a plane ticket to Bangalore, to join his wife in adventure.

She forced herself back to the jungle, with its screaming bugs and brilliant stars. "Sam," she said, "for what it's worth, the girls and I have been trying to get Sarah to move on for years."

"Yes, well, good things come to those who wait, and I've been waiting. Oh, I've been waiting. Burundi is a hard place, Kate—it breaks you down like no other—and these past months, I'd been giving some serious thought to leaving." His mirthless smile looked more like a grimace. "I stayed for the chance to wear Sarah down with my ruthless charm."

You're the better man, Sam.

"'Course," he continued, "things got a little weird when I got the letter from your friend Rachel."

Kate startled. "Wh—what?"

"Yes. A little white envelope from a woman I met only once. Rachel told me to stay close to Sarah in the next few months. So I tracked Sarah's movements like a good Boy Scout. Now here I am, an unwilling witness to her undoing."

"Don't feel so bad. Rachel made me jump out of an airplane."

"Bloody hell." Sam flexed his elbows, then stretched his arms flat against the ground. "I might've preferred that to watching the damn doctor rip Sarah's heart out again."

Damn Rachel. Interfering, worldwide.

"You know, in the weeks before Sarah left Burundi, things between us were heating up. In a very encouraging way." Sam shifted on the blanket. "I thought I was finally, *finally*, breaking through the wall she kept throwing up against me. Because of Rachel's letter, that wall now has a name."

"Well," Kate said, "that's hopeful...isn't it?"

"I'm not so sure. When a woman like Sarah falls in love, she falls in love forever."

> Memorial Sloan-Kettering Cancer Center
> Rockefeller Outpatient Pavilion
> Chemo Ward

Dear Sarah,

All these months, I've wished over and over again that you weren't half a world away. I'm a mess, sweetie. I've got cancer. I've had it for a while and it has hit me hard. I'm writing this in the chemo ward, in my one last desperate attempt to conquer the disease. Since you're reading this letter . . . well, I guess the cancer won.

I'm so, so sorry for not telling you sooner. I'm so, so sorry for breaking the news like this. I could have handled so many things better, I know, but there's no use regretting the past. I'm trying to focus on my friends and my family now, and what I can do with the time I have left.

I've been thinking a lot about you lately, Sarah. Do you remember when we first met? It was the first day of the rock-climbing club. You wore Birkenstocks and an ankle-length skirt, and you swept into the room like a warm breeze. There's serenity around you. All of us—myself, Jo, Kate—we all need that. When you're around, our worlds are put into the proper prospective.

But, Sarah, there's one thing in your life in which your perception is distorted. Yes, darling. It's Colin. Years ago, when you two first split up, it was reasonable for you to mourn for a time. But that time has long passed. Your grief has morphed into something hard. It shields you from heartbreak, but it also shields you from true joy. You've become blind to love. You wouldn't recognize it, even if it stood tall, dark, and handsome right in front of you.

You mustn't hide from love, Sarah, no matter how difficult your world will become after. You need to find Colin. You need to face him. You need to win him back, or finally say good-bye.

Please, Sarah. I want you to do this for yourself. But if you can't . . . then do it for me.

Love,
Rachel

~~~ chapter nine

I have loved you forever.

Sarah lay still and quiet, exquisitely conscious of the fibers of the cotton sheet grazing her naked skin. A fan whirred above. Pale light seeped through the blinds. If she got out of this bed, padded across the room, and opened them, she'd see nothing but monsoon-washed Indian skies. But there was no reason to open them. Her world—her entire life—hung in the balance right here, right now, in this king-sized bed. Beside her, Colin lay on his back, his broad chest rising in a slow rhythm.

She'd forgotten so much. The darkness of his eyelashes, tipped in gold. How quickly the stubble of his beard grew. And the range of colors in it—deep blond, little-boy red, and, sprinkled here and there, a bit of lucid white.

I have loved you forever.

She said it to herself out of long habit—she said it to herself because she didn't dare say it aloud—not yet, not now. He stirred in his sleep, and she thought, *Don't wake.* She wanted to lock this moment into her memory—this sweet, fragile sense of sleepy communion—where she could pretend that the last fourteen years hadn't happened and that they were still young and alone in Paraguay. If he woke now, then he'd awaken that other presence as well. That ghost of the other woman.

Suddenly he opened his eyes.

"Sarah."

She kissed him to drown the soft incredulity in his voice. His mouth felt hot. She grasped his jaw to hold the embrace. Stubble prickled against her palm. She slid her knee up his leg. It had been fourteen years since she'd been with Colin, but her body remembered.

They'd made love three times last night. The first time they'd done it desperately, tearing off only what needed to be torn off. He'd taken her up against the wall by the door, with her skirt bunched around her waist and her underwear twisted around an ankle. She told herself it was because of a physical hunger she'd suppressed for so long. She told herself it wasn't to beat the rising of his conscience or to commit the sin before either of them could think. The second time they made love, staring at one another in the darkness and breathing heavily, they had abandoned all pretenses. They'd stripped off each other's clothing and rediscovered each other's bodies. The third time she woke to feel him pressing against her, Colin her lusty demon in the darkness, as if they were young again and the rain thrummed on the thatched roof, and before them stretched hours and hours of languid South American time.

And now, with daylight seeping in between the blinds, she intended to remind Colin what it was like to have her warm and willing in his bed. She'd always been wanton with him. In Paraguay, she'd often wondered if Pombero, the lustful, mischievous imp of the night, had taken hold of her spirit.

But in her heart, she admitted there was more to this urgency than passion. In this strange situation with her and Colin and the ghost of that other woman, she found herself—the minister's daughter—in the odd position of acting the aggressor.

It didn't take her long to notice his stillness. His hands on her waist didn't roam. The kisses she gave him coaxed no response. She paused, tracing his nose with hers, only to pull away far enough to see his expression.

Then she wished there wasn't so much light in the room.

He eased her aside, and rolled up in one fluid motion. The muscles of his back tensed as he rifled through the clothes on the floor, found his underwear, and pulled it on. Sarah pulled up the sheet, but there weren't enough blankets in the world to stave off the chill.

"It's nearly nine." He spoke in a brisk, husky voice. "I'm due at a symposium in thirty minutes."

She curled into herself as if each word were a blow. She willed herself to be calm and remain quiet. He'd flown halfway across the world to take part in this conference. She couldn't expect him to drop everything—busy doctors, needy patients—just to be with her.

But she was never good at lying, even to herself. Colin could be speaking a Zulu dialect and she would still understand the international body language of a man feeling guilty after spending a night with another woman.

"I can't get out of it," he continued, avoiding her eyes as he wrestled into his pants. "I'm on a panel of two."

She stretched over the edge of the bed, letting her hair shield her face as she searched the floor for the coral splash of her skirt. She seized her bra. On the long plane ride to Bangalore, with Kate whispering encouragement in her ear—*All is fair in love and war*—she'd conveniently ignored the fact that Colin was a good man, an honorable man, a man whose word could be trusted, and who would naturally feel guilt over infidelity, even outside the bonds of marriage. Would she have wanted him any other way?

"It's a damn thing." He found his shirt, tugged it on, and fumbled intensely with the buttons at the wrist. "I'm doing something for the conference every day this week. A surgical demonstration this afternoon, a lecture on—"

"Colin, enough." With a swipe of her forearm, she pushed her wild hair off her face. "I don't expect you to change your schedule for my sake."

With a frustrated sigh, he stopped fussing with the buttons. He swiveled on one foot and walked to the windows, feigning interest in the dust on the closed blinds. "For God's sake, Sarah, you think I wouldn't, after *this*?"

She crumpled her skirt in her lap. She could take almost anything except his anger. "I ambushed you last night. I know that. I am sorry—"

"Don't." He raised the back of his hand in the air, as if to swat back her words. "Don't apologize."

"I know there were better ways to contact you. I could have called your office in California. I could have e-mailed you—"

But I needed to see your face.

"It wouldn't have mattered." He planted his hands on his hips. "Seeing you last night was like a shot of adrenaline. Any way it happened, the result would have been the same." He turned abruptly and fixed his gaze on her, across that terrible distance. "The timing is just unbelievable. Why now?"

She shifted the sheet up higher, knowing that the fine cotton didn't do much to hide her freckled nakedness. She searched her conscience, painfully aware of how careful she had to be. She sensed that if she mumbled her mantra right now—*I have loved you forever*—he would retreat deeper into this angry confusion.

"Do you remember my friend Rachel?"

His brow furrowed, then he shook his head. She was surprised he didn't remember. They'd had so many long, lazy conversations in Paraguay. She was sure she'd mentioned all her friends and family, especially the girls of the rock-climbing club, especially the wildest of the bunch.

Then again, when she and Colin had been together, conversations had a way of melting into more visceral, more physical forms of communication.

"She was one of my best friends. She died." She told him about the fateful envelopes and how her task had been to seek him out. "I couldn't say no, not to a friend's dying wishes."

"That's it? That's why you hauled yourself across the world?"

"You left me, Colin." She spoke without reproach. "I had to assume it was because you'd lost interest."

"I didn't. Lose interest." He paced in a tight circle. "Obviously."

The little hairs on the back of her arms danced.

"It's just..." He scraped his fingers through his hair. "Once I left Paraguay, and started my surgical residency, there wasn't an easy way back."

"I'm not digging for an apology."

"Oh, but you deserve one. That, and a hell of a lot more." He stopped pacing, leaned against the corner, and sank into a crouch. "Sarah Pollard, after all these years. Showing up in India, of all places. Like the Ghost of Christmas Past."

She needed to find her blouse. She scanned the carpet, but he'd cleared it of all garments. Sweeping up her skirt and bra, she frantically sought the white muslin amid all the tangled white sheets. She told herself she would leave this room— Colin's room—in a moment, just one more moment. Dressed and out of his sight, she would acknowledge her guilt, she would succumb to the trembling, and she would catch the next flight to...to someplace. Anyplace. Not here.

"I followed your career, you know."

His voice stopped her short.

"After you left the Corps," he said, rubbing the bristle along his jaw, "you earned your nursing degree at New York University. I couldn't imagine you in that big city."

A tingle walked up her spine.

"You joined Doctors Without Borders. I remember thinking—that's just where you belong." He shifted his weight, sprawled against the wall, and tilted his head back to face the ceiling stucco. "Do you know how many times I thought about you, working all alone in that muddy village in Paraguay, picking up Guaraní like you were born to it? You slipped right into their world. Never once did you get pissed off that nothing ever worked, and nobody ever showed up on time, and there was never any money."

The tingling spread, and a new weakness threatened her senses.

"At the hospital, I'd be watching surgery and I'd tell the guys in my residency, This is nothing, you should try surgery in a mud hut. I'd tell them, Go work in the third world, you'll get more surgery practice in two weeks than you'll get in two years here. I'd tell them, There's this girl I met, she's got a face like a Botticelli but she's got a backbone of iron, didn't even flinch picking leeches out of a kid's shredded muscle—"

"That boy—Werai—he's married now," she interrupted, needing to stop him for a second so she could breathe. "Last I heard, he had two kids. He named his oldest son Colin."

"So he did." Colin managed a breathy gust of a laugh, then raised his face to meet her gaze. "I still can't believe you're here. It's like you've been sent."

Her blood pounded. Black spots threatened at the periphery of her vision. She *had* been sent. By Rachel. And maybe, through Rachel, she'd been sent by a higher power. Her prayers had been answered once, when Colin arrived to save Werai...and now she and Colin were here, together.

Maybe, after all, Kate had been right about fighting for love.

Then, suddenly, he slapped his hands on his knees. "I can't think about this now." He glanced at the clock on the bedside table. "As awkward as this is, I *am* telling the truth about the nine-thirty panel." He eased himself up, the edges of his shirt billowing open. "I have to wash up, gather my notes, prepare."

Sarah nodded, trying to regulate her breathing. She sensed his mind working, triaging the issues so they could be dealt with in the proper order. "I'm on temporary leave from the camp," she said, wanting her turn among his priorities. "I can stay here two days...or two weeks."

Or two months. Or more. Her supervisor, at Doctors Without Borders' satellite office near Bujumbura, had made that clear. He understood what it was like to live in a refugee camp. Furthermore, he knew about the wounded girl, the one with the crooked braids, the broken little girl that Sam had pulled from that dirty alley and brought to the clinic for Sarah to nurse. So, when Sarah requested leave to attend Rachel's funeral, the supervisor told her she could take what time she needed.

How much time, she now realized, depended on Colin.

He walked to the edge of the bed. His gaze slipped over her bare shoulders, a touch as hot as a hand. It followed the hollow of her throat, then cascaded down the pattern of freckles to the edge of the sheet that she'd let slip, perilously close to her breasts, where he'd scraped his cheek against her last night, until she'd moaned.

"If I were a better man," he murmured, "I would tell you to go home, right now."

She held her breath, watching the struggle on his face, watching his features settle—just as she remembered they did whenever he made up his mind about something important.

"The day after tomorrow," he said, "I'm going to a village about eighty miles from here. Just a couple of the local doctors and myself. There's a clinic, and we're operating on three kids. We'll be using a new craniofacial technique—" He cut the air with his hand, stopping his speech mid-sentence. "Anyway. What I'm trying to say is . . . we could always use an experienced nurse."

She drew in a slow, careful breath. It was a strange invitation, a working invitation, but an invitation nonetheless.

"Yes, Colin. I'll go."

chapter ten

India?! Sweet Holy Mother, what do you mean, she's in India?"

Across the doctor's waiting room, a mom with a pageboy haircut gave Jo the hairy eyeball. Jo cradled the cell phone against her shoulder, grabbed her purse, and headed for the privacy of the hallway.

"Paul," she said, as she closed the waiting-room door behind her, "you're not making a lick of sense."

"Of course not. It doesn't *make* any sense. I was the one raised in a hippie commune, remember? *I'm* the one who should be taking off to India—just like my father did, taking off to study under some guru in Nepal."

"Paul—"

"Instead, it's Kate dumping me—Kate, from the stable Midwestern home, for God's sake!" In the background, a child squealed, and something fell hard. "Michael, take that basketball outside *now*. Jo—she didn't tell you?"

"Not a word." Kate went to India? *Without the kids?* "When did she leave?"

"About fifty years ago, on Tuesday. Find the cleats, Tess.

You wore them. You took them off. Find the damn cleats yourself."

Jo leaned against the wall. She hadn't wanted to make this call at all. She'd jettisoned a boatload of pride just to punch in the damn number. But she was in a doctor's office, seeking medical help for the second time in a week. She couldn't let pride get in the way any longer or Grace would end up in the morgue. So here she stood, ready to concede defeat, to admit she'd been a clueless jerk to Kate for eleven straight years, ready to prostrate herself before the Great Mother and bow to her superior wisdom, and Kate wasn't even there to gloat.

". . . If you didn't lose the cleats the last time you wore them, then we wouldn't be late for your soccer game."

"Paul, when is she coming back?"

"Good question. She's got a return date of a week from Wednesday, but she's going to see 'how it goes.' She hasn't yet seen the Tipu Sultan's Palace. And you never can tell when old flames get together—Sarah might need a little more *moral support*."

"A week from Wednesday." Jo's big presentation was in six days. She'd yet to find a nanny after Grace's explosive fit. She couldn't even get a service to return her calls, leading her to conclude that nanny services were networked like IBM. "Paul, I can't wait until a week from Wednesday."

"Neither can I. That's when my mother goes back to the commune, laughing all the way. I'll have to quit my job to take care of these kids, because when I work from the dining room Lola the Mistress of Kundahar ends up throwing frying pans instead of balls of flaming gas— Tess, what do you mean, it's our turn to bring the snacks? Look in the pantry and see what's in there. Anna, I'll make your sandwich in a minute, so don't stick your finger in the peanut butter— Look, Jo, I've got to go—"

"Wait! Do you have her phone number? In India?"

"Don't bother. Last time I called, she cut me off. Told me if I couldn't find a bar of soap in the house I could 'bloody well go out and buy it.' Where the hell did that come from?"

"Now, you just give me that number, Paul. She'll take my call."

"She's staying at The Chancery in Bangalore. Sarah had tried to book her at some dump with bedbugs and no flush toilets. I'd rather she took up skydiving again." He rustled some papers while yelling at Tess to get the cleats on and get into the car. "And if you get through to her," he said, after he reeled off the phone number, "ask her where she keeps the lightbulbs, and where's Anna's sock puppet, and why the hell are we out of laundry detergent?"

"Sure."

"Hey, wait a minute— Jo?"

"Still here."

"You're a woman."

"Sugar, believe me, I haven't noticed lately."

"Where can I buy Styrofoam balls and wooden clothespins?"

Jo pressed her forehead against the wall. She could hear Tess shouting in the background, Anna crying, and the distinct sound of a ball being bounced on wooden floors.

Paul released a long, haggard sigh into the silence. "Yeah, yeah, stupid to ask. I thought, you know, you being a woman and all—"

"Paul, I'll tell you one thing I've discovered. Talent in motherhood? It doesn't come with the boobs."

Jo disconnected, flipped the phone shut, and set it to vibrate as she walked back into the waiting room. She tried not to envision Paul, a father for over a decade, losing his mind after a few days alone with his own kids. How was she, never a mother, supposed to take care of a half-psychotic orphan?

Moments later, a woman in a vintage Nurse Ratched getup poked her head around the door to the examining rooms. "Ms. Marcum? Dr. Maria Rodriguez is ready to see you now."

Dr. Rodriguez turned out to be about half Jo's age, a fact she tried to hide by slicking her hair back and wearing oversized tortoiseshell glasses. As Jo entered her office, the doctor jumped out of her chair, rounded the desk, and thrust out a hand so full of false fingertips that it could be classified as a weapon.

"Ms. Marcum. I'm Dr. Rodriguez." She displayed bleach-whitened teeth. "You've got one heck of a daughter there."

"Well, she's not really mine—"

"I know, I read the file." Her nails clacked as she waved off Jo's explanation. "Grace is just great, open and smart as a tack. But she sure as hell has been through a lot. Tell me, how did she get those stitches?"

Jo blinked. That was the third time she'd been asked that question since coming through the shrink's door. "She fell down the stairs in my condo. She hit the edge of a table."

"You've got to get that padded," she said, clacking her fingers again. "There's this stuff called Glasswrap. It'll fit right around the edges. How did she fall?"

Jo's phone vibrated but she ignored it. "It was the first time she slept at my place. I guess she didn't see the stairs—"

"Sleepwalking, probably." The doctor nodded, then rounded the desk, sat down, and wrote something on her pad. "Yeah, sleepwalking. It fits the profile."

"Profile?"

Dr. Rodriguez shuffled forward in her seat. She pulled off her glasses and laid them on the file. "Ms. Marcum, you have nothing to worry about. What you have there," she said, gesturing through the large window to Grace, who was playing in a room such a bright yellow it could produce seizures, "is a totally, completely, absolutely normal child."

Jo should have felt relief, but instead she felt terror. She couldn't shake from her mind the sight of Grace's contorted face the other day as she threw the plate of three-cheese macaroni across the room.

"Now, that's not to say she doesn't have issues." Clackety-clack went the nails. "Oh, boy, does Grace have issues! I mean, think about the disruption in her life in just the past two weeks. A mother dead—a concept she's hardly old enough to grasp, by the way—an abrupt change in location, severing her not only from her lifelong caretakers"—here the doctor slipped the glasses on long enough to read the file—"but also severing her from whatever network of neighborhood friends and pets she may have had."

Pets?

"Of course she doesn't know which way is up and which way is down. Can you blame her? But the biggest thing of all is the loss of her mother, and that's what she's trying to work out when she throws bowls of pasta at you."

"Actually, she threw it across the—"

"Whatever. Look. Here's what you've got to understand."

Clackety-clack. "Children are special, different from adults. That's why there are people like me," she said, waving to the wall full of framed degrees, "who specialize in the unique challenges of children's psychology. A child won't grieve the way you and I grieve. It's like this: My *tia* Maria, she'll go to every funeral in Queens just to get a good cry. Sure, she's related to most of the dead, but she's not going there for that. She's going for the cry. And I mean *cry*—absolutely wailing, hurling herself over the coffin, whatever. It gets the grief out of her, you know, she lets it free. She knows it for what it is. But a child of seven years, she's too young. She can't bend her mind around 'gone forever.'"

"Now, wait—wait. Grace doesn't understand that her mother's dead?"

"Not really. I got a cousin that age who still thinks Goldie is coming back, even though she saw the bloated fish go swirling down the porcelain chute. Of course, it doesn't help that my uncle keeps buying her look-alikes and calling them 'Goldie.' She's had seven of them. My cousin's got an understanding of divine resurrection better than anyone at St. Joseph's Parochial."

Jo leaned back in her seat, as much to get away from the finger-daggers as to try to grasp what this doctor was telling her. Her phone vibrated again, making a whirring noise in the small office.

"Can't do that with a mother, though—can't keep Grace thinking her mom's coming back—because she isn't, and as time goes by, she's going to understand that more and more. That hard realization, it'll come in spurts. Yesterday you saw one of those little 'spurts.' Maybe the first."

"No, no," Jo objected. "It had nothing to do with her mother. She lost her marbles over macaroni."

"Transference. It wasn't the macaroni and cheese. That's not true—it *was* the macaroni and cheese, in the sense that it was a trigger."

"A trigger."

"That's her favorite food, right?"

"That's what her aunt told me."

"Well, maybe you didn't give her the right kind."

"Right kind." She felt like a freakin' zombie, repeating everything.

"Listen." Clackety-clack. "Children are creatures of habit. I got a patient who'll only eat Land O'Lakes yellow American cheese, right from the deli. You give him any other brand, or the kind that comes in plastic, and he totally loses it— I'm talking about a full-blown, blue-face, end-up-in-a-seizure kind of tantrum. Whatever kind of macaroni and cheese you gave Grace, it was the wrong kind. Your job is to find out what kind she likes and then serve that to her next time."

Jo sank deeper into the chair.

"You've got to remember, too, that this is only the first incident you've noticed. She's probably been doing all kinds of weird stuff. Sleepwalking, for example. It's very common for young children under emotional stress to have a hard time sleeping. Her eating habits might be disrupted, too." The doctor searched the file again. "Didn't you say she wasn't eating much and that you suspected she might be chewing on something weird?"

"Cardboard."

"Totally in profile. I'll warn you: It's going to go on. Every child acts differently, but she might act out in school, too. Fighting in the playground, being disruptive in class. They'll try to diagnose her attention-deficient but be wary—that's not it. Grace will be a Ping-Pong ball of emotions. She'll hit you with one, and then she'll veer off, and there's no telling in what direction. Your job as her guardian is to be alert for the moments, steer her away from self-destructive and violent behavior, and let her grieve in her own way."

Jo's insides went liquid. She was going to faint. She really was going to completely pass out, and not in a Southern-girl kind of way.

"Because it's not going to end anytime soon," the doctor continued. "Grace lost her mother, and that's forever. She'll be thirteen and getting her period for the first time and suddenly she'll burst into tears because her mother's not around to share the moment with her."

A red haze passed over Jo's vision. Dr. Rodriguez started writing something on a little blue slip.

"This will help, for a while." The doctor tore off a prescription. "It's mild, but it'll help with her sleep." She started writing another one, rat-a-tat-tat with the nails. "And this can tide her over the worst of the shock. When you bring her back for a re-evaluation in eight weeks, we'll see about adjusting the dosage—"

"Dosage?" Jo stared at the papers. She knew the drug—lately, she'd considered getting some for herself. "You're going to give Grace antidepressants?"

"They're very mild. Hardly have any effect. She's traumatized. Grace needs time."

"No."

She hadn't thought she'd said it out loud.

"It's your choice—but consider it. On a temporary basis. For both your sakes."

The doctor put on her glasses and stood up. The interview was over. Jo stood up, too, on unsteady feet, her phone dancing in her bag. She clutched the two blue prescriptions in her hand. Dazed, she walked out of the office and around to the playroom to fetch Grace.

"Okay, Grace," Jo said, staring at the smudge of her thumbprint on the little blue papers. "Time to go."

Grace didn't say a thing. She bent over a pile of blocks she was building into a castle.

"Grace—"

"I'm almost finished."

Jo crushed the papers in her hand. She'd had Grace for barely two weeks and already she was considering drugging her. Everything in her gut told her that wasn't right, but how could she trust her gut? What did she know about raising a normal, happy kid, never mind an emotionally and psychologically traumatized kid? What did she know about different kinds of macaroni and cheese? What did she know about the long-term care of a potentially violent and grieving child? How could she possibly deal with the day-to-day demands of a needy kid when her Martha Stewart friend had a husband who could barely control his own three-kid brood?

Her hands shook. More than her hands were shaking. She was shaking, from the top of her head to the soles of her feet. She sank into a red plastic molded chair too small for her Kentucky ass. She trembled, and trembled, like the damn phone in her pocket.

She snapped it open to Hector's frantic voice.

"Listen, Jo, you gotta be straight with me. Are you lying on a beach on some tropical island? Because if you are—"

"Gawd, I wish I were."

"Then when are you coming *in*?"

"Soon."

"If you don't come in *real soon* you may as well kiss your client good-bye."

Jo closed her eyes and pinched the bridge of her nose. "What now?"

"Miss Sophie is moving in on this presentation. She's got the whole office rooting for Miss Crackhead to be the face of Mystery, and all the graphics guys are working off her specs—"

"What, you haven't come up with an alternative? Do I have to come up with everything myself?"

Hector went silent. She could hear his hurt through the connection. In the background, Jo could also hear the clicking of fingers on keyboards, the rumble of adult conversation, and the hum of a printer. The noises were like a lullaby to her. She wanted to go to the office. She wanted to tell Hector it was okay and she was sorry for being a bitch. She wanted to be in the office—and away from *this*—so badly that it hurt.

She'd never been one to take drugs, but now she was wondering if she shouldn't order some of Grace's medicine for herself.

"Hector...I'm sorry." Jo forced herself to stop shaking. "That was unacceptable, and completely unfair. I know you're under pressure, and I do appreciate that you're covering for me."

"You need to show your face, boss." Hurt lingered in his

voice. "Because, if you lose this client, you might lose your job, and if you haven't noticed, this young man has hitched his wagon to your star."

"I'll come in today." She gazed at Gracie's bent head, her knotted hair, and her too-short jeans. She took a deep breath. She would go to work. She would get her mind off all this. She would have a lively discussion among creative individuals. She would talk about last night's episode of *Law & Order* by the coffee pot. "I've got a few things to do first, but I should be in by lunch."

When Jo flipped her phone closed, she understood three things, in swift succession.

First, she remembered last year, when one of the publicists had brought her two-year-old boy into the office. Her usual day care had fallen apart, and the employee had had no more vacation or personal days left. She'd sequestered the kid in a conference room with *Sesame Street* and then stepped out for a meeting. When she got back, the kid had scribbled all over the walls with a Sharpie. Cost fifteen hundred bucks to repaint the room, plus they lost the use of it for a week, and though Jo, like all the rest of them, had murmured words of understanding, out of earshot she'd made herself clear. Next time, the woman should take an unpaid day and stay home with the kid.

Now it would be Jo herself dragging a kid into the office. A kid that could potentially do a spew-the-pea-soup, spinning-head kind of thing over something as small as not getting the right pencil. And, like that flush-faced, exhausted publicist, Jo had little choice.

Second, she remembered vividly the sight of her mother

coming home every night with her shoes splattered with blood. Telling Jo that it was nothing but a poultry-packaging factory, but it paid better than the five-and-dime, and it kept a roof over their heads and food on the table and clothes on Jo's own back. If her mother kept at it, maybe she'd move up to supervisor, and then they could finally fix the curling linoleum on the kitchen floor.

Third and last: Jo understood, fiercely, why Kate had blown her cork and taken off for India. The wonder was that it took so long.

"Are we done now?"

Grace stood in front of her with unblinking brown eyes and a mouth the color of a wild strawberry.

"Yeah, kiddo." Jo stood up and slipped Grace's coat off the purple peg. One-handed, she helped Grace into it. "We're done, all right, just like burnt toast."

"I don't like burnt toast."

Things Grace doesn't like: (1) Benito's mac and cheese. (2) Burnt toast. (3) My sense of humor.

"Well," Jo said, "I'd bet my best pair of shoes that you'll like the next place we're going."

"Aunt Jessie once said that to me. And I told Aunt Jessie I don't like Lots o' Tots."

"What?"

"It smells funny from all the babies. And they cry all the time."

"Grace," Jo said, casting a nervous smile at the receptionist as they wound their way out of the office, "we're not going to Lots o' Tots."

"Aunt Jessie left me there *forever*."

"I'm not leaving you, kiddo. In fact, you're coming to work with me."

Grace went silent. She wandered down the stairs. Her shoe-laces flopped around, untied. *Can't seven-year-olds tie their own shoes?* At the bottom of the stairs, Grace gave Jo a shy look. "Do you work on mountains?"

"Uh...no." Jo held the door open into the bright October day. The kind of day Rachel would have spent biking through the Adirondack trails. "I work in an office. With phones and faxes and big rooms where you can play—"

"You got 'puters?"

"Lots of them."

"At Lots o' Tots they had 'puters. I liked the 'puters, but they wouldn't let me play *at all*."

Jo scrambled: Was there an extra computer in the office? And did they have any games on them? Could she dig out a laptop she could set up and install some game onto it?

"I just started whacking the moles," Grace said, "and I got all the A moles and most of the B and I was working on the C moles and teacher told me I'd had 'nuff. And the C moles were the *funniest*. They had long legs, and they were *quick*."

Jo caught sight of a taxi with its light on. She hailed it, clasping Grace's hand. "Well, I know just the place to hunt down that very game, Grace, and then we can set you up at my office."

And maybe, at least, I can save my job.

J. C. Richards was one of the biggest specialty toy vendors in the city. Its flagship store sat in prime real estate on Fifth Avenue. Jo had been there a few times, buying presents for the children of office staff, and Kate's kids, but whenever possible she sent an assistant to do the deed. For it always was, just as it was today, an absolute screaming madhouse of over-sugared kids.

Appropriately, a jungle was the theme for the first floor. An enormous baobab tree swirled up from the center, with tile paths curved around its base. Stuffed pythons hung from the branches. Colorful birds perched among the silken leaves. Monkeys swung on wires from one branch to another, and a nine-foot giraffe stretched its neck toward the greenery. Chirping and screeching and the roar of a lion played on a looped soundtrack, piped in through discreetly hidden speakers, just loud enough to hear over the screeching of kids.

Grace's eyes widened. "Whoa..."

"This place is hog heaven, eh, kiddo?" Jo crouched to her level. "And guess what? Today's your lucky day. I'm going to let you pick out one toy—anything you want."

She squeaked, "Anything?"

"Anything."

Here comes the nine-foot giraffe.

Grace slipped out of Jo's grip and raced to the seventy-pound hippo. Jo wandered after her, wondering how she was going to get that in a cab and to her office; she wasn't sure this place had delivery. But as soon as she reached Grace's side, Grace zipped off to the lion, and then reached for a snake. She wrapped it around her neck like a—well, like a boa—then flung it off, just to race off in another direction, toward the building blocks. Then toward the science sets. *Oh, God, please don't let her pick the chemistry set.* Jo imagined the conference room in flames. But Grace trotted off to the action figures, and then to the costumes, and then she discovered the escalator to the second floor and a whole other world of clay and plastic beads and tiny interconnecting building blocks and computer games and aisles and aisles of dolls.

They found the "Whack-A-Word Educational Computer Game (Learn to Read!)." The specs showed that it should run with no problem on Jo's laptop. Jo tucked it in a basket and told Grace that it didn't count as a toy. Grace raced off to the next aisle. Jo took the opportunity to answer another one of Hector's calls, plugging one ear and trying not to scream to be heard. Jo remembered that she'd seen a hot young Kenyan crooner on a late-night show last night. He'd been billed as a "black Frank Sinatra." Who said the face of Mystery had to be a woman? Wouldn't that blow everyone's minds, and bring more attention to the campaign? She sent Hector off to find his agent and contact him with a proposal.

By the time she dropped the phone into her purse, Grace had paused over a play table full of railroad tracks and magnetic trains. She was rolling one of the cars in her palm.

"Is that what you're going to choose?" Jo asked, thinking that the wooden set cost more than she'd spent on toys in her entire life. "Because that sure looks like a whole heap of fun."

Grace didn't answer right away. She put down the car she was playing with and picked up another. She perused it like she was trying to read hieroglyphics on the side. "You said I could get anything, right?"

Here comes that nine-foot giraffe. "Anything you want, kiddo."

Grace put the train down. She turned on one heel and walked back toward the aisles, passing the arts and crafts, the shelves full of pre-school toys, the Play-Doh, and the baby dolls you could feed, change, and make fart. Grace walked to the very back row of the store, until she reached the corner. Then, rising up on her toes, she fingered down the third box from the wall. Not the second, not the first. The third box, on the fourth shelf up from the floor.

What Grace held in her hands was an old-fashioned Barbie doll, complete with sweeping blue eye shadow, flowing golden locks, and a pink organza ball gown strewn with golden sparkles.

Jo looked at Grace's face as she'd never looked before. Looked at how hungrily Grace eyed the doll with its oh-so-perfect figure and its high cheekbones and arched feet shoved into faux glass slippers. Looked at *Grace,* with her flyaway long hair and floodwater pants. Noticed the dirty pink ribbon she'd tied around her wrist like a bracelet, and the pink canvas sneakers that had seen better days.

Grace mumbled, "Can I have her?"

The realization came to Jo like a splatter of puzzle pieces whirling into a new and unexpected design.

She imagined Rachel, passing this aisle with Grace in tow. Imagined what Rachel would say, catching sight of a fashion doll. *Look at these, Grace. No woman in the world looks like this. Freakishly skinny, huge boobs. And who the hell wears dresses like that anymore? C'mon, let's go to the Rollerblades.*

She imagined Jessie, exhausted from driving one relative or another to doctors' offices, tugging Grace into the day care. *No, Grace, you can't come today. You'll be staying at Lots o' Tots. Maybe tomorrow old Mrs. Henson will keep an eye on you. No, Gracie, it's after-care for you. Don't you like the snacks they serve? Then you can play in the playground. Grace, bring your GameBoy, honey, we'll be at the doctor's office for a while. . . . Grace, your mother's tired. Go ride your scooter outside, okay?*

She imagined Rachel losing all her dark pixie hair as the chemotherapy for the cancer ravaged her, as the fast-moving disease sucked the glow from her face and the softness from her skin. And she took to wearing a blond wig, because that would be Rachel's sort of humor, going blonde before she died, and anyway she wouldn't want to frighten Grace with the balding truth.

Rachel, you should have told us. We could have helped.

Jo fell to one knee. Grace still wouldn't meet her eye. Her knuckles whitened on the box.

Jo said, "Now, there's some beauty queen for you."

Grace couldn't keep her eyes off the doll. "She's got pretty hair."

"It comes with a brush," Jo said, eyeing Grace's own wild mop. "It'd be fun to brush her hair. You made a great choice, kiddo."

No one had noticed this before. Not Jessie, or Grace's grandparents, or even Rachel, all so overwhelmed for so many months. Who would have expected that a child of Rachel— the super-athlete, the adrenaline junkie, the most tomboyish of tomboys—would grow to become a girlie girl?

It really couldn't be this simple. Children were complicated, irrational, and uncontrollable. She must be fooling herself to think she could solve all problems so easily. It wasn't the purchase of a simple toy that put this glow on Grace's face. Jo sensed she could buy Grace every overpriced gadget in the store and it wouldn't make the kid any happier. Grace loved the doll, yes, but what she loved more was the attention.

Someone was listening to her, hearing her wishes, acknowledging them as important.

The phone jumped in her purse. Jo reached in and curled her hand around it. Held it tight.

She thought about her job: the vice-presidency she'd worked eighty-hour weeks to acquire; the paycheck that bought the caramel lattes and single-malt scotch that washed away the lingering, bitter taste of the canned vegetables and two-day-old bread of her youth; and the swelling F-U fund that would someday secure her freedom from drudgery and obligation—twin traps from which her own mother escaped only by dying.

Jo's phone vibrated violently in her hand.

Grace looked at her with Rachel's fathomless brown eyes, full of unguarded, quivering hope, and Jo did what she had to do.

She shut off her phone.

~~~ chapter eleven

With unguarded, quivering hope, Kate lounged on the queen-sized bed in her hotel room. Paul was coming. Kate *knew* it. The last time they'd spoken, he'd promised to look into flying to India. There'd been a warmth in his voice she hadn't heard in all their other angry telephone conversations—two a day since she'd arrived—a warmth and promise that had melted her bones.

He hadn't called her since. It had been forty-eight straight hours. Which could only mean one thing: He was—right now—on a plane to Bangalore.

Rubbing her knee with her bare foot, she toyed with the ribbon of her red silk negligee. Make-up sex between them was always hot and intense. She'd bought this nightgown just for him, just for that. The tissue still lay crumpled on the floor, the bag discarded in a corner. Last night, online, she'd checked airline flights between Newark and Bangalore. Taking into account a change in Frankfurt, and half a day for settling things at home and work, she'd calculated that he should be sweeping into her hotel room any minute now. She would have to remind him to bolt the door behind him, so

Sarah's usual early-morning arrival wouldn't interrupt them in the lusty middle of things.

She wondered if he would bring flowers from the airport. She wondered if he'd remembered to bring the chocolate body paint going stale in the drawer of their bedside table. She wouldn't care if he came empty-handed—because, without a doubt, the man who walked through that door would be the one gift she ached for the most, the Paul she'd married, the surfer boy with the wicked sense of fun, and the man who would bring excitement back into their lives.

She'd already forgiven him for all the nasty things he'd said to her since she'd come to India. That had been nothing but noise and fury fueled by shock, confusion, and frustration. Any sharp transition such as this was like birth; the pain was necessary to remind you of its importance. She hadn't forgotten that it had taken a jump from eight thousand feet to shock her back to herself.

The doorknob rattled, and Kate leapt out of the bed. Her hair, loose and freshly blow-dried, swung across her vision. She tripped over a pair of her running sneakers, lying in the middle of the floor, and the door swung open before she reached it.

"Sa—Sarah!" Kate stopped short. "You're here!"

Sarah froze, blinking, with her key card in hand. She wore the same tie-dyed brown skirt and crinkled white cotton shirt that she'd been wearing when she'd slipped out of the room the night before. Her face looked freshly scrubbed.

Sarah gave Kate a steady gaze, like she was rising up from deep water. "Hey." She raised one eyebrow as she took in the sight of Kate's negligee. Then, with a sudden tight expression,

Sarah glanced toward the bed. "Is there something going on that I should know about?"

"No, no, not yet." Kate kicked away the jeans she'd shucked on the carpet last night. Then she ducked around the edge of the door and looked up and down the long hallway. "It's Paul. He's due to be here any minute."

"Oh? Paul. Lucky man." Sarah did a strange little shake and then slipped into the room, tracing the ochre stain on Kate's forearm as she passed. "Is that for him?"

Kate glanced at the vine that climbed up to the third finger of her left hand. "Yes, I had it done in the marketplace yesterday." She closed the door on her disappointment and leaned back against it. "Sam found me the best henna artist, a woman who must have been a hundred years old." Kate gave Sarah a thorough look-over, from the pinched skin between her brows, to the stiffness of her shoulders, to the careless way her wrinkled skirt dragged on her girlish hips. "Sam and I wanted you to get hennaed, too, but you were sleeping so soundly I didn't have the heart to wake you."

"You washed it too soon." Sarah strode deeper into the room, ducking under the strap of her hemp purse before tossing it on the bed strewn with her rucksack and scattered sandals. "It's supposed to be darker than that."

"I know." Underneath the red silk, Kate had a deeper-ochre image—one she hadn't yet washed—of an intricately scaled snake. The reptile wrapped up her side and stretched halfway down her groin, its mouth open and its forked tongue pointing south. "It's done for brides, you know." Kate steadied her gaze on her mysterious, terribly uncommunicative friend. "You should have it done, Sarah. For your and Colin's pending...engagement?"

Sarah stiffened over her rucksack, its mouth spilling clothes. "I'm not Tess, Kate. Find someone else to mother."

"I'm not *mothering*." Kate pushed away from the door and slid a hip onto her own bed, upending the spread of a newspaper, whose pages fanned to the floor. "Well, all right, maybe it comes out that way. Hell, that's all I've been doing for *years*. But, honestly, Sarah, I'm trying just to be a *friend*. Isn't that what I'm here for? You're spending so much time with this guy, yet you're tight as a drum about him. What's going on? Has he mentioned anything about his fiancée?"

Sarah yanked off her shirt with more force than necessary. Her bra was held together by one hook, and the elastic on the band was beginning to fray.

"Oh, Sarah." Kate sighed as the silence stretched. "This is *not* good—"

"Kate, I really don't want to talk about it now."

"What's it like," Kate persisted, "sleeping with a man who has another woman on his mind?"

"We don't talk about her." Sarah pawed through her bag and tugged out a skirt the color of a tropical sky. "We don't talk about Stateside. At all. We talk about Paraguay. We talk about his conference and my work in Burundi. We don't get much opportunity to talk anyway."

"Hot sex will shut a guy right up."

"Will it? I wouldn't know." Sarah tossed the skirt on the bed and searched for a top to match. "Colin and I had 'hot sex' the first night, and since then he hasn't really touched me."

Kate stilled. Certainly she couldn't be serious. Kate didn't think there was a single day in the first five years of their relationship when Paul and she didn't go at it like nymphomaniacs. They couldn't keep their hands off each other. It was one of the simple truths of their marriage.

Her breasts were suddenly heavy; her lips, moist and swelling. *Hurry to me, Paul.*

"C'mon, Kate, despite what Jo believes, not everything is about sex." Sarah balled up her old shirt and hurled it into the corner of the room vaguely designated for laundry. "Colin wants me there. In his bed. He told me so. And in the middle of the night, things can get..." Sarah pulled the band out of her ponytail, shaking her hair free. Her face started to redden as only a freckle-faced minister's daughter's face could.

This Kate understood. "He's fighting it, then."

"Hell if I know." Sarah grabbed her clean clothes and pressed them against her midriff. "The Hutu have it right. Just build a hut and offer the father some cattle and a goat. It makes things so much simpler."

Kate scooted out of the way as Sarah strode toward the bathroom. The last time Colin broke Sarah's heart, it took a good year and a half for the girl to recover. Sarah had spent six months with her family in Vermont, chopping firewood and feeding chickens and wandering the paths of the Green Mountains. It was Rachel who'd finally pulled her out of it and brought her to New York. Sarah had thinned to a wraith by then, hollow-cheeked and haunted.

Rachel wasn't here anymore.

Kate reached out, tracing Sarah's arm as she passed. "I'm worried about you, Sarah-belle."

"Clearly." She swiveled on one foot and gave Kate a weary, winsome smile. "But I really can't talk now. I need to shower and get downstairs. Colin's leading a surgical team to a village south of here. It's been delayed but they'll be operating today. He asked me to join them—they could use an extra nurse. I have to meet them in about twenty minutes."

"Oh."

Sarah looked at her, sharply. "Is that a problem? Looks like you won't want me around once Paul arrives."

"Will it be dangerous, this trip?"

"Listen to you." With the edge of her foot, Sarah shoved aside an empty bottle of water, then paused with her hand on the bathroom doorknob. "It's dangerous only in that it's India, Kate—civilized, democratic, overpopulated, and totally unpredictable. I'm not in the least bit worried," she said, closing the bathroom door behind her, "and so neither should you."

Kate chewed on the edge of her lip as Sarah turned on the shower. Paul was due today, but Kate didn't know when. Planes could be delayed, connections missed. Perhaps he'd had some difficulty clearing his desk at work. She didn't relish the idea of lounging around all day in a state of heightened sexual tension, just waiting for him to show up. Yet here in Bangalore she'd done every touristy thing: all the gardens, the marketplace, the Hindu ruins, and the palaces. She wouldn't mind pushing her adventure just a little further and taking the rare opportunity of seeing Sarah at work. And digging more information out of her, too.

She'd just have to ruin Paul's surprise.

Ten minutes later, after punching in two dozen numbers to put the call through, Kate held the phone to her ear, waiting for someone at home to pick it up. Paul's mother answered.

"Barbara? It's me, Kate."

"Ah, the runaway bride." Barbara paused, and through the crackling of the connection, Kate heard her suck deeply on a cigarette—probably a Virginia Slim. "You still in India?"

"Can't you tell by the connection?"

"Good for you, good for you." Barbara exhaled loudly. "So—have you seen my no-good thieving ex-husband yet? He's probably bald, with a paunch, and wearing one of those red togas."

"Barbara, I told you before, I'm in India—not Nepal. Slim chance I'll see him here."

Not that Kate would even know what he looked like. All Paul had of his father was a few thirty-year-old photos of a full-bearded, scrawny, shirtless guy in low-slung jeans.

"You never know where the bastard is. If you do see him, punch him for me. A couple of times. And let him know who it's from."

"Sure will."

"And take a few extra days while you're there. Have yourself a good time. Now I understand why you called me here, sounding like a maniac." Barbara made a hoarse, deep sucking noise again. Kate hoped she was smoking on the deck and not in the house. "This place is a madhouse. Phone rings all the time, the mail is six inches high, the doorbell rings constantly, strange women come and drag your kids around, and the laundry grows in the basement like 'shrooms in manure."

Kate closed her eyes. She didn't want to know. Didn't even want to imagine. Barbara—who had raised Paul in a

California commune—lived quite carelessly in clutter. An attitude, Kate thought—as she scanned the dirty glasses and discarded clothing and shoes and candy wrappers of her hotel room—she was only beginning to appreciate.

"But keep away from the opium dens out there, Kate. It's not like weed. Opium will ruin you."

"Don't worry, Barbara, I'll stay clean."

"You want to speak to the grumpy old man?"

"Right." Kate grinned. "Like he's around."

"Oh, he's around, all the time. Underfoot. A damn nuisance. Pissed at you, oh, he's pissed at you, girl."

"I know."

"He can't keep away from this house, though. He took three days off work this week."

"Um-huh." *She's covering. Just in case I call the office.*

"Right now he's doing some project with Anna. Something about making a loom to weave cloth—crazy stuff. In my day, Paul wove a few strips of colored paper into a placemat, and it was done. Ten minutes, tops. And he did all the work. He spent his three hours in kindergarten singing 'Kumbaya.' He turned out all right without all this institutionalized brainwashing busywork. Hey, here he is now. Want to talk to your woman?"

Kate stilled. In the background, she heard the rumble of a voice.

No.

Paul couldn't be there, in New Jersey. Right now, he was on a plane thirty-two thousand feet above her hotel, slowly descending into Bangalore's BLR airport.

They fumbled with the phone. Kate shot up, flexing her hand over her belly, fighting a sudden swell of emotion.

"Hey," he said, his voice eager. "Are you at the airport?"

She tried to swallow. "Paul, I thought that you were coming *here*."

"Newark or LaGuardia?"

"Here, Paul. *Here*." She paced along the edge of the bed, scraping her knee against the sheets they were supposed to be making love upon, all the long day. "To Bangalore. To The Chancery. The last time we spoke, you said you'd think about coming—"

"You're still in India?"

"Of course. Waiting for you."

He made a short, angry noise that cut cleanly through the crackling of the satellite connection. "Well, I'm here waiting for you, Kate, because you said you'd think about coming home early."

"You told me you'd think about coming here!"

"And I did. I thought about it. For about *ten seconds*. And then I realized, Hey! We have kids! One of us has to take care of them!"

She squeezed her eyes shut. She didn't need the mommy-guilt. She'd taken care of things before she left, as she always did. Running the house like a well-oiled machine even when she was not there. Running it so well that all anyone noticed was the rare screw-up.

"The pantry is full of food." She filled her hand with the silk of her negligee, then pressed her fist against her racing heart. "The bills are paid for the month. I did every scrap of laundry I could before I left. Your mother is there—"

"She doesn't *drive*, Kate. She's 'limiting her carbon footprint.'"

"I made arrangements—"

"Things keep coming up."

"You could ask—"

"I don't *know* these women. I could be sending the kids out with serial killers and pedophiles—"

"I've been waiting for you, Paul." She swallowed, her throat dry. "I've been waiting for you for twenty-four straight hours."

"I've been waiting for you for over a week." His anger vibrated through the wavering connection. "I've been waiting for you to climb back on a plane, make your way here, and *come to your senses.*"

She wandered to the window and pulled the rope to open the blinds. Below spread the grand, well-tended boulevard that faced the hotel. Beyond, she could see the spires of two mosques, and the tarps that marked the edge of the marketplace.

"Paul, if you were here, we could rent a motorbike." She smiled, dreamy. "We could wander through the city. Everyone rides on them here. Even the women, in their saris. They ride sidesaddle, behind their husbands. They hold on tight."

"You do that, Kate, you go do that with Sarah. Scoot around on motorbikes through the streets of Bangalore. Meanwhile, I'll shuttle Mike to practice, cook dinner, dash out at eleven p.m. to buy that *special* shampoo for Tess, yank a comb through Anna's *ridiculously* long hair, and burrow through the mess in the playroom looking for Tess's lost cleats."

Through the opened slats of the blinds, Kate looked up at the blue sky streaked with high, white clouds. Just after Tess was born, when Kate had felt so weak, so vulnerable, so helpless—when she was so sure she couldn't possibly take care of this tiny little baby—Paul had morphed before her eyes. He'd opened his long-fingered hands and held Tess so perfectly. The baby's small head had filled his palm, and his hands didn't tremble like Kate's did. They'd been living near Malibu at the time. She'd been so grateful when he told her he was swearing off surfing for a while.

Is that when it happened?

Or was it when he contacted the headhunter who found the job in New Jersey? The one that paid a good deal more than what he was making at a struggling start-up. He'd taken it, though it meant shucking the blue jeans and buttoning into a collared shirt—because the corporate position meant they would have the financial freedom to let Kate quit her job and stay home. Raising kids in day care, he'd said, reminded him too much of his wildly unconventional youth in the southern-California commune.

She twisted the rope that closed the blinds, cutting off the view. "Call Kathy Hayward to drive Mike. Her boy is in the same class. The phone number is on the board." She turned her back to the window and clutched her arm as if she were cold. "Use lots of detangler for Anna's hair, and wash it every other day. Tell Tess to check for her cleats by Hannah's trampoline—that's where she usually loses them. And your mother is there for one reason: to cook dinner."

"Spaghetti squash with raisins. Okra. Vegetarian lasagna I couldn't even get the dog to eat."

"Might do them some good to try someone else's cooking." She kicked the pile of dirty clothes into a tighter pile in the corner. "They might learn to appreciate mine. And the world won't end if they miss a soccer practice or two."

"Tell that to Tess."

"Tess needs to *know* it." She gave the pile of shirts a last, vicious kick. "Do you even *miss* me, Paul? Or do you just miss having your shirts show up on hangers, and a home-cooked meal on the table every night?"

"I miss having a partner in this marriage."

"So do I." Striding past the bureau, Kate crushed the phone between her cheek and shoulder and swept up old newspapers and candy wrappers, dumping them in the garbage at the other end even though she knew the maid would be coming soon. "The kids will do just fine for a week in your mother's care—"

"My mother? The woman you wouldn't allow to stay here when the kids were young? You said she stank of smoke. She swore too much. She let them stay up too late, didn't keep them on a schedule—"

"You don't even want to come, do you?" She swept up two pairs of her shoes, then shoved the closet open with her foot. She slammed the shoes onto the closet floor, as hot tears bit at the back of her eyes. "You have a chance to have a week alone with your wife for the first time in fifteen years, and you're just standing there waving as it passes by."

"Here's what I want to know: Is this how it's going to be from now on, Kate? You taking off whenever the mood moves you?"

"I'd rather take off whenever the mood moves *us*."

"You haven't even asked me about the kids. About how your actions have affected them—"

"I'm not your freakin' father, Paul. I'm not leaving you and the kids to go meditate on a mountaintop."

"Good. Because I want my old wife back. The one who takes care of her responsibilities. After this past week, I don't know who the hell you are."

Her joints went loose. She dropped onto her bed, abruptly,

bouncing as she landed. She waited through the crackling connection for him to whisper a hoarse apology, tell her that he was simply overwhelmed, that he remembered, too, what they'd had, what they'd shared, a long time ago.

"Apparently, you've forgotten me." She gathered a handful of silk. "Or maybe you've just stopped..."

Loving me.

She let the phone fall upon her lap. It slid across the silk of the red negligee and tumbled onto the floor. She heard him calling her name with increasing irritation. When she didn't respond, he broke the connection.

A hundred years later, Sarah stepped into view. She picked up the receiver, placed it in the cradle, and sank to her knees in front of Kate.

Sarah's hands were warm and still moist from the shower. Her face was soft with compassion, framed by tight wet curls. "It's not good news, is it?"

Kate shook her head.

I don't know who the hell you are.

"Oh, Kate." Sarah tightened her grip. "I really don't want to leave you here alone."

Kate stood up numbly. She walked to the bureau and pulled open the drawer beneath the television. The day before yesterday, she'd gone to a sari seller and sat shoeless on a white cotton mattress while the seller tossed bolster after bolster of brilliant fabrics upon it. She tugged out the freshly stitched sapphire-blue Punjabi suit she'd had made—chosen because it reminded her of the color of Paul's eyes.

"Then take me with you, Sarah," she said, un-self-consciously stripping off her negligee and kicking it under the bed. "I need a little perspective."

~~~~

The lobby bustled with activity. Two men argued with the concierge. Porters lugged medical bags to a waiting van. A cluster of doctors talked heatedly near the doors. An Indian woman in a traditional sari stood apart from it all, calmly smoking a cigarette, and watching with an expression that conveyed boredom and amusement at the same time.

Kate trailed out of the elevator behind Sarah, still battered from the conversation with Paul, now numb, as if she were moving within a cotton cocoon. Sarah strode into the confusion of the lobby and headed directly to the clutch of doctors by the door, then grazed the arm of a broad-shouldered American.

This must be the infamous Colin O'Rourke. As if from a very distant place, Kate eyed him. She'd been too bleary to get a bead on him when he'd examined her when she first arrived at the hotel. She knew Jo would expect a report. Sarah didn't have any photos of the doctor, and after he'd left her, it had been painful to even bring up his name, never mind milk her for a physical description. Given his antics in the jungle, they'd all pegged him as a gritty Clive Owen type. Someone craggy-handsome. Stubbled and sweaty. A dirty-under-the-nails loner, intense in his work.

Certainly not anything like the khaki-wearing all-American turning to her now, with his pristine pressed shirt and Brooks Brothers yellow tie. Just a few wrinkles away from the corporate uniform.

Like Paul's.

No. I can't think of that now.

Colin grasped Kate's hand and granted her an easy smile. A blinding smile. Clearly, a bleach-strip-enhanced smile. "Last time I saw you," he said, raking her face with his striking gaze, "you were dreaming of unicorns."

"I'm feeling better now."

"You look better. How do you like Bangalore? I heard you went into the jungle to ride elephants."

"Camped overnight, actually. Heard tigers roaring beyond the ditch."

It seemed like a very long time ago, and oddly unimportant.

"I haven't done that in years," Colin said. "Which preserve did you go to?"

He was very good at pleasantries, Kate thought, as they chatted under Sarah's nervous scrutiny. But all the while, Kate was thinking, *Is this really the legendary Dr. O'Rourke?* Sarah could have met his type on the campus of any university that had an NCAA lacrosse team. A little older than herself, he was lean and strong, but with a grain-fed bulk. He just looked so...American. He sure as heck bore no resemblance to the whip-lean international relief workers she'd encountered, perpetually underfed and constantly in motion.

Like Sam, who suddenly arrived in all his tall, dark, and handsome glory. "It's all settled," Sam said, speaking to Colin. "My car is available for whatever you need."

Sarah's face stiffened. "Your car, Sam?"

"It's a damned inconvenience," Colin explained, "but I asked Sam if we could commandeer his car. One of the vans broke down, stranding some important equipment. We've already had to reschedule this twice. Something like this happens every time I do one of these gigs."

"I volunteered," Sam explained, eyeballing Sarah. "I've no plans, so I figured I'd join all you merry crusaders."

"It just burns me." Colin scraped his hand through his hair. "Something always gets in the way of the work. In this case, we can fit the people in the cars we have, but not all the gear. And we're so late that if we wait for a new car to come on Bangalore time, there will be that many fewer kids we can treat."

Kate sensed an undercurrent of guilt in the flurry of details, but she was still too numb to sort it all out.

Sam gestured to his white rental car, idling just outside the hotel. "Sarah, you and Dr. O'Rourke can ride with me. Just like old times."

Kate asked, "Is there room for me? I'd love to see the real India."

Sam, Colin, and Sarah exchanged swift glances. A wordless three-way exchange that absorbed her bazaar-bought Punjabi suit, her damp messy hair, and her inexperience. She'd seen wordless three-way exchanges like this before. At cocktail parties, whenever she responded to the query "What do you do for a living?" with the bland truth, "I'm a housewife."

"Are you sure you want to do this, Kate?" Colin asked. "It's very primitive. There'll be things you might not want to witness. And we'll all be working like lightning to get to every patient."

Sarah slipped a hand around her elbow and drew her close to her side. "Kate can help me. I could always use another set of hands."

"Well"—Colin shrugged and gestured to the front desk—"let me see what's holding us up."

As soon as Colin was out of earshot, Sam turned on Sarah. "Bloody can't help yourself, can you?"

"Me?" Sarah tightened her grip on Kate. "You can't bloody help *yourself,* Sam, interfering in everything—"

"You're on the first real holiday you've taken in years, and within days you're working again."

"It's for a—"

"—good cause. I know. It always is." Sam rolled his wrinkled sleeves above his elbows. "Did you ever consider just sitting in one place and sipping a drink, maybe twirling the umbrella in it?"

"Did that once. The Paraguayan sugarcane liquor, remember? It left me unconscious for days."

"You're exaggerating. And you were cracking funny that night."

Kate stood like an observer at a tennis match, watching their fevered back-and-forth with increasing interest.

"You could always skip the booze," Sam suggested, "and just lie on a beach, take in the sun."

She pinched her freckled forearm. "I don't have your skin. I'd burn to a crisp."

"You'd rather bloody burn yourself out working."

Sarah cocked her head, nearly dislodging the pencil-pierced roll of hair at her nape. "You are aware that I already have a mother and a father? Seven brothers as well?"

Sam planted his hands on his lean hips. "Then you should know how to relax."

"Take me out for a beer later."

"Oh, I'm sure the good doctor has you booked for this evening, like every other." Sam eyeballed Colin, who strode across the lobby toward them. "Give him a few more days and maybe he'll whisk you away from the business altogether."

Colin, oblivious to the tension stretching between Sarah and Sam, slapped his hands together. "Good news. We're free to load up and follow the van." He handed Kate a slip of paper. "For you. I heard them take the message at the front desk and figured you'd want it now."

Kate sucked in an uneven breath as she took the paper. She held it in her hands like a communion wafer. Relief quivered through her. What a fool she'd been. She never should have worried. Fifteen years of marriage couldn't be shaken by one week apart. Of course Paul would call her again, right away, apologizing. Maybe even promise to join her.

Gripping the message, she followed the crowd through the hotel doors into air thick with humidity. She tossed her bag in the car, settled in the passenger seat next to Sam, and reverently unfolded the paper.

To a crushing disappointment.

Sarah suddenly gripped her shoulder. "Kate? Is everything okay?"

She swallowed, nodded her head, and refolded the paper. "It's nothing. I thought it might be from home." Into the bag at her feet, Kate tucked the message, along with her hopes. "It's just from Jo. No explanation. She just wants me to call."

"Oh." Sarah groaned. "Things must be going badly."

"With what?"

Sarah said hastily, "Sam, you got the directions?"

"Of course I have the bloody directions."

Sam pulled into traffic, keeping on the tail of the swift-moving white van they were to follow.

Kate sat for a moment, knowing something was wrong. Knowing something was out of place. Something else, something beyond her own marriage.

"Sarah," Kate said, "what do you mean, things must be going badly?"

"It's nothing." Sarah leaned forward, peering out the window. "It's green. Kate, you'd better help Sam navigate the lights."

"You," Kate murmured, "are a terrible liar."

"I'm not supposed to tell you. Watch, Sam—the rickshaw." Sarah gripped the back of the seat as they swerved. "What the heck. Jo can't get to me here. And maybe you can help."

"Help?" *I can't even save my own marriage.* "Help how?"

"It's Grace, Kate. Jo has custody of Grace."

"What?!"

"I'm sure Rachel had a reason."

"But . . ." Kate struggled to break free of her own issues, to remember Rachel's child-care arrangements. "But why didn't Grace stay with her grandparents?"

"They're pretty bad off, apparently. Medical issues."

"But why would Rachel want Jo of all people—"

"You know, you and Jo really ought to sit down and talk. The two of you just don't understand one another. Trust Rachel, Kate, I'm sure she put a lot of thought into who was going to care for her daughter—"

"As much thought as she did when she was inseminating herself with a stranger's sperm?"

"Whoa!" Sam cut off another driver to a cacophony of beeping. "Did somebody say 'sperm' in my car?"

"Rachel had a daughter," Sarah explained, "through artificial insemination."

Sam shook his head. "You Americans."

"It doesn't make any sense!" Kate grasped the dashboard to keep herself from surging into the door with every swerve. "It should have been *me*. I should have been charged with Gracie, and Jo should have jumped out of an airplane!"

Then Kate would have gone on in blissful ignorance, in the pleasant, if not very exciting, routine of her marriage.

" 'You Americans,' what's that supposed to mean?" Sarah, ignoring the seat belt, gripped the back of the front seat to confront Sam. "Is artificial insemination any worse than, say, the Hindu practice of suttee? Or the Malawian tradition of sexual cleansing—"

Sam raised his finger. "The difference is choice, Sarah. The difference is choice."

"Colin," Sarah said, slapping his arm, "help me here."

"I'm with Sam on this one. I once had a patient from L.A. ask me to reconstruct his entire jaw just so he could look more like Judy Garland in his drag-queen show. Haven't come across that in any developing country."

Kate, ignoring the conversation, grappled with the news. "The lawyer must have mixed up the envelopes."

"Jo checked." Sarah tucked a drying, frizzing curl behind her ear. "And, Colin, if you think that's strange, you haven't been to Bangkok."

"Actually, I have. The thing I remember most was standing outside the Grand Palace and there was this Thai kid selling food for the pigeons. I bought a bag, and in the thirty seconds

I spoke to him, he lifted my watch, my wallet, and my hotel key card. Absolutely amazing."

"The Thais are some of the best cons," Sam added. "Almost as good as the Gypsies in Madrid."

Kate tried to concentrate while the car swerved and Sam launched into a story about European Gypsies. Why hadn't Rachel given her Grace? The only reason Kate could come up with was that Rachel thought she'd screw it up. So Rachel sent Kate skydiving, knowing it would trigger a series of events that would have Kate end up a world away from her husband and abandoned children, who were probably cursing her right out of their lives.

What the hell am I doing here?

She hunched in the car, balling herself up against the violent swerve-and-sway of Bangalore traffic. Tuk-tuks and rickshaws flew by. As they reached the edge of the city, cows grazed on the verges and wandered into the street. They passed hulks of abandoned trucks rusting by the side of the road. Around her, the conversation danced from comparing the driving skills of Americans and Southern Indians, and the cleverness and ingenuity of spare-parts dealers in sub-Saharan Africa. The conversation went to places she'd never been, to subjects she knew nothing about.

What had started as a niggling sense of panic had grown, by the time they reached the clinic, into a throat-tightening anxiety attack. It didn't help that a huge crowd gathered around the squat building, and the mob raced toward them as the cars approached. Young boys clambered on the hood. Women, crying out in Hindi, held their babies up to the windows. Thin-ribbed babies. Babies with oddly deformed feet. Babies with cleft lips so deep they split through the nose.

Sarah squeezed Kate's shoulder, sensing her panic but mistaking the source. "It's always like this. The news travels that doctors are coming, and the mothers bring their children hoping the doctors will be able to look at just one more patient."

Sam parked the car carefully on the grassy verge. He got out and started shouting, waving his arms, and urging the crowd to make way. Colin and Sarah edged their way out and started unloading the trunk. Kate sidled out, took what equipment they gave her, and followed them blindly through the throng into the clinic, where a dozen medical workers busied themselves setting up two makeshift operating rooms.

She dropped her load where they directed. Young doctors barked orders at one another, cursed at the flickering of lights as more and more equipment drained the system. Colin, all business, directed the placement of the instruments. Sarah fussed with a clipboard's worth of paperwork. Sam hauled in another load, then disappeared into a back room, promising to hook up a mobile generator.

Kate stood in the middle of the room, awaiting instructions, but she was buffeted by rushing medical workers until she retreated, knock by little knock, to an unobtrusive place against the wall. She became piercingly conscious of the curious stares of the locals, whose gazes went from the brilliant sapphire silk of the traditional Indian attire to her blond hair.

And there stood Sarah—little Sarah, the baby of the crowd—the one they were always helping out Stateside. Sarah worked her way through the throng while a translator dogged her footsteps. Sarah leaned into the sore-ridden face of an ailing child, smiling and tugging a lock of his hair, as she sent an orderly to fetch a particular antibiotic. When she reached Kate's side of the room, Sarah glanced up casually and said, "I'll give you something to do in a minute, Kate." She swiped a piece of hair off her face. "I've got to triage these cases first."

Kate leaned up against the wall and felt her senses spin as if she were falling from eight thousand feet but her chute hadn't deployed, and all she could see was blue sky and green earth, blue sky and green earth. Below loomed the concrete face of the target zone and it was coming up fast—

Kate started, and her eyes flew open, and—here she was—slumping against the wall, a useless American standing in a rural Indian clinic doing absolutely nothing but gaping at all the world's misery.

What am I doing here?

She knew what she was doing here. She'd come here with Sarah. She'd wanted to walk into Sarah's impossibly exciting life. She'd wanted to see exotic places and eat strange foods. She'd wanted to come a hairbreadth away from danger. She wanted to gather tidbits for future dinner parties. *I once rode an elephant through the jungles of Mysore when...* She wanted to unfurl *National Geographic* tales over canapés so Paul's overeducated business associates and their fabulously chic working wives wouldn't avoid her like the jean-wearing, spittle-shirted, mushy-minded housewife she'd become.

So *Paul* would look at her—really *look* at her.

Kate buried her face in trembling hands. She'd taken Rachel's leap, but it had blown her so far off course, halfway across the world, to a place where she was more useless than ever.

It was too much. Her skin prickled from the miasma of sickness and antiseptic, and a haze came over her eyesight, threatening her with another swoon. She strode away from the waiting room to get her blood pumping. She didn't know where she was heading. She only knew that she couldn't stand here any longer. She strode past the two operating rooms with their flickering lights and clusters of white-jacketed doctors. She strode with no destination in mind except to get away from herself.

She ran smack into Sam.

"Ruddy hell!" He gripped her by the arms. "Kate? Where are you going in such a hurry?"

She met his gaze. The scars that traced his cheeks gave him character and strength, like the pits and chips on the face of an old Roman statue. Sam was opinionated, and funny, and competent, and lived a life so full of meaning and interest, and so much more important than hers.

His hands curled around her arms. "You look wretched. Come here." He drew her into a room full of old equipment and wiring, scattered with tools. "Are you not feeling well? You're paler than usual."

She couldn't speak. She couldn't put her thoughts together. She kept looking at his mouth and thinking it had been so long since she'd been with Paul. Sam was tall and excitingly unfamiliar, all of him. He was handsome and kind. He tightened his grip on her arms, even as these thoughts flickered through her mind.

"Kate, don't go barmy on me. You know there's only one woman I want looking at me like that. Did something just happen out there?"

She shook her head. In the dim room, her wedding ring glinted. *Her wedding ring.* She thought of Paul, somewhere in New Jersey, struggling with the three kids. Tess. Michael. Anna.

"I'm sorry." She rubbed her face with her hands, wishing she could rub away the shame. "I don't know what's come over me."

"Don't be so hard on yourself. Only the coldest heart comes to a place like this and leaves unaffected. Clearly, it's time for you to go home."

"I hope I still have one."

"Of course you'll have one."

No, Sam. It's not that simple. Paul is so angry.

"Come on." He drew her into his embrace and patted her shoulders. "Nothing is ever as bad as you think it is."

She pressed her cheek against his chest. His heart beat steady and sure. Sam was a good man. She was a fool. She didn't belong here. This was Sarah's life. Whoever Kate had been once, long ago—before she'd given up her job and her freedom for a husband and family—that woman was gone. Maybe, despite Rachel's urgings, despite Kate's own feelings of excitement these past weeks, maybe that woman should have stayed dead and buried.

Suddenly, Sam went rigid.

Kate looked up. He stared, lock-jawed, at the open doorway, where Sarah stood in the hallway, watching.

~~~ chapter twelve

What the *fuck* is going on?"

The words slid out of Sarah's mouth like slivers of steel.

"Easy, Sarah," Sam said. "Kate is having a hard time of it."

Sarah glared at them. Why didn't he loosen his grip? Kate looked pale, but perfectly capable of standing on her own. "Hard time of what?"

"She can't take it all in. She's a green recruit. She's not like you."

What the hell did that mean? Not dreamy and disconnected? Not short and frizzy-haired and socially awkward? Not fashion-challenged or blithely ignorant of important details? No, Kate was the fierce and capable one; all tasks done impeccably with taste and style; even her kids turned out flawless. She never did anything half assed or by the seat of her pants, like Sarah was trying to do right now, searching for candy to give to a kid with late-stage lymphoma because she had nothing to offer that would really *help*.

Sarah glared at Kate. To think she'd been worried about Blondie during the drive. To think she'd been worried that, in spite of the vaccinations, Kate had come down with malaria or typhoid or some other tropical malady. Instead, Kate had succumbed to a different kind of fever—with the strapping black Brit who had the irritating ability to unnerve Sarah with nothing more than his tall and brooding presence.

Kate ducked away, muttering something about finding a bathroom. Sarah didn't bother warning her that the only bathrooms were the squat-toilet kind and not a place for lingering. She'd find out soon enough, and Sarah was still reeling over the vision of Kate and Sam embracing. A red haze threatened the edges of her vision, even as Sarah told herself that Kate hadn't been herself in weeks, not since the first skydive. The angry haze lingered even as the softer part of her nature argued that Kate was crashing, finally, to earth.

But Sam should know better.

Sam stepped closer, then leaned in the doorway, crossing his arms. "What are you more angry at, Sarah? That I might have kissed Kate? Or that I might have kissed her instead of you?"

"Stop." Sarah pushed the memory deep, deep inside. She thought she'd made it clear to him: What had happened on the trip to the mountains was irrelevant—just a lapse of judgment in a time of stress. "Kate is a married woman."

"And vulnerable," Sam added. "And missing her husband. A heart is a fragile thing."

Sarah drew in a tight breath as a thought assaulted her. "Did you two have crusader sex in the jungle?"

"Only one of us is indulging in crusader sex," he retorted, "and it's not me."

If her face got any hotter, her skin would sizzle right off

her bones. Surely it must be written all over her body, Colin's kisses like bruises on her throat, the imprint of Colin's hands all over her skin, and, mostly, the guilt she felt, and the shame.

"Don't change the subject. This is about you taking advantage of my friend—"

"Oh, no, Sarah-belle, it's about a lot more than that." Sam pushed away from the doorway. He took one step too close. Close enough for her to see his bitter chocolate eyes, and the intensity brewing in them. "It's about getting entangled with someone you hardly knew, at a time when you were lonely and vulnerable—"

"Exactly. You know better than to do that to Kate."

"—and then dreaming that experience into some great bloody opera-love, dreaming it bigger with each passing year, until the weight of it suffocates you. Blinds you so much you can't even see what's right in front of your eyes—"

"You're wrong, Sam."

"You should have put him up on a shelf. You should have labeled the relationship for what it really was: a great shag overseas. But, no, not you, Sarah, not the minister's daughter who has only one heart to give, one big heart, who made the terrible mistake of giving that heart to a man who took advantage of you when you were vulnerable and lonely—"

"*Enough.*"

She swung the clipboard as if she could strike the words right out of the air. A pen shot out, clattered against the wall, and slid down the hall. The red haze dimmed her vision, thankfully, because she didn't want to see Sam's face and look into those fierce eyes. This Sam unnerved her. She'd encountered him once before, under an acacia tree on the border of

Lake Tanganyika, when he'd seized her rain-wet face in his hands and kissed her until she couldn't think straight.

She seized the clipboard to her chest, shielding her heart. "I should expect no better," she said, hating the husk in her voice, "from you."

His nostrils flared. "Someday you will forgive me for those rifles."

"It's a hard thing to forgive, when a gunshot patient bleeds out on the table—"

"I was given two choices: The guns go through, you get your medical equipment, and I survive—or the guns go through, your equipment is sold on the black market, and I'm dead in a ditch. Tell me, which moral choice is the better?"

She shut her eyes. She didn't want to hear it. Didn't want to argue the point. The world she lived in was riddled with ugly moral compromises. You want the bags of flour driven inland? Pay a bribe at the port, bribe the driver, bribe the sentinels at every one-mile-marker checkpoint, and don't forget the armed rebels greeting you at the end, who'll take all the food for their own soldiers. A harsh world chipped away at her hopes and expectations. A harsh world bred impossible compromises.

"And since we're speaking of moral compromises," Sam said, leaning in, "why don't you tell me, Sarah-belle, which is worse: me kissing a married woman, or you banging an engaged man?"

~~~~~

Hours later, Sarah found Kate crouched behind the clinic with her head between her knees. The face she lifted to Sarah was blotched with misery.

Sarah absorbed the jolt of guilt like a quick shot of bitter medicine. She hadn't been very forgiving this afternoon. When she'd turned on her heel and left Sam, she'd made no effort to find Kate. Instead, she'd stepped right back into work, losing herself in the much larger problems of patient after patient after patient. Now she meandered to Kate's side and leaned against the wall.

The plaster exuded heat; Sarah felt the burn through her shirt. "You've been here all day?"

"Pretty much."

Sarah gestured to the edge of the jungle, not ten feet away. "See any tigers?"

"Saw a couple of monkeys." Kate scraped her hands through her tangled hair. "That's all the wildlife back here. A couple of monkeys and a big blue jackass."

Sarah slid down the wall. The rough surface of the plaster caught the fibers of her shirt. She rifled through her skirt pocket, then pulled out a lighter and a thin hand-rolled cigarette, tied at both ends with colorful string. Licking the tip, she put it between her lips and flicked the lighter.

Kate managed to cock a brow. "Hard day, huh?"

"Not really." Sarah blew a stream of sweet-smelling smoke. "Not any harder than most."

"You're smoking a joint."

"It's a *bidi*. A poor man's cigarette." The fragrance of cloves curled around her. "They spice it to mask the taste of cheap tobacco. The patients kept foisting them on me. It's rude to refuse. Want one?"

"Will it make me forget the day?"

"No. But it'll keep away the flies."

Kate reached for it. "That'll do."

They sat in silence, enjoying the perfume of the clove ciga-rette. Sarah made a smoke ring and watched it wobble and widen as it rose into the canopy. "So," she said, feeling low and unworthy, but unable to help herself as the mild narcotic hit her system, "Kate Jansen's got a thing for Samuel Roger Tremayne."

"Oh, no, no, no." Kate covered her face and then just as quickly lifted it from the cradle of her hands. "I'm an idiot. Sam just caught me as I fell."

"Yeah," Sarah said, eyeing her through a smoky drag, "he caught you with his lips."

"Lips? No! We didn't kiss. Sarah! We didn't kiss! He just held me. It was a nonevent—really."

Relief was a wicked, treacherous thing.

"Listen, I'm a mess." Kate grasped her hair in two fistfuls. "I've jetted off and abandoned my husband and kids. I'm the most reviled creature in the world. I'm the Bad Mommy."

"That's a little harsh."

"I've got to go home. I've got to make things right."

"Kate, I'm sure they've adapted."

"You don't understand." Kate crossed her arms, grasped her shoulders, and squeezed. "Everyone thinks I spend my time at home watching soap operas and whipping up gourmet meals...but I'm usually draining pots of pasta and tossing in bottled sauce, or I'm racing around town looking for poster board and the right kind of cleats, or I'm patching the crum-bling walls, or managing a fever while I'm on the phone plan-ning the next school fund-raiser. I'm always on the edge of losing it. I came here thinking I could revitalize my marriage, and all I've done is dump all that on Paul."

"Finally, you're crashing."

"I'm changing my flight when we get back to the hotel. I want to leave tomorrow morning."

"Frankly," Sarah said, twirling the *bidi* between her fingers, "I thought you'd have crashed long before now."

"What are you talking about?"

"After finals, your junior year of college, you rented that beach house on your father's credit card. Invited half the dorm. Introduced mosh-pit diving at the local bar." Sarah adjusted her unwinding ball of hair so it lay in a pile on one shoulder. "You partied like an animal for four days. Two of them on a sprained ankle."

"I just blew off a little steam. I had finals and GMATs practically the same week."

"Then you completely popped your cork senior year. Remember when you climbed that ridge topless, and those two rangers—"

"Hey, it was a tough semester."

"Kate, I don't know much about your home life, but something tells me that this breakdown was inevitable. And a long time coming."

A crease deepened between Kate's brows. She plucked a thread loose on the hem of her Punjabi suit, now wrinkled and sweat-stained.

Sarah nudged her with a fist. "For what it's worth, when you go off the deep end, you're a hell of a lot of fun."

Kate laughed in a way that was half a sob. Then she sank

her head on Sarah's shoulder. The sun dipped in the sky, taking the keen edge off the day's heat. The tops of the trees danced with a rogue breeze, shifting the dappled light, and the air was charged with the threat of a late-season rain shower.

Kate asked softly, "How do you do it, Sarah? How can you be so calm, so unruffled... doing *this*?"

Sarah rolled her eyes and avoided answering by filling her lungs with smoke. After her conversation with Sam, this was the last thing she wanted to discuss. Right now, she didn't feel very much like a stouthearted, self-sacrificing, morally incorruptible relief worker.

She released a long fragrant plume of smoke. "I get paid."

"In cigarettes," Kate muttered, reaching for the flaking remnant. "Nasty ones, too."

"Kate, I tell you about this stuff all the time."

"No, you don't. You just ask for money."

"For food, for supplies, for bribes. If I actually talked about this," she said, waving a circle in the air, "I'd spoil everyone's appetite for Pinot Grigio and bacon-wrapped dates."

"Ouch."

"Look." Sarah rubbed her eyes with the butt of her hand. Her lower back ached. Even crouched against the wall, she couldn't stretch out the pain. "You and I look at the world with very different eyes."

Kate jerked with a humorless laugh. "Hey, I don't think rose-colored glasses could filter out any of this."

"That's not what I mean." Sarah took back the cigarette and rolled its wet tip between her fingers. "Do you remember when I stayed with you and Paul one year, over Thanksgiving?"

"Sure. Your parents were overseas doing a missionary stint."

"Tess was only a few years old. I think you were pregnant again." Sarah pushed her skirt between her knees and slipped so she was fully seated on the ground. "You had this incredible centerpiece. You filled a bowl with wheatgrass, and evergreens you'd clipped from the neighborhood, then piled on blue-and-silver ornaments."

"To match the chair covers. Saw it in *Family Circle*."

"All weekend I kept looking at the thing." Sarah took a final deep draw on the cigarette and pressed out the butt as she exhaled the last of the smoke. "I kept thinking: How much time did you spend on it? And where in the name of God do you find wheatgrass? And why were you trying so hard to make your house look like the cover of some magazine?"

Kate shrugged, bewildered.

"Do you know what Jo once said to me? She confessed that her job in this world is to set up impossible ideals. To create an image so powerful that even good, honest, striving people—people like you, Kate—will do anything to attain that unreachable expectation."

Kate went very still. Her lips parted, and she searched some place well beyond the jungle.

"That's what I meant when I said that you and I look at the world differently." Sarah patted the wall over her head. "This clinic, this place—just imagine how crazy I'd be if I thought all the problems here could actually be solved."

In Sarah's mind rose the memory of that sweet little girl with the crooked braids, lying bloody on a pallet in the clinic.

"But," Kate muttered, "that's different. I just want what's best, for Paul, for the kids—"

"What *you* think is best? Or what Michael's teacher thinks

is best, setting up that ridiculous log-cabin project? Or what those magazines think is best?" She nudged her with a shoulder. "You have to trust your instincts more or you'll sacrifice your sanity. You'll be trapped chasing rainbows."

"Geez, Sarah. Where the heck did this come from?"

The memory struck Sarah like a fist.

Rachel sprawled against a mud wall in Burundi, blowing a smoke ring in the blue light of the moon.

For a girl elbow-deep in all the world's muck, Sarah, when it comes to love you waste a lot of time chasing rainbows.

Rachel, when you've spent three hours digging shrapnel out of the leg of an eight-year-old, then we'll talk, okay? Until then, let me keep my hot, handsome rainbow.

Kiddo, there's this thing about rainbows. They're perfect from afar. But when you get real close to them they just disappear.

"It came from Rachel." Sarah turned her face away, toward the patients still milling on the road, and toward a slow-dawning realization about her own impossible expectations of one particular man. "When she visited me in Burundi, she had a lot to say about rainbows."

"Sarah-belle." Kate wrapped her hands around Sarah's arm and pressed her cheek against her shoulder. "For what it's worth, I think you might be the most incredible woman I know."

~~~

Kate and Sarah were still sitting like that sometime later, when the back door to the clinic squealed open.

Colin poked his head around the edge. "There you two are. I've been looking for you. We're just finishing up." He squinted through the trees. "We need to pack up. If we don't get on the road soon, we won't reach Bangalore by dark."

Sarah gently shifted Kate off her shoulder. "That last boy, is he out of surgery?"

"They're closing him up now." Colin's shirt, once pressed and pristine, now hung limply from his broad shoulders. Sweat stained the collar. He walked toward them, unrolling the sleeves, buttoning them around his strong-boned wrists. "Incredibly complicated case. We had to balance the muscle forces on the lip and nose without repositioning the nasal septum. Kid's going to need a rhinoplasty in a few years, but at least he won't be aspirating milk into his lungs anymore." He shook his head. "Don't see many cases like that in L.A. You know, Sarah, you were absolutely incredible in there. I never understood why you didn't study to be a doctor."

"Not her calling." Kate pushed herself to her feet. "I'll go help Sam pack." Kate ran her hands down her wrinkled suit and gave Sarah a meaningful look that said, *I'll leave you two alone.*

Not that it mattered, Sarah thought. With his hair tousled, sweat gleaming on his forehead, and his face bright with excitement, Colin looked, more than ever, like the young man she'd loved in Paraguay. But even as her heart moved in that familiar, painful way, she told herself to stop. Now, as he had all day, he'd fixed his professional expression tight on his face, the one she'd come to dread. Despite his bright, affable voice and plenty of harmless talk, his eyes warned, *Stay back.*

Colin gestured to Kate with his thumb as she slipped inside the clinic. "Is she all right? She looks wrung out."

"It's complicated. It has to do with another of Rachel's letters."

"Ah."

Down came the wall. The subject of Rachel's letters was rife with treacherous emotional currents—involving him, and her, and this strange, tense relationship—and, as usual, Colin avoided, quite deftly, swimming in those waters.

Sarah plunged on. "Kate's going to change her flight plans when we get back to the hotel. She wants to leave Bangalore as soon as possible—even as early as tomorrow morning." Her throat tightened, but the words came out before she could stop them. "Colin, I'm going to leave with her."

She lifted her chin and faced him. She tried to modulate her heartbeat and the rate of her breathing. She had to leave. They couldn't go on like this. *She* couldn't go on like this.

Physically, she wanted him. Even now, she couldn't help noticing how light dappled his skin and cast in shadow the vale by his sturdy collarbone. The collarbone she'd bitten last night, just before he'd seized her hips to stop her from doing what they both wanted.

But emotionally, they were still continents apart.

He took a few steps back, then thrust his hands in his pockets. He swiveled away and found interest in the jungle canopy, rustling in the breeze above their heads.

She hadn't expected him to protest. Nor had she expected him to plead with her to stay. But as the silence stretched, disappointment came anyway. She swayed slightly where she stood. She'd known since she'd received Rachel's letter that this day would come. She'd imagined the scenario in a dozen different ways. But no imagining could brace her against the sudden unhinging, and the deepening sense of vertigo.

"Ah, Sarah." He'd lost the affable voice. "I haven't been much of a superhero this time around."

"You were a superhero today, to the kid whose face you just reconfigured." She credited the huskiness of her voice to the lingering effect of the clove cigarette. "And you were a superhero to those medical students who hardly breathed while you taught. You're still the best surgeon I've ever seen."

That wasn't the absolute truth. Dr. Mwami in Burundi could work miracles under the light of a flashlight, with gunfire in the distance. But it was different. Sometime during his years away, Colin had developed a skill so specific and so fine-tuned that it was a sort of magic.

"I'm not talking about work." He crossed his arms and glanced around, taking in the dirt road, the rough plaster of the clinic, the shivering greenery of the jungle—anything but her, standing still in the shade. "I intended to handle this better. Every morning I told myself I'd be straight with you. But then you'd look at me with that wonderful expression on your face. You seduced me with that look, Sarah. Back in Paraguay. And here." He shrugged, then shoved his fists in his pockets. "What can I say? I let myself be seduced by my exotic, adoring nurse."

Exotic? With her pale, freckled skin and mouse-brown hair, she considered herself perfectly ordinary. Certainly not an instrument of seduction. Overseas, she always felt like plain vanilla next to rocky road or marble swirl or butter pecan or almond mocha.

Or rich, dark chocolate.

"Tell me, my Vermont-bred minister's daughter," he said,

tracing a pattern in the dirt with his foot, "what kind of sin is it, to want to be the man you think I am?"

She shook her head, uncomprehending.

"Is it vanity? Or is it pride?"

"It isn't a sin to want to be a good man."

"That's the real reason I didn't come back to Paraguay. I'd made choices you wouldn't approve of. If I had come back, you would have been disillusioned completely. It's pretty hard to keep the cape on, Sarah-belle. It weighs a ton. Rather than destroy what we had... it was easier to just put your memory away."

On a shelf, she thought, flinching. Labeled "Passionate Affair in the South American Jungle."

"And now, of all times, *now*, when I'm halfway around the world; when back home I'm starting a new business, and my entire life is in flux—"

And, Sarah added silently for him, you're about to marry another woman, by the name of Victoria Lee, the toast of southern-California society.

"—and here you appear. Out of nowhere. Reminding me of the life I once had, and the better man I used to be."

"You're too hard on yourself." It was true. Colin still could work magic on the operating table. He still gave his time to international relief. He still hated petty annoyances like broken equipment, rickety cars, or ignored schedules. He still counted strokes when he brushed his teeth. And he still had the terrible habit of ignoring—and avoiding for as long as he could—an uncomfortable emotional situation. She didn't think any less of him for these all-so-human faults. "Honestly, Colin, you haven't changed a bit since Paraguay."

"Oh, I have." He pulled a strange smile. "Superheroes don't lie, Sarah. And they certainly don't cheat on a fiancée."

And there it was, acknowledged. The engagement that had been announced at such length in the *Los Angeles Times*. He and his fiancée had registered for silver and crystal at Tiffany's. Sarah had considered saying good-bye to Colin by sending him a gravy boat from their china pattern, but the piece cost more than four months of rice for the camp.

Which is worse, Sarah-belle, me kissing a married woman, or you banging an engaged man?

Sarah shook the dust from her skirt. "I should go." Permanently. Crawl back to the States and find a way to forgive herself for tempting a man away from his promise to another woman. "Sam may need help with the equipment—"

"Don't go."

Suddenly he stood before her. He reached out and cupped her tangled mop of hair in his palm.

"Colin, don't."

She curled a hand around his wrist. It was a strong wrist, a surgeon's skillful hand. His touch made her ashamed of herself and oddly disappointed in him. She didn't want him to kiss her. Not now. Not anymore. Something had shifted in her heart, something fundamental. The change was still too fresh to bear examining. Jo would understand, if she were here. Jo would handle this just the right way. Jo would say her goodbye and kiss him off and walk away, letting the velvet chains of commitment fall into the dirt behind her.

All Sarah knew was honesty. "It was wrong of me to chase you down like this, Colin, when I knew your heart was committed elsewhere."

"You wanted to find me." He tugged gently on her hair. "I know you did."

"Had Rachel not sent me that deathbed letter, I would have kept your memory on the shelf, too."

Pristine. Perfect. And forever unchallenged.

That would have hurt a whole lot less.

"Maybe." His gaze drifted to her throat. "But in your heart, you wanted to find me."

"And I'm glad I did." That was a platitude, but she let it stand. She didn't know how she felt right now, with Colin more intense than he'd been all week, more open and intimate than she wanted him to be. "But it's time for me to leave. What I really want—the only thing I should have ever expected from you in the first place—is a proper good-bye."

The amber rings around his pupils contracted. "You don't mean that. We made love."

"Yes," she said, damning her voice for breaking. "We did. It was sweet, but it was wrong."

"No. No." He shook his head, working up the words. "It was *not* wrong."

"Colin—"

"I'm not ready, Sarah Pollard." He stepped in to her. "Damn me for a fool, but I'm not ready to let you go."

~~~

chapter thirteen

"Kate!" Jo fumbled with her phone and then struggled up off the couch. She tossed the cashmere throw over Grace, who lay rapt, watching the animated movie *Cinderella*. "Sugar, are you finally home?"

"I wish I were." The connection crackled. "I'm calling from Bangalore. At about six trillion bucks a minute."

"Stay on the line. I'll *pay you* for the charges—just don't hang up!"

"Hanging up is Paul's job. He's done it to me twice today. I'm counting on you to tell me if my children are still alive."

"Last time I called your house, they were just fine." Jo raced to the pile of papers spread across her kitchen table, searching for a particular yellow pad. "Tell me you're drinking yourself blind and belly-dancing in hotel lobbies."

"Jo, it's India, not a Bollywood movie, and I haven't seen a single one of those stars with the great hair and the unpronounceable names." She paused. "There is a hot black Brit, though. A friend of Sarah's."

Jo started, remembering Paul's crazy suspicions from their

last phone conversation. "Kate, you know I'm all for the easy loving—but you're very married."

"I know. Yes. I *am* still married."

Jo paused, hearing the fear in Kate's voice. The last time Jo had spoken to Paul, asking him about—of all things—macaroni and cheese, there had been such a furious, unrelenting undertone to his narrative that she'd given up trying to convince him Kate hadn't lost her mind.

"Sugar, if you're wearing the ring, you're still married." Jo couldn't imagine any other situation between the two of them. "Now, tell me, did Sarah finally spill?"

"Yeah. You got Grace."

"The surprise behind door number three." Jo glanced into the living room. All she could see was Gracie's tousled dark hair against the arm of the sofa. Right now, the mice were struggling to bring the key up the stairs to save Cinderella from missing the ball. No wonder mothers had the TV on all the time. It gave them a moment of peace. "That's Rachel and her twisted sense of humor."

"Any bones broken yet?"

"Five stitches."

"You, or her?"

"Her. She was sleepwalking, right down my stairs. The psychiatrist says that's normal for a grieving girl."

Across the satellite connection, Jo heard an ominous hiss. Maybe it was just a hitch in the line. "Kate? Are you still there?"

"First things first," Kate said. "For the love of God, get her out of the psychiatrist's clutches."

"I—"

"Look, some kids definitely need them. Maybe Grace will

need one, too. But I just think there's a whole lot you can do before...before the third-person therapy and the drugs."

Jo felt a strange settling. Maybe she'd done something right. "I refused the drugs. But she's still sleepwalking. I've got gates everywhere. You know, those baby-gate things? The place looks like a damn kennel."

"That may be overkill. But better too much than too little. Is that why you called me?"

"No. Well...yes." Jo glanced down at the papers strewn across the table, bloody blue with ink. Phone numbers of nanny services, laundry services, tutoring services, local schools, pediatricians. Books on raising the seven-to-twelve-year-old child. She had her laptop open to every mothering Web site she could find. Not a single one could tell her how to decipher children's clothing sizes. "I called because..." She braced herself for taking the hit. "I called because I could surely use your help."

Jo held her breath. She wouldn't blame Kate for tearing into her. She expected it. Jo had just handed her a golden opportunity for avenging years of insolent and snarky remarks. Jo'd been remembering each and every one of them: *Honey, remember the rules? No talking about husbands or children over wine. Tell me, Kate, is Paul incapable of shuttling a kid to soccer? Sugar, if you want to sacrifice yourself on the altar of motherhood, that's just fine, but don't expect me to delay the appetizers because of it.*

But Kate was the only serious at-home mother she knew. Oh, there were women at work, pushed onto the mommy track, but she'd made a point of avoiding them, because they were always so frazzled and overwhelmed. As for her own mother . . . well, Jo hadn't been out of her tweens when the car accident happened.

Through the crackling of the line, Jo heard a muffled sound. Then another. "Get it out of your system, Kate. It's ridiculous, I know. *I'm* ridiculous. You should have seen the freaks that showed up for the nanny job. I mean, one of those women walked in *without shoes.*"

"Jo—"

"And just taking care of the hair. The hair! I thought Grace combed it herself. Turns out she doesn't. Well, that means it hadn't been combed for about five days! I gave up and went to that salon Bangz—yes, *the* Bangz, in SoHo—just to pay some-one to run a comb through it, without her screaming like I'm murdering her. I got Mario, who has about the same amount of sense as me when it comes to kids. Get this: They gave me my three hundred dollars back just to hustle the kid out of the salon." Kate was still making strange hiccupping sounds. "I guess Rachel was popping mushrooms on top of some snowy mountain when she made this decision. She probably thought this was a great joke, but I tell you I just think, when it comes to a kid, you've got to make a well-thought-out *choice,* and here she has thrust that choice upon me. If I get through the next week without destroying the poor kid, I'll kiss your ass in a window."

"Welcome to my world."

Something in Kate's strangled voice made Jo pause. Above the noise of the television and the breaking up of the con-nection, she listened more closely to the muffled, rhythmic sounds.

"Geez, Kate. You're crying."

"No, I'm not." Kate blew her nose. "Well...yes, I am."

"Honey, are you drunk?"

"Hell, I wish I was. I'd go to the bar downstairs and get myself a drink if I didn't look like someone just wrung me out. I'm not crying because I'm sad. I'm crying because I'm happy. Someone actually *needs me*."

"Girl, what happened to you over there?"

"Later. It's a really long story. Let's take care of Gracie first." She cleared her throat. Jo envisioned her straightening up on the hotel bed, pulling down her oversized T-shirt, slipping on the reading glasses she didn't like to admit she needed, and getting down to work. "Now. What do you need?"

For the next half-hour, Jo scribbled furiously. She wrote lists of medicines she needed to have at hand at all times: cortisone ointment, antibacterial lotion for cuts, Band-Aids of all sizes, a thermometer, liquid acetaminophen, liquid ibuprofen, pectin drops for coughs, and Benadryl and Caladryl lotion for mosquito bites and allergic reactions. Kate asked if Grace took medicine orally, and when Jo hesitated, she horrified her by reminding her that there are always anal suppositories.

The advice came hard and fast. If a kid doesn't want to take a bath, promise bubbles or let her go in her bathing suit, and if she doesn't have one, let her go in her underwear. I mean, really, Kate said, what's another piece of wet clothing? Since Jo's tub didn't have a sprayer, Kate advised buying a special tube that fit over the faucet and ended in a rubber ducky spray. It'd help when she needed to wash Grace's hair. Combing hair? Do it while she's watching TV or eating breakfast or otherwise distracted, use a wide-toothed comb, keep it in braids to reduce knotting, and you have to do it every day.

When Jo told her about the adventure with Benito the cook, Kate whooped with laughter. "Oh, Jo, you didn't try to feed her gourmet mac and cheese?!"

"Sugar, I'd have fed her truffles dug with my own hands if I knew she'd eat them."

"Get her boxed mac 'n cheese. The orange powdered stuff, in the blue box with the cartoon characters. That's what kids want."

Kate confirmed that kids ate freaky things. She suggested apple slices dipped in peanut butter for lunch. *For lunch?* Why not? Fruit and protein. She rattled off some tricks: Call broccoli "trees" and cauliflower "snow trees." Play "shoot the pea into her mouth" at dinnertime. Make bologna faces. Avoid fancy sauces. Keep things pure.

Jo's hand cramped over the yellow pad. She shook it out. Kate was still talking.

Clothing sizes mean nothing. An eleven-year-old can fit into a size eight if she's slim. Go by weight more than age. Don't get fixated on jeans or fancy shoes or tights; some kids just don't like them. Try sweatpants, simple cotton T-shirts, things that are sturdy and will wear well. Buy sneakers and shoes a half-size bigger. Kids grow in spurts, and you never know when it's coming.

"You know," Kate said finally, "we've been talking nearly an hour. You're making me feel like a freakin' genius."

"Taking care of this kid is worse than pampering some runt pig for the 4-H fair."

"You poor soul. It isn't like that at all."

"Jesus save me."

"Tell me you're not sipping wine."

"Perrier." Jo eyed a bottle in her glass cabinet. "Though the Jack Daniel's is winking at me."

"Resist. You've got to be on your toes."

The line crackled, then went silent again. Jo knew Kate was still there; she could hear her breathing. Could hear her across thousands of miles, and wished—wished with an ache—that she were sitting right here beside her.

"You know what really burns me about this, Kate? In my real world—the working world—if you do something well, then you get a raise or a promotion. You move up, you feel appreciated, you feel valued. And if you suck at your job, well, soon you'll be pounding the pavement with a lot of motivation to do better next time. But at home, here, playing 'mom'? Strangers glare at me if Gracie cries. People roll their eyes at me if she plays in the grocery aisle."

"I hear you."

"I mean, really, where's the payback? Someday, at Tess's wedding, I'm sure she'll raise a toast to you and Paul—but that's, what, thirty seconds of validation? And where are the limits? Honestly, if a kid goes to Harvard, then her mom did exactly what she was supposed to do, no big deal. But if the kid ends up smoking cigarettes behind the machine factory, then the mom is scum of the earth."

No, those weren't tears in Bobbie Jo Marcum's eyes. Bobbie Jo Marcum was a tough son of a bitch, a Mistress of the Universe who, through creative wizardry, was responsible for a good number of the commercials on major network TV stations. Bobbie Jo Marcum was no longer the ungrateful young girl who nursed a resentment because her mother worked two jobs yet wouldn't buy that pretty china doll for her birthday.

"You're preaching to the choir, Jo."

"Oh, honey, don't put me in your league." She glared at the tissues, across the room, through blurring eyes. "What this Kentucky girl owes you is an apology. A great big spanking one. And as soon as you get your tanned ass back here, I'm serving it up to you in a frosted glass with a rim of salt and two cherries speared on a swizzle stick."

"Jo..."

"No, don't make it easy on me. I've been an unforgiving, arrogant bitch who's just beginning to understand what you've been going through. And I'm simply not going to be able to do this without your help."

Kate hiccupped. Her voice was raw with tears. "You have no idea how much I need to hear that right now."

Beside her, on the table, Jo's cell phone began to ring.

"Holy cow, Jo, you've got a real job. How are you working with all this going on?"

"Working? What's that? Oh, is that the cell phone that's ringing every five minutes, and my team screaming we're going to lose an account because I haven't shown my face in the office more than twice in the past ten days?"

"I take it you didn't hire the barefoot nanny."

"No. But I may have someone." Latoya ("Mom named me before the Jackson girl went all freaky"). She was a student at a community college uptown, working on getting her teaching certification. She'd taken a semester off to make some money because she was paying her own way. Jo had liked the frankness of the girl, her no-nonsense toughness. And she possessed that quality that had been left out of Jo's own DNA—the ability to charm a child in a millisecond. *Gracie, girl, that's one kickin' haircut you got there."* Gracie had beamed. Jo had hired Latoya on the spot. "I'm trying her out tomorrow. Then I can get a few hours in at work."

Not that it mattered. The Kenyan singer hadn't worked out, and the dearth of ideas coming out of her crew made it pretty much a non-issue. Her work nemesis's idea of using Miss Sure I'll Do Some Blow as the great "Mystery woman" was the only idea anyone had—and so it was on. Jo had had a moment of inspiration last night, when she woke up on the couch to the noise of an all-night music channel. In the video, a raven-haired vixen writhed to the updated beat of a funky sitar. When Jo heard the same music blaring from Latoya's iPod later that afternoon, she realized that her muse had finally woken up: The perfect face of Mystery was an up-and-coming Indian-American pop singer whose single was only now hitting the airwaves. Jo had found the perfect face for Mystery—but too late.

Which was pretty much, in Jo's estimation, a guarantee that they wouldn't get the account for which she'd been fighting for six straight months.

"Jo," Kate said, misinterpreting her silence, "Grace will survive. Kids are pretty tough."

"Yes, yes, I know. If she doesn't crack her head open sleep-walking tonight."

"Just go with your instincts."

Instincts were precisely the problem. Jo could smell a business opportunity from three thousand miles, but she didn't have a single mothering instinct. "Kate, you know it should have been you."

"I'm not so sure of that. Maybe Rachel could see the future, and see how I'm fucking up my family so badly right now."

"You needed a vacation."

"Moms don't get vacations."

"Don't tell me that! I'm booked for St. Lucia in February."

"I'll take Grace for that week. In the tiny run-down apartment I get after Paul throws me out on my ass."

Jo cradled the phone against her shoulder, hearing loud and clear the insecurity in her voice. "You haven't spoken to him recently?"

"I'll have a chance soon." Kate blew her nose. "I've changed my flight. I'm coming home the day after tomorrow."

"What time are you coming in?" Jo scribbled the flight number and arrival time in the margins of the pad. The plane arrived well after the scheduled pitch meeting. She'd need to get the hell out of the office after they screwed up that deal anyway. "Listen, how about I pick you up?"

"Why? Do I need moral support?"

Jo weighed the value of a little white lie. Jo could give her a few more days of peace. After all, if Paul wasn't returning Kate's calls, then there wasn't a darn thing Kate could do from halfway around the world.

Then again, Kate deserved to be warned.

"Sugar, I spoke to Paul today."

"Oh, God."

"Strap yourself tight, Kate. After that plane lands, you're in for some serious turbulence."

~~~~~

After she hung up the phone, Jo realized she'd made a colossal mistake warning Kate about the extent of Paul's fury. She shouldn't have burdened her. Paul and Kate had ties that ran deep—but Jo knew enough about relationships to understand that, the tighter the ties, the more they chafed under pressure.

One of the better reasons never to get married.

The TV swelled with music as Cinderella rode off into the sunset in the Prince's carriage. Gracie stirred on the couch. Jo mentally shook herself. She couldn't think about Kate right now, not when another problem loomed: getting Grace to go to bed—and actually sleep.

She scanned the six pages of notes she'd taken. Routine. That's what Kate had emphasized. A solid, predictable bed-time routine.

"Hey, kiddo," she said, rising from the stool, "did you like that one?"

"Too much mice," Gracie said, yawning, "and not enough Cinderella."

Jo grabbed the remote and flicked off the TV. Gracie had flopped back down on the couch. One of her socks lay on the floor beneath the coffee table.

"What d'ya say about a nice bubble bath and a book before bed?"

"Okay."

To Jo's surprise, Grace scampered upstairs and stripped down to her birthday suit without the abashed look she'd given her yesterday while trying on clothes at the stores. Testing the water, she let Grace sit in the bathtub as it filled, while she gathered the clothes for the cleaners and scrounged through her linen cabinet for some bubble bath. She had bath salts and bath oils and shower gels—and massage oils and personal lubricants, pushed to the back like her love life. She was about to give up on the idea of a bubble bath altogether when she read the back of the shower gel and realized it could also be used for bubbles.

She hoped Gracie didn't mind the scent of passion fruit. Squirting it into the tub, she went to fetch a swim Barbie from the pile of bags. By the time she returned, Gracie was chin-deep in bubbles.

"Oops. I probably put in too much, huh?"

Gracie smiled.

Gracie smiled.

Unwilling to risk the rare good will, Jo backed out of the room and let Gracie play in the tub. While on the phone with Hector, she glimpsed the little girl through the doorway, making beards with the bubbles and covering her shoulders like Cinderella's big puffy sleeves. Water splattered all over the tiles and sloshed onto the floor. Jo was thrilled with the peace. She let Gracie play until she complained that the water was too cold, and then she took her out, poured warm water all over her to wash off the bubbles, and wrapped her in one of her huge towels. Only when Gracie was dressing did Jo realize that her collection of Ruth Rendell crime fiction, with the blood-splattered covers, would not be the best reading material for a seven-year-old.

Then her gaze fell on a photo album gathering dust on the bottom shelf. She bit her lip and wondered. It might be a good idea. It might be an all-out disaster.

Follow your instincts.

Oh, Lord, help this child.

"Hey, kiddo," Jo said, coming around the door as Gracie wrestled into her nightgown, a blue silky thing she'd chosen herself. "I thought we could read a book before bed."

She shook the dress down, not meeting Jo's eye. "My mother used to read me *The Poky Little Puppy*."

"Well...I'm afraid I don't have *The Poky Little Puppy*. Or many books like that. Maybe you and I can go to the bookstore tomorrow to pick out a few."

"Okay."

It seemed to be the kid's favorite word. "But I do have something else you might like." *Take a deep breath.* "It's about your mother."

Gracie stilled. "Really?"

"Yes." She pulled the photo album from behind her back. "From when your mother and I were in school together, long before you were born. We were both a lot younger. Not as young as you, but young like...like Latoya."

Jo lowered herself to the floor, bracing her back against the bed. Grace plopped down beside her. The photo album opened with a crack.

Once upon a time...

There was a girl named Rachel. Fit and strong and full of life. She had hair like yours, Gracie. All brown, except hers was curly when it was long. It's a mess in this picture because she just finished rowing a boat in a race. That's her and the crew team after beating the regional champs. Sarah, Kate, and I had joined her on the road trip—*not so much for moral support as to meet the Dartmouth guys.* Yeah, that's Sarah Pollard, she hasn't changed at all, has she? *All that clean, saintly living.* And this is Kate—Mrs. Jansen. Do you remember her? She has a boy named Michael about your age. That's her right there. What's your mom doing in that picture? Well...she's drinking from the victory cup. It's a special game you play after winning.

Look, Grace, here's another. Did your mother ever tell you she started a rock-climbing club? That's how we all met. We all had different reasons for joining. Kate—Mrs. Jansen—she's a real bookworm, and I think she just wanted something to get her outside. Sarah's from Vermont and an outdoors kind of girl. She drifted into it but she stayed because we all got along so well. I joined because...because of your mother. I meant to go to a meeting for future businesspeople. I ended up in the wrong room. But your mother and I, we got to talking. She convinced me to join. She told me I was the kind of person who needed to stand on mountaintops once in a while.

For perspective.

Just give me a minute, Gracie. I've got something in my eye.

Look, here we all are again, climbing up a sheer face of stone in the Shawangunks. There's Kate. Doesn't she look like a Texas cheerleader? We're all laughing because her harness is digging into her bottom. She's got powder on her hands to help her grip. If you look closely, you can see Sarah at the top, sunburnt, the sky pink beyond her hair. Look at this one, Grace. There's your mother, framing us all in for a hug. We made a pot of brown beans over a fire that night, and it got burnt so badly on the bottom we had to chip it out with our knives.

Look at all these mountaintops. Pages and pages of them. *Lots of chances for perspective.* We were so bad with the camera, I can hardly tell who is who, and we're all just a bunch of silhouettes against the rising sun. Look—there's your mother. Do you know what she's doing? She's heading into the bushes with a roll of toilet paper. When you camp, you have to go to the bathroom outside! Just ignore the rest of these pages,

Gracie; we got silly as the night went on. That's why there are so many bad shots of thumbs and half-heads.

Except for that one. Boy, your mother sure did have a smile.

Gracie ran a finger across the close-up of her mother. Rachel had been such a strong spirit, such a fierce presence, and there she was, fixed on photographic paper, so very full of life. How could Rachel be gone from the earth? It still didn't fully register with Jo—a part of her still expected to get a phone call from her, from some exotic port. Then, noticing how Grace sat unmoving, how her little pink finger lingered on the photo, Jo wondered how this small bundle of a girl could handle the void when it was threatening right now to swallow Jo up.

Grace...let me show you one more.

Jo shuffled through the pages until she reached the one she wanted. Look at this, she said. Do you recognize anyone? Yes, that's me, and that's Mrs. Jansen, and there's Sarah. Why are we dressed up like black-and-white bunnies? It was a Halloween party. We thought we'd go as black-and-white Easter bunnies. Can you guess who that is in the middle? Yes. It's your mom.

As Tinker Bell!

A laugh burst out of Gracie, a bigger sound than you'd think a little girl could make. It was a spontaneous eruption of pure hilarity, so unexpected and unfettered that Jo couldn't help it, she laughed right along with her.

Gracie keeled over against her shoulder, her belly heaving, and Jo let it happen. She slipped her arm around the little girl and squeezed her. Grace's warm, damp hair soaked her shoulder, and Jo felt the vibrations of Grace's laugh shiver her very bones. The scent of passion-fruit bubble bath rose from her skin, and Jo breathed it in as a strange, warm bubble swelled in her chest, fragile and very, very frightening.

...and they all lived happily ever after.

With shaking hands, Jo closed the book. She left the photo album on Grace's bedside table as she swung the little girl's legs under the covers. She shut off the light and left the door ajar to the hallway. Padding barefoot down the stairs, Jo strode directly to the kitchen, where she perused her choices in the liquor cabinet.

A little Kentucky bourbon should do it.

She poured a healthy swig, thinking of her own youth. Most of the fairy tales Jo remembered were less Disney and more Brothers Grimm. The fundamental lesson being: When a mother dies young, Lord help the orphans. More often than not, they're eaten by the witch in the forest.

Or shuttled among foster homes, where tired foster mothers try earnestly to absorb another lost soul into a motley collection of wounded, abandoned creatures they have tried to forge into a family.

Jo closed her eyes as the bourbon seared her throat. It wasn't working. The memories were stronger than the alcohol. She poured a little more, but then just stared at the amber liquid in the glass. She suspected there wasn't enough bourbon north of the Mason-Dixon Line to help her forget what it was like to be the unwanted one.

She'd never given much thought to all those women before. At the time, they'd just been a series of strangers: authority figures foisted upon her to make sure she stayed in school, ate decent meals, learned her Bible, and stayed away from those boys who smoked cigarettes and drank applejack around the back of the machine shop. They must have been good souls to take on such a thankless burden. But as an abandoned, orphaned twelve-year-old, she'd convinced herself never to bind up her emotions with any other soul. Like her mom, these foster mothers might be here today, but gone tomorrow. So she'd been the prickly, unapproachable one. She'd completely shut them out. That way, she'd never get hurt again.

Groaning, Jo closed her eyes and slid her head onto the countertop, still gripping the glass. It'd be better for poor Grace if wolves raised her. They roamed in packs. They cared for their young. Better a pack of wild wolves—than a woman who'd forgotten how to love.

chapter fourteen

Sarah closed her eyes and tilted her head against the head-rest. Twenty hours of travel, and she hadn't managed more than a few hours of sleep. The airplane had just made its first queasy drop in altitude, presaging the long slow descent toward Newark Airport. The fact that this leg of the journey was almost over gave her no comfort. She knew she still had so far to go.

Her body ached. Not just from the discomfort of the seat, but from emotional exhaustion. She needed a full night's rest, uninterrupted by plane changes, and, more important, the dog-chasing-its-tail cycle of endless moral uncertainties. She wasn't the only one absorbed in her own internal battles. Kate squirmed beside her, pressing her forehead against the window, as if she could will the clouds to pass more quickly. Waves of remorse billowed from her hunched frame.

Sarah nudged one of Kate's tense, tight shoulders. "I could ask if they have a parachute for you."

Sarah knew Kate had had even less sleep than herself. Kate had been frantic trying to rearrange flight plans for the two of them, to get them home as quickly as possible.

Now Kate kneaded her swollen eyes with the butt of her hands. "Why don't I just jump without a parachute? It'd be quicker. And less painful."

"I wouldn't try that." Sarah tilted her head toward the buzz-cut guy two seats ahead of them, sitting on the aisle. "Mr. Air Marshall there will tackle you before you reach the door."

"Maybe I'll get lucky and he'll shoot."

"I don't think that's what Rachel had in mind when she wanted you to skydive in the first place."

"Huh, so you've figured it out? What Rachel had in mind?"

Sarah's throat tightened. She'd been thinking about Rachel a lot lately. One memory kept haunting her—the image of Rachel, in full climbing regalia, grinning down at her from the top of a craggy rock face as Sarah struggled across a difficult pass.

Hurts like hell, doesn't it, Pollard? Push through it, kid, because heaven's all the way up here.

"Rachel knew change was hard," Sarah said. "She knew none of us would change our lives without a good push."

"Yeah, and who's to say change is always *good*?"

"It isn't." The plane banked again, and the view from the window was an autumn patchwork and the shimmer of the setting sun against the city in the distance. "Not always, anyway. Honestly, Kate, I think Rachel didn't know how this was all going to work out."

"What?!"

"After her push, I think she figured we'd all be on our own."

Kate made a noise like she'd been hit in the solar plexus. "Don't tell me that."

"C'mon. You didn't really think Rachel was some all-knowing yogi, leading us to enlightenment?"

"Actually," she sputtered, "after my first jump, I *did*. I've been doing all this on faith."

"Well, maybe she knew that's how you'd react." Sarah sighed as she pressed her head back against the seat. "I might be reaching, Kate, but I know this much for sure: Every single day of Rachel's life, she confronted her own fears, and it made her happier."

"Oh, God."

"So I suppose, in Rachel's point of view, if she pushed us to do the same—confront exactly what we feared most— then, ultimately, we'd work it all out. We'd find the same joy." Sarah shifted her gaze to the blue, blue sky, as understanding softly unfurled. "I think Rachel was just trying to give us happiness."

"While destroying my marriage?" Kate made a sound somewhere between a snort and a sob. "Making questionable choices for her own daughter? Risking Jo's career? Sending you into the arms of that two-timing—"

"Hey, I know it destroys your saintly image of me, but I'm the Jezebel in this situation." Sarah unfolded her legs, then curled them under her. She'd been on this plane so long she swore she was developing a bedsore on her hip. "And I always thought it would do Jo some good to rearrange her priorities anyway."

"Well, Rachel sure as hell rearranged mine." Kate balled her fists in her oversized sweatshirt. "About all I'm getting out of this is bragging rights. Now, over an appletini, I can talk about elephant rides in the jungle and bouncing in a rickshaw through Bangalore."

"You'll be the life of the party."

"I can start conversations like 'While I was getting my hands hennaed in the souk...'"

"The snake on your belly is more interesting."

"And I can always mention Sam, the color-blind Nigerian gunrunner."

Sarah tugged her skirt from under her thighs, feigning interest in the folds she gathered on her lap. Memories of Sam—unexpected, and unexpectedly vivid—washed over her. In Burundi, when Sam pulled into the camp with a jeep full of sanctioned supplies—as well as a trunk full of what they *really* needed, bought on the black market with money from a questionable source—the villagers considered it a time for dancing. She remembered the wicked flash of Sam's smile when she'd given in to his insistence on accompanying her on an unauthorized trip into the mountains to reach a localized epidemic and isolate it before it spread. She remembered Sam, standing in the rain outside the clinic, anxious for news from Dr. Mwami about the wounded child he'd smuggled across the border.

Mostly, she remembered Sam cradling a bottle of banana wine by the light of a kerosene lamp after he'd brought in the girl with the crooked braids. He'd talked, that night, about leaving the business altogether, returning home to cricket matches, decent housing, and warm beer. And she'd found herself battling a fierce urge to stop him—to beg him not to leave.

Kate's nail-bitten hand slid over her knee. "I assume I don't have to tell you, Sarah, that Sam's crazy for you."

Sarah thought of the acacia tree on the border of Lake Tanganyika. The way the wet branches traced cracks against the gray sky. His kiss had tasted like rain.

Sarah shook the memory from her mind. She couldn't think about Sam. Or Burundi. Her senses were in chaos, her emotions too bruised, and the ghost of Colin lingered. "It won't work, Kate. The timing's wrong. Or maybe the pieces just don't fit."

The plane landed and taxied to the gate. Walking through the terminal with her backpack cutting into her shoulders, Sarah couldn't help scanning the gates as they passed, looking for the ones marked with the destination Los Angeles.

Colin had stated it so boldly.

I can't let you go.

Sarah had convinced herself that he didn't mean it. Not really. If he'd meant it, he'd have taken her into his bed that last night. He'd have made love to her without guilt. If he'd meant it, he'd have done more than just urge her to come visit him—he'd have made definite plans. Even though she knew that just wasn't his way.

Departing now, Gate 117. Flight 776 direct to Los Angeles. Priority seats only, please, and passengers who need assistance...

Jo waited for them at baggage claim, barking into a cordless earpiece jutting across her cheek. She high-heeled over to Kate, talking loudly all the way, stopping only as she engulfed Kate in a hug.

They hugged for a very long time. When Jo pulled away, Sarah noticed that both their faces were wet.

"Sugar, you look like hell." Jo braced Kate an arm's length away, then glanced at Sarah. "For the love of sweet Jesus, what did they do to you two? I swear right now, I'm never traveling to a country that requires shots."

Sarah smiled wanly and neglected to tell Jo that even the

U.S. required shots for some visitors. Personally, she thought Jo looked jittery and sleepless herself—and told her so.

"Double-shot lattes," Jo explained, as they searched the carousel for Kate's overstuffed luggage. "More than one. I had to pull an all-nighter getting the presentation in shape."

Kate spotted her suitcase, dashed over, and used all her strength to yank it off the carousel.

Sarah asked, "Well, how did it go?"

"Discordant and unorganized." Jo summoned a porter with nothing more than a pointed look. "We gave dueling presentations—mine was better, of course—but I suspect we did nothing but make ourselves look fractious and unco-operative." She gave a tight shrug. "Six months of work over and done with, and I tell you, all I really want is a good night's sleep. Today is Grace's first evening alone with Latoya."

Kate heard the last part of the conversation as she dragged the suitcase behind her. "Is Grace adjusting?"

"Honey, she's alive. That's about the best I can ask for."

"Are my kids alive?"

Jo paused, gave Kate a pained look, and slung an arm around her neck. "Your kids are fine, kiddo. They're healthy and looking forward to seeing you. Paul and your mother are still at the house. He knows you're coming in tonight. He's been taking my calls."

Kate brightened. "Then he'll keep the kids awake for me!"

"No, sugar, he won't."

"He will, he will." She bobbed her head, her limp ponytail flying. "He's mad at me, but he won't—"

"This isn't the place to talk about this." Jo gestured to the porter and led them all toward the elevator for the parking garage. "We'll have plenty of time to discuss this tonight," she said over her shoulder, "because, Kate, you're spending the night on my couch."

Kate stumbled. The skin of her throat began to blotch—the spots growing a more and more alarming shade of pink. She found her footing, then skittered to Jo's side. Sarah heard the torrent of Kate's desperate words.

"I want to see my kids, I need to see my kids!"

Jo was disturbingly firm and unbending. "You need to pull yourself together, Kate. You want your kids to see you like this? Honey, you're practically unhinged. You're in no condition to face them now. Get a night's sleep. I've got a nice, comfortable couch—I know, I've been spending a lot of time on it. You need to brace yourself, because Paul's not exactly in a good mood."

Sarah followed, listening to them with growing distress. Kate and Paul couldn't be having *real* troubles. They were perfect for each other. Sarah had noticed it on their very first date. She'd always envied Kate for finding her soul mate—and keeping hold of him.

Then, glancing up, Sarah came face-to-face with a monitor right next to the elevator. A monitor that showed plane arrivals and departures. Los Angeles blinked back at her.

"Sarah, darling, can you stop dreaming of the third world already? There's a double bacon-cheeseburger waiting for you at a cheap diner down the road, and, personally, I'm so hungry I could eat half a side of pork myself."

Colin's voice in her head.

If you decide to come, come soon.

Kate, shaky and pale, tugged on Sarah's arm. "Sarah, c'mon—the elevator."

The elevator doors yawned open. People filed onto it, filling it up with their luggage, muttering as they cursed their way around the three women and a porter standing smack in the path. Jo and Kate blinked at her, puzzled. Sarah knew if she went through that gaping doorway right now she'd never come back.

Sarah blurted, "He told me to come to Los Angeles."

Kate stared, slowly ascending from her own misery into a dawning comprehension. "Oh, God," she murmured, squeezing her eyes shut. "What fresh hell is this?"

Sarah's gaze drifted to the monitor. "He told me to come soon."

Jo tugged the headset out of her ear, as if she hadn't heard right, then directed the three of them and the porter away from the elevator doors, where they wouldn't be in the direct line of traffic.

"Sarah, I thought this was over." Kate's neck flexed tensely with each word. "You told me you'd made your decision."

"You saw him yesterday morning, Kate. He was there, in the lobby, at five a.m." Looking unshaven and sleepless. Sarah plunged her hand into the hemp purse on her hip and rifled around until she felt the familiar hotel letterhead. She pulled it out, dirty with newsprint. "He gave me this paper. It's his home address in Los Angeles. The address of his office, his cell-phone number, even the number of the hospital where he's on call—"

Jo glanced at it curiously. "Why didn't he just give you a business card?"

"It's a new office, a new business. He says he's in transition, so there's a lot of phone numbers—"

"That's what people do, Sarah, when they break something off." Kate hugged her midriff. "It doesn't mean he really wants you to visit."

"But—"

"Jo," Kate said, squeezing her bloodshot eyes shut, "help me here, will you?"

Jo eyed the piece of paper as if she were assessing the photo qualities of a new model. "I'd say, usually, that Kate is right. Handing you some contact information is a clean, if rather cold-blooded way to break it off. It leaves open the possibility of a reunion, but makes no messy promises. But he went to a heap of trouble to write all that down and to meet you in the lobby at an hour suitable only for larks."

Kate's eyes flew open. She made a frantic cutting gesture at Jo.

Jo ignored her. "He could have stayed warm in bed and avoided the situation altogether."

Sarah nodded. "That would have been more his style. That's why this was such a surprise."

"Sarah," Jo said, "tell me exactly what he said to you."

"He just told me to come to L.A." She ran a thumb across his name, written in his own hand. "He told me that he knew it was crazy to ask, but that he really wanted me to see his home."

"Sweet Jesus."

"Sarah!" Kate all but stamped her foot. "Twenty hours in the air, and you didn't tell me any of this!"

"I thought I'd made my decision. I spent those twenty hours rolling it around in my mind."

Jo gripped a fistful of Kate's sweatshirt to keep her quiet. "Did you tell him you'd go, Sarah?"

"No. No!" she insisted, as Kate rolled her eyes. "I didn't know what to say. I thought I'd made it clear that I couldn't do this. I couldn't be the other woman."

"Ah." Jo fiddled with the Bluetooth in her hand. "And he still asked you to visit him in L.A."

"He did." Sarah folded the paper and tucked it back in her purse. "You know, it'd be a lot easier if he'd just bring a cow and a couple of goats, and then the whole village could sing and dance and drink beer—"

"Well, sugar, it's good that I know the *American* customs." Jo twisted her wrist so she could see her watch face. "And I'm thinking you'd better catch a flight to L.A., the sooner the better."

"No." Kate slashed the air with her hands. "No way. Sarah has made her decision. Why should she trot across the country just because he can't make one of his own?"

"Because," Jo drawled, "clearly that man has something he wants Sarah to see."

"What? His fiancée?"

"Dr. O'Rourke never struck me as a fool. If I were placing bets in Vegas, I'd say he wants you to come to L.A. to see if you can be transplanted."

Kate pressed her temples. "You don't know the whole situation, Jo. You don't understand—"

"Sugar, I might not know a thing about child-rearing, but I know a boatload more than both of you about men." She laid her hands on Sarah's shoulders. "But you have to listen to me very carefully, Sarah-belle. When you come back from L.A., I don't want to hear any hero stories anymore. You know that a relationship with a man can't be just passion and roses, or sex with tigers roaring outside the mud hut walls—you've got to put up with the tough stuff, too. I want to know if he snores, or if he leaves the bathroom towel on the floor. I want to know how he reacts after a root canal—"

"Or," Kate interjected, "how he reacts when faced with gunrunners and a trunkful of medical supplies."

Jo whistled. "Boy, I sure missed some fun."

Sarah hugged her arms. "Life would have been so much easier if my father had just sold me off to those Bedouins when I was twelve."

"And I know just enough about your parents to be frightened by that story. Now, come on, let's get you on a plane."

Sarah followed Jo blindly toward the ticket counters while Kate tipped the porter and then took the luggage herself. As they stood in line, Jo glanced at Sarah's canvas backpack. "I'm assuming you've got the sum total of all your worldly possessions on your back there?"

"Passport, clothing, a few rupees."

"Not enough, I suppose, for a plane ticket."

She hadn't thought about that wrinkle. She'd used up most of her cash in Bangalore, and she'd blithely abused so many credit cards over the years that she no longer allowed herself to carry one. She mused on the problem for a moment, then said, "I can call—"

"No one." Jo plugged the Bluetooth back in her ear. "I'll take care of it."

"Jo, you've already—"

"Don't mention it." She steered Sarah to a counter while Kate, muttering, struggled with her luggage trying to keep up. "Just remember this—at the wedding, make me the maid of honor."

"Hey!" Kate stopped short. "That's my job!"

"And promise me one more thing, Sarah-belle." A strange expression passed over Jo's face. "Promise me that when you get back—*if* you come back—you'll let me know if the risk was worth it."

"Of course it's worth it, Jo." Sarah's throat swelled, raw and dry. "I think, maybe . . . it's worth any risk to love."

~~~

Sarah appreciated that Jo had thought of everything. She really did. Jo had arranged for a driver to meet Sarah at LAX, a sleek young man in a dark suit who drove her to a Best Western in a car that smelled like patchouli. Jo had even pre-paid for the room. Money always smoothed the path to what you wanted, but Sarah hadn't appreciated the perk for herself until she'd spent over twenty-four hours traveling halfway across the world.

I mean, geez, Sarah, by showing up you're essentially telling him you'll bear his babies. Don't show up bleary-eyed and stinking like a cow.

So Sarah felt a little guilty when she checked out of the hotel the next morning to hop into a battered twenty-year-old Volkswagen driven by an old friend from the Corps. He was spending a few months in a rental in Venice Beach with seven other buddies, taking some time off to surf. Sarah figured it was as good an opportunity as any to step off the grid for a few days. Look for answers within, without the influence of anyone else's expectations.

The days she'd spent on the white sand beaches, digging her toes in the surf—feeling overdressed and over-pale—had revealed to her one essential truth: Her relationship with Colin had always taken place in *her* world—in the rural isolation of the little village in Paraguay, and, last week, in the chaos of Bangalore. She suspected Jo had figured out in seven seconds what it took Sarah two days to understand. Colin asked her to come to L.A. to see if their relationship—whatever it was— could be transplanted to *his* world.

Los Angeles. A strange village filled with tanned blondes and men with chiseled abdomens. Freakishly wide, clean streets stretched in all directions, rumbling with shiny new cars. In Gatumba, if someone was seen marching alone down the road talking to himself, the villagers would treat him kindly but with fear, for madness was considered a kind of oracle. Here everyone sported ear antennas like Jo's, and they all talked to themselves, loudly, even among company. Too many times she caught herself staring at the women. Some looked so smooth-limbed and strategically swollen that the only thing that distinguished them from the fashion dolls she'd played with as a child was the lack of leg and arm seams.

When she could delay no longer, she borrowed the old Volkswagen and drove it to the office address Colin had given her. She parked it in the lot of a sleek, mirrored building. She squinted up to the winking windows, against the beating of the southern-California sun. Behind one of those windows, Colin sat in his office in a white coat, ministering to his patients. Somewhere in there, Colin sat in his everyday world.

The front doors whooshed open to a blast of air conditioning. Her plain rubber-soled sandals made no noise as she walked through the vaulted lobby. A guard sat behind a low, shining counter, very far away. She'd been in L.A. a few days now, but she couldn't shake the dislocation she experienced whenever she returned to the States. It was sensory-deprivation shock. These buildings had no odors, little color, so much shine and stone, so very few people, and so little exuberant chaos. All was so calm here, so open, so...clean.

Even the guard had a well-scrubbed look.

"I've come to see Dr. O'Rourke." She leaned over the massive leather-bound guest book, which he then gestured her to sign. She unwound the hemp purse from her shoulder, noticing, as the guard gingerly searched inside, that it was gray with dirt, and that unraveled fibers stuck out at strange angles. Pushing it back toward her, the guard handed her a name tag and directed her toward the elevator banks. There she stepped aside as a bevy of not-so-natural blondes wearing huge glasses breezed past her, as if they'd stepped right out of *Baywatch* on a sixty-two-inch flat-screen television set.

She gazed at them with curiosity worthy of an anthropologist. Surely, this sort of female decoration was no different from the scarification tattoos of the Nigerian tribes, or henna patterns on Indian brides, but to Sarah, the stream of nearly identical blondes looked impossibly exotic.

The office of Colin and his partners covered half of the top floor of the building. The elevator opened to the sight of a tall sheet of glass. Colin's name, along with his partners', was stenciled in big black letters, below the words "Center for Reconstructive Surgery." As Sarah slipped through the door, a slim young woman raised her head from her work. The scarlet frame of the receptionist's glasses matched her button earrings and string of oversized beads.

"I'm Sarah Pollard. I'm here to see Col—Dr. O'Rourke."

The young woman frowned. She searched a blue-inked appointment book on her desk. "I'm sorry. I don't see your name."

"I don't have an appointment."

Those eyelashes—they couldn't possibly be real. Neither could the breasts stretching the odd word BOTOX in rhinestones across her chest.

"I'm terribly sorry," the young woman began, "but none of the doctors can see you unless you make an appointment."

The receptionist took in, with one glance, Sarah's batik cotton shirt, loose flowing skirt, and unpainted fingernails. Sarah ran her thumb under the strap of her bag and recognized the kind of scrutiny that took place all over the world: Sarah was being assessed for importance—and she was coming up short.

"He'll be expecting me," Sarah added. "We were in Bangalore together, just last week. I know he's only been back a day or two. Perhaps he forgot to tell you I was coming."

With some reluctance, the young woman tilted her chin toward a plush leather couch. "Have a seat. He's with a patient now, but when he's free, I'll let him know you're here."

Sarah perched on a couch with her back to the receptionist. She didn't need to see the odd glance the BOTOX girl shared with the nurse who checked in moments later. The whispering was bad enough. She didn't know why it bothered her, since she spent most of her time as a pale curiosity in the refugee camp.

She perused the tastefully framed posters advertising chemical peels and laser refinishing. She'd never heard of either of those techniques and briefly wondered if she was falling behind in her medical knowledge in reconstructive surgery. She fingered the magazines scattered across the glass coffee table—*Glamour, Vogue, Condé Nast Traveler, People, Cosmopolitan*—and was soon lost in a fascinating perusal of advertisements that mostly involved, to the best of her discernment, freakishly bony pre-pubescent girls.

She lifted her head from the pages when a perfectly proportioned blonde breezed into the office. The receptionist leapt from her seat, fluttered and squealed, then shuttled her straight through to an examining room. That's when Sarah began to worry. She began to wonder if Kate hadn't been right, and Colin had only been polite in his invitation. Sarah began to worry that Colin was back there in his office fretting about how to get rid of her, before his fiancée showed up for lunch. Perhaps that perfectly proportioned blonde was his fiancée. Sarah wondered if she'd spent Jo's money fruitlessly, chasing a one-sided dream clear across the world.

"Sarah."

There he was, looming before her, all clear eyes and astonished smile. No stethoscope hung from his neck, and the lab coat she expected he'd be wearing was, instead, a very well-cut lightweight business suit.

He grasped her hand and pulled her off the couch. "I'm so sorry you waited so long—I had no idea you were here. When I'm with a patient, I don't like to be interrupted—"

"You don't have to explain."

"Well." He dropped her hand, then ran those fingers over his head and grasped the back of his neck. "Yeah, actually, I do." He didn't have to glance at the receptionist; Sarah knew that they were being watched. "Come into my office, Sarah. We'll catch up."

She followed him past the receptionist's desk, past the nurse in full white-capped regalia, past rows of closed doors and quiet murmurings behind them, through a lemon-antiseptic scent, to the end of the hallway, into a corner room luminous with southern-California light. He clicked the door shut behind him, then wandered to one of the floor-to-ceiling windows that looked out on a fantastic view of greater Los Angeles.

Sarah stepped deeper into the room and clasped her hands. Her gaze slipped over the shiny wooden surfaces, the abstract print on one wall, the raw silk curtains discreetly tucked on either end of the windows, billowing in pools on the patterned carpet. She felt like a dust mote caught in the sun.

Then she stopped abruptly. On his desk stood two medical models: one of a woman's breasts and another of buttocks.

The truth didn't come immediately. Sarah stared at those medical models, not believing her own eyes. She kept thinking she must be mistaken—maybe they were oversized models of a palate, or a jaw, or some interior facial organ. That's what Colin specialized in, wasn't it? Face and jaw surgery. They couldn't possibly be models of . . . tits and hips.

She slipped her fingers over the back of the chair that faced Colin's desk. The leather sucked heat from her skin. She struggled to absorb the strange broken pieces of information now just swirling together. In most tribal communities, the elders were honored. Their arthritic fingers, the bow of their shoulders, the gray in their hair, the darker spots on their faces, and the stretched sag of their breasts—all these things stood as a tribute to how many years they'd survived in the sun, as well as a lifetime of knowledge and experience. Those youthful *Cosmo* images assaulted her now, and the parade of blondes, and the *Vogue* advertisements for creams and anti-aging unguents, and she began to comprehend a new and terrible meaning for the phrase "reconstructive surgery."

Colin stood like a soldier with his back to the window, watching her, until he saw the first glimmer of realization dawn on her face.

"Colin." She tightened her grip on the back of the chair. "I don't understand."

"I know. But maybe, if I explain, you will."

She stood silent, barely able to breathe.

"This all started in Paraguay. With Werai, and the surgery I'd performed to save his leg."

She'd helped in the surgery. She'd watched with awe. She'd sensed in him a powerful need to succeed, an emotion so fierce that for six hours it emanated from him in waves. It enveloped her in its intensity, made her blind with a primitive sexual need she'd never known before.

"I was so proud I'd fixed it that day." He reached for a ball sitting on his desk, a black leathery thing that he squeezed in his hand as he talked. "I was so proud I'd succeeded in front of you, too. But as the weeks passed and Werai started to walk again, I saw how grotesque his leg looked, how crude my handiwork had come out, despite all my efforts."

"Colin—it's a miracle he *lived.*"

"Maybe. But I should have done better."

Sarah remembered Colin's growing frustration in the weeks after the surgery. She'd attributed it to his overwhelming desire to improve the living situation for the villagers. His frustration had spilled over into other things, such as annoyance over supplies delivered late, and irritation over the village's resistance to the measles vaccinations. She'd kept telling him, *Tranquilo*. Werai is alive and walking. *Tranquilo*. The supplies will come. Colin hadn't yet accepted, as so many of the Corps workers had, that you just can't change everything. That's what made him different, she'd thought. She admired how hard he strived.

"I'd proven to myself that I could make a difference, but it was a crude difference. My surgery skills were rudimentary." He flexed open his hands, balancing the ball in the hollow of one palm. "I wanted more than to just save a life or fix a limb. I wanted that limb to be as perfect when I was done with it as it had been before the accident. That's why I left, Sarah. I went back to the States and did my two-year residency in plastic surgery. I spent another year in craniofacial surgery. And then . . ." He squeezed the ball. "It was a path. Stretched out before me. I took one step at a time—each one a little higher and a little harder—and then I looked up, and here I was." He laughed, shortly and without humor. "Nose jobs and cheek implants."

"And correcting cleft palates," Sarah said, "for kids whose faces are so malformed they can barely eat."

"Two weeks a year. On training junkets where I spend seventy-five percent of my time in bars and only about twenty-five percent in the OR." He planted the ball back on the desk, then clasped his hands behind his back. "Though it's just like you to make it more than it really is. That's what I always loved about you."

Love.

"Here's the difference between us—you haven't changed, Sarah." He took a few steps toward her but paused at the side of his desk, trailing a finger over the shiny surface. "When I saw you in that hotel in Bangalore, I thought I'd conjured you right up out of thin air. I mean, there I was, out in the wild again. Bringing the cutting edge of medical technology to the hinterlands. Feeling the way I used to feel, when we both were young and working for the Corps. Feeling generous—like I was really making a sacrifice with my two weeks abroad. Like I was really making a difference in the world, fixing a couple of kids' mangled faces—"

"Success," Sarah said, huskily, hearing the echo of the same words she had spoken to Kate, "comes one patient at a time."

"And in the middle of all this—you appear." He looked at her as if he didn't dare to reach for her. "Do you have any idea what you do to me? You're so pale—it's like you're made out of some angelic stuff. None of the troubles of the world have ever touched you. All these years, and the places you've been, and the things you've seen—the suffering and the insanity and the whole wretched world of problems that can*not* be fixed, no matter how much money you throw at them—and there you are, standing there in the flesh, like the dream of something I gave up a long time ago."

Sarah went very still, because the man standing in front of her, the man talking like he couldn't get the words out fast enough, was the Colin she remembered from Paraguay. The Colin who grappled every night with the big questions of what they were doing, and what good they were doing, when what the people really needed was a decent sewer system and a road through to the city, not a couple of health-care workers who'd fix broken bones and hand out some pain reliever and do no long-term good. How she loved to listen to him then, hear his determination to make the world a better place.

"You stood there like my conscience. I had no business touching you. For more than one reason."

The major reason, Sarah figured, was pictured on his desk in that gilded frame she could only see the back of.

He swiveled, gesturing to the broad expanse of the bright and airy room. "I couldn't tell you about this, Sarah. I couldn't look in your eyes and see the disappointment. Then I wouldn't be your heroic savior anymore. I'd be just another guy who sold out."

She took a sudden interest in the straight, even stitching of the leather armchair. She shouldn't be thinking this way, but she couldn't help herself. What a waste it was for all of Colin's surgical talent to be put toward giving wealthy women bigger, firmer breasts, fuller butts, clearer skin, and smaller noses. All that talent frittered away on the ridiculous perfectionist goal of chiseling vain women into somebody else's version of beauty. What kind of goal was this, when the world was full of women suffering post-natal complications, and children dying of appendicitis, and farm laborers suffering from stran-gulated hernias gone gangrenous?

"I never was a hero." He unbuttoned his suit jacket, sweep-ing it aside to plant a fist on his hip. "I couldn't deal with the bureaucracy and the *ugliness* of it all, the great heaping weight of the problems. You know what they are. Some organization is set up to deliver the needed services. You go out there and talk about the issues and solicit money for them. Then the organization becomes a monster of its own that swallows a good part of that charitable giving. Even the fraction that goes through, what is it used for? You know. You've bribed dock-workers. You know the transportation rules that require high-cost carriers to foreign countries. You've mollified warlords with cash. You've seen whole truckloads of grain stolen by the very military that is causing half the problems the populace is facing—"

"*Tranquilo,* Colin." Her voice was whiskey-soft, and tears pricked in her throat. "No one can save the world alone."

"Yeah, well, that's my arrogance. If I couldn't do it myself . . ." He gestured to his corner office and all its gleaming furniture. "Then why bother doing it at all?"

Sarah wandered to the windows. Los Angeles sprawled as far as she could see, a series of neat, compact buildings and long paved roads, and in the distance, the brown of gentle hills.

It usually took about a year and a half for charity fatigue to set in among relief workers. They all came into the job so fired up and so excited and a little scared of what they were going to face. Eager for the gratitude they were sure was going to be rained down upon them. Determined to change the way things were done. Like puppies, overexcited and proud of their schoolroom multicultural knowledge. It was no wonder so many people overseas couldn't stand Americans. Every-one knew puppies needed a few whacks to the head with a rolled-up newspaper before learning how to behave with the proper humility.

Why didn't she recognize that in Colin when they were in

Paraguay? She supposed she'd been new to the experience, too. Fresh and excited and not afraid to admit she was scared. But, yes, now, standing here in his fancy office and thinking about their conversations, those long talks naked in a mud hut in the jungles of Paraguay, thinking about his growing annoyance with the mothers who refused to have their children vaccinated, thinking about the impatience which she'd taken—or mistaken—for dedication, for passion, for drive. Now she saw, all too clearly, that he'd had all the signs of charity fatigue a long time ago.

She'd blinded herself to it. To admit it would be to destroy the perfectionist image she'd come to love, of the heroic surgeon saving a boy's life in a mud hut in a rain forest.

He approached behind her. Carefully. Close enough that she could feel his warmth and the swelling aura of his personality. "I'm not proud of the way I treated you after Paraguay. I should have made a clean break. But it wasn't so easy. I liked the way you looked at me. I held on to the knowledge that, somewhere in the world, someone I respected still considered me a hero."

And you are, for Werai, at least.

"What made it harder was that I knew you didn't feel the same way I did. Even all those years ago, I knew you'd stay in the business. You wouldn't leave the work, disillusioned like everyone else. You never saw charity as work. For you, charity was a state of mind."

"I get paid, like everyone else." She swallowed a growing lump in her throat. "And I haven't been any angel. I've traded whiskey for safe passage. And I've allowed worse—"

"You never gave it up. Do you have any idea what you could make in a year by hiring yourself out as a private nurse?"

She started. "So—it's all about money?"

"Yes."

Without hesitation. She stared at him. In the unforgiving light, she noticed his perfectly trimmed hair, the barber-smoothness of his cheek, and the flawless weave of his dark-blue suit. Was he really doing this for the money? Sculpting perfect bodies for the ladies who could afford it? Inserting saline implants? Padding buttocks? She wondered if Colin, while making love to her, had ever envisioned slicing a half-moon just under the rise of her tiny breast and slipping in an implant to give her better proportion.

She crossed her arms. She should never have come to Los Angeles.

"Don't look at me like that, Sarah. You know money always helps. Money allows me to work a couple of weeks a year for The Smile Train." A muscle worked in his jaw. "Money allows me to make a real difference—"

"Colin, why did you ask me to come here?"

"I wanted you to see this."

"Why? We said our good-byes in Bangalore. It was over. It didn't work out. I was going back to my life, and you," Sarah said, gesturing to the photo on the desk, the one whose face she could now see, "you were going back to yours."

She was Asian. Probably Thai or Vietnamese. Exotically thin, wearing something slim and black and elegant. The photo was taken from slightly above, and she wasn't looking directly in the camera. Her hair fell across her shoulder like a blue-black waterfall. Colin stood behind her, raising a glass of champagne, his eyes crinkling in laughter. The woman was laughing, too, her teeth unbelievably white against red lipstick.

She had a nice face. Open. She wasn't afraid to wrinkle her nose as she laughed.

"I always had a hard time saying good-bye," he explained, running his hand over the top of the frame, discreetly turning the picture away. "And you're not an easy woman to forget."

She felt easy to forget. Standing there in her comfortable worn cotton, she felt like a little brown wren. *That* woman would know what clothes were appropriate to wear to a plastic surgeon's office; *that* woman would know how to act in a country club.

He dropped his voice, and it rumbled over her. "You must think I'm an absolute shit."

"Honestly, I don't know what to think anymore."

"The two of you, you're like the two halves of me. Both of you—better halves. I'm not being fair to either of you. I'd made my choice, without reservation, until you took me by surprise. And suddenly I was in *your* world again, and I was back there—in Paraguay—all over again. Revisiting decisions I'd made in life, decisions that I was not sure were the best."

Sam had been right. The sex between her and Colin had been brief, hot, and memorable. It had been crusader sex. And that was all.

She shuddered with the realization that she'd wasted so much time...on a fantasy. "I still don't know why you asked me here."

"To see if it's real, if this is real—if we are real—in *my* world. Listen." He paced restlessly. "Money is not always a bad thing. It's necessary—it's the oil that makes the gears move in any business."

Money again.

"I mean...if you have money, you can direct it any way you choose." He ran a hand through his hair, and every strand fell, maddeningly, right back into place. "I can't do what you do. I can't spend months, years, off in underdeveloped countries, administering the care that so many people need. But I can provide the means for others to do it by proxy. That's partly why I'm in this business, Sarah. It's not just so I can have a Jaguar and a villa in Beverly Hills. It's so I can use the money to make a real change. I could use someone to help me spend my money."

Oh, heaven help her. He was bribing her with a donation. "Colin, you know who I work for. You can make any donation you want—"

"I'm not offering to finance your work, Sarah, I'm offering something bigger. I'm offering you a chance to be the one who distributes that money, to be the one who helps raise it, and gets it into the hands of the people who really need it."

"What?"

"It's what rich women do around here," he said, gesturing to the great stretch of Los Angeles outside his window. "They start charitable organizations. Hold fancy luncheons. Raise funds. See to it that the money is spent wisely, that it gets to where it has to be."

She gestured to the photo, twisted askew. "Sounds like her job."

A muscle flexed in his cheek. He'd gone pale, but she could see the shadow of his beard on his cheek. "I did plan...But if you were to tell me that you could live this kind of life...if you were to tell me that, after everything you've seen today, you could still look at me and see Superman..." He smiled sheepishly as he spread his arms and made himself a tall silhouette against the southern-California sky. "If you could do that, Sarah, then things would change."

She wasn't looking at the photo, but she felt nonetheless the hot gaze of the woman within. The elegant laughing woman with the glass of champagne, obviously enjoying herself at a formal function. There'd be a lot of formal functions as the wife of such a successful doctor. Charity balls, hospital fund-raisers, nights at the symphony. Cooking dinner for colleagues and attending the functions of high-profile clients. She could see it, suddenly, as if she were the woman in the slim elegant black dress, sitting at tables eating overcooked chicken and regaling the guests with tales of Africa and India and South America, telling them about Guinea worm and cases of polio still extant and other tropical diseases that should have been wiped off the face of the earth long ago. She'd be trotted out—the oddity, that little brown wren that snared Dr. O'Rourke—the public-health nurse who has *been there* in the developing world, who has cleaned the oozing sores of the afflicted. She could see them: the powdered and hatted women, the smooth-browed fifty-year-olds, the young tennis-skirted wives of power moguls. She could feel their stares upon her, gazes full of disbelief and shuddering horror. Surely they'd sign plenty of checks to hear her tell them what the world is *really* like outside their arctic offices and high-ceilinged homes. She'd gather a fortune in international aid. Then she could take that money and send it directly to someone who could really do something about a situation, someone still on the ground.

Someone competent and strong and wise.

Someone like Sam.

She squeezed her own arms. She couldn't mock this. It was honest work; it was *good* work. She wasn't a fool. She knew that, without money, there'd be no insecticide-embedded nets or donations of rice. But her head ached thinking about the tight high-heeled shoes and the dresses she'd have to wear, and the glasses and glasses of liquor. Her jaw started to ache thinking about the talking and the talking and the talking. And her heart started to ache, too, because, though worthy, this kind of work best belonged to elegant young women who could wear black strapless dresses and wrinkle their noses while laughing over a glass of champagne.

She'd sensed it would come down to this, since the very first moment she'd Googled him in that apartment in New York City. What she'd feared most of all was disillusion and heartbreak, and she wasn't feeling either of them now.

She felt gratitude that he still cared for her enough to offer her his life, and himself, in spite of all their differences. She felt regret, solemn and sincere. Regret that they hadn't remained in contact over the long years, a contact that would have diminished the fantasy she'd built up of the man she'd known briefly—but intensely. She felt grief, too. Grief that they'd both willingly, and for capricious reasons, let go of a passion that could have blossomed into a rare and wonderful thing. And the strongest emotion of all, the one that overtook all the rest—was a profound sense of relief.

Relief.

"Sarah?"

Oh, Colin. Rachel was right. I'd housed my heart in a cage all these years. A lovely, gilded cage, but a cage nonetheless.

She walked toward him. She reached for his face. She slid her fingers along his jaw, then she curled them behind his neck. His gaze flared as she pressed against him, her batik cotton ridiculously bright against his sober suit. She let her eyes flutter closed, and she breathed deeply.

Yes, he was wearing cologne or aftershave or whatever men wear, and it was subtle and strangely intoxicating. Inside began the familiar quiver, the growing desire, and she let herself feel it with an almost scientific detachment. She blindly arched her neck for the kiss. He scraped his chin against hers, and it startled her, the slickness of the move and the lack of stubble upon his face. He rubbed his lips against her mouth, then released her long enough to thrust his fingers through her hair, to hold her head fast as he closed his mouth more tightly over hers.

Colin. The only man she'd thought she would ever love. The memories came thick and fast, unfurling like an old eight-millimeter tape crackling through a projector, like the ones her parents had saved of their early trips abroad. She remembered Colin driving up with Sam in a cloud of dust, and she remembered the six tense hours of surgery. She remembered Colin, sweaty, running his fingers through his disheveled hair, yearning to help, and irritated at how easily his best intentions were thwarted. She remembered Colin leaving in Sam's car without saying good-bye—and leaving Sarah behind.

She'd spent the next fourteen years dreaming of him, while he was on another continent, thinking she was his better half.

It would have been pretty to think that it was the sound of the intercom that finally ended the kiss—that it was the smooth and efficient voice of his secretary alerting him to the arrival of his next patient. Sarah knew Jo would say that would have made a better story. The truth was more powerful. Long before the secretary buzzed Colin, Sarah had pulled away from Colin's kiss.

Colin's kiss didn't taste like rain.

With a low growl, he separated from her, leaned over, pressed the intercom, and, switching to his professional voice, told his secretary to get his next patient settled in room three.

He took a minute before looking up at her. "I can't say I'm surprised. I didn't think you'd stay."

"I'm honored that you asked. But I think we both know that this is not going to work out."

"I'm fourteen years too late."

"Maybe." *Maybe not.*

She felt lightheaded and woozy, but not from the kiss. She trailed her fingers along the edge of his desk for balance, to keep herself steady. The door was not so far away.

He straightened and buttoned his suit coat closed. "Where will you go now?"

"I don't know." She couldn't think that far ahead, not yet. "I suppose I'll go back to New York. I'd like to spend a couple of days with my friends."

She'd like to visit Rachel's grave, too. Let her know how it all turned out. Maybe ask for a little advice.

"Sarah."

She paused with her fingers on the doorknob. She swallowed, through the thickness of her throat. Colin stood silhouetted against the window, solid but a little smaller, now that he'd mentally shrugged off the cape.

"I know I've come up short for you."

"No, you haven't." Her fingers tightened on the knob. She wanted to be honest. She wanted to be kind. "You're finding your own way to change the world. Just because it isn't the same as mine, doesn't mean it's wrong."

Trust your instincts.

"Sarah-belle, I'm glad you came."

"I am, too." She meant it. She'd needed to see this. A girl can't heal without taking the full dose of bitter medicine. "I got what I wanted, Colin. I finally got a proper good-bye."

He gave her a wistful smile. "In that crazy, dangerous world you're going back to, if you ever find yourself in need of a hero..."

Oh, no, Colin. I won't be calling. It's long past time to put you up on a shelf.

"...if you need a hero, go look in a mirror."

～～ chapter fifteen

P lease, Jo, just don't go blaming me if you get fired for taking another day off, okay?" Kate said, as Jo steered her rented BMW into the Lincoln Tunnel. "I appreciate you driving me home . . . but I just don't have any more room for guilt."

"Hell, sugar, no one is going to the office before noon today anyway." Jo downshifted as the lanes converged. "We all worked like dogs prepping for yesterday's disaster; no reason for any of us to hurry in and face the blame. Besides," Jo said, letting go of the gearshift long enough to reach over and squeeze Kate's hand, "I'll be damned if I'll let you face that angry wolf of a husband of yours all alone."

Kate's gaze fell to the tissue she was crushing in her hand. It was dry; she'd used up her tears last night, sobbing into the arm of Jo's white sofa. Silently, so she wouldn't disturb Grace. Silently, so she wouldn't rouse Jo—after the two of them had stayed up past midnight sharing a bottle of wine.

Jo had come right out with the truth last night, without even the thinnest layer of sugar. Jo told her that the family had run out of peanut butter, and Tess missed the Friday game because of the lost cleats. They were getting calls about over-due videos, and Michael's robot project was already days late. A pile of papers teetered on the dining-room table, and Kate's mother-in-law refused to deal with it. Anna had been eating Pop-Tarts for breakfast every day because Paul kept forgetting to pick up milk.

Nightmares roiled Kate's few restless hours of sleep. Rocking in a canoe littered with empty bottles, lost sneakers, and fluttering permission slips, she searched in vain for the oars. The canoe wobbled dangerously, and she tried to grip all three of her screaming kids as the tip of the canoe turned toward the rapids.

Jo flicked on the windshield wipers as they emerged on the Jersey side of the Hudson River to a quick, short-lived splatter of rain. "Kate, plug in my iPod. I'm itching for some music."

Kate perused the music on Jo's iPod, then plugged it in and chose some bluesy Nina Simone.

Kate settled back in the seat and brushed the tissue fuzz off her jeans. She'd deliberately chosen the soccer-mom outfit today—jeans, sneakers, a comfortable sweater. She'd resisted Jo's entreaties to wear something sexy and slip down to the local salon for a quick blow-out, opting instead for a ponytail and a pill-worn sweater borrowed from Jo's closet. She wanted to look familiar to Paul. Unthreatening. She wanted to show him she was ready to take up right where they'd left off.

Not that he really missed me.

Tucking the tissue between her knees, Kate tugged the sleeves of the sweater over her knuckles as Nina wailed through the speakers about a marriage gone wrong.

"Stop mooning over there," Jo said, nudging her shoulder.

"I told you: The situation isn't beyond repair. Fifteen years of marriage and three kids isn't going to go away with one wifely nonsexual transgression."

Kate managed a wan smile.

"Whatever happens," Jo said, as she took a sip of her coffee and licked the foam off her top lip, "you can always come and crash with me."

"We can share expenses. Raise cats."

"Oh, no, honey, no cats. I've got enough trouble raising Grace, thank you very much." Jo glanced at her phone. It vibrated on the console between them to the tune of Ray LaMontagne's "Trouble." "It's the office. Gotta take this, Kate."

Jo slipped her coffee back into the cup holder, pressed a button, and put on her work voice. Kate picked up her own cup—a hot chocolate, complete with whipped cream—and cradled the comfort in her hands.

Strangely, while flying down a Jersey highway with its orderly lanes and enormous signs and polite drivers using their directional signals, she couldn't quite work her mind back to the state she'd been in after she'd made that first jump from an airplane. Why had she thought that dumping all her responsibilities, so suddenly, was such a great idea? Why did she think she could improve her marriage by walking away from her family for nearly two weeks? Now, with her butt planted firmly in a fancy foreign car, looking out at gas stations and office buildings and neatly trimmed landscaping, the idea was as exotically foreign as a herd of cattle leaping over the guardrail and wandering onto Route 3.

Unforgivable.

She rolled her shoulders and flexed her head, trying to

work out the kink in her neck from using an armrest as a pillow. For two full days, she'd gone over it and over it and over it, trying to figure out how to make things right. She felt so thinly stretched that, if it weren't for the windshield of the car, the gusty October wind would cut right through her bones. She knew this much: What was done, was done. Today she must try to look to the future, and change things for the better, from this moment forward.

She would. She would go back to her family. She would have a long talk with Tess's coach. She'd barter with Michael's teacher for time, patience, and a bit of indulgence. She'd keep Anna home from school one day and spend the morning with her so they could romp in Anna's favorite park. She'd scrub the house from attic to basement, fill the pantry to bursting with food, cook macaroni and cheese and roast a chicken and bake honey-wheat bread from scratch. She'd handle the paperwork, one piece at a time, and make lists of what needed to be done. With time, and the captain back on deck, the Good Ship Jansen would be sailing smooth waters again.

That would be the easy part.

Jo disconnected the call with a heavy sigh. "No word yet on the Artemis account." She pulled out the earpiece and tossed it on the console. "It's just a delay. I know *I* wouldn't hire us. We looked like a bunch of squabbling hens yesterday."

Kate shifted, laying her cheek against the back of the buttery leather seat, glad for a distraction from her own toilet-swirl of a life. "Is the account important?"

"Oooh," she said, "it's the biggest catfish in the pond, girl. It'd keep the revenues in the black for another year. It'd be a nice trophy for me, too. But in the grand scheme of things,

Kate—you know, poverty, hunger, Grace's mental health—it doesn't make a darn bit of difference how many people buy a perfume called Mystery."

Kate's lips curled into a smile. "You've become a mother."

Jo nearly spewed a mouthful of coffee all over her nicely tailored suit. Seizing the steering wheel and her coffee with one hand, she groped for a tissue with the other. "Well, Lordy sakes, Kate. You can't just up and say things like that to me. Messes with my self-image."

"I watched you with her last night." When Kate had arrived at Jo's place, she'd had to resist the urge to gather Grace into her lap and smother the poor child with hugs and kisses. That urge had been more for *her* than for Grace, whom Kate pegged right away as a prickly-pear type. "Her gaze followed you all over the room. And you noticed the moment she got tired. With one word from you, she marched up into her bedtime routine like she'd been doing it in your apartment all her life. Shoot me for thinking it, but I didn't expect it out of the Mistress of the Universe."

"Well, I'll tell you one thing, this mothering thing has got me thinking." Jo patted her chest and lap blindly with the tissue, searching for splatter. "It got me thinking of that associate we lost last year, Laura Henley—sharp as a tack, imaginative, came up with the idea of the cliffhanger commercials for that clothing line. She left because my boss wouldn't let her telecommute two days a week so she could spend some time with her newborn. It reminded me of Ginger Schein—a brilliant graphic designer—sidelined after she had to cut her hours to take care of her aging mother. It's got me thinking there's a lot of talent going out the door."

"I smell a business plan."

"I might be needing an exit strategy after we lose this account," Jo said, "but it's more than that. With Grace in my house these past few weeks, it's been a real challenge to do my job and take care of her in the way that she needs. There doesn't seem to be enough hours in the day."

"Proud of you, Jo."

"Hush you up. I'm still going to St. Lucia in February."

"Good for you. I'll be spending my February at basketball games in middle-school gyms that smell like old sneakers."

"You're not going to really do that, are you, sugar?"

"Yes, I am." She curled deeper into Jo's sweater, wishing she could curl around Anna, Tess, and Michael, wishing she could just see them *right now*. She raised her knees and contracted into a ball, trying not to let panic seize her again. "Right now, I'm looking forward to sausage-and-pepper heroes and seeing that fat basketball referee with the limp—"

"No, I don't mean basketball—I mean, you're not going to completely cave in to Paul, are you?"

Kate tucked her hot chocolate back in its holder. She avoided Jo's eye by perusing the Joss Stone songs on the iPod. Kate knew that Paul—no matter how furious he was right now—would allow her back in the house. He needed her to pick up his suits from the dry cleaner and make the kids' lunches every night and to settle the kids back into their routine. If there was one thing she'd learned from this whole disaster, it was that she'd mastered something over fifteen years: running a household and raising kids.

And there loomed the dangerous eye of the vortex. For the kids, she would make any sacrifice. She'd submit to her old life—give up skydiving, anything—just to be able to care for them again. For the sake of Tess, Michael, and Anna, she'd even continue in a marriage to a man who might not be so sure he loved her anymore.

"Kate!" Jo nudged Kate's shoulder. "You're not just going to cave, are you?"

She cocked her head. "Define 'cave.'"

"Sugar, you know he's not the only one wronged here—"

"Paul's going to see it that way."

"Then it's your job to make Paul see sense." Jo reached over blindly, yanking the sleeve of the sweater Kate was wearing. With one manicured fingernail, Jo tapped the fading remnants of the henna design on Kate's hand. "This is a sign of the old Kate," she said, "and I *love* that girl. I *loved* that you hurled yourself out of an airplane. I loved that you rode an elephant through the Indian jungle. I'm thrilled that you spent some time with a Nigerian gunrunner—"

"English, actually. Schooled at Oxford. But it's hard to think about that," Kate said, as she tugged the sleeve down over her knuckles again. "Especially when the bill for my forbidden pleasure is about to come due."

"Honey, it wasn't exactly a sex tour you took in Bangalore. No. No more, Kate." Jo seized the iPod out of Kate's lap and ran a thumb over the menu. "No more Nina, no more Joss, no more Amy Winehouse. No more wailing, whining women. You're depressing me."

"Hey, it's your iPod."

"Hon, you just can't cave. You can't do that to yourself. Or to me." Jo ran her thumb around and around, searching the menu as she steered one-handed. "If you give in to him without fighting for your relationship, you'll be no better off than before you jumped out of an airplane."

"Life before skydiving was pretty damn good," Kate muttered. "I had a nice house. Great kids. Insurance policies. Sex on Tuesdays and Saturdays—"

"I'm not listening to this. Don't you dare tell me you can't have it all. I've got a kid of my own now, Kate. I'm counting on you to show me I can still have a full life."

Kate reached for her hot chocolate again. She didn't know what to say. She'd thought she had a full life until Rachel had sent her skydiving. Maybe Rachel had realized, long before Kate did, that her relationship with Paul was dying.

No.

"Here, let's listen to this." Jo pressed the play button and tossed the iPod back on Kate's lap. "And, girl, I want to hear you sing."

"Why? You like bad singing?"

Jo's grin spread. "Remember that karaoke bar we used to go to when you were working downtown? You always got the most applause."

"I was blonde." She stretched out a strand of hair. "*Naturally* blonde."

"And you sounded like a wounded hound. Come on, don't worry, this BMW's soundproof. Sing at the top of your lungs, honey. I want you to feel it."

Kate glanced at the iPod as the music started. Gloria Gaynor. "I Will Survive." She rolled her eyes. "Hold on, let me blow the dust off this one."

"Go ahead, sugar, mock it. But George Michael's next. And you know every word."

Kate suddenly remembered a time years ago, when the kids were small, and she and Paul had driven to Ohio to visit her mother, and they were so punch-drunk from listening to Disney tunes that they started making up their own raunchy words, until Paul could barely breathe he was laughing so much.

Kate's singing stalled on a sob.

"Hell, Kate." Jo took the exit ramp off the highway. "That was supposed to cheer you up."

"Memory's a bitch." She peered out the tinted glass at the sign that welcomed her to her hometown. "Let's get this over with, huh?"

~~~~

The house came into view. Kate's gaze skimmed across the peeling paint and the streak of greenish moss on the roof shingles by the gutter. Anna's bike sprawled in the driveway next to Michael's skateboard and an overturned bucket of bubbles. The front yard sported an elaborate maze made of lawn chairs, towels, and a pup tent, bound together with jump ropes and anchored with border stones pulled from around the rhododendrons.

Jo pulled the car close to the curb. With a sore, fluttering heart, Kate unfolded her aching body from the front seat, seized by the sudden urge to freeze this moment in time. She wanted to capture the sight of her home, just as it looked right now—standing solid amid the buffeting winds—in all its weathered, vibrantly flawed, and gloriously chaotic beauty.

"Hey! Mom's home!"

The front door flew open. Tess raced down the walkway.

She dropped to her knees to crawl through one of the towel tents and then flung herself out the other end so hard that Kate tumbled back against Jo's car.

"Finally! Mom! I'm so glad you're home. *Finally!*"

Kate squeezed her—she couldn't help herself, she held on tight, because she knew in a minute Tess would pull away, embarrassed—but Tess only jumped more, vibrating in her excitement.

"I'm so glad you're back! You wouldn't *believe* the trouble we've had! Grandma was such a *pill*! And I nearly got kicked off the team! But I didn't, because Daddy had a long talk with the coach and told him all about you going off to India and all, and then he let me stay. And we *won Saturday's game*—"

Kate drew away long enough to smooth the bangs off Tess's brow and gaze with love at the flash of her braced teeth.

"—that means we're going to the semifinals next week! Can you believe it? Helena says we're never going to beat Caldwell East, that they've got players head and shoulders taller than us, but I—"

"Mama's home!"

Anna sprung out of a pup tent wearing a tutu of purple tulle. Squeezing herself under a draped towel, Anna ran toward them and shoved every ounce of her fifty-two pounds between her sister and Kate's knees. With one arm around Tess's back, Kate crouched down and pulled Anna against her, crushing the tulle. Anna gifted her with a small, wet kiss.

"Look, Mom!" Anna opened a fist to reveal a pile of candy corns, white and orange like the ring around her mouth. "I've got Halloween candy!"

"Yum," Kate said, drowning in those enormous brown eyes. "How did you convince Grandma to let you have that?"

"Grandma doesn't know." Anna leaned in with a secretive little grin. "Daddy said I could have them."

"Mom, Mom," Tess said, "can we have sausage and peppers tonight? Or *real* lasagna? Grandma's been feeding us stuff you wouldn't *believe*, and Daddy said..."

Through the barrage of Tess's narrative, and above Anna's head, Kate glimpsed Michael, who'd come around the far side of the family minivan and now fretted with his skateboard in the driveway. Catching his eye through the flop of his bangs, she raised her hand. With an uncertain smile, he returned her breezy wave. Then, abruptly, he slapped the board onto its wheels, shoved off down the street, and thrust his hands deep in his pockets.

"Are you listening, Mom? Because Helena *really* wants to sleep over tomorrow night to study math but also she needs a ride to soccer the next day...."

But Kate wasn't listening, because the front door had swung open, and Paul stood framed in the doorway.

She tightened her grip on the girls as she straightened up. He wore a Caltech T-shirt, the black logo faded and cracked, and the fabric so softened by washings that it clung to his chest. A dishcloth lay across his shoulder, as if he'd just come from the kitchen.

Jo came up beside her. "I'll hang out for a while." She reached over to mess Anna's hair in greeting, muttering for Kate's ears only, "Just to make sure there are no serious incidents of domestic abuse."

Paul loped down the stairs and strode across the flagstones, pausing just on the other side of the pup tent that crossed the walkway. "Girls," he said, pulling the dishcloth off his shoulder. "Find something to do in the house."

Paul's voice forced Kate's heart rate up into aerobic territory. Tess and Anna sensed the tension—after an exchanged glance, they skittered off.

Kate watched them go, not just to drink in the sight of two ponytails swinging, but because her pulse was pounding dangerously and she wasn't ready to look Paul straight in the face. It was as if her whole body were wired, and someone had just flicked the switch. Though he stood a good five feet away, with a stretch of nylon tent waist-high between them, he was so *here*. It was the intensity of his concentration. She hadn't experienced this kind of laser-beam awareness from him in a very, very long while.

She tightened her grip on the strap of her carry-on bag to maintain balance. "I appreciate," she said, in a voice too hoarse to be her own, "that you kept the kids home from school today."

"Half-day." He wiped his hands in the dishcloth like he was pulling off skin. "Teacher conferences."

She winced. "Well, at least you didn't send them all on play dates."

"You can bet I thought about it."

Her gaze flew to his. She felt the shock of his bright-blue eyes. She felt the shock of the sight of him, too—how tightly his skin stretched across his cheeks, how rigidly he held his shoulders, how thick the scruff had grown on the line of his jaw. She'd seen him like this once before—when he'd been under job-threatening pressure to deliver a beta version of a computer game, and she'd found him asleep twice in his office chair, his cheek on the keyboard. It was fury that kept him upright now, but Kate could see that Paul was approaching the point of utter exhaustion.

Guilt came in waves.

"Hey, Paul." Jo slapped a protective hand on Kate's shoulder. "Can't say I haven't seen you looking better."

"Jo."

"Don't you think that it might be wise to bring this show inside?"

"Nope." He flung the dishcloth over his shoulder. "I don't give a damn about the neighbors. If I did, I wouldn't have left this mess here up for three days to kill my lawn. If my wife has anything to say, she can do it while I take care of this house and this family."

His words cut deep. She stood wincing as Jo's hand slipped off her shoulder, and her friend backed away. With shaking fingers, Kate shoved her hair out of her eyes. She'd had twenty hours on an airplane to think about this first conversation. Yet now, with Paul reaching across the tent to work the knotted rope that held it to a chair, the explanations she'd practiced over and over caught behind her teeth.

Well, at least she knew how to begin.

"Paul... I'm so very, very sorry."

Paul's expression flickered. The tiny contraction of small muscles was barely discernible—except to her, the one who loved him best.

"I know that sounds really lame," she said, "but I really mean it. I never should have left you, or the kids, so abruptly."

"That is the first damn thing you've got right in weeks." He yanked the rope free and let it drop. "But 'sorry' isn't going to cut it."

"I know."

"You left us—"

Left us.

"—and I keep waiting to hear a reason *why.*"

"I've been trying to tell you—"

"Over satellite connections," he retorted, working on the knot on the other side of the tent. "From the back of a damn elephant, while riding motor scooters through Bangalore—"

"—and if you'll just stop and listen for a moment, I'll try to do it better."

He gave her a smoldering look as he freed the pup tent and moved stiffly to the next section of the maze. Tentatively, Kate shuffled parallel to him. She fingered the knot of a jump rope tied on the edge of a lawn chair. The rope was damp, and the knot pulled tight. It'd be just as hard to unravel as the truth about their marriage.

"That T-shirt, you wore it on our honeymoon," she said, glancing briefly at a pale spot upon Paul's shirt, where she'd dripped bleach in one of the early years of their marriage.

He shrugged one shoulder impatiently.

"Do you remember our honeymoon, Paul? Do you remember when we took that walk to the lava fields of Volcano National Park?"

She knew he remembered. She saw the memory playing across the angry lines of his brow. That night, they'd walked carefully with flashlights along the marked route after dark, getting closer and closer to the heat, the smell of sulfur, and the dangerous red glow of the lava. They'd watched how the molten rock sprayed sparks, how it hissed every time a rivulet touched the sea, where new land was born.

"I remember everything," she murmured. "I remember standing next to you in the darkness. I remember holding your hand. I remember thinking about the years to come, and the new life we would someday make together. The baby we'd call Tess—"

"Kate." Words dammed behind his lips; she saw the angry red swell of them in his throat. "Get to the point."

"This is the point. It's what I've been trying to tell you all along." Kate felt a moment of dizziness. It was the same sensation she'd felt approaching the open door of an airplane, just before stepping into the void. "I think the problem with our marriage might have begun just after Tess was born."

His head shot up. His fingers stilled on a knot. His pupils widened, and he swayed back on his heels.

"A good part of it was my fault." She let the words tumble, while he was still processing, knowing she might not have a chance to say anything more if she didn't say it now. "Having that baby scared the hell out of me. I was so afraid of screwing up. Send me into a company that's kept handwritten records for thirty years, and I'll get the whole thing straightened up in a few weeks—but this? Ten pounds of mewling infant? There were no guidelines for that, there were no semi-annual reviews, there was no ladder to climb, and I was lost—"

"Since Tess?" His cocked his head. "Since *Tess*?"

"—and so I overcompensated, like I always do. I read every freakin' book and played Mozart while she napped and bought every educational shape-sorting toy. And I just couldn't stop when Michael and Anna came along. It just intensified, it built upon itself, and before I knew it I was running the PTA and shuttling them to soccer—"

"Now we're getting somewhere, because *that's* what this is about." He yanked a freed rope and sent it whirling across the yard. "You doing too much with the kids."

"I know."

"Michael in two sports, Tess on a travel team." He hurled a damp towel to the ground behind him. "Anna in gymnastics—"

"I never meant for it to get so—"

"—and you," he continued, kicking a bucket of pebble soup out of his way, "you treating sex like it's something to cross off your list."

From somewhere far away, Kate heard Jo make a strangled little sound, but only in passing, because now it was her turn to reel with the impact of his words. The truth pinched hard. She remembered writing it down once. "Have sex with Paul," she'd scribbled. Right after "Tess's soccer practice" but just before "Anna's bath."

"That's going to change." Her words came out in a shaky, breathy rush. "I'm going to cut back . . . with the kids."

"Right."

"I am, Paul. I've made that decision already."

She had, long before the plane touched down in Newark. She'd talk to the teachers next week. She'd resign as PTA president after the end of the term. And she wanted to have sex with Paul again—often—fiercely—the way it once had been—sex on the dryer—sex in the shower—sex like they used to have, spontaneous, frequent, and raw.

"Yeah, well, maybe you will," he said in a low, grim voice.

"Maybe you've decided this is all you have to do to fix this. Cut back on the kids' schedules. Get life back to normal."

"Yes!"

"I know how much you love the kids, Kate. No denying it. They're your whole world."

Tears prickled at the back of her eyes. "Yes," she said, around the lump swelling in her throat. "Yes, they are."

"So, for the past two weeks," he continued, "I've been running our marriage through my head like a damn slide show, trying to remember something—a single argument, a single betrayal, anything big enough to make you want to put half a world between us, because it's become as clear as glass that you didn't go to India to get away from the kids." His voice roughened. "You did it to get away from *me*."

Time stopped in a sort of buzzing haze as Kate found herself remembering a toy Paul had bought Michael when he was young, a three-foot blow-up clown that was weighted at the bottom so, no matter how many times you punched the thing, it would wobble back up again, ready to be smacked anew.

And yet even in this gob-smacked state of mind she felt Paul's pain. She'd hurt him. She was gripped with the urge to take his face in her hands and look into his eyes and tell him that she loved him, *loved him*, and nothing else really mattered.

She took a step toward him to do just that—but he grabbed a lawn chair off the ground and folded it flat, keeping it between them.

"You forget," she said, gently, "that I begged you to follow me to India."

"It's an easy enough demand to make when you know damn well that I couldn't leave work and the kids."

Paul turned his back to her. He kicked the rocks off the edges of the next set of draped towels. Numbly, Kate pulled at the nearest lawn chair, tied up on both sides with more towel-and-jump-rope tents. She searched her own heart as she slipped into automatic, twisting the knots out of the ropes. Had she been fooling herself? No, no, she had definitely wanted him to join her. Desperately, in fact, she'd ached for him every day. But now, standing on her own lawn, she began to wonder if she'd expected the impossible.

Doubts worked on her mind. Absentmindedly, she folded a lawn chair. Maybe Paul was right. Maybe, after the heat of the skydiving experience, she'd been entirely unreasonable, and this rift between them was all her fault, born of some crazy idea that they could have a different sort of marriage, a wildly romantic, idealized love life only found in novels. Her actions suddenly seemed so idiotic—just make a plane reservation, and off to India we'll go! But they lived in the real world. Maybe every couple comes to a point in life when marriage by necessity morphs into little more than a working partnership, centered on raising kids.

Jo cleared her throat and pinned Kate with a significant look.

You're not just going to cave, are you?

Kate looked away so fast she nearly threw out her neck. *Damn.* She squeezed her eyes shut, trying to still the whirling of her thoughts, but no sooner had she done that than a gust of wind slapped her hard. It whipped her hair off her cheek. A gust so sudden it reminded her of free-falling from eight thousand feet. It reminded her of feeling weightless and exhilarated.

It reminded her of Rachel.

And in that instant, Kate opened her eyes and saw herself and the world as if she were seeing it from above. She saw the house and the broken-down maze and Paul's stiff back and frustrated gestures as he gathered everything up. She saw herself following in silence, helping him with the chore, nothing between them right now but a fierce need for everything to go back to normal, to avoid talking about what hurt most.

And just like that, her mind cleared. Kate *knew*. She *couldn't* cave. She could see the consequences if she did, as clearly as she saw the wind chasing shadows of the clouds across the lawn. Oh, yes, she could see the unfurling of the long years passing in clockwork predictability, and nothing would change. Nothing would change, and she and Paul would become that old couple eating out on Saturday nights with absolutely nothing to say.

She shoved the last towel on the pile with the others. She gripped the determination twisting up inside her, and she held on to it as she strode across the yard, kicking rocks aside, trotting around the folded lawn chairs until she reached Paul's side.

He jerked up in a spasm of long, lean muscle. He glared at her through eyes of heartrending blue.

"Paul, this is not all about me." She seized the strap of her carry-on bag, fisting it for courage. "After Tess was born, you changed, too."

He shook his head, swiveled on his heel, and took one long step toward the house—away from her, away from explanations, away from the ugly truth. Just then, Jo cleared her throat. Loudly.

Paul stopped. He paused with is back toward her, his shoulder blades knife-sharp against his T-shirt.

Surprised, Kate glanced at Jo. Jo leaned against her car with her arms crossed, giving Paul an intense glare. Suddenly Kate remembered that Jo had been talking to Paul all week. Kate realized that Jo had been *working* on him, using all her people skills to coax him from an angry ledge.

Later, Kate thought, with a quiver of gratitude, she would have to thank Jo for trying.

Then she turned back to Paul, and took advantage of his sudden quiet.

"You did change after Tess was born," Kate said, "and most of the changes were wonderful. I'll never forget the way you cradled Tess's head in your hands, just after she was born. You just . . . you seemed to know exactly what to do. Not every man adapts so well."

He gave her his profile, squinting down the street at Michael doing skateboard tricks with a friend, but she knew he was thinking of his own father.

"But you also quit your job around that time. I used to tease you about becoming Mr. Corporation, but it wasn't easy leaving southern Cal, leaving that start-up company, and coming here. It's a whole different attitude, the whole nine-to-five, meeting-after-meeting thing, and you worked hard to adjust." She remembered, oh so well. "I know, Paul. I watched."

"I had to get a real job." He shuffled in a tight half-circle, bracing his hands on his hips, stopping and then starting again, like he did at a soccer game when a referee made a bad call. "I wasn't going to raise the kids on some commune, planting okra and collard greens, having Tess dig latrines and Michael learn to tie-dye—"

"You wanted a better life."

"Yes, and I gave it to us—to *all* of us."

"You did, Paul, you did." She leaned toward him, willing him to understand. "But somewhere along the way, we both started thinking that a 'better life' was like a Ralph Lauren ad."

He blinked at her, blankly.

"Think about it. Haven't we become so tied up in our kids—so determined to give them some Nick at Nite version of a stable life—that we forgot to take care of *us?*"

She watched him as he processed what she'd said, in his infuriatingly logical way, as he stared so intensely at the ground he might as well have been taking inventory of the weeds. She trembled so violently that it took her a minute to realize that the stinging feeling in her hand was where the buckle of her luggage strap had cut through the skin of her palm.

She loosened her grip and then dared to close the space that separated them. She paused, gauging his reaction to her nearness. When he didn't move, she put her hand on his shoulder.

She felt his muscles tighten under her palm.

"Someday Tess, Michael, and Anna will be grown." She pressed her nose in the hollow just by his shoulder blade. "Someday they'll be out of this house, living lives of their own. It'll just be you and me then, with all the time in the world." He smelled of cut grass, of old cotton, of dish soap. "I know what kind of marriage I want. I want us to be the couple caught slow-dancing to the music of street musicians in Barcelona. I want to be the couple that is the life of every party. I want to be the old twosome that still holds hands." She felt moisture and realized that a tear had slipped out. "That's what I want, Paul, that's all I ever wanted. A life, with you, full of adventure and love. The way we once were. Tell me"—her voice caught—"tell me that's what you want, too."

She pressed her cheek against his back, willing his spine to soften as she waited in free-fall, ticking down the seconds, waiting while her heart threatened to burst in her chest, along with all her hopes and all her dreams.

Abruptly, he stepped away, turned around, and fixed her with a steady, wary gaze. She tried to hold it through the shimmer of her own tears.

His face was like stone, his jaw fixed, his mouth a tight white line, but beyond his eyes, Kate saw a flood of emotions—a roiling, fluxing deluge that stopped her breath. In those blue waters she read all the things that he wouldn't say—all the pain he couldn't admit. She saw the hurt of a boy who'd been abandoned by his father, and the struggle of a young man determined not to make the same mistakes. She saw what she'd never anticipated when she'd trotted off to India—how much her actions had wounded him, and how deeply he'd buried his scars.

"Oh, Paul."

"Damn it, Kate."

"You must have known," she whispered, "that I was going to come back."

"Yeah, I must have known that," he said dryly. "Just like you must have known that I—"

He swallowed his own words. His gaze flickered away. A muscle in his cheek flexed.

"What, Paul?" She tried to draw his attention back to her. "What should I have known?"

"I tell you all the time."

"Tell me what?"

Paul planted his hands low on his hips. His brow knit in confusion. "I *do* tell you all the time. At least, I mean to."

Then he met her gaze. Searching, searching. Kate's throat closed up. Her heart began to race.

"I love you, Kate." His voice hitched. "It's that simple. All I ever wanted in life was *you*."

Kate met his blue, blue eyes and tried to absorb what he'd just said, but then there was no more reason to think. His arms wound around her. She smelled the shampoo he'd used that morning. She felt the throbbing of his pulse in his throat. His hair tangled in her eyelashes, suddenly damp with tears.

A little while later, when she could speak again, she whispered, "I missed you, Paul."

He flattened his hands against her back. "I'm still angry at you."

"I know."

"We need to talk about this."

"I know."

"My mother is still here," he said. "She could watch the kids one more night."

"Okay."

"We'll go out. Just you and me." His voice grew gruff. "I'll even make the reservations."

She laughed, a husky and uncertain sound, and then she burrowed closer to him. "That sounds...perfect."

Gently, he rocked her back and forth, right there on the front lawn.

Jewish Hospice Institute
Room 300-C
New York City, New York

Dear Jo—

When you get this, I'll be gone. I hope you'll forgive me for not sharing this last adventure with you, because it hasn't been joyous like the others. Imagine—cancer, after the life I've led. What a kick in the head, huh?

So I've got these letters spread across my hospice bed, and I'm so glad that I wrote them. They remind me of what good friends we've been, you and me and Kate and Sarah, how different we all are and yet how perfectly matched.

I keep remembering that trip we took to the Finger Lakes a year or so after graduation. Sarah was about to leave for the Peace Corps, and so we arranged to take that last trip together to an upstate music festival. Kate had mapped out the whole thing, brought water bottles and aspirin and a camp stove, a new tent and spades. You'd made a reservation at a nearby hotel, you told us, because now that you had a job you weren't camping ever again. I'd been eyeing a nearby mining site where I could spelunk into some limestone caves. And Sarah planned to spend every moment worshipping at the feet of that Christian band from Vermont. As we talked about our plans on the way up, I remember thinking, This is the end. We're spinning off in our own directions.

You remember that weekend, yes? How much it rained, and how someone screwed up your reservation, and how they closed the caves for flooding, and Sarah's favorite band canceled. I remember sitting in the car, all of us quiet, just about ready to give it up and go home, watching all the other cars heading out. I don't remember whose idea it was. I think we all thought it up at the same time, as we looked out the window at that muddy hill. I remember Sarah saying something about "monsoon slides" and you saying you sure could use a drink and me saying, "I wish we had cafeteria trays," and Kate saying, "Garbage bags will do." Then Kate, Sarah, and I were struggling through the rain to the top of that hill, clutching green Heftys, hurling ourselves down into the widening puddles, laughing, wiping the dirt out of our eyes, watching other cars stop, other people stream out. Only when we struggled back to the tent hours later did we realize you'd spent that time at a nearby grocery, stocking us up on beef jerky and bourbon. Then, impossibly, Sarah had found someone she knew, a musician, who settled by the camp stove and played his acoustic guitar like a dream, and we slung our arms around each other and sang songs, our crowd growing as mud caked on our skin and the rain subsided and the moon came out. That night I knew it wasn't the end for us—that the thing that bound us together, the thing we all understood deep down, was that life—however we chose to live it—was something you embraced with open eyes and a full heart—and that if we made an effort, we could be friends like this forever.

Jo, of the four of us, you were always the strongest—stronger than you'd even let on, with all your smirking and no-commitment hookups. I knew that the first day I laid eyes on you at the meeting for the rock-climbing club. All those Southern wisecracks and flippant irreverence came from a heart that had known terrible trouble, and by sheer force of will risen above it. So I wrote all the rest of the letters thinking of other people's lives and other people's needs—but for this letter to you, I've been selfish. What I'm asking you to do is going to be the hardest job of all, and it isn't so much for you as it is for me.

There's never enough time, you know? I tried so hard. After Gracie was born, I cut back on the skydiving and the BASE jumping, I joined the adventure travel company and spent way too much time in an office, booking flights and making arrangements for strangers, but I thought I'd managed a balance, somehow, between the life I'd been living and the precious young life I was responsible for. But it was never enough, really, and it seemed every time I returned from a trip I was coming home to a little stranger, a daughter I had to get to know all over again.

What I'm asking you to do, Jo, is to succeed where I've failed. I know you are going to think this is a mistake, but it's not. This isn't the disease talking, either, because, though my hand is trembling and I can barely grip this pen, what I'm writing comes from that sure, solid part of me that cancer hasn't yet touched.

Jo, I want you to be mother to my child. I'm making you her legal guardian. Take Grace. Take care of her, better than I could.

Love her, as I always will.

Love,
Rachel

chapter sixteen

A children's tea at the Carlyle hotel on the Upper East Side was not the kind of activity Bobbie Jo Marcum would normally have in mind for a Sunday afternoon. But today's Bobbie Jo was not the same woman as the Bobbie Jo of a month ago, who'd spent most Sundays listening to Rascal Flatts while leafing her newsprint-stained fingers ever deeper into *The New York Times*. The Bobbie Jo of today sat across from a little girl dressed in a red plaid jumper over a neat white shirt with a Peter Pan collar. Atop her head, Grace wore a wide-brimmed yellow hat with a red ribbon, which she stubbornly refused to take off.

The room was filled with such hats. The children's tea was a theme-inspired meal based on the *Madeline* series of books by Ludwig Bemelmans. The familiar tale about that smallest of French schoolgirls, who lived in a little brick house in Paris, and whose parents were always "away," had thrilled Grace as much as it had Jo, who, as a foster child sleeping in a series of trundle beds, had once incurred nearly three dollars in fines for keeping *Madeline's Rescue* under her pillow rather than returning it to the library.

Jo gestured to the man who'd just gathered a new bunch of girls on a plush carpet to read. "Do you want to join the group, honey? Looks like he's going to do *Madeline in London*."

"Nah," she said, swinging her legs as she reached for a miniature burger. "He didn't do *Madeline and the Bad Hat* nearly as good as Cousin Jessie. And that's my favorite—because of Pepito."

"Pepito?!" Jo pulled a mock grimace. "When you're a teenager, Gracie, remind me to keep you away from psychopaths."

"What's a s-aye-co-path?"

"It's someone *really* scary. Like a teenage boy."

"Pepito isn't scary!"

"Gracie, honey, do I have to remind you that he sets a cat loose among a pack of dogs?"

"That was *before*."

"And he builds a guillotine for chickens?"

"He says that he's *sorry*." She stopped swinging her legs long enough to lean into the table, waving her half-eaten teeny burger at Jo. "And Madeline forgives him and tells him he's not a bad hat anymore."

Jo took another sip of lemonade and narrowed her eyes at Grace, wondering if it was too early to worry about this tendency to go for the bad boys.

Jo slid her cup back on the table. She needed to take it one nightmare at a time. "Well," Jo said, "my favorite character is that mutt that pulled Madeline from the river. What was that pup's name, now? Something ridiculously Fifth Avenue—"

"Genevieve."

"Ah, yes. Genevieve." In Kentucky, dogs were called Rover or Pooch or Butch. Princesses were called Genevieve.

"Ooh, I love Genevieve, too! And Miss Clavel let Madeline keep her!"

"And all her puppies."

Yes, all those sloppy puppies in that old house in Paris, covered with vines. How Jo had yearned for such a place, while wearing stranger's hand-me-downs, and devouring the stories under worn bedcovers. She'd wanted to be transported there, where she could pretend that she wasn't really an orphan—that her parents were just rich and busy and mysteriously away.

"Do you need some more tea, Aunt Jo?" Grace reached for the perky white teapot. "I'll pour it for you."

"Fill her up, kiddo." Jo slid her delicate china cup within Grace's reach. "I've gone plumb dry."

Gracie lifted the teapot. Holding the lid with her other hand, she poured the tea—well, lemonade—in the general direction of Jo's cup. Fortunately, the linen tablecloth was very absorbent.

Jo took a sip of the strongly sweetened brew. The way they both were drinking, they'd have to make another trip to the ladies' room soon, and not just to peruse the bunny-with-umbrella wallpaper, designed by the same man who'd authored the books. On the table stood a three-tiered platter with a pretty lineup of miniature food. Jo picked up one of the shrimp arrayed in two straight lines. "Hey, this is the smallest." Jo held up the shrimp. "Do you want to eat Madeline?"

"I like Pepito's veggies better," said Gracie, seizing a slim sliced carrot. "Especially the dip."

Jo popped the shrimp in her mouth. She'd been trying to get Grace to eat sliced carrots and celery with ranch dip at home—to no avail—but serve the same thing up on silver and call it "Pepito's crudités" and suddenly it was meal-worthy. Kate would appreciate that.

Kate, who was finally home with her kids, neck-deep in domestic suburban life again. Kate and Paul had come a long way, if that heartrending scene on the lawn was any indication, but Jo knew it was just the beginning. Apparently, even the truest of loves needed tending.

"Well, sugar," she said, finishing a quick prayer, "my favorites were the teeny burgers. Not enough for this Southern girl, though—I could have eaten ten dozen more. But I was saving room for one of those." Jo nodded discreetly toward the next table, where a redheaded little Madeline and her mother, in vintage Chanel, hunkered over a heaping bowl of ice cream. "What do you think, should we get the Eiffel Tower Hot Fudge Sundae or the Petite Banana Splits Fontainebleau?"

Grace craned her neck in a very unladylike way to get a good look at her neighbor's Eiffel Tower sundae. Jo spotted a Fontainebleau a few tables over and pointed that out to her, too.

"I'll make you a deal," Jo said, as Grace bit her lip in indecision. "I'll get one, and you get the other. Then we'll share."

"That's what me and Cousin Jessie used to do," Grace said, making an excited squiggle in her seat, "whenever we went to the Dairy Princess at home."

Jo paused with the teacup halfway to her lips. "Home" for Gracie still meant back in New Jersey, at her grandmother's house. Jo felt a twinge in her chest, like the sink of a sharp splinter.

"Well, kiddo," Jo said, clearing the husk from her voice, "I can eat twice as much as skinny Cousin Jessie, so you'd better be quick with your spoon."

Waddling out of the hotel six thousand calories later, Jo

gamely suggested a few blocks of walking. Motherhood could pack on the pounds more easily than two weeks' worth of late-night take-out. So they braved the frisky wind and strolled toward Central Park. Gracie buttoned her blue wool Madeline coat right up to her neck, and Jo wrapped herself in her cashmere pashmina. Skipping along in her Mary Janes, Grace followed the skittering of the leaves along the sidewalk. Ablaze with russet and gold, the trees of Central Park rustled in the wind as the feeble November sun warmed their heads. Winter was soon to come, but right now New York City was as lovely as it could get.

As they crossed Fifth Avenue, Gracie slipped her hand in Jo's. Grace's hand was weightless—so small, so warm, and slightly damp.

And though she strolled on a busy street in a busy city, with yellow cabs rushing by, and trucks rumbling over the pitted streets, and double-long buses squealing to a stop, Jo experienced a sudden, muffled silence, like a cocoon—like the drift of a soft, familiar blanket around them.

No reason to rush home.

Jo leaned down to catch the little girl's eye. "Hey, Gracie, what do you say we work off some of that ice cream in that park over there? I hear it's got a kickin' twisty slide."

Grace burst into a smile, and then darted toward the opening in the stone wall. Jo followed her through the gap, watching the ribbon on the little girl's hat flying in her wake. Gracie raced for the park bridge, only to squeal in delight as she spotted the granite spiral slide.

With a twinge of guilt, Jo flicked her wrist to glance at her watch. Grace's cousin and grandmother—Jessie and

Mrs. Braun—were due to visit today, within the hour. Sarah was crashing at Jo's apartment so she could let the Brauns in should Jo and Grace be late, but Jo's concern extended beyond the threat of tardiness. Jo was looking forward to the visit with about the same enthusiasm as she was looking forward to her "performance review" at work on Monday, and for much the same reason. She'd spent the last weeks trying to do two very important things: land a new client, and try to make a home for an orphaned little girl. She'd bobbled the first, and the jury was still out on the second, though her spare room was starting to look as if it had been conquered by a tribe of fluffy bunnies.

As she hauled her Kentucky butt around the park, chasing Gracie from slide to stone bridge, Jo pushed the guilt from her mind. She and Gracie were having a wonderful day so far . . . and a pretty darn good week. Gracie had only walked in her sleep twice; she'd started to expand her food choices beyond sliced apples and macaroni and cheese; and there'd only been one tantrum, over the wrong brand of toothpaste. But Jo had a terrible dark Southern sense of foreboding about the upcoming visit with Nana Leah and Cousin Jessie. It would be the first time Gracie had seen them since Jo had swept her away from her home in Teaneck.

Jo remembered her own "family visits." She closed her eyes and saw her twelve-year-old self on the third Sunday of every month. She'd made a point of getting filthy by the creek, and wearing her most tattered clothes. She'd listen for the crunch of wheels on the graveled drive, the signal that Aunt Lauralee had arrived in her blue pickup truck. Then Jo would slouch into the parlor late, glare at her aunt from under overgrown bangs, and secretly hope Aunt Lauralee would stop looking at her watch long enough to notice Jo's Dickensian appearance. What she really longed for was a sudden change of heart—that Aunt Lauralee would take Jo back to the neat little ranch house and her four rambunctious cousins, the only family Jo had left.

No—there was no use rushing home today.

Gracie paused at the edge of a skateboard park, where she watched what appeared to be a gang of young Goth pincushions risk total paralysis on skateboards. ("Look, Aunt Jo, psychopaths!") Despite the Mary Janes and plaid jumper, the little girl had more than a bit of her mother in her, and Jo suspected that after today a skateboard would be on her Hanukkah wish list. Veering away from the show, Grace managed to be in just the right place when a kid abandoned a swing, and, seizing it, she called for Jo to push her—which she did, until Grace was flying back over Jo's head.

By the time they tumbled out of the taxi much later and headed into Jo's apartment building, the yellow bow at Grace's throat had come undone and she'd scraped the knee of her tights, but she was pink-cheeked and chattering all the way up the elevator to their floor. Jo's stomach clenched more tightly each time the bell rang, marking the passing of another floor.

The minute Jo swung the door open to her apartment, Grace tore away from Jo's side.

"Nana!"

Mrs. Braun was a hefty woman, incapable of sudden moves. As Gracie hurled toward her, the elderly woman shuffled forward on the couch in an effort to brace her legs to stand. Grace threw herself at her before she managed. Laughing,

Mrs. Braun wrapped her plump arm around Gracie's back and pulled her onto her lap.

Jo felt that sliver of a splinter slide a little deeper into her heart.

"Mrs. Braun, Jessie," Jo said, as she tossed her keys in the bowl by the door. "Are we late? How long have y'all been here?"

"No, no, you're not late." Jessie jolted off the chair and then shoved her fingers into her jean pockets. She looked bony, and her hair was in desperate need of an appointment at Bangz. "We're early. My aunt couldn't wait. She was nervous about the traffic. She said in this part of town it would take an hour to find a parking spot. Your houseguest—Sarah—was kind enough to let us in."

Jo met Sarah's eye. Sarah shrugged where she sat curled in the corner of the couch, looking fragile but serene after the disastrous visit with Colin in L.A. "I offered tea," Sarah said, "but for ten minutes I stood in front of your stovetop, and I still couldn't figure out how to turn the thing on."

"The dang thing's computerized," Jo said, sweeping up Grace's discarded hat. "I'll get it started in a minute."

Mrs. Braun had managed to pull Gracie away from herself long enough to get a good look. Gracie unbuttoned her blue wool coat, smoothed her hand over her red plaid jumper, and wiggled her Mary Jane–clad toes. She sat inches from Mrs. Braun's face, grinning, her body pliable and molded to her grandmother's form.

"So you went to Central Park, did you?" Mrs. Braun asked. "And you went to a playground with a twisty slide? And before that, you were eating with Madeline?" Mrs. Braun's grip on

Gracie tightened. "You've been having quite a time for yourself here, haven't you, Gracie?"

"Hey, do I get a hug?" Jessie dipped to her knees and opened her arms. Gracie slid off her grandmother's lap and flung herself at Jessie. Jessie squeezed her tight, then launched into one of those kiddie monologues that Jo knew she would never, in all her life, master.

"So how's my kitten-girl, huh? You've been causing problems for Aunt Jo, I bet. Sure, you've been nothing but trouble, putting tacks on her chair and glue in the locks and playing tricks with the toothpaste, haven't you? What? You haven't? Well, then, who are you? You can't be my Gracie-girl, then. Did the gnomes come and take my good girl away and leave you instead...?"

All the while, Gracie smiled and shook her head and laughed and lost her little fists in Jessie's hair. Jo unwound her pashmina and reached for Gracie's discarded coat and the jackets Sarah had left on the back of the couch, all the while struggling with a strange feeling just by her heart, an aching, lonely little twist.

When Jo hung the last hanger onto the pole, she made a beeline into the kitchen, as far away as she could get from the Norman Rockwell scene. "Anyone have a tea preference?"

"You got Lipton?" Mrs. Braun asked. "Tell me you got Lipton. I can't stand that fruity stuff."

"Lipton it is."

Sarah piped up. "Got any coffee?"

"You, Sarah? Coffee?" Jessie sank back into the couch. "I had you pegged as a green-tea type."

"I hate the herbal stuff." Sarah pulled the mass of her hair off her neck and braced it atop her head, with her elbow resting on the back of the couch. "Give me coffee, straight up. The stronger the better. At the camp we're spoiled—we get Burundi beans from the hill plantations—costs a few francs for a kilo."

As Jessie and Sarah chatted about free-trade coffees, Jo pulled down the decidedly non-free-market coffee beans she had and poured some in the stainless-steel grinder, an act that couldn't drown out the sound of Mrs. Braun chattering.

"Let me look at you now, Gracie. Go ahead, stand in front of me. Look. Look! You're up to here now. That's a lot bigger than you were last time I saw you. Jo, what are you feeding this kid? She's shot up like a rocket. Are you eating steak every night and finishing your vegetables, or are you sneaking sandwiches when Aunt Jo isn't looking?"

"I ate Pepito's crudités today."

"Did you, now? Well, that must have helped. Or does Aunt Jo have you on a bed where she ties up your arms and legs every night and stretches you a bit? Is that what she's doing?"

"No, you're being silly, Nana!"

"I think that's why you've grown three inches since I last saw you! I just can't get over you. And look at your dress. Jo, how'd you get this kid in tights? Remember Passover, Jess? We tried to get her in tights, and, oh, there was no putting those on your legs—no, sir."

"Nana, I was just a baby then!"

"Oh, you're not a baby anymore, sure, not anymore. Now here you are all prettied up and going to teas like Eloise. Madeline? Well, then, like Madeline..."

Jo shoved the stainless-steel teapot under the Kohler faucet and pushed the knob so the water would come out fast and loud. That aching little twist by her heart was coiling into something slit-eyed and shameful. This was Gracie's *family*. Of course Gracie would be thrilled to see them again. Of course Gracie would liven up and laugh and loosen up into her own little-girl self, and wasn't that a hundred times better than what Jo had dreaded from this visit—a full screaming red-faced throw-the-macaroni-across-the-room tantrum?

She clattered the teapot on the stove to boil just as the coffee began to percolate, and then she forced herself to look into the living room. She watched Mrs. Braun pull a tattered, stuffed empire penguin from a bag. Gracie's eyes widened; then she pressed the stuffed animal hard against her face.

Jo watched, with a shiver of worry.

"It's one of Grace's favorite stuffed animals," Jessie explained as she sidled up by the kitchen island. "Rachel bought it for her years ago, after her first trip to Patagonia. My aunt has spent the past weeks in knots of worry, sure that Gracie was crying herself to sleep every night, missing it."

"Grace never mentioned it, not once."

"That's funny." Jessie shoved thin fingers into the hip pockets of her skinny jeans. "She couldn't sleep without it at home. Screamed for it every night, even if it fell off the bed."

Jo turned her back to pull open a cabinet. "You hankering for Lipton, too?"

"Whatever you got." Jessie planted a booted heel on the lower rung of the chair, her face turned away to the scene in the living room. "Jo, she sure looks happy."

"Yeah, well, I cut her a Prozac before you came."

Jessie started.

"I'm kidding." Jo pulled down four oversized mugs. "Though I might not have been if I'd listened to that therapist."

"Therapist?"

Sliding the cups on the counter, Jo tugged open the silverware drawer, debating how much of the truth she should burden Jessie with. *Oh, hell.* "After Gracie's first serious meltdown," Jo said, "I had enough sense to seek professional help."

"Meltdown?!"

"What, she didn't melt down with you at all? She never threw her macaroni and cheese across the table? She never ate cardboard? Never got caught wandering around like a blind pig in the middle of the night?"

Jessie found sudden interest in the pattern on the polished granite countertop.

"The shrink said it probably had been going on for weeks." Jo placed a spoon in each cup and darted a glance toward the living room, as Gracie burst into high, tense laughter. "Don't worry—I said no to the drugs. For Gracie's sake. I've yet to decide whether I need them myself."

"Raising a child is a full-time job," Jessie murmured, her gaze scanning the room with its Glasswrap and covered outlets. "I can't imagine how you're doing it and working, too. You've gone to a terrible amount of trouble."

"She's my best friend's daughter." Jo pulled out a few tea bags. "And, for whatever reasons, this is what Rachel wanted."

Jessie tucked a stray lock of hair behind her ear, then ran her fingers over the counter's ogee edge. Back and forth. Back and forth. "It is really strange. Rachel always talked about you as this go-go material girl. No time for commitments."

Jo had opened her mouth to retort when Gracie's sudden,

sharp laugh stopped the words in her throat. This time, Grace's laugh was higher and tenser than before. Sarah caught Jo's eye. Sarah had heard that quavering pitch in Grace's voice, too—the day before yesterday, right before the toothpaste incident.

Jo took three steps into the living area and made a quick assessment. That penguin—full of memories—was probably the source of the distress. Gracie needed a quick change of focus.

"Hey, kiddo," Jo said, "why don't you bring your grandmother up to see your bedroom? You can introduce your penguin to all those rabbits. Then you can change into your Eloise outfit. Or show her your Tinker Bell costume from Halloween."

Gracie slipped off her grandmother's lap with a bounce and seized the older woman's hand. "C'mon, Nana, come see my room. I've got a 'puter of my own. Just a baby one, not like Aunt Jo's, but it plays Ping-A-Pig and Typing Torpedoes."

"Goodness, Jo," Mrs. Braun said, as she pushed herself off the couch. "What a place you've made for this girl! Call me down when the tea's ready."

Sarah watched the interaction with a steady gaze, then exchanged a glance full of meaning with Jo. Sarah had proved to be a great help during the toothpaste incident. Her aura of calm helped coax Grace out of her tantrum and revealed to Jo the oasis of serenity Sarah must be in the refugee camp.

"Coffee smells good, Jo." Sarah pulled the cashmere throw across her shoulders, uncurled herself from the couch, and joined Jessie at the kitchen island. "Quick, too. It's a treat for us at the camp, because it takes so long to brew. We have to grind the beans with rocks."

Jessie laughed a nervous little laugh, and then she stopped abruptly. "You're serious, aren't you?"

Sarah hoisted herself onto a stool, the wooden beads at her wrist clanking. "Takes a lot of firewood to boil the water, too."

"Hold on to your wallet, Jessie." Jo placed the sugar bowl next to the milk pitcher. "If you let Sarah tell you stories, she'll have you writing a check before the day's over."

"Oh, I'd write you a check," Jessie said, shrugging. "But it would bounce as soon as it hit the table."

Jo caught sight of a bottle in the glass cabinet just by the stove. "Hey, girls—the devil's on my shoulder. How 'bout a Mexican coffee? What do you say?"

"Not me," Sarah said. "A glass of that and I'll be like the drunken uncle, snoring on the couch."

"I'd love to," Jessie said, managing a small smile, "but I'm driving."

"Sugar, one small cup in a two-hour visit doesn't make a drunk."

"Yeah, but I don't even want to be buzzing, not when Gracie's in the car."

"Bunch of Girl Scouts." Jo dropped the tea bag into a cup and grabbed another. She tore open the wrapping and was reaching for a third when she paused, her hand hovering over the third cup.

Not when Gracie's in the car.

"Jessie . . . are you planning to take Gracie out to dinner or something?"

"Oh . . ." Jessie stiffened. "Shoot."

"Because that's not such a good idea. Grace needs to keep to her routine and get a good night's sleep for school tomorrow."

Jessie leaned back against the wrought-iron backing of the barstool. "Hey, Jo, I didn't mean to blurt it out like that. We *did* make some plans, but..."

"Listen, sugar, Gracie's your cousin. I may be the legal guardian, but, trust me, I'm not going to play this as if I'm a divorced mom, negotiating with her ex about visitation rights. By all means, take her out, do something special, but just tell me ahead of time. Sarah will back me up on this: Gracie doesn't take well to change these days."

"Amen," Sarah added.

"You know, this whole situation just doesn't make any sense." Jessie leaned her elbows on the counter. "It's just one of a lot of ridiculous things Rachel did. And not the most insane, either."

"Hey, it's a molehill, not a mountain." On the stovetop, the teapot started to burble. "Just get her home by seven-thirty."

"This is not about taking Grace to dinner, Jo. That's just the problem." Jessie let out an exasperated-teenager type of sigh that shuddered her entire body. "God, this is so *hard.* I don't even know how to say it. So I'll just say it. Jo, this is about taking Grace *home.*"

Jo stared at the tea bag in her hand, waiting for Jessie to continue. The wrapping bore the familiar red logo. Inside, there was that green tag at the end of the string, the kind she'd seen so many times hanging, brown-stained, off the edge of her mother's own cup in the evenings, after a long day at the factory.

"What do you mean," Jo asked, tearing the top of the paper, "you're going to take her home?"

The teapot started to wheeze. A soft whistling that, as Jo stood frozen over the empty cups, built up to a scream.

From upstairs, Mrs. Braun's faint voice, "So the tea's ready?"

"Soon, Aunt Leah." Jessie came around behind Jo and shut off the gas. "Listen, Jo." Jessie wrapped a dish towel around the teapot handle and hefted it to the counter, where, with quick, jerky moves, she sloshed boiling water into everyone's cup but Sarah's. "I know this might seem sudden to you. Out of the blue."

"Out of the blue."

"Like, all those weeks ago, when I dumped Grace on you—I feel rotten about that. I just put on her coat and shoved both of you out the door, and I apologize for that. I didn't handle it well. I never meant to do it with so little ceremony, without giving you the papers and all that, without preparing you... well, for Gracie. And all her quirks."

"Quirks."

"Try to put yourself in our shoes, Jo. Life was just crazy." Jessie used the dish towel to vigorously dry the spots she'd spilled on the counter, leaning in close, elbows flying, as words tumbled out of her. "We'd just buried Rachel. My uncle was bedridden, and my aunt was half out of her mind with worry. And there were bills, and paperwork, and the fuss of settling Rachel's estate, and sorting her athletic equipment, and donating her clothes to the local Jewish Community Center. And for my aunt, just getting out of bed in the morning was difficult. We just didn't handle it well. We haven't handled a lot of things well. When you showed up that morning," Jessie continued, "well, it was just a dream. We *so* needed help. Gracie was getting pushed aside, over and over, because we were so overwhelmed with Leah's doctors' appointments and Abe's mobility issues. And there you were, to take on the responsibility."

A brain freeze. That's what this was called, Jo thought, this strange inability to comprehend what was being spoken to her. It was what kept Hector, for all his talents, from being a project manager; he said that standing in front of all those suits put him in a brain freeze every time. Until now, Jo hadn't really understood what he was talking about. Jessie was chattering on—babbling—and though Jo could hear the words, she couldn't completely comprehend. The thought that kept overwhelming Jo was that Latoya was coming tomorrow, and Jo had to remember to tell her to start Grace on two-digit subtraction so the little girl would catch up to the other second-graders.

"I know you didn't expect the responsibility, Jo. I know you thought the whole thing was a mix-up." Jessie threaded the dish towel through the handle on the refrigerator door, tugging the ends even. "I saw it in your face that day. I know Rachel didn't give you a clue until you got one of her letters."

"Making me Grace's guardian," Jo said, through lips gone strangely numb. "Her legal guardian, fixed in ink."

"Rachel made some crazy choices." Jessie ran her fingers through the thatch of her hair, now falling completely out of her ponytail. "I just can't believe what she wrote in mine. But this thing with Grace, this tops them all."

"Jessie," Sarah interrupted, "I've been here three days, and I can tell you that Rachel made a smart choice. Jo's been amazing."

Jo sent a silent hug her way.

"I don't mean any disrespect." Jessie paced the length of the island, swiveling on the toe of her sneaker at the demarcation between carpet and tile. "You have done such an unbelievable job, I can tell. The arrangements you made, the therapist, even selecting a Jewish school for Grace—I can't tell you how much that means to my aunt." Jessie paused and met Jo's gaze across the length of the island. "It's just that we—my aunt and myself—figured it was time to relieve you of this responsibility, a responsibility that probably should never have been yours. Maybe Rachel...wasn't thinking straight when she wrote the letter to you. She *couldn't* have been. After all, Gracie still has family. She still has *us*. We thought today might be a good day to... Well, not too much time has passed since we sent her here, so it would be like a little vacation to Grace. Just a little time away from home. Even the lawyer suggested that now would be a good time—"

"Lawyer?!"

Jessie froze. The blood left her face. She hugged herself, tightly, and turned away to avoid Jo's eye. "I...wasn't supposed to say anything," she mumbled into her hand. "It was just a consultation. To talk about...options."

Options.

"He told us...it was best to be amicable. He said we should work with you. Do what's best for Gracie. Contesting a will takes time..."

Contesting a will.

Jo reeled away from the island, then swiveled on one foot to turn her back to Jessie, to *options*, to *lawyers*. She braced her hands on the opposite counter. Her fingers changed color before her eyes, went white around the edges as she leaned harder upon them, to keep herself from hitting the floor. Black spots exploded in her vision, but she couldn't faint now—*she couldn't faint now*—not even in a Southern kind of way. She had to keep her wits about her and try to figure out what was going on.

Breathe.

Here was the first simple truth: Life would be so much simpler without Grace. Without Grace, Jo could bring the full force of her concentration to work again. She could find a project for that Indian singer she'd contacted about the Mystery project. She could remove the baby gates that kenneled the condo, reclaim the spare room as a repository for her dry cleaning. She could call up that guy in Accounting with the crest of silky dark hair and bring him home to the massage oils going stale in her bedside drawer and have acrobatic sex with him on the stairs.

Here was the second simple truth: Grace was an orphaned little girl who clearly loved her family. Grace still referred to her nana's house as "home." And, unlike when Jo was orphaned, Gracie still had a family who wanted her.

It all made perfect sense.

Just let Grace go.

It was the right thing to do.

But here was the last simple truth: For reasons she didn't completely understand, Jo's whole body, spirit, and mind balked fiercely at the idea of some *lawyer* telling her—Grace's legal guardian—that the best thing to do would be to slip Grace's arms through her Madeline coat, pat her on the cheek, and let her walk out the door with the Brauns.

"Let me get this straight. You're telling me," Jo said, through her teeth, "that you came here on a lawyer's recommendation, thinking you'd bring Grace home today. Without even calling me. Without even discussing it with me."

"I know, I know. I'm not the bad guy here, Jo, believe me! I know we should have talked with you first." Jessie shoved the sleeves of her sweater up to her elbows and paced in a tight circle behind her chair "Believe me, I *wanted* to. But it's been back and forth with my aunt and me, back and forth. I kept telling my aunt that maybe we shouldn't bring it up yet, that we should let Grace stay here a little longer...and then she'd argue with me. We'd make plans to talk to you, and then something would happen—a bad blood test for her, or my uncle nearly slipping in the driveway—and she'd concede a few more days. But the issue kept coming up. She won't let go of it. She insisted on seeing the lawyer."

Jessie gripped the back of the stool, bracing herself to continue. "For the past weeks, my aunt has done nothing but worry, worry, worry. She can't cope with the empty house. It's not like she doesn't have enough to deal with, but the house just isn't the same without Grace in it. Now that Rachel's gone...well, Grace is really all that's left in my aunt's family—she's the only grandchild. And though my aunt is grateful that she's had a few weeks to put her own house in order, now that things are calming down, she really wants Gracie back."

Sarah stood up and fetched one of the teacups. She brought it to Jessie, urged her to sit down, and then placed the cup into Jessie's hands. Jessie curled both hands around the warmth, her shoulders sinking. All the while, Sarah's practiced gaze swept over Jessie's pale face, tangled hair, rib-fitting sweater, and heavy eyes.

Sarah gave Jo a long, meaningful look as she rubbed Jessie's back. "Your aunt isn't handling Rachel's death very well, is she?"

"No," Jessie conceded, after daring a sip of the hot tea. "None of us are. Aunt Leah and I, we're just trying to pull things together, one issue at a time. Up until we walked into this apartment building today, I thought I'd convinced her not to bring this up. Honestly, Jo, my aunt thinks Grace's stay here is a mistake. She just can't wrap her mind around the fact that Rachel gave custody to you, and she won't accept it—"

"But Rachel *did* give me custody," Jo insisted. "Legal custody, which will take a heap of time to *contest.*"

Jessie flinched.

"And Rachel did it," Jo persisted, "because of all you've been telling me—because of the pile of issues your aunt and uncle are dealing with." Information-gathering. That's what she needed to do. Gather all the facts before making a decision that her heart was resisting with all its might. "Your uncle—is he still bedridden?"

"He's better. He's using a walker now."

"And Leah," Jo insisted, "is still fighting diabetes."

"She'll deal with it for the rest of her life. But all that doesn't matter. We'll cope with that. Because I'm in the house now, permanently."

"Taking care of Abe and Leah?"

"And Gracie," Jessie added, "when she comes back."

Sarah stopped rubbing Jessie's back for a moment. "I thought you were looking for a job? You told me you wanted to be a teacher."

Jessie shrugged, finding interest in the tea bag floating in her cup. "I'll wait for the right position. Family comes first."

"So I'm to understand," Jo said, "that you're taking care of two elderly people, and now you want to add a child to that?"

Jessie's chin tightened, in a way achingly similar to Gracie's. "I'll manage."

"*My* lawyer," Jo countered, "might disagree."

Then, abruptly, a wail emerged from Gracie's room, high-pitched and piercing. The door to Gracie's room swung open, so hard that it banged against the wall. Gracie tore out of the room, a blur of plaid. She screamed as she ran down the hall to the bathroom, and then she slammed the door closed behind her.

Mrs. Braun shuffled out of Grace's bedroom, befuddled, grasping the doorjamb for balance. "I don't know what happened. I don't understand."

Jo strode into the living room and glared past the rail. "Did you talk about taking her home?"

"I said nothing," Mrs. Braun said. "I didn't even suggest it!"

"Then why is she so upset?"

"I don't know, I don't know!" Mrs. Braun shuffled to the railing and grasped it, out of breath. "She was showing me her room. The dolls that blink. The computer. That Barbie you bought her—oh, Rachel would have your heart on a platter if she saw that, Jo. She's got a purple blanket on her bed, so I mentioned her room at home, that we'd done a little redecorating—"

Sarah, from behind Jo, hissed in a breath.

"—we got her a purple cover with the penguins on it, two things she loves, I couldn't believe it when I saw it in Target. Then—this."

"Change," Jo said, understanding. "You changed things."

"She just collapsed. Right in front of me. Never seen her do that. Not even when..." Mrs. Braun covered her mouth; then, using the railing for balance, she shuffled down the hall toward the bathroom. "Gracie, love, Gracie," she said, her voice quavering. "Let Nana in now. Be a big girl—"

"Mrs. Braun," Jo said, forcing her voice even, "I suggest you leave Grace alone for a while—"

"But—"

"She'll come out of it." Jo planted her fists on her hips. "And we have to talk."

About change. And a seven-year-old orphaned girl.

"She's crying," Mrs. Braun said. "I can't leave her crying alone in the bathroom."

"Maybe I can help." Sarah slid off the barstool and let the blanket fall to the floor at her feet. "Grace and I had a good time yesterday, pretending her Barbie was a doctor and her stuffed animals the patients." Under the scrutiny of three women, Sarah shrugged. "I have some experience dealing with kids who are recently orphaned."

Sarah glided across the room, swept up the stairs, and laid a hand on Mrs. Braun's back. Mrs. Braun left with some reluctance. Sarah sank into a curl against the bathroom door, whispering soft words Jo couldn't quite hear—words that seemed to have a calming effect on the sobs.

"I never saw her like that," Mrs. Braun kept saying, as she made her way across the room to sink heavily onto one of the island stools. "One minute, she was fine, and then the next, boom!"

"It's the change," Jo explained, shoving a teacup toward Leah, as her mind—snapped awake—raced on how to handle what was sure to be a very difficult situation. "You went and made changes to her bedroom."

"She loves purple. She loves penguins!"

"Maybe before." Jo shoved the sugar and creamer down the table. "But now change is a very bad thing. She's plumb full of it."

"Don't I know it," Mrs. Braun exclaimed, tugging her tea bag in and out of the hot water. "But after today, that will be done. When she gets home, everything will go back to normal."

Jo tugged the dish towel off the handle of the refrigerator and tossed it across her shoulder. "Okay. First, we have to talk about that. About the idea that you're just going to take Gracie home today."

Jessie stood up. "Jo—"

"Because, with all respect, Mrs. Braun, I just can't let that happen—no, ma'am. I don't give a fig about that lawyer's recommendation. The last thing Grace needs right now is being yanked out of another home."

The memory hit her, full-force, the memory of Jo's very first foster mother. *We can't handle her anymore. She doesn't get along with any of the kids. She goes her own way, and laughs when I suggest otherwise. She won't respond to me at all.*

Jo turned her back to the room, trying to contain the anger, because it wouldn't help the situation, it wouldn't help *Grace*. Jo glared at the stone-tiled backsplash with its edging of green glazed tiles, the ones the designer had chosen to bring out the sage in the granite countertop. She pressed her palms so hard on that countertop that they began to throb, as the hurting words played back in her head.

You need to take her away. Today.

"I don't understand." Mrs. Braun sounded baffled. "Jessie, you told me Jo would agree, that it would be a relief for her, that she didn't expect to have custody. I thought this was settled."

"Aunt, don't you remember? We talked about this in the car—I suggested we wait another week."

"Why another week? A week is forever in a kid's life. Gracie should be back with her family."

Jo closed her eyes. And saw, in her mind, the montage of foster homes, one trundle bed after another, one weary, well-intentioned foster mother after another, one school after another. Jo always felt like the mutt in the dog pound, shuttled from one shelter to another because no one really wants someone else's old dog.

"I agree," Jo said suddenly, surprising herself. "Grace should be with family." She twisted to look at the two women. Mrs. Braun squeezed out her tea bag against the spoon and placed it on the saucer. Jessie looked pale and tense. "I agree," Jo repeated, "that, in a perfect world, that's the best possible thing."

"I always knew you were a sensible girl, Jo," Mrs. Braun said, clattering her spoon on the table. "I'm glad it's settled."

"But you have to be strong and healthy enough to take care of her. I mean *really* take care of her. Drive her back and forth to softball games. Bring her to the county fair. Help her with homework. Go clothes-shopping."

"Jessie's good at shopping," Mrs. Braun said, over the edge of her teacup. "She's always trying to get her into dresses, don't know how you did that, Jo—"

"And I don't mean just for a few weeks or a few months," Jo continued, pressing against the island counter. "I mean for years and years to come. It's not fair to Grace to take her home, only to have to send her away again."

"We'll manage." Mrs. Braun waved her wrist, waving away the trouble. "We've always managed, haven't we, Jessie?"

Jo caught Jessie's gaze before Jessie could drop her lids over her eyes, hiding her thoughts. Clearly, Mrs. Braun did not realize the extent of the burden she was putting upon the frail shoulders of a twenty-two-year-old girl. Mrs. Braun, like Gracie, had not yet truly absorbed the extent of the changes in her life since Rachel's death.

That's what was going to make this so hard, Jo realized. It was inevitable when a mother—or a daughter—dies. Denial was a powerful tool to stave off the grief, to stave off the difficult process of accepting change.

Sometimes it takes a whole lifetime to come to grips with the loss.

"It's the changes that got me in a knot, Leah," Jo said, carefully, swirling her cup. "I know what it's like, being shuttled around from one home to another." Never knowing, when the social workers show up, if they're just checking up on you, or if you're going to be sent away because you spit out your peas at the dinner table. She swallowed a dry, growing lump in her throat. "It's a hell of a way to grow up."

A memory struck her like a bolt of lightning.

Rachel, lying on the couch with her legs hiked in the air after coming back from her first bout at the fertility clinic, grinning as she enjoyed a final beer, while Jo sucked on a Marlboro, shaking her head.

Rachel, I still don't understand you. You're going to be hugely pregnant—you can't skydive anymore; you can't hike over the tree line, and that's your last beer. Why are you doing this?

Baby fever. I caught it from Kate.

Well, sugar, that's one fever I'll never catch.

Oh, Jo, don't rule it out so quickly. I think you should adopt.

What, a puppy?

A child, Jo. A child. Who'd know better than Bobbie Jo Marcum how to take care of an orphaned little girl?

With trembling hands, Jo sipped her tea. It scalded her tongue. She sipped it anyway, to hide her face and the tumbling realizations. She had convinced herself that Rachel had chosen her because—more than any of Rachel's other friends—Jo could afford to raise a child. Now Jo realized that money had *nothing* to do with it.

Rachel knew that this situation was going to happen. Rachel knew how much her mother loved Gracie, how insistent her mother would be about being the sole guardian. Rachel knew how soft a touch Jessie was, how devoted to family, how easily she subsumed her own desires. Rachel, losing weight in her bed, had had plenty of time to think about what to do for little Grace—sweet Grace, forgotten Grace in the whirl of doctors' visits and home health aides and prescription changes and mountains of laundry. Rachel knew her death would bring a whole new set of problems she couldn't even imagine.

But Jo could imagine them. Jo knew what happened to orphaned little girls. Who better to take care of an orphaned little girl than a woman who'd once been an orphaned little girl herself?

She looked over the rim of her teacup at the two women sitting in front of her. Her heart moved. Both loved Grace, that was clear. They wanted her to be back in their home, back in their family—even to the point of consulting a lawyer. Two openhearted, well-meaning women sat before her, but they did not completely understand the effect of their own actions on Grace's well-being—and *couldn't,* not in the way Jo did.

"I'll tell you one thing, ladies." Jo slid the cup back on the counter. "Grace is a lucky girl to have so many people who love her."

In the silence, they heard Sarah's quiet footfall through the living room.

Jessie glanced up at the bathroom door. "Grace isn't crying anymore. Is she coming down, Sarah?"

"Not right now." Sarah's face looked strangely bright. "She needs a few minutes."

"Why was she crying?" Mrs. Braun asked. "What was all the fuss about?"

"She kept saying something about 'lots of tots.'" Sarah crouched to pick up the blanket she'd left on the floor and then swept it around her shoulders. "She kept saying she didn't want to go back to 'lots of tots.'"

Jessie exchanged a guilty look with Mrs. Braun and muttered, "Did we use them too much?"

"No, no." Mrs. Braun shook her head. "She needed to be with other kids. That's why we sent her there."

"All those doctors' appointments." Jessie sank against the back of the barstool. "And the physical therapists."

"No, no, Jessie, don't think that way," Mrs. Braun insisted. "It wasn't good for Grace to be alone all the time."

"I was late once—"

"She liked the place, she did." Mrs. Braun's voice caught. "She told me she liked it. She told me she liked the computers."

Mrs. Braun's chin started to tremble.

"Listen," Jo said, taking a deep breath, summoning her inner executive warrior. "We don't need a lawyer to work this out. We'll decide, together, what is best for Gracie. But not today, not right now. Okay? Today is a visit, just as Grace expected. Can we agree on that much?"

A wave of relief passed across Jessie's face. She leaned in to her aunt, put her hand on her shoulder. "Auntie . . . I think Jo's right."

"But she belongs home." Mrs. Braun pulled a tissue out of her sleeve and pressed it against her cheek. "She belongs with her family."

Sarah spoke up, suddenly. "Grace told me one more thing, Mrs. Braun. Something she was very sure about."

Jo heard the creak of hinges. She glanced up to see, through the balusters, the door of the bathroom widen just a crack. Wide enough for a little girl's face to peep through, wide enough to show one pleading, tear-filled eye—blinking and fixed on Jo.

"For now," Sarah said, "Grace would like to stay with Aunt Jo."

~~~ chapter seventeen

On a road ten miles northwest of Gatumba, Sarah hauled herself out the window of a moving car and planted her butt on the rim of a door that had lost its window decades ago. Opening a bottle, she leaned across the windshield and sprayed the driver's side with water, so the driver could clear the glass with her one working wiper.

"Better? *Mieux?*" Sarah asked, dipping her head to speak to Ninette, an acquaintance from UNHCR who happened to be at the airport in Bujumbura yesterday to pick up supplies. "I have a little more water—"

"*Oui, ça va,* that's fine." Ninette took one hand off the wheel long enough to adjust the knot of her orange-and-green head-scarf, which had gone askew when the car lurched into an enormous mud hole, coating the whole front end with a third layer of muck. "I will have to go more slowly," she said. "One more hit and—*pftt!*—no more suspension."

"The camp is just around the bend."

Though every bounce jarred her bottom, Sarah lingered on the edge of the door. She'd left Boston two days ago in a snow-storm, after spending Christmas and most of January with her family in Vermont. Now she breathed deep of the humid air, sharp with the scent of ozone and rich with the smell of earthy decay.

As they passed the last hillock, the refugee camp loomed into view. It sprawled up the gentle slope of a denuded hillside in all its strange beauty. At the sight of it, she dug her fingers into the metal rim of the car's roof. Years ago, this camp had been a tent-strewn temporary way-station for refugees from the wars in Congo and Rwanda—an oasis in crisis, to be abandoned as soon as everyone had been repatriated. Now, as she gazed upon the exuberant patchwork of makeshift houses created from bent saplings, thatched hay, and tarps, she realized how fully it had become a village, complete with—she counted the roofs—a dispensary, a clinic, a maternity unit, and three schools.

The ragged ribbon of her heart clenched. After all the weeks in New York, helping Jo settle the situation with Gracie, and then, after staying in her family's rambling farmhouse, Sarah had toyed with the idea of leaving Doctors Without Borders for good. Strangely, it had nothing to do with Colin. She'd shut the door on him in L.A. Her weariness and uncertainty ran deeper than that; and it had been growing long before she received Rachel's letter. She'd collected too many terrible memories. She'd finally filled herself up to overflowing.

She'd come a whisker away from quitting the business forever. Until she heard the news that Sam had returned to Burundi.

At the sound of shouts, Sarah saw a crowd of children racing toward the car—a gaggle of excited boys. Sarah recognized the biggest, Misage, who'd grown at least a head taller in the months she'd been gone. Niboyu, Misage's younger brother, tottered barefoot, trying to keep up, sporting his big brother's muddy Red Sox baseball cap. The kids spread out across the road like stampeding antelope, shouting her name.

"Mwaramutse." Sarah greeted the boys in Kirundi, reaching into her woven bag for the hard candy she'd brought as gifts. When they got close enough, she tossed the first amber candy to Misage. *"Eh, Misage, bite?"*

"Hello, Miss Sarah," he replied, in English, as he deftly caught the candy. "Welcome back to Burundi how are you today I am fine thank you."

Show-off. Clearly, he'd been made leader of the crowd, though she knew he was barely twelve and had a weakness of heart due to a bout of scarlet fever when he was a toddler.

"You've been studying hard," she said, as the kids swarmed around her side of the slow-moving car, reaching eagerly for the candy she doled out as fairly as possible. "Where are you all going today?"

"We go to market."

"Ah." The market was four miles away, and not much more than a crossroads to Bujumbura, the capital. "Did you find anything good on the heap?"

He shrugged, indicating the sack against his back. "Kool-Aid very sweet. Pretty shoes. Very high." He struggled as he searched for words for the things he had scavenged from the refugee garbage, and then he sank his free hand into the pocket of his shorts and pulled out three small tubes. "This, too."

Sarah stared at the tubes and frowned as she tried to remember the words for "lip balm" in Kirundi. Doubted the language had such words. In this humid, muddy climate, there was very little need for lip balm or stiletto heels, or for many of the odd donations that occasionally made their way to the refugee camp. Yet these little entrepreneurs could earn some coin hustling such flotsam in the marketplace—usually to prostitutes. Their efforts kept whole families afloat.

"*Pour les lèvres,*" she explained in French, the lingua franca of the camp, as she rubbed her mouth in imitation. "*Pour les jolies filles.*"

For the pretty girls.

A couple of the boys hooted. Misage quickly shoved the lip balm back into his pocket. Tugging on the fraying sleeve of Niboyu's oversized sweatshirt, he barked orders to the rest of the boys, who made motions of not paying attention even as they headed back down the road, waving, vigorously sucking the butterscotch candy.

"*Nzoz'ejo,* Miss Sarah," Misage shouted over his shoulder. "I will come tomorrow."

To the clinic. To learn more English from her, as he surreptitiously watched Dr. Mwami pierce a boil or stitch up a swipe of a machete. As if Sarah had been away for a few days, not four months.

Time passes very differently in Burundi.

The small group proved to be only a fraction of the welcoming committee. As they approached the steep road that led to the camp's main building, a flood of children poured around them, splattering mud with every excited step. Despite leaning on the horn and shouting at the kids, with her head outside the window, Ninette was forced to bring the car to a complete stop at the base of the hill.

"*Ça va,*" Sarah said, sliding inside the car to gather her bags.

"No one ever makes it up the hill. You don't want to attempt that slope anyway," she said, gesturing to the steep, muddy incline. "It won't be solid until the rainy season ends."

"You trust this swarm with the boxes?"

Sarah eyed the crowd. "Some."

"*Bon.*"

Ninette shoved the car into park, kicked the door open, and waded through the throng of kids toward the trunk. With a jerk, she lifted the dented hood and handed Sarah's duffel bag, following Sarah's direction, to a tall Tutsi girl with a regal bearing.

"*À ma chambre,* Aline," Sarah said, "if I still have that room by the dispensary. Then come to me after—for a gift."

Sarah had made sure to stock up on gifts. Her duffel bag bulged with beads to braid into cornrows, flip-flops decorated with colored glass, Bic pens, and cigarettes made of real American tobacco.

Ninette handed box after box into the arms of the chosen, barking at them in fluent Kirundi to take the boxes directly to the doctor. "Tell Dr. Mwami," Ninette said to Sarah, piling a second, smaller box into a young girl's arms, "that these are all the salt tablets we can spare for now but there's another shipment coming in soon."

"I have a few boxes arriving by plane also." Before leaving the States, Sarah had stocked up on alcohol prep wipes, bandages, IV tubing, and other simple necessities. "Maybe I can send Sam..." She choked on the name. It fell off her lips without thought, and then caught as the sound reached her ears. "...or someone from the camp," she added, recovering, "to pick everything up at once."

"D'accord."

Ninette embraced her, kissed her on both cheeks, and then shooed the children away from the Peugeot as she slipped back in. Sarah plunged her hand into her bag and lured the swarm away from the old car with the sound of crackling wrappers. They rushed her so fast that she nearly fell.

Sarah found her footing and headed up the incline while the children yanked on her skirt, patted her arms, ululated, and cried out in that high pitch only young children can reach. *Miss Sarah Miss Sarah Miss Sarah Miss Sarah,* they cried, hands raised, as she tucked a single candy into each palm, the number of palms never slacking, the number of faces never easing, and she recognized most of them: tall, slim Tutsi girls, the wide cheekbones of a child of the Twa tribe—*Have you finally lost those front teeth, Shabani? Is that you, Nadège, with all that hair? Egide, have you had your measles shot yet?* The mud sucked at her sandals with every step, threatening to steal them from her feet.

Then, drawn by the noise, the women emerged, ducking beneath the doorjambs to straighten like long streaks of color against the stick-and-mud construction of their refugee homes, or rising from their cooking pots, smoking over wood fires between buildings.

Sarah waved at Solange, noting the swell of her belly. Sarah called a greeting to Raissa, surreptitiously counting her toddlers, and wondered about the littlest one—the one who'd been sick with measles when Sarah left—the one she did not see.

She wondered, too, about the young girl she didn't see, the one with two crooked braids standing up on either side of her head, tipped with wooden beads. She'd been sent away, no doubt. To a place with no bad memories.

"Miss Sarah, you are back!"

Sarah glanced over her shoulder to a woman trudging up the hill, balancing a heaping thatch of firewood on top of her head.

"*Bonjour,* Safi," Sarah said. "How are your children?"

"Yvan has a sore, and Mamy drank bad water, but the others fare well. Did your travels pass well?"

"Thank you, yes."

"And your mother and father, are they in beautiful health?"

"Yes, Safi, thanks for asking. How are your lovely mother and respected father?"

Sarah continued to hand out pieces of hard candy as she and Safi traded the expected morning salutations. Finally, after she'd asked about Safi's parents and children and aunts and goats, Safi said, flatly, "*Bon,*" and got to the true business of her blessings.

"Now that you are here," Safi said, flashing a sly grin, "are you hiding an American husband among those children?"

Sarah reached deep in her bag, scraping the bottom for the last few candies, letting her hair screen her face. No doubt Dr. Mwami had explained her sudden absence in a way the Banyamulenge women would understand—that Sarah had gone home to see her family, a family that would undoubtedly marry her off before she became too old, because she was already, in Tutsi terms, the oddest of creatures: a woman without a husband, away from home.

"What need do I have for a husband," Sarah said, "when I already have so many children?"

"How can that be, you come back alone?" Safi paused, to hitch the weight of sticks on her head. "The men in your tribe—they must be..." She made a motion with her hand, indicating her low opinion.

"Maybe none could pay the bride wealth," she said. "My father asks for too many cows."

Safi cocked her head. "It is good to have a father who values you."

"It's a blessing upon me."

"But a father is no husband." Safi leaned toward her. "You know my son, Sarah. Young and strong. Almost of age." She winked. "*Tuyage twongere.*"

Let's talk.

Safi's laugh told Sarah the woman had managed to make Sarah blush even harder, a feat of endless fascination among the refugees. She'd better brace herself; no doubt there'd be more of such teasing coming.

The children swarmed even after the last candy was gone, roiling around her, asking questions, their small hands stroking her arms. She approached the main building of the camp and noted the moss growing on the edge of the roof, and the chunk of mud that had slid off the wall in the humidity. It would soon need repair.

And she couldn't help herself. She couldn't help scanning the open area, looking for a very specific jeep, wondering if he was here now, having delivered some supplies, perhaps boxes of donations like the ones the boys had filched from to bring to the market, but there were no cars here, nothing but a couple of loose goats. It was better this way, she told herself. She needed to brace herself, get a good grip on her senses, before she laid eyes on Sam.

She gave the last candy to the youngest in the crowd, and

then said her good-byes as she slipped into the coolness of the main building. It served as the registration area for refugees, as well as a hospital and living quarters for herself, Dr. Mwami, and a collection of other employees of various NGOs. If it weren't for the flies, the mud walls, and the humming of the generator, the room could be mistaken for a back office somewhere in Iowa. An iron-haired woman in khaki scowled over a monitor, her features bathed in a blue glow, as she pounded a single key over and over.

"Be with you in a minute," she said, sliding under the table to unplug the CPU. "Dang operating system, freezes the whole drive," she muttered, "couldn't bring us a Mac, had to give us some virus-ridden office reject with a processor speed in the kilobytes—"

"Hello, Maggie."

The woman poked her head up over the rim of the desk and blinked behind her square-rimmed glasses. "I'll be damned if it isn't Sarah Pollard." She hauled herself up. "You just cost me two bottles of banana wine."

Sarah cocked her head.

"I made a bet with that hunk o' man with that bed-nets organization. Told him, after you left, that we wouldn't see your skinny ass again. Can't say I'm sorry I lost." She spread her strong, wiry arms. "Come give Maggie a hug."

Sarah braced herself for Maggie's powerful squeeze, and was sputtering when Maggie finally let her go long enough to give her a good look-over. "You're supposed to come back from the States fattened up and tanned, darling. What the hell you been doing, hibernating?"

"On airplanes," Sarah said, ruefully. "It's a very long story."

"Well, there ain't a hell of a lot doing around here, so you can fill me in on the gritty details over the next ration of mush, what d'ya say?"

"Sounds good." Sarah thrust her chin at the computer. "More trouble?"

"Than it's worth." Maggie rounded the desk and gave the monitor a good swipe on the side. "The monitor's got a burn-in. I think it's porn. Ever try reading Banyamulenge profiles through the shadow of an angry penis?" Maggie gestured over her shoulder to the suite of machines humming behind a tarp. "The real problem is that I can take all the pictures I want of these lost souls, but without access to the refugee database, I can't match orphans. Ah, you don't want to hear this. It's nothing Maggie can't fix." Maggie eyed Sarah's bulging bag. "Wouldn't happen to have a nice hummin' black-market processor in that bag, would you?"

Sarah pulled out some magazines. "No, but I did bring you three months' worth of *People* magazine."

"Child," she said, with a deep-throated laugh, "you just earned yourself an upgrade on your firewall."

Sarah spread the magazines on the desk, and then cocked her head toward the hospital wing. "Is he in?"

"Is Brad Pitt crazy?" Maggie pulled the top magazine toward her. "Beyoncé is what? When did *that* happen?" She gave her head a shake. "I've got some reading to do. Why don't you go on back to the clinic? Dr. Mwami could use the help. The last girl Doctors Without Borders sent, he demoted to firewood duty."

Sarah shrugged her much lighter bag over her shoulder and made her way through the open doorway to the clinic. She followed the strengthening scent of disinfectant and bleach, which did a heroic job of masking the less pleasant scents of a room that housed fevered patients. The room itself, nothing more than a large open space, had its own separate entrance. Six of the eight beds were currently occupied, and she was relieved not to find any children lying on the floor pallets they kept stacked in the supply room. Yet a full bench of patients waited for Dr. Mwami's attention, and one woman paced just outside the clinic, clutching her swollen abdomen against the labor pains.

She heard Dr. Mwami behind the single curtain.

"...I tell them, never drink still water. Still water is bad water, full of bugs and sickness. Fast water is better, if you must drink. Yet over and over again I see this. You will remember what I am telling you, won't you, Dieudonné, the next time you go by that pond when you're gathering sticks?"

Sarah came around the edge of the curtain to see the boy, thin and weak, manage a nod.

"Two of these a day." Dr. Mwami grabbed a bottle from the shelf by the bed, checked the label, and handed it to the mother, Inès—a young and lovely woman who had named her child "God-given," in spite of the less than loving way he had been conceived. "Two a day," Dr. Mwami repeated, "one at sunrise and another at sunset. *Comprenez?*"

Inès nodded.

"You have no other children, yes? Then take the bed at the end of the row, so I can observe him. Maybe, in a day or two, he'll be strong enough to go home." Dr. Mwami raised his head and saw her. "Ah, Sarah. You are back."

"Yes."

"Good." Dr. Mwami pressed the plunger of the antibacterial

gel on the bedside table, filling his palm with the quick-drying liquid. "That's the eleventh case of bloody diarrhea I've seen today—but it's not from the tanks. In every case, they drank out of that cow pond about a kilometer west of the camp."

Sarah started. "Cholera?"

"No, but that's why six of them are still here, for monitoring." Dr. Mwami vigorously rubbed his hands together until all the antibacterial lotion dried. "The other two beds are taken by women who've just delivered. There's a third on the way"— the laboring woman cried out, punctuating his words—"and if my instincts are right, little Claude out there has broken a rib from his foolish idea to climb the water tank."

Sarah couldn't help the smile that pulled at the corners of her lips as Dr. Mwami continued to catalogue the cases as if he were standing in a white-tiled room in a city hospital and she'd just come in for a new shift. She kept mum as she nodded, feeling slow in the head. Absently, she thumbed the strap of her bag off her shoulder, took the familiar stained lab coat off a peg on the wall, and hung her bag in its place.

"For now," he said, "you'd best fetch Lynca out of her mother's arms—the screaming one. She'll need about a dozen stitches and a tetanus shot for that gash on her foot."

Sarah shoved her arms into the sleeves of her lab coat. She walked around the curtain and glanced at the bench-full of patients, trying to pick the right sobbing girl from the crowd. Sarah led the girl behind the curtain. At first, she couldn't find a pail or a clean cloth, though the soap was where it always was, and she felt Dr. Mwami's slight impatience as she fumbled for supplies. She cleaned the girl's foot as the doctor flourished a frighteningly long needle. Then Sarah held the girl's hand while she told halting stories about America: about dogs who slept in feather beds, and machines that sucked away dirt, and houses that did not need fires to be kept warm. Dr. Mwami finished the stitches and called the next patient while Sarah did her best to keep up.

The next time Sarah lifted her head, it seemed, the bench was empty of patients, and the dried banana fronds on the roof rustled in the night breeze. Dr. Mwami shoved a bawling newborn into Sarah's waiting arms and then turned back to take care of the exhausted mother.

Sarah brought the newborn to an empty pallet and gently cleaned the birthing fluids off the tiny girl. As she tucked the child into the box that would serve as a cradle, Dr. Mwami dropped a hand on her shoulder.

"Sarah—we've missed you." He gave her a curt nod before turning away. "Glad to have you back."

Sarah stared down at the infant, swaddled tight, as evening insects buzzed outside, as the light dimmed to the rose-purple of a Burundi evening, as the scent of cooking fires and roasted goat filtered through the open door. She felt, somewhere deep inside her, a certain fundamental shift of gravity, like a cart dragged through the mud finding sudden purchase on a straight and solid road. She stood quiet for a moment and let herself experience the growing lightness of being.

Yes. It was very good to be home.

~~~~~

A full week passed before Sarah finally heard the familiar pitch of a revving motor as a vehicle labored its way up the hill to the main building. She was pacing in the clinic, patting the tense back of a screaming infant who'd just received his first immunization, when she recognized the distinctive grinding of metal as the driver forced the jeep into a lower gear.

Sam had returned.

Her stomach dropped right to her feet. She patted the baby's back a little faster as prickles of heat and shame erupted all over her. Sarah knew she'd have to face him, sooner or later. He was, after all, the one fragile thread that had been strong enough to pull her all the way back to Burundi. She knew this wasn't going to be easy. They'd parted on such bad terms in Bangalore. He had been so angry with her.

With reason, Sarah reminded herself. Sam had been right. She'd made the wrong moral choice in India. She'd thrown herself at Colin, knowing he was promised to another woman, when she should have just said good-bye.

The devil had a million excuses, but Sarah took none of them. She couldn't blame her behavior on Rachel, or Kate's urging, or Jo's encouragement: Sarah had made the decision all on her own. In the months past, she'd made her peace with God and her own conscience. She just wasn't sure she could bear Sam's terrible censure. Especially when she'd been such a virulent holier-than-thou about so many of Sam's own difficult decisions.

"Dr. Mwami!" Josette, a young woman who happened to be herding some goats just outside the clinic, poked her head around the door. "Dr. Mwami! Master Tremayne is here! Come, you must see!"

"A moment, a moment—"

"He is asking for you," Josette said excitedly. She spoke toward the doctor, but her eyes danced on Sarah. "He wants to see you, Dr. Mwami!"

Sarah glanced at the doctor. He was inoculating an older boy against measles, a boy of about nine who sat with his eyes squeezed shut. The doctor finished the shot, pressed a cotton ball on the welling dot of blood, and tossed the needle in a sharps container.

"And doesn't Sam look fine," Josette said, her smile so wide her cheeks bulged like plums. "A fine man he is, tall and strong! And no wife of his own!"

Sarah turned away to lay the babe in the box they used as a crib so the young woman wouldn't revel in seeing Sarah's face redden even more. She hoped the teasing about her lack of a husband would taper off soon, but she supposed Sam's arrival would only make it worse. Half the women of the camp considered her and Sam married in all but tradition. Didn't they argue like husband and wife?

They did. All the time. It had taken her months to accept the realization that she was angry around Sam because he stirred within her a flood of dangerous feelings. Feelings she'd only dared to examine when an entire ocean physically separated her from him.

Dr. Mwami told the waiting patients that he'd be right back and headed out of the clinic. The patients, curious, quickly followed. Sarah fussed with the baby, arranging the cotton bedding, until she heard a voice in her head—part Rachel's, part her own.

Coward.

Yanking off her lab coat, she tossed it across an empty cot and strode through the registration area to the main door of the compound.

The usual confusion of goats, children, cattle, and the curious had gathered in an arc around Sam's jeep. Sam had managed to drive the vehicle all the way up the soggy hill, but the front wheels had sunk in the mud to the rim, and the vehicle was so splattered only a few spots of white paint and windshield glass shone through the muck. In stark contrast, Sam stood apart, straight-backed, wearing a blindingly white button-down shirt and a pair of belted, starched khakis.

She curled her hand around the bent sapling that formed the doorjamb. He looked fit and strong. The dark skin of his chest gleamed through the fibers of his shirt. He'd rolled the cuffs up, exposing the ropy strength of his forearms. He stood still, visibly uneasy, waiting for something.

She slipped outside to stand at Dr. Mwami's side. Sam's gaze shifted. It fell upon her. She braced herself for anger, censure, dismay—or, worst of all, lack of interest—but his look was a sudden flare, shifting and unreadable.

She shifted her feet to balance herself. She really must remember to eat her rations.

"Sam," Dr. Mwami said sharply, "what's all this about? I have a dozen patients waiting."

Sam answered by turning away and nodding to a tall young man, who promptly slipped away. Then, leaning forward, Sam motioned to a boy by the other end of the jeep, who shot off in a different direction. The boy returned a moment later, trailing four young goats, just as the first man muscled through the crowd, gripping a leash and one horn of a brown Ankole cow.

The crowd murmured admiring noises, drawing around the beast, and the women grinned with new excitement.

"Dr. Mwami," Sam said, "I've been thinking of how best to do this for some time now. I've decided it's you who I must approach, to make an offer."

"Speak plainly, Sam, is this another one of your grand jokes?"

"No, no joke." A muscle flexed in Sam's dark cheek, catching a gleam of sunlight. "You are considered the foster father for many of the fatherless daughters in the camp."

"Well, what of it?"

"I've come to make an offer," he said, gesturing to the goats and the cow, "of bride wealth."

"Bride wealth." Humor flickered across the doctor's usually strong, expressionless face. "Burundi tradition. You wish to marry."

Sarah swayed, sucking in a slow, long breath. The sagging belly of rain clouds rumbled across the sky, like Burundi drums in the distance. The first faint patter of raindrops rustled the dried roof fronds. A breeze brought the sweet tang of fermenting bananas from some hidden mash-pot.

She dived into Sam's dark-chocolate stare. Fathoms deep, those eyes; she kept tumbling deeper.

Sam spoke, loud and clear. "I make an offer...for Sarah Pollard."

Around the clearing, the women squealed and clapped their hands, and the children laughed, and suddenly everyone was moving, dancing, clapping, and stomping in circles. All but she and Dr. Mwami and Sam, three stiff figures amid the madness. Sam watched her steadily, his hands curling in his trouser pockets, ruining the sharp creases, while her heart started a steady, heavy pounding.

"A cow?" Dr. Mwami said suddenly. "Four stinking goats? What use do I have for these beasts, Samuel Tremayne?"

The crowd's exclamations ended abruptly. The women stilled and watched Dr. Mwami with wide, unbelieving eyes.

"Of all the things you could bring me," the doctor continued, "syringes or alcohol, iodine or bandages, salt tablets, antibiotics—you come to me with animals? Animals?!"

Sam spread a hand toward the jeep. "There is more."

"There'd better be." Muttering, Dr. Mwami left Sarah's side to pull open the filthy door, revealing a pile of boxes. He patted his lab coat for his reading glasses, but Sarah didn't know if he found them, because, while he looked, Sam crossed the yard, closing the space between them.

"Sarah-belle."

She broke eye contact, then took interest in her muddy flip-flops, and filled her lungs with air, because it was too much, really—too much all at once—a great volcano of feeling. She didn't deserve this. She'd done nothing but fight him since the first day he'd driven up the hill, over a year ago, and announced himself with a grin and a wink. She'd struggled against him the whole time, fought his tactics, even as he brought her equipment they had never been able to get before, despite all their efforts with grants and the requisitioning and the bureaucracy. She'd tried to drive him away with her holier-than-thou disapproval and her arguments about moral reckoning, but he kept coming back. She'd ignored him and yelled at him, even as she shamelessly chased another man—yet he persisted, solid and unyielding and sure. Sam scared her—she'd never really understood why, not until now.

His fingers were suddenly under her chin. She yielded to the soft pressure. Dared to look at that face, only inches from hers, as she had dared once before, under an acacia tree on the shores of Lake Tanganyika. Intense and searching. The spattering of pits on his cheeks was like so many stars in the night sky, a counterpart to her own freckles. Sam, her dark reflection.

"I thought," she said, her voice breathy, "that you were leaving Doctors Without Borders. I thought you wouldn't come back."

"So did I." His nostrils flared as his gaze drifted over her head for a moment to the mountainous jungle around them. "But this place, these people..." His jaw worked. "It's my calling."

"You're not angry with me?"

"For having a loyal heart?" He shook his head, sharply. "I can't fault you for that. It's one of the reasons I love you."

She watched his throat move as he said those words. Fearlessly. She raised her hand and placed it flat on his chest, just over his heart. Beneath the warm cotton, she felt the strong, steady beat.

"Kate tells me," he said, in a strangled voice, "that you are done with him."

It took her a moment to remember who.

"Yes. I am."

Sarah flexed her fingers, feeling the curve of his pectoral muscle, hard and tense beneath her touch. She wanted to caress him without the roughness of cloth between them. Wanted to feel him—Sam, who was *real*, flesh-and-blood, heart and soul, standing in all his warm, yearning glory before her.

Sarah knew that Sam could have gone anywhere. He could

have transferred within the organization to another area altogether. He could have left the business and returned to England to work in an office, or anything. He could have washed his hands of her, of Burundi, and spent his days watching cricket on the telly and eating bangers and mash. He'd been talking about it for weeks after they'd rescued the girl with the crooked braids, and she had listened with some of the same yearning in her heart.

But he chose to come back. To all of it—the good and the bad and the beyond—because he was stronger than she was. He was a man of good heart and unwavering loyalty. And it made her think that maybe there was someone in the world perfect in his own imperfect humanity, and she'd been a fool all this time, looking in the wrong direction, for the wrong man, even as the right man walked calmly right beside her.

She closed her eyes and pressed her nose into the hollow of his chest. His shirt smelled like soap warmed in the sun. "There's something I have to tell you."

"Let the past lie," he said. "It doesn't matter anymore." He thrust both hands, fingers splayed, through the tangled mess of her hair, gathering the great weight of it up at the back of her head and letting her shift position against him, his chest her fulcrum. "You've been gone so long. I was afraid you wouldn't come back. I've missed you, Sarah-belle."

"Sam."

"Shhh." He buried his face in her hair. "There is time enough."

"But I want you to know this." She turned her face, so she could feel the bare skin of her cheek against the bare V of his chest.

"Sam, I came back to Burundi—for you."

~~~~

Sam shifted the jeep into fourth gear as Sarah raised her chin to the breeze. They'd made it off the rough mountain paths onto the firmer roads approaching Lake Tanganyika. She slid her fingers over his, where he gripped the gear shift, so he could drive and she could touch him at the same time. She tilted her head and managed a tentative smile, and he gifted her with a laugh that made her toes curl.

They'd escaped their own celebration. After Dr. Mwami had announced the bride wealth acceptable—to the jubilation of the crowd—Sam had informed everyone that several boxes of sorghum beer cluttered the back of his jeep, and they should be promptly unloaded. The women ululated, the boys ran for their drums, and everyone began to dance. No sooner had the last box been removed than Sam gripped her hand and urged her into the passenger's seat. Maggie shot out of the clinic, tossed a duffel bag through the window, gave Sarah a salty, weepy kiss, and said, "Git, now, both of you!"

Now bouncing around in the jeep, Sarah sensed where they were going. Anticipation was doing strange and thrilling things to her. Her grip on his hand tightened. Sam nudged his fingers between hers, until she relaxed.

They pulled up to a scattering of well-made huts centered on a low, long, whitewashed building, well tended with pots of flowers in exuberant bloom. A friend of Sam's owned the establishment, which was luxurious for Burundi, but considered by international travelers a "rough and rustic" retreat for environmental tourists interested in viewing the lake hippos or doing a little sport fishing in the narrow native canoes. Behind the main building, she glimpsed the deep-blue waters of the lake, shimmering silver now, reflecting the threatening clouds.

"I'll register," Sam said, grabbing his bag and hers from the backseat. "I'll meet you by the lake."

Sarah ran her fingers through her windblown hair as she sauntered around the edge of the building. A few fat drops of rain pattered, leaving spots on the back patio and sinking into the thatched umbrellas that shaded the few small tables. Beyond, a grassy slope spread to the edge of the lake. On a little hillock, just by the water, an acacia tree spread its low, wide branches. She walked directly to it and leaned up against its rough bark. It protected her from the sporadic rain.

She heard his footsteps in the grass, long before he came up behind her and pulled her into his embrace. She sank into him. How they fit—the back of her head in the crook between his jaw and shoulder, her back flat against his strong torso, his forearms tight beneath her breasts, his breath warming the hollow below her ear.

"I'd convinced myself," she whispered, remembering the last time they'd embraced under this tree, "that it was just another kiss for you. That it was nothing to you, a bit of flirtation."

"I frightened you."

"I didn't expect it," she admitted, "and then I couldn't explain...how strongly I felt."

He turned her toward him and claimed her mouth. He took what he'd taken before—her lips, her balance, her senses—but he didn't stop this time. He deepened the kiss and drew out the last of her lingering fear, the last of her doubts, coaxing from her the passion she'd been too afraid to give until right now.

"The people in the camp," he said, pausing to press his lips against her temple, where a vein pulsed wildly. "They consider us married now."

"I know," she said, huskily. "So do I."

His grip tightened.

"And though my father will appreciate the Burundi tradition," she added, sensing what Sam was trying to say, "being a pastor, he'll want a more formal Western ceremony eventually."

"So will mine."

She pulled away to look up at his face in silent query.

"Didn't I ever tell you? He met my mother on a mission." His smile was soft, teasing. "He's a clergyman in the Anglican Church."

Her smile warmed into a gentle laugh as the rain pattered around them, big messy drops falling from the leaves. She wondered at how much they still had to learn about each other, and how lovely it would be to do just that in the weeks and months and years ahead.

A drop of rain fell upon his cheek. She touched it, and with her finger she traced the tiny scars along his cheekbone, then followed the curve of his ear and the strong length of his jaw, watching as he grew silent and still and very intent upon her face.

I will be afraid no more.

She whispered, "Do we have a room?"

"A whole hut, Sarah-belle."

He claimed her lips again. Bending, he lifted her off the ground, leaving the shelter of the acacia tree as he walked in the direction of one of the stilted huts. He twirled her as he carried her, making the whole world blur beyond his head, blur beyond the fall of the rain, which was steady now. It soaked his head and her hair and his shirt as only a tropical rain could.

He pushed the door open with his back. She fumbled with the buttons of his shirt, pushing the wet cotton off one broad shoulder, letting her palm linger on the perfect mahogany swell of muscle, as he finished the job. He skimmed his hand across her waist, then slid his fingers under the hem of her T-shirt. He traced a trail up her spine, dragging the shirt up with his wrist, exposing her stomach to his, so that she couldn't resist pressing them together from navel to breast.

Their clothes fell in sodden heaps on the floor. With eyes wide open, she took wonder in their nakedness, marveling in the long sinews of his frame, the strength and coiled power of his lean body, the stark contrasts of their skin. He held himself back for her—she sensed it in the subtle trembling of his muscles as he drew her onto the bed and in the swiftness of his breath as he scraped his palm across the bone of her hip. With his lips and tongue and teeth he brought her to the tight edge of all sensation and held her there until, her whole body atremble, she wordlessly urged him close—even closer.

Sam. Loving, wonderful Sam.

And she felt lightness in her heart, like a soul washed clean by rain.

~~~~ chapter eighteen

Jo sat on the bench and tilted her head back to soak in the September sun. The light dappling through the trees couldn't be more golden, the sky more blue—or the rolling hills more green. It was the kind of day that would have made Rachel insist on a climb. Twenty years ago, Rachel and Jo and Kate and Sarah would have blown off their classes, piled into Jo's Jetta, and set off for the Shawangunks. Today they gathered at Rachel's grave, one year after her death.

Jo's gaze drifted about twenty yards away, to a plot now surrounded by mourners. She was glad that the grave was covered with grass, and that the traditional Jewish ceremony would be confined to the unveiling of Rachel's headstone. Jo never did like funerals of any kind. They brought back too many painful impressions: the choking smell of Kentucky clay, the big gaping hole, and the lingering smell of cigarette smoke in the folds of Aunt Lauralee's dress. Today's ceremony would be the last in Rachel's honor, and Jo couldn't help feeling that it was time for closure.

She hazarded a glance at Gracie, seated on the bench beside her and swinging her legs. The little girl still gripped the seat's edge with tight white hands. They'd come early to pay their respects, but now the crowd had grown too thick for the girl, too full of clucking and pitying gazes, so Jo had drawn Grace away. They'd ended up on this bench by a gravel path, which was close enough to watch, but far enough away so they could avoid direct contact.

Jo stretched an arm across the back of the bench and tugged a lock of dark hair to get Gracie's attention. "Your nana sure is looking forward to spending the holidays with you, kiddo. I could smell the honey on her clothes." Jo hoped, by turning Grace's thoughts to the upcoming visit to the Brauns, she could help Gracie get through the next difficult hour. "She promised me some of her honey cake for Rosh Hashanah, so you'd better not eat it all, you hear?"

Grace continued to bob with each swing of her legs.

"Maybe," Jo added, fingering the open edge of her bulging purse to check one last time that she'd remembered to bring tissues, a granola bar, and a lollipop, "I'll ask Jessie for that applesauce recipe, too. Then, when we go apple-picking in October, you can teach me how to use my stove again."

Gracie stopped swinging her legs. She twisted her right foot to scrape the sole of her Mary Jane against the concrete brace of the bench. "Jessie's applesauce is okay. I like the challah better."

"I hear you, kiddo. I'm a carb girl myself." Jo shifted her weight, subtly turning her body toward Grace. "Cornbread's my preference, but challah will do. Did you remember to pack your Cinderella toothbrush?"

"Uh-huh."

"And the new underwear, the princess ones still in the package?"

"Aunt Jo!" Grace turned her face up. "No talking about underwear!"

"Well, why not? A girl's gotta have it." Jo pinched the lapel of her black suit and pretended a playful peek. "Mine's red."

Red and lacy and downright raunchy. Because Rachel would have hated to see them all gathered here like a bunch of crows. Only respect for the family—and Grace—had kept Jo from striding into the cemetery sporting a leather miniskirt and stilettos.

Gracie's roll of eyes didn't quite hide the hint of a smile. "I packed enough for a whole two weeks, Aunt Jo, just like you told me."

"That's my girl."

Fortunately, Grace had become very good at packing. The arrangements Jo had made with the Brauns meant a lot of shuttling back and forth between New York and New Jersey. Only a month ago, Grace had returned from a summer in Teaneck. Jo knew the summer had been difficult on Mrs. Braun, though the older woman refused to admit it. Mrs. Braun was still struggling to come to terms with the idea that Grace's primary home was in Jo's condo. Thank God, the older woman wasn't fighting the custody arrangements anymore, and was by degrees becoming more amenable to compromise. In time, Jo hoped, Mrs. Braun would come to accept the new situation as the best one possible in an imperfect world.

Now the Jewish holidays loomed, and Grace would be going back to Jersey again. That would give Jo an opportunity to put in some serious face-time at work—and prove to her boss that the flextime she'd negotiated was just that—flexibility in her hours, so she could be a real mother to Grace.

Yep. It'd been a long, hard road, but she'd finally gotten this working-mother thing down.

"Aunt Jo?"

"Yeah, kiddo?"

"Where will I go when you die?"

Jo sucked in a breath so fast that spit hit the back of her throat. Her body spasmed and then she coughed, covering her mouth with her forearm. She motioned for Grace to wait as she turned away to root through her purse for tissues, continuing to cough long after she needed to, as she desperately searched for an appropriate response.

You're not going to get rid of me that easily, kiddo, so no worries.

No worries. Jo knew she couldn't tell Grace that. Gracie had been told that before, when her mother first went into the hospital, and look how that turned out, with them sitting on a bench in a cemetery.

After Jo got her coughing under control and wiped her watering eyes, she looked back at Grace. There were Rachel's eyes, big in the face of Rachel's daughter, as deep and brown as her mother's but without the laughter, without the wisdom, and with more innocence and twice the sorrow.

Jo should have seen it coming.

In that instant, Jo followed her instincts and went with what she would have wanted to hear when she was sitting on a bench near her own mother's grave, all those years ago.

The truth.

"That's a good question, Gracie girl." She wadded the tissue and shoved it in her purse. "I'm not planning to go anywhere soon, but," she added, as she gestured to the mourners with her chin, "there's no harm in looking at your options."

By the graveside, the rabbi began the ceremony by reading psalms. The lilting Hebrew wafted to them on the breeze. Jo eyed Leah and her husband, Abe, standing close to the gravestone. Abe leaned on his walker. Leah, her head bowed, gripped the head of her cane.

"Well, you already have your nana and your grandpa." Jo quietly slipped the tip of her finger across the part in Grace's hair, fussing with that one stubborn strand, and gently combed it to the other side. "You have a room in their house, here in New Jersey. If something were to happen to me, you'd still have a place to stay."

At that moment, Leah's cane wobbled, and the elderly woman leaned in to Jessie. Gracie caught sight of her grandmother's physical weakness, and then looked pointedly at Jo.

"Well," Jo said, as the lock of hair that Jo had been fussing with twisted right back into place, "there's always Aunt Jessie."

"She's got a boyfriend now." Grace turned away and took an interest in peeling a sliver of green paint off the seat of the bench. "He's over at the house all the time. And they're always *staring* at each other."

Jo smiled as she noted Jessie's companion, a tall, rather gawky young man with Clark Kent glasses, whose body language screamed, *She's mine.* It'd be a while—and maybe a wedding—before those two matured out of the cow-eyed phase.

Then Jo's gaze fell upon another relative, Rachel's buff, bachelor older brother. "There's always Uncle Artie—"

"His house smells like gym." Gracie shook her head hard. "And he keeps *rats* as *pets*."

"Gracie girl, you gotta help me here. I'm plumb out of ideas."

Gracie shrugged. She toyed with a sliver of rubbery green

paint, but Jo noticed that the little girl's gaze drifted beyond it, to a point just to the left of her mother's granite gravestone.

To Kate.

Kate, a slim silhouette in a black Liz Claiborne suit, stood close by Paul. On one side stood her older daughter, Tess, clutching her elbows tightly. Michael, a smaller version of his father, stood frowning at the rabbi in concentration, as if he were trying to figure out the Hebrew. Anna swayed in front of her parents, blithely playing with the ruffles of her velvet dress.

A perfect nuclear family. What more could any orphan want?

"Ah, Gracie."

Jo slipped her arm around her and pulled the warm bundle of girl against her side. She held Grace tight, so the little girl wouldn't see the brightness of Jo's eyes or the trembling of her jaw. Death was an ever-present thing. Yet, to live a full life, you had to face your fear.

Like Rachel did.

"I'll tell you what, my girl: I'll have a talk with Mrs. Jansen later today." Jo scraped her fingers over Gracie's head, messing that crooked part and all those dark locks. "Your ma took good care of you; now I'll do the same. If something happens to me, don't you fret. I'll be sitting on a cloud, sipping an appletini with your ma. And you'll be here, in the very best of hands."

～～～

Staring at the gravestone, Kate rolled the pebbles in her palm. The rocks slipped smoothly over one another, like oiled massage stones. A long time ago, she'd taken a pile of them from a brook in the Shawangunk Mountains, from a stream she,

Rachel, Jo, and Sarah had all bathed in during a brutally hot summer jaunt. She liked the way they felt in her hand. Over the years, they'd become her worry stones, clicking between her fingers as she studied or worked or fretted.

Time to give a few of them up. She leaned down and slid the first pebble on the granite base of Rachel's gravestone.

One.

This is for opening Sarah's eyes to what was right in front of her. And for teaching Jo what is really important in life.

Two.

For restoring my sanity, and my marriage.

Three.

And for you, Rachel. For reminding all of us that we have to jump out of airplanes every once in a while, for perspective.

Kate straightened. Paul's hand felt warm on her shoulder. He'd been sweet today—attentive, accommodating, and a source of comfort and support. She slipped her hand in his and squeezed his fingers, to let him know how much she appreciated it. As they rambled down the hill, Kate saw a car stop on the road just beyond the green. A woman stepped out of the passenger's side, dressed in a coral tie-dye sundress. Kate's heart leapt: Sarah had arrived. Late, as usual, and wrinkled, as if she'd just tripped off an international flight. Sarah waved at her briefly, then struggled to tie a black mourning band around her upper arm as she wound her way through the gravestones toward the huddled crowd.

Paul dropped his hand from her shoulder. "I'd better get going if I'm going to get Tess to her soccer game."

She tugged the lapel of his navy suit jacket. "Thanks, hon. I really need this afternoon with the girls."

"You can pay me later."

She couldn't resist a slow, wicked smile. "Oh, I will."

She watched him for a while, as he herded their three kids into the car.

"Sugar, didn't anyone tell you the rules?" Jo sauntered up behind her. "You're married. You're not supposed to drool over your husband."

"Clearly, you've been given the wrong information."

Kate turned and embraced Jo, who looked very much as if she could use a cigarette.

Jo spoke into Kate's shoulder. "I take it things are still improving?"

"Oh, yeah. And the make-up sex is great." Any marriage, Kate had come to realize, was a work in progress. Kate glanced around. "Where's Grace?"

"She's going to Leah's house for the High Holies." Jo brushed at a dusty little handprint on her skirt. "It's a perfect arrangement. I can concentrate on the new launch, and I may even squeeze in a love life."

Kate grinned. "Do spill."

"Surely you know who it is."

"Really?"

"Down, girl. The accountant and I have been out to dinner twice, real casual, to talk about the new account after hours."

"An account your buddy Hector is handling now, I hear."

"Well, yes. I *did* insist he be promoted. Somebody has to handle the travel and the talent after hours, now that I've got Grace at home."

Kate gave Jo a soft smile. Six months ago, Jo had quit her job. Jo said she had enough money to keep her and Grace comfortable for at least a year, and she needed to sort things out. Grace's little episodes had worsened over the winter, and though Jo made Herculean efforts to handle both the job and the grieving little girl, the strain had proved too much.

"Rachel would say," Kate said, "that you got a big dose of reverse karma when your boss begged you to come back after you quit."

"I can't say I didn't enjoy hearing that my clients were bailing when they heard I had left the company."

"So is it working—the flextime, working at home one day a week, the whole new situation?"

"Oh, it's working. But, sugar, I'm no fool. I won't make CEO before fifty." Jo gave Kate a wink. "But there's a good chance I'll get something better. Gracie will raise a glass in my honor at her wedding."

Kate laughed, a little laugh, a laugh that went husky and wet.

"Don't you start, Kate Jansen," Jo said in a shaky voice, "because then there'll be no stopping."

Sarah came toward them, glanced at both of them in concern, and then opened her arms for a hug.

Kate embraced her. "Hey, Sarah. Welcome back to the real world."

"Is that where I am?" Sarah burrowed against Kate and then gave Jo a squeeze. "I can't think. My head is still in Burundi time."

"We're glad your body's here."

Then they held on to one another as they talked, the three of them in one loose circle. Kate couldn't stop looking at her friends. Marriage was treating Sarah well, for her cheeks flushed when she spoke Sam's name, and she looked peaceful and happy. Jo let out a hearty laugh at something Sarah said, and the oh-so-familiar sound made Kate's breath hitch a little. Her thoughts turned—inevitably—to the one whose laughter was missing.

Rachel.

Suddenly they all fell silent.

Jo was the first to speak. "You know, girls, I've been doing a bucket load of thinking lately."

Kate felt a teary weakening. "If you cry, Jo, I swear, I'm going to lose it."

"You know all this trouble Rachel caused us?" Jo blinked rapidly. "The skydiving, the hunting of old boyfriends, the raising of small children?"

Kate and Sarah, in unison: "Oh, yeah."

"Well, this much I know is true." Jo looked at each of them. "Rachel didn't want us to go through it alone."

Kate tightened her grip. She pulled them all close, until all that was left was a small space between them, a space just big enough for one athletically slim mountain-climber with a big heart.

Then Kate lifted her head and smiled up at the blue, blue sky.

Dear Reader,

If you've been to a college reunion lately and noticed a bunch of crazy women in the local pub singing bad eighties rock . . . and, if you're in a certain upstate New York college town, then it's a good bet that those are my friends, and I'm the one in the middle, dancing badly.

We've been doing this every five years since we graduated. As a group, we celebrate the memorable times we spent together lolling on grassy quads, as well as the years after graduation, where, cash-strapped and struggling, we suffered through one another's horrid first jobs, romantic relationships, and roach-infested apartments. Now we're scattered all over the country and settled into marriage, mortgages, careers, and family life. When we get together, we tend to embarrass our children.

We're an odd and varied bunch: One raises money for charity by biking in 100-mile marathons; another, a gregarious working mother, juggles incredible responsibilities yet throws fabulous parties; and a third started her own landscaping business in midlife.

Honestly, I don't remember how we were drawn together all those years ago. We're a jumble of religions and races and socioeconomic classes and political beliefs. There are rough edges, old hurts, and fundamental disagreements. There's also respect, humor, and empathy. It's a recurring miracle that we've maintained our bond despite the distances of both time and geography. We know we are blessed. That's why, every five years, we make Herculean efforts to reunite at our alma mater.

Magic occurs when we are in a room together. We talk about politics, sex, money, religion—all the things you're not supposed to talk about in polite company. We roll out the old stories, and then tell new ones until we laugh ourselves to tears. By the wee hours of the morning, we're at the college pub singing hair-band power-ballads and dancing as if no one is watching. And by the time we return exhausted to our regularly scheduled lives, we are sure of one essential truth: Life has taken us in very different directions, yet we all strive for the same goal—joy in our work, our marriage, our parents, our children . . . and our friends.

This novel, The Proper Care and Maintenance of Friendship, is my little valentine to all of them.

reading group guide for

The Proper Care and Maintenance of Friendship

1. Which of the four women do you most relate to? Is it the one whose lifestyle most resembles yours? If not, why?

2. Rachel chooses not to tell her friends about her illness because she feels she is sparing them. Was this the right decision? Is it ever right to keep the news of a potentially fatal illness from your loved ones?

3. Toward the end of her life, Rachel thought long and hard about what her friends needed to do to improve their lives. Do you think Rachel understood the full consequences of what would happen to them if they followed her last wishes?

4. One of the themes of this book is that friends know you better than you know yourself. Rachel, in particular, has a good bead on each of her friends, but Kate, Jo, and Sarah also, in some cases, see each other more clearly than they see themselves. Do you know your friends better than they know themselves? What advice would you give a good friend on how to improve her life? What advice do you think she'd give you?

5. Kate's fifteen-year marriage faces a crisis born of the stresses and responsibilities of raising a modern family. Do you relate to her troubles? Would your parents relate to her troubles? What about your grandparents?

6. Do you consider Kate's behavior—skydiving and traveling to India—to be irresponsible for a mother of three young children? If you were in Kate's position, caught between a deathbed promise to an old friend and the responsibilities of family, how risky a task would you be willing to do? Where is the acceptable line of risk for a mother? Is that line the same for a father?

7. Paul reacts very negatively to Kate's choice to take a sudden vacation to India. Was his reaction justified? What are the factors that complicate his response? If you are married with a family, how do you think your spouse would react, if you did the same?

8. Why do you think Sarah clung to the memory of Colin for so long? Why did she resist Sam despite the strong physical attraction? If Rachel's letter had not forced Sarah to seek Colin, do you think she and Sam would have ever gotten together?

9. Rachel chooses to have a child as a single mom, using a sperm donor. Knowing her lifestyle, what do you think about her choice? Why do you think she chose to have a child at all?

10. Jo's attitude toward Kate's busy life is skeptical and dismissive but changes quickly when she is forced to be a full-time mother to Gracie. Have you seen friendships between mothers and their working peers disintegrate under the same pressures?

11. Jo's early life as a foster child, as well as the memories of her mother's struggles as a single mom, would perhaps make her the worst candidate to adopt an orphan. What factors encouraged Rachel to choose Jo over Kate, and did she make the right choice?

12. Motherhood is often described as sacrifice. What sacrifices did Kate, Rachel, and Jo make in order to raise their families? How did they each feel about their sacrifices? Is it ever possible to be fully comfortable with the choices a woman must make when she chooses to have a family?

13. Rachel mentions that the friends have grown apart because they didn't properly maintain their friendship. Rachel's three best friends have become so busy with their own lives that they don't realize what is happening to their friend. But Rachel seems to understand. Do you understand?

about the author

Lisa Verge Higgins

Friends who know me as an author are often surprised to find out that I was once a chemist. In fact, when I wrote my first novel, I was studying for a PhD at Stanford University. That kind of smarty-pants revelation tends to grind conversations to a halt, so it's easier to just stay mum.

The situation isn't as crazy as it sounds. While I was in graduate school, teaching, studying, and working in a lab, the creative side of my brain was simply withering. So much analysis, so much math! Writing a dramatic story about lovers in revolutionary France was just, well, *therapy*. The real surprise came when a charming editor in New York decided to pay me for my labors. Until then, I hadn't even considered the option of writing as a career.

If I hadn't met a certain hot rugby player, I probably would have tinkered at both professions forever. We'd connected the year before, in the last few weeks before we'd graduated from our East Coast college. Apparently smitten, he decided to move clear across the country just to be with me in California. After he finished law school, he made me an offer. If I'd move back east, he said, with a lusty twinkle, he'd support me while I continued my burgeoning writing career. But here's the catch: I had to marry him.

Then, in a glorious flash—and that's how I remember a few years in Manhattan—I was living in the wilds of New Jersey, married, mortgaged, and with multiple small children. Though I had twelve books to my credit, writing fell to the wayside as I focused on the care and feeding of the lovely little moppets who filled my days. But writers never really stop gathering material, and suburban family life turned out to be richer than I'd ever imagined. When my kids entered school, I was bursting with ideas, and I knew I had to write again. *The Proper Care and Maintenance of Friendship* is the result.

As for my former career... well, I still devour the Science section of the Tuesday *New York Times*. I read, wistfully, of chemists working on breakthroughs in drug synthesis. But writing has afforded me the opportunity to work and stay at home. For my kids, and for me, that has been the greatest blessing.